MAFIA BRIDE

L. STEELE

For those who love fictional men over 6 feet,
with dark hair,
and with questionable morals...

1

Olivia

"Another shot of tequila, please."

The bartender flashes me a grin, then snatches up the bottle of Patrón.

"Oh, no, I can't afford that brand," I protest.

"But the man who's paying for your drink can." He nods at the space over my shoulder. I resist the urge to glance back. No doubt, whoever offered to pay for it will ask for something in return. And while I'm not above the occasional one-night stand, I prefer for it to be on my terms and with my choice of a partner. If a man has to pay for my drink before he introduces himself then, sorry, he's lost my interest already.

"No, thank you." I narrow my gaze on the bartender. "I'm good with Jose Cuervo."

The bartender reaches under the counter to grab the bottle of Jose. Good ol' Jose, he's been a good friend to me all these years. When I left home at eighteen, it was like the metaphorical chains around my wings had been lifted. I went a bit crazy those early days, partying at every opportunity. I had to make up for the time my family had cloistered me and tried to hold me back. Well, fuck them. I made it out, didn't I? Despite my brother's and my mother's opposition. Only my father supported me.

He asked me to think carefully about my choices, and if I still felt this was the way forward for me, he wouldn't stand in my way. I didn't have to think twice, to be honest. Becoming an actress is my dream; it's what I've lived for since I was five years old when I acted in a school play. I stepped on stage, and I knew this was it for me. My calling. My profession. What makes me happy. So, I left, with my father's blessings.

That was three years ago, and I've been back once. It was when my father dropped dead of a heart-attack. If only I'd gotten to spend more time with him. Was I selfish to leave when I did? And if I had stayed, would I have regretted it?

The bartender tops up my shot glass, then pops the bottle back in its place under the counter. I nod at him, and he moves away to attend to another customer. I toss back the glass of tequila and warmth explodes in my stomach. A pleasant heat suffuses my skin, and I toy with the rim of the second glass.

When I signed up to be the understudy in *Beauty and the Beast,* I had no idea it would be opening in Palermo. In Italy, the place of my birth. The place I left to pursue my drama studies in LA, and had hoped not to return to until I was a successful actress and proved myself.

I changed my last name, and because my father had sent me and my siblings to an American school, I already spoke English with an American accent. It ensured no one could trace my roots.

I met Jeanne and Penny at drama school, and when they moved to London to pursue opportunities in the West End, I moved with them. The two of them, along with my other friend Declan, who studied with us in LA, have been my support network since I left home.

The only person outside of my father I've kept in touch with is my sister Solene. It pained me to leave her behind, but if I'd stayed, it would have meant following in the footsteps of my older cousins—married at eighteen with two children by the time they were twenty-one, and already settled in the ways of their mother and their grandmother before that. Nope, that wasn't going to be me.

So, I made it out, and wouldn't have taken this part, but for the fact that roles don't come easily. That, and the fact that Jeanne and Penny are also acting in it. It's the first time since graduating from drama school that we'll be acting together, so when I got the offer, I couldn't say no. Now here I am, stuck on my own, on a Friday night, no less.

To be fair, Jeanne had invited me over to her place to watch a movie. I'd briefly thought about accepting the offer when Penny had, but this is the only free night I'm going to have in a while, and I wanted to de-stress. My plan is to down a few drinks, perhaps pick up a one-night stand for a quickie, then drive back tomorrow. And if I don't find a one-night stand? I'll simply find a room in the hotel attached to the bar, sleep off my booze-addled high, and leave tomorrow.

Maybe it's a little dangerous I decided to come without informing my friends about where I was going; but I'd rather not have my best friends around to judge my actions tonight. It's also why I didn't go to any nightclub in town, for fear of running into someone I know from my family or friends' circle. Instead, I opted to come to this bar in Monreale, an hour's drive from Palermo. Weeks of rehearsing, followed by constant monitoring of what I ate and drank, left me with the need to break free. I left home wanting to lead a life where nothing held me down. I landed in a profession where my every move is scrutinized on stage and on screen. Go figure.

Jeanne and Penny don't seem to have the same need to let loose once in a while like I do. I love my friends, but my idea of a fun Friday night is not watching Netflix, with no chill. I need… something more. Something that challenges me, makes me think differently, excites my brain cells and the cells between my legs, ideally at the same time. What's a girl got to do to find someone who'll stimulate both her brain and her clit, hmm?

The bartender refreshes my drink and I snatch up my second—no, if I'm being honest, it's my third glass of tequila this evening—and raise it to my lips when thick fingers circle my wrist. "You've had enough."

Static electricity zings up my arm, then arrows to my core. The hair on the back of my neck rises. *What the—* I whip my head around in his direction. "What do you think you're doing? How dare you touch me, you—"

Colorless eyes, gray like an impending snow storm. Flickers of gold spark deep inside like distant thunder. The irises are rimmed a dark blue, and the pupils are so black, they're like the bottomless pits of hell. The breath catches in my throat. I try to drag in air, but my lungs burn. Try to drag my gaze from his, but it's like I'm held in tractor beams. Every cell in my body hums. My nerve endings seem to fire all at once, sending a bunch of signals to my brain which I can't interpret.

The skin around his eyes creases. He seems as confused as me, for his eyebrows draw down. A crease dents his perfect forehead. It draws my attention to his nose that juts down over his mouth. And what a mouth it is. Jesus-fucking-Christ, that perfectly-bowed, thin upper lip with just the right hint of cruelty to send a shiver spurting down my spine. The pillowed lower lip, which I want to chew on and bury my teeth in. That jaw of his, which is square enough to give Superman a complex. And those cheekbones. Surely, it's not possible that someone is blessed with such razor-edged facial architecture that he could hurt me with it. *He* could hurt me. If I gave him the chance. I try to pull my arm from his grasp, but he holds on to it.

I try to speak. I honestly do, but the words are lost somewhere between my brain and my mouth. Stupid braincells that seem to have melted and congealed beyond recognition. He rubs his thumb across the pulse that drums at my wrists, and I feel it in my core. My breasts seem to swell, my nipples tighten, and a throbbing flares to life between my legs. What madness is this? How can I be so attracted to this stranger?

"You were saying?" His voice is darkness coated in sin, dipped in vanilla ice cream. *Stop it. Have you gone crazy? He's just a man... A very good-looking, spectacular specimen of a man who you happen to find very attractive.*

I tug on my hand again, and his lips twitch. Is he smiling at me? He's smiling at me. Probably laughing at my reaction to him. *Jerk.*

"Let go of me," I snap.

"Okay." He releases me so suddenly I slide back on my barstool.

I raise my hand to slap him, then pause when he shakes his head. He smirks. A twist of his lips that is so hot, so lethal, liquid heat coils low in my belly. I blink. "This is insane." This response to him is beyond weird. It's like nothing I have ever encountered before. Not with a stranger; not with anyone. If I stay here, I'm either going to try to hit him, or kiss him, or worse. My thighs clench. Shit, the thought of sleeping with him is far from hateful. My toes curl, and my ovaries seem to burst into a happy dance, similar to the one I was practicing before I left rehearsal today. That's it. I've officially lost it. I grab my purse, pull out some bills, and drop them on the counter. Then I turn to leave—

"Running away?" His deep rumble chafes my skin.

I ignore him and move away, when I hear him drawl, "Didn't take you for a coward."

Excuse me? I pause. He's baiting me. I know he's trying to get a rise out of me. I should leave without paying him any attention, but my stupid pride doesn't let me. I spin around and scowl. "What did you say?"

"You heard me." His grin widens. "You're leaving because you can't face the music?"

"Music?" I tilt my head as if listening to the tune playing over the speaker. "The only music I hear is the eighties' hit by Tina Turner—"

"Remixed by Kygo."

"Excuse me?"

"She came out of retirement to release the single remixed by Norwegian DJ Kygo."

I laugh. "You're kidding, right?"

"I assure you, I am not. You can look it up if you don't believe me."

I shake my head. "This entire conversation is insane. Now, if you'll excuse me, I have something urgent I need to take care of." I turn to leave.

I hear his footsteps behind me a few seconds before he plants his body in front of me with such speed that I almost bump into his wide chest. He's so massive that he blocks out the rest of the bar behind him. And his scent, sweet baby Jesus, his scent. It's spice and citrus and something smoky like firewood. I sniff again, fill my lungs, and my head spins. My knees turn to jelly and I stumble. Why am I turning into a klutz around him?

He grips my shoulder to steady me, and once more, pinpricks of heat bleed out from the point of contact.

I freeze; so does he. I pull away, and this time, he lets me go without protest. "Look, I didn't mean to scare you in any way. I simply want to talk to you." He raises his hands, palms facing toward me.

"I don't want to talk to you." I glance down, only so I can avoid those piercing gray eyes of his, and end up taking in his jeans. Hoo boy, does he fill out those jeans, or what? They might have been blue at one point in time, but the color is almost white now. The fabric is threadbare at his knees and at the edges of the pant legs. And his feet, OMG, his booted feet are huge. A size thirteen at least. Which means, the size of what he's packing must be quite substantial. I raise my gaze to his crotch and almost groan at the column outlined over the left side of him.

"I believe this is when I say, my face is up here?" he drawls. I flush. Sweat beads my hairline. Is it hot in here or am I having a hot flash decades before going into menopause? I gotta get out of here before I say or do something to embarrass myself further.

"I believe this is when I excuse myself." I duck past him, but he moves with me, so I have no choice but to pause.

"You have to stop doing this," I say through gritted teeth.

"You've got to stop trying to escape me." He chuckles.

"I'm not trying to escape you; I'm trying to leave," I snarl.

"From where I am, it looks like you're trying to run because you are scared of what you're going to find out if you stay," he retorts.

"Oh yeah?" I tip up my chin, all the way up, and then some more, so I can see his face. Gosh, he's tall. I mean, I had a sense of his height when he was sitting down, but standing, he's an absolute behemoth. He's possibly the biggest brute of a man I've ever seen. His beaten-up leather jacket stretches across his shoulders. I can't miss how his biceps stretch the sleeves, hinting at powerful muscles underneath. The overhead light bounces off of his longer-than-fashionable length hair, picking out hints of brown among the coal dark strands. A hint of a tattoo peeks out from under the neckline of his T-shirt. With his day-old stubble, he comes across as someone who'll always look effortlessly sexy. A look that adds to his appeal. A look which I definitely don't fancy. Not at all.

"And what is it I'm going to find out?" I scowl.

"That the two of us have something in common."

"We have nothing in common." I toss my hair over my shoulder.

"We sure do." He bends his knees and peers into my eyes. "We want to fuck each other's brains out."

2

———————

Massimo

She opens her mouth to speak, and I'm sure she's going to deny my earlier comment. Which is what most women would do. But I should have known she's not like anyone else. Her expression turns angry, then contemplative. "You have me there. I do find you attractive. All the more reason I should leave."

"You should stay." I search her features. "If not, you'll always wonder how it would have turned out if you had, and you'll forever regret that you didn't."

She bites the inside of her cheek, and this time, anger glints in her eyes. "It's bullshit that you'd say that to me. It's even worse that I can't help but believe it."

"I always endeavor to call it as I see it," I murmur. *And what I see is a woman who's so appealing that I can't let her walk away from me without getting to know her better.*

"Shall we?" I hold out my hand, indicating the booth in the far corner of the bar.

She looks at it, then at me.

"And if I refuse?"

"You know you don't want to."

"Don't I?" She tips up her chin, and juts out her lower lip. Fuck, if I don't want to bend over and bite down on her mouth right now.

I tilt my head. She glowers at me, then blows out a breath. "Fine, but *you'll* follow me." She pivots and marches off to the booth. I follow her, getting a good eyeful of her sweet, pear-shaped butt poured into skin-tight jeans.

My pants feel tighter by the second, and I reach down and adjust myself. How the hell am I going to sit opposite her when all I can think of is throwing her on the table, shoving her thighs open, and feasting on the delicious flesh between her legs? The blood drains to my groin. Every muscle in my body tenses. I manage to tear my gaze off of her, and reach the booth to slide in opposite her. Uncomfortable as fuck, given my tightened pants, but what-fucking-ever.

A waiter instantly materializes.

"Whiskey, on the rocks," I order.

"Would you like to order food?" he asks.

"Get us the drinks first."

When he leaves, she arches an eyebrow at me. "Thought you didn't want me to drink anymore."

"That's not for you; that's for me." I smirk.

She scowls. "How very chauvinistic of you to think I'm going to sit here and watch you drink and not drink myself."

"I haven't had a drink all evening. You, on the other hand, have been chugging down tequila like the bar is going to run out of it."

"Been watching me all evening, have you?" she asks lightly.

"I have, actually, from the moment I walked into the bar," I say without hesitation.

She blinks. "That's very honest of you."

"I already told you, I don't believe in wasting words."

"Yet, here you are." She places her elbows on the table, locks her fingers together, and rests her chin on them.

"Oh, this is not a waste of either of our time, since we both know where this is headed."

She glances away. I can practically hear the wheels spinning in her head. She stays that way for a few more seconds, then turns to me. "You're right, I want to fuck you."

"You're wrong." I nod toward the bartender who places the whiskey in front of me and the water in front of her, then leaves. I take a sip of the whiskey. "*I* am going to fuck *you*."

She laughs. "Awfully confident, aren't you?"

"Only when I know the odds are in my favor."

"Aren't you getting ahead of yourself?"

"Am I?" I tap my finger against my glass.

Her gaze narrows. Once more, she seems angry... At me? At herself? Then, just like that, it seems to drain away from her face. "No, you're not."

The tension fades from my shoulders. Fuck me. Had I been that unsure of myself? At first. I've never had to proposition a woman before. Most of them can't wait to jump into bed with me. All I have to do is crook a finger and they'll come running. This woman, though, is making me work for it, and fuck, if it isn't increasing the anticipation of where this evening's going to end.

She leans forward in her seat. "But for this to work, there are rules which need to be followed."

"Oh?"

She nods. "No names. No addresses. No contact details. One night. We fuck, and then we go our separate ways."

"Hmm." I contemplate the whiskey in my glass. It's what I want, isn't it? No complications or problems. A straightforward sexual encounter. The kind which would be blistering, given the chemistry between us. It's exactly what I'm looking for. I'm not looking for a long-term relationship, or indeed, to get married. Not like my brothers who have, one-by-one, found the loves of their lives and settled down. I'm nowhere near ready for that. What I'm looking for is a good fuck—the kind of sex that'll allow me to forget the responsibilities I carry on my shoulders for the *Cosa Nostra*. It's why I drove out to this bar, a place I tend to frequent because it's far away from my brothers' usual haunts.

Over the years, I've tended to come here when I need to get away from it all. I normally book a room above the bar for the night and sleep off my hangover before returning home. Only the owner knows my identity, and he swore to keep it secret.

Maybe the bartender suspects I'm *Cosa Nostra*. If he does, he's never given any indication. And I'd prefer to keep it that way. Normally, I prefer to keep a low profile and not talk to anyone, but today, I walked into the bar and spotted her instantly.

Her tight jeans and blood-red corset had made my balls tighten. I knew, even before she turned her head, she'd be beautiful—her auburn hair curling down her back, her luscious hips thrust out as she leaned forward to take a drink. I knew then, I wasn't going up to my room alone. I'm going to have her. Things are working out. I'm going to fuck her, and then walk away in the morning. So why am I not satisfied? Why do I want more?

"What about hard limits?" I murmur.

"Excuse me?"

I glance up to find her gaping at me. "Did you just ask—"

I tilt my head. "About your limits. Is anything off the table tonight?"

Her nostrils flare. Color sears her cheeks. In the dim lighting, red highlights glimmer among the strands of her gorgeous auburn hair.

"If I say no, would you accept it?" she finally asks.

"No," I say flatly.

She reaches over, takes the glass from my hand, and sips from it.

"Should I have a safe word?"

"When you're with me, you won't need a safe word. You'll trust me to handle your body the way I think you'd want me to."

"That's a lot of trust you're asking me to put in a stranger." She wrinkles her nose.

So damn adorable. "The very fact that you're here talking to me means you trust me," I point out.

She seems to think about it, then nods. "About the hard limits then..." She juts out her lips. "No anal—"

"Unacceptable. And that's not what I meant. You know that."

"Wait, what?" She opens and shuts her mouth. "How am I supposed to know that?"

"I plan to take your pussy, your ass, your mouth, every hole in your body, and many times over before the night is out. We clear about that?"

She swallows. Her breath hitches. Her chest rises and falls, and if I glance at her breasts, I'm sure I'll find her nipples outlined against the corset-like top she's wearing.

"Are. We. Clear?" I ask again.

She nods. "So, if I don't have a safe word, and if we're not establishing hard limits, how do we proceed?"

I rake my gaze over her features, then reach over and take the glass from her. "We'll have to play it by ear."

"By ear?"

"I won't do anything outside of what I outlined earlier."

"So, no hard-core S&M, then?"

I stiffen. "You know what I'm talking about?"

"I read, I go on Pornhub, so yeah, I know what S&M means. I've never gotten excessively kinky with a partner, so I don't know if there's something I wouldn't enjoy; not until I try it, I suppose."

"I promise not to go into the hard-core stuff." I hold up my hand.

"So, you have been into the more hard-core stuff?"

"Why do you want to know? Are you jealous?"

She scoffs. "Why would I be jealous? I was merely curious."

"Don't ask questions you don't want to know the answers to." I allow my lips to widen in a grin.

"Your attitude is annoying." She reaches across the table, grabs for my glass, and I hold it out of reach.

"I don't want you to be drunk. I need to you to be wide awake, alert, and in full possession of all of your faculties when we fuck." I drain the glass and place it on the table with a snap, then rise to my feet.

Her cheeks turn fiery. Her pupils dilate. "Anyone ever tell you, you're a true gentleman, the way you speak?" Her voice comes out rough, and she clears her throat.

"You didn't come here to pick up a gentleman. You want someone who can fuck you hard, someone who takes you with enough passion that you see stars. You want—" I reach over and run my knuckles down her forearm. "Someone who can fuck the attitude out of you. And trust me, when I'm done with you, you're going to be feeling the shape of my cock in between your legs for many days to come."

3

Olivia

Oh, my god, he hasn't even fucked me, and I can already imagine the shape of his rigid length between my legs. Feel his taste in my mouth, smell his scent in the air as I follow him up the stairs to the room he has for the night. Good thing he has it, too, because, no way was I going to go to his home, nor was I going to bring him to my place. I've had one-night stands before, but something about this man tells me this encounter is going to be different. And it's not only due to the hum of electricity that sizzles between us every time our eyes meet. Doesn't mean this encounter is going to be anything but strictly transactional. *I* am going to make sure it's purely transactional. Exchange of bodily fluids, and some old-fashioned banging meant to let off steam.

There will be no intimacy, nothing to blur the lines about what this is. A one-night stand, purely carnal, where we enjoy each other's bodies. That's it. End of story.

I can't help but train my gaze on his butt as he walks up the stairs ahead of me. And oh, God, what a butt it is. Tight and hard, it stretches the seat of his jeans as he stalks forward. My fingers tingle, and my mouth pools with saliva. What I wouldn't give to lean in and squeeze his flesh. I curl my fingers into fists.

As we reach the corridor at the top of the stairs, he prowls forward until he reaches the single door at the end of the short hallway.

"There's only one room here?"

"And it's ours for the night." He pushes the door open and gestures to me. I walk in, very aware of the heat of his body as I brush past him. My scalp tingles, and the soles of my feet burn. Goodness, and I haven't even touched him. He slaps on the light, and I walk into the room. He shuts the door behind him, and the quiet snick echoes around the space. I shiver, and the hair on my forearms rises.

The room—well it's a suite really—is nicer than I would've expected—a double bed, with bedclothes that appear to be clean, next to it a bed-stand, then a door that leads to the bathroom. Pushed up against one wall is a single mirror with a dressing table and stool in front of it. Next to it a window, with an armchair pushed up near it. Adjoining the area is a bar with stools next to the counter. I glance around the suite and notice there are no other belongings of his.

"You travel light," I murmur.

"I only use the suite to sleep off the alcohol in my system, before I head off the next morning,' he replies from his stance near the door. He hasn't made any effort to approach me, thank God. I just need a little time to gather my wits around me.

"Very sensible of you. Speaking of—" I glance at him over my shoulder, "—you do have condoms, right?"

He glances at the drawer in the bed-stand, then at me. I walk over, pull open the drawer, and spot the unopened box of condoms. "You were expecting to have sex tonight?"

"The staff's instructions are to keep the place fully stocked."

"So, the staff know you use this place for your encounters?"

"Only the bartender knows, and he can be trusted to be discreet."

"Hmm." I straighten and turn to face him. "Why do I get the feeling you're not telling me the whole truth?"

"Just like you aren't revealing why you came here with the intention of picking up someone tonight."

"I didn't—" I purse my lips. Why am I trying to deny it? "Does it matter why I want a one-night stand? Isn't it enough that I'm here?"

"You don't do this very often, do you?"

I sense my cheeks redden and resist the urge to look away. "You don't ever mince your words, do you?"

"Told you, I am forthright in my dealings."

"So, what now?" I twist my fingers together in front of me. "What's the protocol in these situations? Should I strip or something? Or will you take off your clothes first?"

"All in good time." He looks me up and down, and his gaze is so searing, so hungry, that my knees nearly give out from under me. I sit down on the bed and place my hands in my lap.

"Let me get you a drink." He walks over to the bar and busies himself.

I glance around the room, take in the clean-but-faded carpet, the faded wallpaper, and the old-fashioned chandelier in the ceiling. "This place has a certain charm about it; is that why you chose it?"

"I chose it for the location. It's far enough to not be anyone's regular haunt. At the same time, it's not too far away."

"So, you live in Palermo?"

"Do you?" He turns to me with two glasses in his hands. He walks over, hands me one, then sits down next to me.

"Orange juice?" I glance from my glass to his which is half-filled with what looks like whiskey. "I see what you're doing there." I scowl.

"Told you, I need you sober for what's to come." He twists his mouth, and good God, there's so much hidden meaning in the curl of his lips. If every, single, filthy thing I've learned from the internet was distilled into an expression, it would be this smirk.

He clinks his glass with mine, then tosses back his whiskey. He leans around me to set his glass on the side table, and goosebumps unfurl across my skin. My hand trembles and some of the juice spills on my jeans. "Shit." I place my glass on the bed-stand, then look around for something to mop up the juice with.

"There are towels in the bathroom." He jerks his chin in the direction of the door I saw earlier.

"Give me one sec." I jump up and head for the bathroom, shutting the door behind me. I draw in a breath, then another. Jesus, I can't believe how nervous I am. And I'm not a virgin, obviously. I mean, I've done it with my two ex-boyfriends and a few others. But none of them had the kind of presence this guy has. Am I out of my depth here? Did I make a mistake coming here? On the other hand, he'll definitely know how to handle my body. He'll know how to bring me to orgasm, and so far, the conversation has been anything but boring. I glance at my features in the mirror. My eyes are bright, my cheeks flushed. In fact, I'd go so far as to say my skin is glowing, and I haven't even fucked the man yet.

I am going to fuck you.

Yeah, yeah, doesn't mean I can't take the lead in some of our interactions, right? I wriggle out of my boots, shuck off my socks and my skin-tight jeans, then wash my jeans under the tap before I drape them over the shower rod. I reach for the strings of my corset and stop. This could be fun, actually. I walk out of the door, clad in my corset and panties.

Before I can take another step, his gaze locks on me. He takes me in from head to toe, and his nostrils flare. He's lost his jacket, and the black T-shirt stretches so wide across his shoulders, it's as if the fabric is molded to his pecs. His gaze narrows. Those gray irises seem to turn lighter, until they're almost colorless.

I put one foot in front of the other until I'm standing in front of him. He parts his legs and I step into the gap between them. With him sitting down, his gaze is at eye level with my breasts. My nipples tighten, and my flesh aches. A slow burn flares to life between my legs, and I resist the urge to squeeze them together. He raises his gaze slowly to mine, and oh, I was wrong. His eyes aren't colorless. There are flickers of blue and green in their depths, as if hinting at the emotions churning inside. He's not as unmoved as his expression seems to imply.

I bite down on my lower lip, and his chest swells. He raises his forefinger and twirls it, indicating I should turn around. I comply. For a few seconds I stand there with my back to him. The heat from his body wraps around my waist and slides down to the space between my legs. My clit begins to throb. I sense him standing, and the heat in the room seems to intensify. A soft touch on my back has goosebumps smattering across the nape of my neck. He begins to undo the lace that holds my corset together at the back. The edges separate. Cool air assails my back. I shiver.

"You cold?"

I shake my head.

"You nervous?"

I hesitate. "A little."

"Don't be." He pulls apart the ends and the entire contraption slides down my waist until its top end is balanced at the tips of my nipples.

He runs his big fingers down my bare back, and I arch into his touch. That feels so good. He traces lines across my back, probably the marks left in my skin by the bindings. Then, he pushes aside my hair, and a soft touch brushes the nape of my neck. I feel it all the way to my toes. He's not even kissed me, and my body is primed to receive him. Every nerve ending in my body is alive, every cell alert, and every pore on my skin opens as if to absorb his very presence.

He slides his big palms under the corset and around to cup my breasts. Sensations crowd my skin, my toes curl, and I push into his hands wanting to feel the imprint of every finger of his on my skin. He massages my flesh and I lean back and into his shirt-covered chest. I place my head on his shoulder, wind my arm around his neck, and turn my head to glance up at him. He's watching me so closely, with so much intensity. Those gray-blue eyes of his now a dark blue. It's incredible how they change with his moods. His jaw hardens and he pinches my nipple.

I huff.

He tweaks my nipple again, and I groan. My thighs clench, and moisture beads my core. I try turning to face him, but he stops me. He continues to strum my nipple, while with his other hand, he squeezes my other breast. I wrap both of my arms about his neck and pant. A nerve throbs at his temple as he squeezes both of my nipples at the same time. I yell. A shudder grips me as I grind my butt restlessly into his groin. He's thick, and long, and throbbing. The column in his pants feels alive and angry enough to stab into me through the layers of clothes that we're wearing.

"Jesus," I groan, then once more, try to turn. He pulls me flush against him, so every inch of my back is plastered against that hard, unforgiving surface of him.

"Massimo," he growls.

"Eh?" I blink rapidly, not sure what he means.

"That's. My. Name. Now say it."

When I hesitate, he releases my breast, only to shove his hand under the waistband of my panties. He stabs two thick fingers inside me, and I gasp. My gaze widens. I open and shut my mouth, unable to articulate the sensations that scream up my spine. He circles my clit with his thumb, and oh, my god, that's too much. I dig my nails into his shoulders, and a growl rumbles up his throat.

"Do you know how much it turns me on when you do that?"

He adds a third finger inside me and I gasp.

"Oh, god, it's too much. Please, please, please," I pant, mewl, and arch against him. I try to squeeze my thighs together to stop him, but he's relentless.

"My name. Say it." He works his fingers in and out of me, then squeezes my clit and kneads my nipples at the same time, and my entire body trembles. "Oh, my god, Massimo," I cry out.

"Good girl." He releases me, only to turn me around.

"Wait, what?" He tugs on my half-undone corset and pushes it down past my waist, along with my panties. The clothes fall around my ankles, and I kick them aside. He sinks down on the bed and stares at my pussy for so long, I shuffle my feet. He grips my hips to hold me in place, then buries his nose in my center and draws in a long breath.

A tremor grips me. It's so hot, so carnal that my knees give out from under me. I sway, then grasp his hair to hold on. He makes a pleased sound at the back of his throat.

"You smell so fucking good," he says in a low, throaty voice that is a kind of sex in itself.

He glances up at me and his eyes gleam. "I'm going to eat you now."

4

Olivia

"Wait, can we—"

He drags his tongue up my pussy lips, and oh, my fucking god, all thoughts drain from my head. He flattens his tongue and swipes it across my slit again and again. My eyes roll back in my head. *What was I going to say? Doesn't matter; not important.* He takes big handfuls of my ass cheeks and squeezes so hard, I yelp. He softens his touch by curling his tongue around my clit. He sucks on it, and I mewl, hold onto his hair, and tug him even closer. He slurps on my pussy, strumming my pussy lips with his tongue, then stabs it inside my channel. He sinks his tongue inside me over and over again. Each time he mimics how he'll fuck me with his cock, my entire body trembles. My back curves. A trembling grips me.

"I'm going to—"

He pulls his tongue out of my channel and leans back.

I sway a little, then glance down at him. "What, what are you—?"

He grips the backs of my thighs, rises to his feet, and hauls me up with him like I weigh nothing. I'm not light. At five-foot-seven, with curves that I've never managed to control, I weigh more than I should. But he lifts me like it's nothing.

"Hey—" I grab hold of his shoulders. "What are you—"

He merely turns, then throws me down on the bed. I bounce twice, then shove the hair back from my face. When I look up at him, he's staring at me with a fierce hunger on his face. He looks like he hasn't eaten for weeks, and I'm the first morsel he's come across and can't wait to consume. The protest I was going to voice dies in my throat. I gulp; and watch as he wipes the back of his hand across his glistening mouth. He's wearing me on his lips, and oh, God, that's so freakin' hot.

He reaches behind him, and his biceps flex as he grabs the back of his T-shirt and pulls it off. He flings it aside, yanks off his boots and socks, then shucks his pants. When he straightens, my breath catches.

I was wrong. Ripped is an understatement to describe his body. Eight-pack chest and corrugated abs, with the picture of an eagle in mid-flight inked diagonally across his pecs. The beak touches the base of his throat, one of the wings wrap around the front of his chest, and the other folds around his back, embracing him.

The claws of the bird curl down as if pointing to the magnificent shaft that points upward between his thighs. And what thighs they are—corded with muscles and lightly dusted with hair, they frame his thick, pulsing cock. I certainly chose the right man to break my dry spell.

My heart seems to have become a hummingbird, with the way it flaps in my chest. My pulse skitters against my wrists and at the base of my throat. I push up on my elbows and watch as he approaches the bed. Without taking his gaze off of my face, he bends, curls his fingers around my ankles, and tugs me forward until I am poised with my ass on the edge of the bed. One side of his lips twist. He reaches over and pulls out a package from the nightstand. I hear the crinkle of the wrapper then watch as he slides it over his cock, sheathing himself. He locks his gaze with mine, then grabs my thighs and pries them apart, so I am spread wide for him. He leans down just enough for the crown of his cock to nudge my opening.

A moan bleeds from my lips.

"Tell me your name," he growls.

I shake my head. "No names."

"I gave you my name; it's only fair you give me yours."

"Is that even your real name?"

"What do you think?" He drags the tip of his cock up my pussy lips, and I jerk my pelvis forward, trying to capture it with my slit.

"I think you should stop teasing me, and fuck me."

He laughs. The sound is dark and silky, and so mean, it tugs on my nerve endings. I dig my fingers into the cover as he strums my pussy lips with his dick. He prods my slit with his cock, and I gasp. "Please, please, please," I blubber. God, how demeaning is this? And it's not fair that he asks my name when I told him specifically that I didn't want to share what it was. He pulls back and my ovaries cry with desperation. My guts twist, and my belly clenches. "Massimo, fuck me already."

"Your name, *Stellina*." His lips kick up.

Little star. He called me little star. Why would he do that? It's such an unusual and beautiful endearment, it feels like it means something. But it can't. This is just a one-night stand, and I intend to keep it that way.

He places his knee on the bed, and leans over me to cup my breast. He places his mouth over mine, his nose almost bumping mine, sharing my breath. He peers into my eyes, then whispers, "Please, tell me your name."

Maybe it's because he says please, or it's because I want to hear my name from his lips, but I can't stop myself from whispering, "Via." I squeeze my eyes shut. "You can call me Via."

"Can I kiss you, Via?" he murmurs.

"Eh?" I snap my eyelids open in surprise. He releases my breast, only to palm my cheek. "May I? I very much want to taste your mouth."

I glance between his eyes, the pupils so dark they seem to take up most of the space in those stunning irises, leaving only a circle of gray-blue around the edges.

"Via?" He lowers his gaze to my mouth. "May I...?" He lets the words hang there between us, leaving it up to me, and somehow, it's as sexy as him licking my pussy.

"Yes, please, I—"

He captures my mouth with his, cutting off whatever I was going to say. Not that it matters, for sparks—no, explosions—fill my mind, then fade away, leaving nothing but the taste of him, the scent of him, the feel of his tongue sliding over mine as he presses his lips to mine and kisses me. I feel his touch all the way to my toes, to my fingertips, to the roots of my hair. Somehow, it's more intimate than him thrusting his tongue into my cunt. This sharing of breaths, of tasting myself on him, the press of his lips, which are both firm and soft at the same time, as he draws from me and opens himself up to me all at once. A groan rumbles up his chest. He tilts his face, deepens the kiss, and that burning in my lower belly erupts into a full-blown forest fire. I throw my arms around his shoulders, and angle my hips so his cock slides in.

My entire body seems to sigh in recognition. It doesn't feel like it's the first time he's made love to me—Fuck! What am I thinking? He's not making love to me, he's fucking me. And it feels like we've fucked before.

He sinks another inch, opening me up even more around his girth, and oh, God, it feels so good. So unreal. I wrap my legs around his waist, push my hips up, and my pussy envelops more of his cock. He throbs inside of me, and all of

my blood seems to drain to my clit. He bites down on my lower lip and I tremble. He licks my mouth, and a moan wells up. I flutter my eyes open to find him
watching me. And this… His direct eye contact is too much.

To see my desire reflected in the spark that ignites deep within his, turns this
entire experience into something different. Something potent. Something I have
no control over. Something that's going to change my life. *Something I am going to
regret.* I widen my gaze, open my mouth to tell him I want him to stop, when he
lunges forward. He buries himself to the hilt, his balls slap against my thighs,
and he hits that spot deep inside. "Oh, my god!" I cry out. Vibrations radiate out
from where we are connected. He pulls out, and still holding my gaze, he slams
up and into me in one long, smooth stroke. The entire bed jerks and I move up
the mattress. He leans more of his weight on me to hold me in place, then he
begins to fuck me in earnest.

5

Massimo

I am breaking every rule in my book. I asked for her permission before I kissed her. I withheld her orgasm until she told me her name. She told me she didn't want to share her name with me, but the moment I tasted her pussy, all the rules exited my head. She tasted so sweet, so perfect, I didn't want to stop eating her. But I wanted her first orgasm to be mind-blowing, so after I undressed her and myself, I reached for the condom. I entered her… And that's the moment everything changed.

To look into her eyes, watching her react as I fuck her, is an almost religious experience. It doesn't make sense. How could someone I've never met before have such an impact on me? The way she mewls when I sink into her and gasps when I pull out of her... How she flutters around me when I thrust into her... How her pussy clenches around my cock... How she digs her fingernails into my shoulders and holds on as I plunge inside her... It's overwhelming.

I slide my hand between us to pinch her clit as I bottom out, and she shoots up off the bed. Her back curves, and she cries out as she climaxes. Moisture bathes my cock, and I continue thrusting in and out of her, fucking her through the aftershocks that grip her in the aftermath of the climax. My dick extends as I plunge into her again. I lower my mouth to her breast and tug on her nipple. She moans.

"Please, Massimo, please—"

"You're going to come again." I lick her nipple.

"No." She shudders. "I can't."

"You can." I suck on her nipple as I slide my palm down to where we are connected. I circle the area and she whines. I continue to suckle the other sensitive nipple, then scoop up her cum and drag my fingers over her butt to play with the knot of nerves between her ass cheeks. She freezes, and I raise my head and brush my mouth over hers. "Let me in."

She swallows, her gaze narrows, and her eyebrows slant down.

I nibble on her lower lip. "Please, I promise, I'll make it so fucking good for you, Via."

She draws a breath, then nods.

I kiss her hard in gratitude, then slide my finger inside her back hole. She gasps, and a tremor shivers down her spine. I continue to fuck her as I move my finger in and out of her, until she settles. Then, I add a second finger inside her as I pick up my pace. She whimpers, and fuck, the sound makes me even harder. I push into her with enough force that my balls slap against her inner thighs, until I, once more, brush against the core of her deep inside. She shudders, digs her nails into my shoulders, and I know she's close again. A hot sensation sweeps my chest and I thrust into her over and over again. I curl my fingers inside her back channel, as I slide my tongue over hers, and she flutters around my cock as she comes. I plunge into her one last time and empty myself into her.

My orgasm goes on and on. I come so hard, I see stars. Sweat clings to my shoulders, and my breath comes in pants. My heart is racing so it feels like I've run for miles. I balance myself on my elbows to keep my weight off of her. She flutters her eyes open and stares at me. I bend to kiss her, and she moves her head to the side. Anger curls in my chest but I push it away. She's right to do that. We're a one-night stand, and it doesn't help to feel anything more for her. I pull out of her, then slide off of the bed, and head to the bathroom. I dispose of the condom, wash my hands, then grab a towel and wet it. I walk over to find she's still in the same position on the bed. A woman who's not afraid of being seen naked. That's so hot. I bend and wipe between her legs.

"Wha—" She sits up. "What are you doing?"

"Cleaning you up." I swipe the cloth across her flesh once more, then toss it aside. I clamber onto the bed and lay back against the pillows before patting the space next to me. "Come on."

"Umm..." She glances at the door, then at me. "I think I should go."

"You're not going anywhere at this time of the night." The moment I say it, I know it's a mistake, for her jaw stiffens.

"You can't tell me what to do."

Actually, I can. I don't say that aloud, though. Instead, I fold my arms behind my head. "Suit yourself, but you and I both know, it's not safe for you drive after the shots you had earlier. Rest up, and you can leave at dawn."

She looks at the door again, then nods. She crawls over onto the other side of the bed, pulls the cover up over herself, and lies down, the breadth of the bed between us.

"I don't bite." I shoot her a sideways glance. "Unless you want me to."

She chuckles. "Does that line work with other women?"

"Sometimes." I turn over to face her. "Do you work out a lot?"

Her shoulders stiffen, then she narrows her gaze on me. "What gave you that idea?"

"Your leg muscles are toned, and you have an incredible figure. Also, the way you move, like liquid gold."

"Liquid gold?" She laughs. "No one has ever given me that compliment before."

"So, you do work out a lot. Is it to do with your profession?"

She hesitates. "I've already broken my promise to myself and told you my name."

"Part of your name," I remind her. "Is it short for Livia?"

She pales, then swings her legs over the side of the bed. I reach over to grab her wrist before she can rise. "Sorry, I shouldn't have asked."

She scowls at me. "We had an agreement, and you've been trying your best to break it. Are you always this untrustworthy?"

"Only when I'm with you."

She tries to pull away, but I don't let go. "Stay, please. I'm really sorry. I promise, I won't ask any more personal questions."

"Can I trust you this time?" She glowers.

"You'll have to try it for yourself to find out." I tug on her wrist, and she tumbles back on the bed. I pull her close and curl myself around her. She stays quiet for a few moments, her muscles stiff. I slide my other arm under her neck and spoon her. Little by little, the tension drains out of her. I pull the cover over both of us, then place my arm around her waist. Her thick hair forms a cloud around her shoulders. I bury my face in it and draw in a breath. Vanilla and coconut, the scent of her shampoo sinks into my blood and I store it away. I'll never be able to smell this particular scent and not think of her. I tuck her head under my chin, match my breathing to hers and drift off.

I come awake to desire pounding in my veins and the sensation of something warm and soft fixed around my cock. I glance down to find she's kneeling between my legs with her mouth around my dick. She locks her fingers around the base of my shaft then flattens her tongue and sweeps it up from the bottom of my steel hard shaft. "*Cazzo.*" I grip the sheets next to me, a burst of heat sweeping up my spine. She holds my gaze as she closes her mouth over the crown of my shaft and sucks.

"*Gesù Cristo!*" My groin hardens, and my dick lengthens. She pulls back until the tip of my cock rests between her lips, then lowers her head to swallow it. Watching my cock disappear inside her mouth has to be the most erotic thing I've ever seen. I push the hair away from her face, then wrap the long strands around my palm. I tug her head back, and she moans around my cock. The vibrations travel up my shaft and my balls tighten. She wraps her fingers around the base of my dick and squeezes. Heat detonates from the contact. The pressure at the base of my spine tightens until my entire body is vibrating with tension. "Fuck! You're killing me, Via."

Her eyes gleam. She hums around my cock, then swallows, and I can't take it anymore. I pull on her hair until she finally relents and releases my shaft with a pop. Then I grab her shoulders, yank her up my body, and close my mouth over hers. I kiss her, suck on her tongue, taste myself on her, and that drives me even crazier. I slide her onto the bed, then flip her over on her front. She gasps, and turns to glance at me over her shoulder as I squeeze her butt. Holding her gaze, I lower my head and bite her ass cheek.

"What the hell?" she yells.

I smirk, then straighten and slap her on the same cheek.

She screeches, "You jerkhole, what the hell do you think you're doing?"

I continue to spank her on alternate butt cheeks, left-right-left, then repeat the motion again and again until her ass is a fiery red, with the marks of my palm clearly visible on her skin.

"Fuck me." I rub the heat into her skin, and she whimpers. A moan bleeds from her lips and I bend and kiss the abraded skin. I sit back on my heels and tug on her waist, urging her up on all fours. In this position her butt is right there in my face. I squeeze her butt cheeks, pry them apart, then bury my face in her ass.

6

Olivia

"Massimo!" I gasp. Heat streaks my cheeks. To say I am mortified is putting it mildly. No man has ever eaten me out there. No one. He stabs his tongue inside my forbidden hole, and a tingling coils in my belly. I try to pull away, not because it doesn't feel good, but the opposite. How is that possible? Are there nerve endings there I'm not aware of? Also, why does it feel sooo good?

He pulls me back, then slides his hand around my hip to play with my pussy. The combination of him tugging on my clit, along with him curling his tongue inside my back channel is too much. I try to pull away, even as I push my butt back, trying to get him to go deeper inside. He releases me, only to reach over and grab something from the bedside table. Something cold trails over my back hole.

I shiver as he works the lube inside my puckered hole, then slides a finger inside. He continues to strum my clit and the vibrations chase each other in my belly. He adds a second finger and works his digits in and out of me. I groan, bury my face in the pillow and give in to the foreign sensations that zing up my spine.

He pulls out his fingers. The mattress shifts. I hear the bedside drawer open, the crinkle of the wrapper, then something much bigger and more blunt nudges my back opening.

I tense, and he slides his other hand to play with my clit. Instantly, my bones liquefy. My muscles tremble, I release the breath I hadn't been aware I was holding, and that's when he slides into me.

Oh, my god, it hurts. "It hurts," I cry out.

He pauses, allowing me to adjust to his size, then reaches up to pinch my nipple. He twists it, and my entire body jolts. The pulse in my center begins to beat faster. Moisture pools in my core and that's when he begins to move. He pulls out, then pushes forward, and again through the ring of muscles.

"Oh, god," I gasp as a trembling seizes me. Pinpricks of electricity radiate out from where we are connected. He continues to squeeze my nipple as he moves in and out of me. Each time he sinks into me, he slides deeper. On the next thrust, he bottoms out and seats himself fully inside me. His balls slap against my tender flesh, sending another burst of heat shimmering up my spine. I dig my fingers into the cover, and tears squeeze out from the corners of my eyes. It's too much. He's filling me up, stretching me, pinning me to the mattress with his cock. He pulls out, then thrusts inside. At the same time, he yanks on my nipple and slaps my pussy with his free hand.

I howl, my back curves, and the orgasm crashes over me. My entire body shudders as I submit to the vibrations that hold me in thrall. As I drift down into myself, I become aware of the aftershocks coursing through me. He fucks me through it, prolonging the high. Still woozy, I reach down between our legs to grab his balls and squeeze. His muscles lock, tension pours off of him, and with a muted roar, he empties himself inside me. When I open my eyes again, I hear the sound of water running in the bathroom. Is he cleaning up? I close my eyes, only to jerk awake to find I'm on my back and he's cleaning between my legs again.

"You're making a habit of this," I say, or at least, I try to, for my brain cells have been blown by that last round of fucking. Instead, I actually mumble something like, "Ya...may...aha...mmm..."

He chuckles, then straightens and tucks me into his side again. My entire body is so relaxed, I feel I'm drifting. Cast adrift in a white space with no beginning, and no end. There's a soft brush against the top of my head, then he wraps his big arms around me. The heat from his body cocoons me, and I close my eyes again.

The next time I'm woken, is to find him inside me again, moving softly. His big body looms over me, his gray eyes almost transparent. I watch myself in them as he thrusts gently into me. He leans and kisses me and I allow myself to sink into it.

It's fine; this is the last time. I'm going to walk away and never see him again. Surely, it's okay to let myself enjoy this time with him?

I wrap my arms around his neck as he coaxes me to wind my legs about his waist. He pushes into me again and again, his every touch so gentle that warmth seeps into my skin. My blood thrums, and my cheeks flush. I push my breasts into his chest, enjoying the scrape of his hair-roughened chest against my breasts. He deepens the kiss as he speeds up his actions. This time, my orgasm wafts up my legs, dream-like in its progress. It creeps up my thighs, curls around my waist, then slides up my spine. A groan wells up, and he swallows it as I float up to the sky. He follows me over the edge, his heartbeat thudding against my chest. We stay there for a few minutes, until my eyelids begin to flutter shut. He pulls out of me, and I hear him slide off the bed. Guess he must be disposing the condom. Within seconds, the mattress depresses, then something cool brushes between my legs before he slips in next to me and pulls me on top.

"Sleep," he whispers.

7

———————

Massimo

I come awake with a start, and even before I open my eyes, I know she's gone. *Fuck, fuck, fuck, how could I have not woken up when she left?* I'm used to sleeping with my awareness at the forefront of my consciousness, ready to awaken at the slightest noise.

Clearly, the sex last night went to my head. Maybe it's good she's not here. This way, I don't have the ability to find out more about her. I glance around and notice something glimmering on her pillow. I walk over and pick it up. It's the chain she was wearing yesterday. The locket is in the shape of a horseshoe, and seems aged with time. An antique of some kind, maybe? I get dressed, slide the chain and locket into the pocket of my jeans, then walk out.

Downstairs, the bar is silent as I walk past it and out the side entrance. I walk over to my Harley and fire it up, then glance around the parking lot. There were too many cars there when I arrived last night. Any one of them could have been hers. Sourcing security tapes from the bar is out of the question, since I made a deal with the owner to turn off the security system when I'm there. It's a precaution I took to ensure no one could track down my whereabouts.

I should let her go, keep our association to the night we shared, but as I drive out, I already know that's not going to happen. The sex was incredible, but more than that, there was something about Via, the way she laughed, how she tried to take the lead over and over again—good luck with that, it's not something I'll ever allow a woman to do—and yet, she managed to surprise me. When she walked out of the bathroom in only her panties and that corset, which nipped her waist in and pushed up her gorgeous breasts, and turned her already generous hips into porn star proportions—I almost came in my pants.

It took everything in me to hold back as she walked over to stand in front of me, as if asking me to undress her. The gall of the woman, she managed to get me to toe the line, and fuck, if that wasn't the sexiest thing ever. She held her own against me every step of the way, responded to my every ministration, opened her heart to me when we made love—when we fucked, I mean. Oh... That gorgeous hair of hers that seemed to have a life of its own; there was so much of it. It brushed my chest and goosebumps erupted on my skin. The taste of her lips, the heat of her pussy, the tightness of her ass—I have no doubt I'm the first to take her there. Fuck. I drag my fingers through my hair, and realize I've been staring at my bike for a while now. Fuck, I needed to get out of here. Maybe the drive home will clear my head.

<hr>

The drive home did not clear my head. In fact, as the days progress, things are getting worse. I can't eat, can't sleep. Can't do anything but redouble my efforts to find Via. Why didn't I ask for her full name? Why didn't I try to find out where she lives? She's from somewhere nearby. Or not. She could have been passing through, but I doubt it. No, she must be from somewhere nearby.

Of course, she could have given me the wrong name, but I doubt that. She was thinking on her feet and probably chose a name similar to her real name. Not that it increases the odds of finding her—I don't know her surname. The fact that her profession is somehow related to being physically active is a clue, but again, it doesn't narrow down the odds of finding her. At least, that's what the private investigator I put on the case told me. Without a picture of some kind to go on, tracking her down is going to be nearly impossible, he said.

I threw more money at the PI and ordered him to do his best. He's someone I trust, and I've used him in the past, so I have no doubt he will. Also, if he doesn't try hard enough, I'll put a bullet through his head. He knows that, too. You don't deal with the Mafia without realizing it's a high-risk, high-return gamble. Like the one I took when I pursued my interest in her and propositioned her to sleep with me.

Just looking at her, seeing something ethereal shining through her eyes, I was caught. There was a light in her I've never noticed in anyone else. A vivacity, a greed for life that came through. There's something undefinable about her, what the French call *je ne sais quoi*, something that made me want to look at her again and again. And then I slept with her, and I knew I didn't want to let go of her. It's why I've spent the last week trying to find her, with no success.

And that's in addition to helping my brother Luca track down the man responsible for attempting to kill my half-brother Seb and his wife Elsa.

In the process, Luca got himself kidnapped. He escaped, along with his fellow prisoner, a woman called Jeanne. Unbelievably, he ended up proposing to Jeanne.

In a last-minute decision, he took one of our private planes to Malta, where they could get married without the need for paperwork, or any of those practical matters that could have delayed it.

And then he roped me in to getting Jeanne's best friends to the airport and on another of our planes so they could join their friend as bridesmaids. But first, I need to take them to the boutique so they can choose their dresses.

Which is why I'm standing next to my car outside Jeanne's friends' apartment building, waiting for them to join me. I should be out pounding the pavement, looking for Via. Instead, I'm playing chauffeur to people I've never met before. The things I do for my siblings. The next time I see Luca, I'm going to make sure he appreciates the favor I've done for him. I pull back the cuff of my jacket and check the time. We need to get a move on if we're to make it to the airport and then onto Malta in time for the wedding.

A giggle reaches me just before the sound of footsteps. I glance up to find a petite woman with dark blonde hair walking toward me. "You must be Massimo."

"Penny?" I shake her hand. Luca shared her contact details with me, and I called her earlier to let her know I was on my way.

"This is so exciting. I'm so thrilled for Luca and Jeanne. Are they really getting married?"

"It would seem that way, yes." I half-smile. Her happiness is infectious. Apparently, Jeanne has genuine friends who don't mind dropping everything in the middle of the day and rushing to attend her surprise wedding.

"Shall we?" I open the back of the car and gesture for her to get in.

"Oh, hold on, we're waiting for—"

"Penny, did you take my passport? I can't find it." A new voice. A familiar voice. The hair on the back of my neck rises.

I pivot to find the woman who's haunted my every waking moment in the past week walking toward us.

She spots me at the same time and her jaw slackens. She blinks rapidly, then shakes her head as if to clear it. Her footsteps slow, until she comes to a pause in front of me. I rake my gaze over her flushed cheeks, her pink lips slightly parted, her gorgeous green eyes, wide with surprise.

"You? What are you doing here?"

8

Olivia

"I'm here to pick you up and take you to the boutique," he rumbles.

Oh, my goodness, that sinfully deep, caramel custard voice which I never thought I'd hear again. What is he doing here? How did he find me?

"You're taking us to the boutique?" I burst out. "Why would you do that?"

"I'm Luca's brother," he replies.

"You're Luca Sovrano's brother?"

"Massimo Sovrano, at your service." He holds out his hand.

I ignore it. "If you're Luca's brother, then—" I stiffen. "You're part of the *Cosa Nostra*," I state flatly.

"My brothers and I *are* the *Cosa Nostra*."

"Do the two of you know each other?" Penny glances between us.

"No," I say at the same time he says, "Yes."

Her gaze bounces between us.

"So, you don't know each other?" Her forehead crinkles.

"Not strictly, no," Massimo says slowly. "What did you say your name was?" he asks.

"I didn't." I brush past him, then walk to the open door of the car and slide into the back seat. I shut the door behind me, and Massimo opens the front door of the car for Penny.

She gives him an apologetic look. "Olivia's not always this rude," Penny explains.

"Olivia, huh?" He glances at me, and his eyes are hot and smoldering.

Had I really thought his eyes were colorless? Silver sparks flicker in their depths, like motes of dust caught in beams of sunlight. My breath catches, and my cheeks heat as I recall... The slide of his skin on mine. Him peering deep into my eyes as he'd taken me, pushed into me inch by agonizing inch. As he'd placed his mouth over mine and shared my breath. As he'd pushed me onto my front and covered my body with his. Moisture laces my core. My thighs clench.

One side of his lips kicks up as if he's remembering the same things as me. *Jerk.*

I glance away, and he shuts the car door behind Penny, then takes his seat behind the wheel. He pulls away from the curb, and I can't take my gaze off of his hands. Broad, thick fingers topped with blunt fingernails that he crammed inside the most forbidden part of me. Sensations well up my spine. I wriggle around in my seat, trying to make myself more comfortable.

"So, you and Luca must be close if you agreed to ferry us around..." Penny prompts.

Massimo snorts. "More like, he realized he had no choice but to depend on someone to help him out."

Penny laughs. "Are you surprised he and Jeanne are getting married so quickly after they met?"

He flips on his indicator and turns the car. The silence stretches a beat, then another.

Finally, he shakes his head. "When you find the person you know you're meant to spend the rest of your life with, you move fast." He raises his gaze to capture mine in the rearview mirror. "When you know, you know."

What the—what does he mean by that? Does he mean for me to guess the hidden meaning in what he said? Is he implying? No, surely not. I lock my fingers together, and turn to glance out the window.

"Oh, how romantic." Penny turns to glance at me. "Did you hear what Massimo said, Olivia?"

I raise a shoulder. "I don't believe in such nonsense. Personally, I think Luca and Jeanne need to think it over before they rush into a marriage, but hey, if it suits them, who am I to stand in their path?"

"I take it you don't believe in falling in love?" Massimo drawls.

"I believe in planning your life out, and going after what you want."

"And what is it you want?"

"To be the best in my chosen field," I retort.

"Olivia's going to play the lead in *Beauty and the Beast,* which will be showing in Palermo, starting tomorrow," Penny chirps.

"Ah, so an actress then?" His lips curve.

He's remembering the fact he guessed correctly I'm in a profession that's physically demanding.

I huff. "I prefer to be called an artiste, actually."

His grin widens. I scowl back at him. Penny glances between us again. "You sure the two of you haven't met before?"

"Positive." I turn to stare out the window, and this time, make sure I keep my gaze averted until we reach our destination. Massimo parks in front of a shop with the most amazing dresses in the window. I slide out of the car and join Penny as we gape at the creations. One of the dresses seems to be made of a sheer black lace with red trim that shimmers in the evening sun. It should look outlandish, but the way the panels have been sewn together, it looks ethereal. The kind of dress a rock star would wear to her wedding. The other dress has a sweetheart neckline, a slim silhouette, and the most amazing, intricate embroidery on it. There is a small discreet sign next to the door that says: Karma's Creations.

"Umm, I don't think we can afford whatever this shop is selling," I mutter.

"Luca insists that Jeanne will be very happy if the two of you accept the bridesmaids' dresses chosen for you."

"But—" I begin to speak, but Penny nudges me sharply in my side. "Ow!" I yelp. "What are you—"

She scowls at me. "It's Jeanne's wedding. Imagine how happy she'll be when we turn up as her bridesmaids."

"But the dress—"

"—Is very important. It's part of the memory we're helping her make." She holds my gaze, trying to convey that I should shut up now and go with the flow.

I blow out a breath. "Fine, fine. I'll do it for Jeanne."

Massimo holds the door open and I follow Penny inside. That very male scent of spice and citrus and wood smoke seems to wrap itself around me as I walk past him. *His fingers around my neck, his chest flattened to my back, every striated pec of his imprinted on my skin as he'd bent me over and thrust into me... Stop it, just stop. He's part of the Mafia.* Part of the life I swore to leave behind. I want nothing to do with his kind.

Mafioso come across as macho and charismatic. You can't resist their sheer maleness. But I've seen how they treat their women. How they cloister them and refuse to allow them to make up their own minds. How they treat them like possessions and deprive them of choice.

My father was an outlier when it came to his daughters. But with his wife, he was as traditional as the rest of the Mafia men. She was an actress, until she met him. She sacrificed her career for him and her children. Grew bitter because of it. Yet, she was so firmly transformed that she wanted the very same for her daughters—security, marriage, staying in the community. Not me, though. I broke down that wall and escaped, and I'm not going to be dragged back into it again.

Something brushes against my ankle. I glance down to see a beautiful Savannah brush up against me. "Hey you," I bend down and rub the cat's head. "Where did you come from?"

"Andy found you, eh?" A dark-haired woman walks over to greet us.

"Karma." Massimo closes the distance to her and kisses her cheek.

"Hey, you!" She smiles up at him, her eyes sparkling.

Something heavy crashes into my chest. It presses down on my lungs, and I can't breathe. I tuck my elbows into my sides and try to regain my composure. Who is she? Wife? Girlfriend? Mistress?

"How's the little guy, or is it a girl, doing?" Massimo touches her stomach. His movements have a familiarity to them that hint he knows her well.

That heaviness intensifies until it feels like my very body is being dragged to the floor. *Is it his? Is she pregnant with his child? And the asshole slept with me?* I curl my fingers into fists.

"It's too early to tell," she laughs, her skin positively glowing.

He takes her hand between both of his, then turns to face us. "Meet Karma, my sister-in-law, and the designer of your bridesmaids' dresses."

"Your sister-in-law?" I blink.

He smirks. "What did you think?" he murmurs, watching me closely.

"I didn't. I mean, I thought... I mean—" I toss my hair over my shoulder and turn to Karma. "Are those your creations in the window."

"They are; you like?"

"Very much." I laugh.

Andy mews and Karma narrows her gaze on him. "You've already had your snack. Nothing more until dinnertime. You're putting on too much weight."

He walks over to Massimo, who scoops him by the scruff of his neck and places him on his shoulder. He nods at Karma. "Why don't you take them inside and show them the dresses?"

9

———————

Massimo

"What do you think?"

I glance up from my phone and my jaw drops.

After Karma took Via—she'll always be Via to me—and Penny inside, the shop assistant showed me to the waiting area. I decided to use the time to catch up on work. With my oldest brother, Michael, wanting to legalize the *Cosa Nostra* business, I've been involved in many of the intricacies that come with that. Before I realized it, forty-five minutes had passed. I was about to ask the shop assistant to ask Karma how much longer it'd take, when Via stepped out from behind the door that separated the waiting room from the atelier.

I take in her curvy figure draped in a dress with long sleeves and a bodice like a corset, not dissimilar to what she was wearing the day we met. It nips in at the waist, and the skirt falls in a straight line to her feet. It's a deceptively simple dress, but the way it's cut, it clings to her every dip and curve. It shows off her hourglass figure, her gorgeous breasts, those curvy hips and thick thighs, with which she gripped me as I drove into her.

"Massimo?" She props a hand on her hip and angles her body so I can see the way the dress molds to her thighs and down the line of her legs. She looks like a picture from yesteryear's Hollywood. Beguiling, alluring, and absolutely ravishing.

"Do I look that bad?" She purses her lips. "Maybe I should change." She turns to go, and I rise to my feet.

"Don't change."

A thick sensation crowds my chest. My belly hurts. My fingertips tingle to reach out and touch her, to make sure she's real.

She frowns as I walk over to her. "You look perfect," I murmur.

The air thickens. Her chest rises and falls. She tips up her chin to meet my gaze and those green eyes of hers are so clear, I can see myself reflected in them. She licks her lips, and the blood drains to my groin. I widen my stance to accommodate the growing thickness in my crotch.

She draws in a breath, and color stains her cheeks. Her eyelids flutter and she lowers her chin so her hair falls over her face. "Uh… I'll… I'll just tell Karma I'm good with this."

She turns to leave, and goddamn it, I am not letting her go. Not again. I grab her wrist and pull her so she falls against my chest.

"Massimo." She plants her palm against me. "What are you doing?"

"Are you going to pretend we've never met before?"

"We didn't meet before. Don't you remember, we said what we had was for one night only? When I left that room, I forgot all about it."

"Did you?" I twist her arm behind her so her shoulders arch back. I glare at her and she pales.

"Let me go," she whispers.

"No." I rake my gaze over her face, then back to her eyes. "Tell me you didn't feel something in that room. Tell me you didn't walk out of there and leave a part of you with me."

"I…" She opens her mouth and shuts it. "I—" She glances away.

"That's what I thought." I walk her backward until her back is to the wall. Then I release her arm, only to cup her cheek. "I can't get you out of my mind, *bellezza*. I can't stop thinking of your lips, your beautiful tits, your gorgeous ass, how you moan when you're close, and your back arches when you're about to come, how your cunt flutters around my dick as you orgasm, how you cry out when you climax, how you—" I lower my face until our eyelashes kiss. "How, when I look into your eyes, I can see the light that shines through you. Your radiance stands out like a beacon on a misty night. There's something about you that is so attractive, it renders me speechless every time I see you. I don't want to want you, but I do."

Her pupils dilate. Her breath comes in little gasps. The pulse at the base of her neck flutters like a hummingbird trying to escape the confines of a cage. I stare at her mouth, and a moan bleeds from her lips. I brush my lips over hers, and her entire body shudders. I lick into her mouth, and she sighs. I nip on her lower lip, and she leans into me. I deepen the kiss, thrust my tongue inside her mouth and suck on her upper lip. She plants her palms on my chest as if to push me away, then rises on her tiptoes and kisses me back. She licks the seam of my lips, and a groan rumbles up my chest. I push my hips into hers, holding her immobile against the wall, and she gasps. She must feel the length of my arousal. I hadn't meant for this to go so far, but seeing her pretend she didn't know me made me mad. How dare she act like we never met? Like she didn't come apart under my fingers, my lips, my cock. I tear my mouth from hers and stare into her desire-filled eyes. "Never avoid me again. I won't tolerate it, you feel me?"

She swallows, then tips up her chin. "Never try to kiss me again. I don't want it, you get me?"

"Not what your body says." I lean more of my weight into her so the tent in my crotch stabs into her core. Color flushes her cheeks.

"I am not my body." She firms her lips. Then she slaps me.

The sound echoes around the space. My cheek throbs, and I can feel every pulse, all the way to the crown of my cock. My shaft elongates. Her pupils dilate. The air thickens with unsaid emotions pressing down on us. Then we move at the same time.

Our mouths collide, our teeth clash, and our tongues tangle as we kiss and kiss. The blood roars in my ears, and my heart hammers against my rib cage. I slap my palm to the wall next to her face and kiss her so hard, my teeth ache. My chest hurts, and my stomach ties itself in knots. *Oh, fuck, this is going to complicate my life immensely.* I tear my mouth from hers, and we stare at each other without saying a word, even as our eyes seem to communicate on a different level. I step back and she slides out from between me and the wall, then turns to leave.

"Via."

She pauses.

"This isn't over yet."

10

Olivia

This isn't over? It never started. Whatever it is he thinks happened in that room... Oh, shit, I know he's right. It did. There was a connection. The kind of sex we had... It was beyond intense. It was potent, powerful, profound, the kind that imprints in your mind and your heart—*fuck, fuck, fuck. I am not going to fall for him.* He gives good dick. Doesn't mean I'm going to develop feelings for him. I cannot develop feelings for him. He's the Mafia, for heaven's sake. He's everything I've spent my life avoiding. I swore I'd never fall for a Mafia guy, and here I am, perilously close to being obsessed about him. I must stop thinking of him. Easier said than done, when he's sitting in a seat up the corridor from me and hasn't taken his gaze off of me since we took off.

After that searing kiss in Karma's boutique, Penny and I chose our bridesmaids outfits in matching shades of blue and Massimo drove us to the private jet where he boarded the plane with us. And okay, I hadn't thought he was coming with us. Somehow, I'd been sure he was going to drop us at the airport and return, but apparently, I was mistaken. Like a coward, I slipped into the seat next to Penny on the plane, hoping being next to her meant I could avoid having to look at him. But sadly, Penny fell asleep as soon as we were in the air.

I'd popped my earphones in and tried listening to some music. When that didn't work, I tried to read my latest smutty romance on my Kindle. Normally, that would have held my attention, but for the first time, my book boyfriends couldn't compete with the allure of the man I'd had a one-night stand with. I finally ditched my Kindle and settled for looking out the window at the clouds, while trying my best not to shoot glances at Mr. Alphaholeness. The stewardess brought us glasses of prosecco, and antipasto to eat. Of course, she shot him a big smile and spent time talking with him. He was too far away so I couldn't hear the conversation, but the bastard smiled and laughed at something she said. Then she leaned over and slid something into the pocket of his shirt.

That bitch! Bet he's going to call her and meet her some time. I was so pissed off, I tossed back the prosecco on an empty stomach—being too on-edge to eat, and now, I'm feeling tipsy. Which always translates into feeling hornier. Maybe it's because I'm more relaxed, and in this instance, very aware of the jerkwaffle sitting not far from me.

I close my eyes and try to sleep, but I can feel his gaze on me. I shift in my seat and cross one leg over the other. At least I'm dressed in comfortable yoga pants and a hoodie. I crack open my eyes and my gaze clashes with his.

Those gray eyes seem almost blue in the dimness of the cabin. He sits there, motionless, manspreading—legs spread, his big arms braced over those trunk-like thighs. He dwarfs the seat, which, unlike in commercial airlines, is a large, comfortable, reclining armchair inviting you to stretch out and sleep. Like Penny. She snores softly in slumber, and I finally give up trying to get comfortable.

If I sit here a second longer, my gaze is going to fall on his crotch—a place I have avoided looking at for so long. But a girl can only resist for so long. I unzip my hoodie and plop it over the armrest of my seat. Is it hot in here, or is it me? Or is it this connection between us that's pulling so tightly, my entire body feels itchy? Best to go to the restroom and cool off. I jump up and stomp off in the direction of the restroom in the rear of the aircraft. I push the door open and step inside, turn to close it, when he plants his foot in the space between the door and the frame of the cubicle.

"What are you doing?" I whisper-scream.

"What do you think?" He steps forward and I slide back. Instantly, he steps inside the cubicle—which, by the way, is at least thrice the size of the bathrooms on commercial aircraft. It's still a small area, and he's so large he seems to take up most of the space.

"There's a bedroom through the door at the back of the aircraft, if you'd prefer?" He smirks.

"No, I would not," I snap.

"Suit yourself." He unbuttons the cuffs of his shirt sleeves and begins to roll them up.

"If you think you're going to join the mile-high club, you're sadly mistaken," I inform him.

His eyes gleam. "We'll see." He moves toward me, and I shuffle back until my back hits the wall.

I put up my hands. "Stop," I say, a tinge of desperation in my tone.

To my surprise, he does. "I'm not going to hurt you."

I swallow.

"You do know that, right?"

I stay quiet.

"Do you, Via?"

"Yes, of course, I know you won't hurt me," I admit.

"Do you want me to leave?"

I glance away.

"If you do, just say so, and I will. And I won't look at you again."

I squeeze my eyes shut. Why, oh, why did he have to be so handsome, so charismatic, so… tender? It came through in the way he touched me in that room. And in how he kissed me earlier and seduced me into opening my mouth to him. The soft and the hard. Chemistry and biology, and every damn thing in between, are at play when we're together.

"Via?" he asks softly.

I put up my hand. "Stop, please, don't say anything else." I flutter my eyes open. "I really don't want to be with you."

His eyes shutter. The gray in them leaches away until, once more, they're colorless, like the surface of a diamond. They definitely look as hard.

"Why not?"

"Because…" I tip up my chin. "Because of what you are."

"What I am?"

"You're in the Mafia."

"So?"

"So?" I throw up my hands. "How can you ask that with a straight face? You kill people. You do illegal stuff for a living."

His forehead crinkles. "Is it me you have an issue with, or is it what I do for a living?"

"Both?"

"What's your issue with me?"

"You… you mess with my head, okay? When I look at you, all I want to do is throw myself at you and ask you to fuck me."

His lips twist. "So, you want me to fuck you?"

I take a step forward so I'm toe to toe with him. "What do you think?"

"I think you can have whatever you want; you just have to ask me for it."

"And if I don't?" I firm my lips.

"But you want to, don't you?" He drags his gaze to my mouth, and it's as if he's touched me there. As if I can feel his breath on my cheek, his big hands on my hips, his tongue inside my mouth, his cock stabbing me where it hurts the most, inside my pussy.

"Just this one time, understand, it's the last—"

He lowers his head and closes his mouth over mine.

11

Massimo

Finally, fuck! If she'd asked me to leave, I'd have turned and gone... Reluctantly, and probably not without trying to persuade her one last time to change her mind, but I'd have left... Probably. Luckily, she met me halfway, and fuck, if I'm not going to make the most of this opportunity. I grab her under her butt and hoist her up. She instantly throws her arms about my neck and wraps her legs around my waist. I lunge forward until I can brace her weight against the wall. I bite down on that puffy lower lip of hers, which has been driving me mad for the length of the flight. She whimpers, then thrusts her breasts into my chest. The feel of her luscious curves against the planes of my body sends the blood pumping through my veins. A pulse flares to life at my temples, over my eyelids, even in my fucking balls. I shove down the waistband of her yoga pants, and stuff my fingers under her panties. I brush them against her clit, and she groans into my mouth. Fuck me, but she's so damn wet. I cram my fingers inside her cunt and curve them. She digs hers into my shoulders. I feel her nails through the fabric of my shirt and my cock thickens. "I need to fuck you."

"Yes." She gasps. "Yes, please."

I lower her feet to the ground, then pull a condom from my back pocket. When I glance up, I find she's already pulled off her yoga pants and her panties. My pants grow so tight, I am sure I'm going to burst out of them.

"Take it out," I growl.

She blinks rapidly, her breathing growing rough. She reaches over and unhooks my belt, lowers my zipper, then shoves down my pants and boxers. My cock springs free. Her pupils dilate, and her breathing hitches. She stares at my shaft like she wants to worship it.

"On your knees."

"What?" She jerks her chin up and her gaze clashes with mine. Her green eyes are stormy. There's a stubborn tilt to her jaw.

"Get. On. Your. Knees." I glare at her.

She pales, then squeezes her thighs together.

"Now, Via."

She huffs, then drops to the floor and reaches for my dick. Without taking her gaze off of mine, she closes her mouth around my cock and sucks.

"*Cazzo!*" I dig my fingers into her hair and tug. She moans around my shaft, and the vibrations travel all the way to my balls. She squeezes them and the blood drains to my groin. The pressure at the base of my spine grows, and goddamn, I don't want to come without her. I release her hair, only to wrap my fingers around the base of her neck. I coax her off my cock, then pull her up. I press my mouth to hers and taste myself on her palate. It's the confluence of me and her which drives me to the edge. I release her, only to tear the condom from the wrapping. She takes it from me and slides it over my shaft. I grab her under her butt again and perch her on the counter. I plant my hips between her legs, hook my arms under her knees and push them up. For a second, I stare down at her exposed flesh. Unable to stop myself, I drop to my knees and lick her from slit to clit. She throws her head back and keens. The sound goes straight to my cock. Straightening, I press my forehead against hers. Then I'm inside her.

She gasps, her entire body one rigid line of want. The heat in the space ratchets up, and a bead of sweat slides down my temple.

"Ma...ssimo," she stutters. Her pussy clamps down on my cock, and my balls tighten. I wrap my fingers around her throat and squeeze just hard enough for her to open her eyes. And there it is. That ever-present connection between us deepens, stretches, and thrums with the kind of electricity that raises the hair on my forearms. The muscles of my shoulders bunch, and my thighs harden. I pull out, then slam into her again with enough force for my balls to slap against her inner thighs. Wet squelching sounds fill the space as I stuff myself inside her again and again. Every time I sink into her, her shoulders hit the back of the cubicle. I slide my other hand behind her head to protect her, then hold her in place with my grasp on her neck as I fuck her in earnest. I increase the pressure on her throat, and she curls her fingers around my wrists and digs her fingernails into my skin as she holds on. She opens her mouth and I thrust my tongue between her lips, drinking from her, sucking on her tongue. I pound into her again, bottoming out inside her.

Her entire body jolts. Her hold on me loosens. That's when I release my grip. With a wheeze, she draws air into her lungs. Her mouth opens in a soundless cry as she shatters. Moisture bathes my cock as I lunge into her one last time and empty myself into her. Specks of black pepper the sides of my vision. I plant my hand on the mirror next to her face, press my cheek next to hers, and struggle to draw in a breath. We stay that way, unmoving, my heart racing in my chest, my pulse still pounding as I come down slowly.

I pull back to peer into her face, but her eyes are closed as aftershocks ripple down her body. I cup her cheek, dragging my thumb across her lips. "You okay?"

"You're a bastard," she says in a low voice.

"Oh?"

"I didn't give you permission to choke me—"

"I took it anyway."

"I don't want to see you again."

"So you keep saying." I drag my fingers down to circle her throat again. Her pulse gallops like the hooves of a horse hitting the hard ground on race day.

"I mean it." She tips up her chin.

I glance between her eyes.

"Do you really?"

She nods. "I can't afford to be messed up with the likes of you. You'll take everything from me, and I'll have nothing left to give to the life I'm trying to build."

I lean in closer, until our breaths merge. "You'll have me," I say softly.

"It's not enough."

12

Olivia

Luca and Jeanne look at each other like it's enough to be in each other's presence. They gaze into each other's eyes, heedless of anyone else in the vicinity. We're in Malta, in the living room of the Sovranos' safe house, where an official is currently formalizing the marriage between the two of them.

After that encounter in the restroom—apparently, I'm a member of the mile-high club now— when I spoke those hateful words to him, he released me. Then he stepped back, tucked himself in, washed his hands, and left without another word. He literally washed his hands of me.

I managed to step back into my panties and yoga pants, then took my time putting myself back together before returning to my seat. Penny was still sleeping. This time, Massimo had chosen a seat right in the front of the aircraft, with his back facing me. So, there's no reason to lock gazes with him again. Maybe he finally got the message. Hopefully, he learned I'm serious about not having anything more to do with him.

You'll have me.

It's not enough.

I lied to him. Truth is, in a very short space of time, he's crawled into my mind. I've been thinking of him to the exclusion of everything else, including the career I spent years building. The career that's going to take off as soon as I step foot on stage as the lead in Beauty and the Beast.

Of course, it's the first in the many steps I need to take to become successful. And nothing is going to stand in my way. If Massimo looks at me again or tries to kiss me, chances are, I'll give in to him. I need another way to show him I'm off-limits. A foolproof way to communicate to him that I'm never going to entertain the idea of the two of us having some kind of a relationship. Not that he spelled it out, exactly, but the way he'd gazed into my eyes when we fucked... It made the act so much more meaningful—a way of speaking to each other with our bodies, of connecting to each other without saying a word. No, it's too dangerous to be around him. I have to convey that things between us were well and truly over. I reach over and pull out my phone, making use of the onboard Wi-Fi to message my friend, Declan Beauchamp.

We met in LA, at one of the many auditions I made the rounds of. I kept running into him, even contemplated sleeping with him once, a notion I'd discarded just as quickly. He's a few years older than me and landed his breakout role a few months ago, which quickly made him media fodder. It didn't change him, though. If anything, it seems to have made him even more appreciative of our friendship. And that's the true test, isn't it? How someone behaves after they become famous? So far, Declan has aced all of the tests in that area. It probably has to do with the fact that he comes from money, and his brother, Arpad Beauchamp, is one of the most respected investment consultants in Europe, not to mention one of the richest.

Other than Jeanne and Penny, Declan is the only other person I'd count on to help me out when in need.

Me: Hey D?

He replies almost instantly.

Declan: Wassup?

Me: What if I told you I need you to back me up in a lie?

…

…

The bubbles jump, showing he's typing out a message, then stop.

Declan: Depends on the lie.

Me: What if I told you it's so I can stop myself from committing a HUGE mistake?

Declan: Hmm. It's a man I take it?

Me: Interesting you'd jump to that conclusion but yes, it's a man.

Declan: You've never asked me for help in that department, so this should be interesting.

Me: Nothing interesting, you ass. I simply need you to play along when the time comes.

Declan: Do I want to know what I have to play along with? *smirk emoji*

Me: Trust me, you don't. Just do as you're told.

Declan: You know I don't take kindly to orders... Except from my closest friends.

Me: I know jerkface. Trust me you, won't regret this. I hope...

Declan: Which means I will regret this but that's okay. Anything for you Olly.

Me: Hate that nickname.

Declan: No you don't. Gotta run.

Come to think of it, there are a lot of similarities between Declan and Massimo. Both are tall and good-looking, and both have that aura of dominance that clings to them, so when they walk into a room, you have to quell the urge to bend and scrape. Only difference, there's this chemistry with Massimo that threatens to detonate every time I meet him. Something I don't have with Declan, charming as he is. More's the pity. Life would be easier if I could fall for Declan. A-n-d... *No, no, no,* I have not fallen for Massimo, either. That would be very dumb of me. A mistake I will not let myself commit.

"I now pronounce you man and wife," the officiant declares.

I jump when I hear those words, then force myself to focus on the unfolding scene before me. Luca pulls Jeanne close and kisses her forehead. She seems taken aback by the gesture. Guess she expected something more passionate. That's the way it is with these Mafia men. They like to keep you on edge. Prefer to take you by surprise, so you'll never know what they're going to do next. I know because I've seen the likes of them up close.

Not that I've revealed my past to any of my friends. It's a time in my life I prefer to keep compartmentalized, and for a good reason. I'm not proud of my roots. Not proud of what my family does for a living. But, perhaps I internalized some traits of my upbringing, for I'm attracted to exactly the kind of man I once swore off. Don't women often marry someone like their father because that's the model for what they expect in a husband? And there are a lot of similarities between Massimo and my father. They are both loyal to their clan, protective of their family, and with a big heart. My dad was also very controlling when it came to my Ma. Would Massimo turn out that way, too? He's possessive, and I admit, I like that trait in him. But if we were to get together, would he stop me from pursuing my career?

Why am I thinking of a possible future with him? I don't want anything to do with him. Definitely not. I squeeze my fingers together.

Luca and Jeanne sign the marriage certificate, then Penny rushes forward to congratulate the newlyweds. She kisses Jeanne on her cheek. I want to do the same. I want to feel happy for my friend, but I worry if I say or do anything wrong, the fact that I'm worried for her will come through. Does she know what she's getting into with Luca? Does she know she's marrying into the *Cosa Nostra*?

I turn away and my gaze is captured by Massimo's. He's wearing the same dark suit he wore on the flight. His chin is dark with a day-old beard. Just how it was when I met him in the bar. Sometime during that night we spent together, he must have dragged those whiskers across my inner thighs; the red marks he'd left behind on my skin were visible when I got home. He took me when I was half-asleep, more than once, and the orgasms blurred into each other. It took me days to recover from the high of the endorphins. That's how thoroughly he fucked me.

Those gray eyes of his grow blue-green. Goddamn, I already know it means he's aroused. He wets his lips, and ohmygod, I can feel the tug on my clit. No one else has eaten me out before him. Now, you know. I didn't feel comfortable being that vulnerable with anyone else. Blowjobs are okay, but having someone go down on me? I need to trust my partner, and apparently, my subconscious decided I did, without checking in with me.

"I know you'll make her happy. I know you love her. I see it in your eyes," Penny declares.

Of the three of us, Penny is the most romantic, the most idealistic, and it shows in her words. Not that I don't want to fall in love, but life isn't always that generous. And even if you do fall in love, there are no guarantees you'll get a happy ending.

The officiant behind us clears his throat again. "I need two witnesses to sign, as well."

"I'll do it." I tear my gaze off of Massimo's, then step forward. I glance around for a pen.

"Here." Massimo pulls a pen from inside his coat pocket. I take it from him with a muttered thanks. I finish signing, then he does the same. When he straightens, our gazes clash. His eyes flash, and a trembling grips me. It's as if a host of butterflies have been let loose in my belly. My fingers dampen. I set my jaw, and a mask seems to fall over his features. He breaks the connection, then we turn to face Jeanne and Luca.

"Everything okay?" Jeanne glances between us.

"Of course." I paste a big smile on my face. I step forward and hug Jeanne. "Congratulations. I hope you'll be happy."

"You still don't approve, do you?" she mutters under her breath.

"It doesn't matter what I think." I kiss her cheek. "If this is what you want, then who am I to disagree? Just remember, if you ever need help, I'll be there for you."

She holds my gaze; a slight furrow mars her forehead.

I squeeze Jeanne's hand one last time, then step back. "We're going to make our own way back to Palermo," I declare.

"But you won't make it back in time for the rehearsal this evening," she protests.

"I already checked the flights. I booked two tickets on the first flight out, which leaves in..." I look at my watch. "Two hours. We'll be back in Palermo in plenty of time for the rehearsal."

"You're not taking a commercial flight," Massimo says in a hard voice.

"News flash: it's how we normal people do things. Which you are not." I look him up and down. "But I wouldn't expect you to understand, given your lifestyle. Also, I am not flying back on the same plane as you. I only agreed to come by private jet because I needed to get here in time to witness my best friend's wedding, which—" I turn to Jeanne. "I have now done." I kiss her again on the cheek. "See you back at the rehearsal."

I walk past them and head for the door, then stop and glance over her shoulder. "You coming, Penny?"

Penny looks at me pleadingly.

I scowl back at her.

Jeanne looks crestfallen.

I bite my lip, then close the distance to her and hug her again. "I am so sorry. I know it's hurtful of me to take off like this. It's just... I can't stand your brother-in-law."

I glance from her to where Massimo is watching us closely.

"Huh? Is there something between the two of you? Something you haven't told us?"

Shit, of course Jeanne would jump to that conclusion, considering how cagey I've been acting around Massimo. And my aggressive statement didn't help.

I hesitate, then lean in even closer. "I can neither confirm nor deny that statement," I mutter.

"Oh, my god. So, you two met before? Did you sleep with him?" she whisper-yells.

"Shh." I peer at Massimo from the corner of my eyes. "Don't worry about it. Anyway, today is not about me; it's about you. I truly hope that you'll be happy." I kiss her cheek. "Please don't be angry with me for leaving, okay?"

She scans my features, then nods. "Fine." She blows out a breath. "Go on, get out of here. But you owe me an explanation."

"Thanks, Jeanne." I squeeze her arm. "I'll see you in time for the rehearsal, okay?"

Penny rushes over, and hugs Jeanne again. "See you in a few, babe. Remember what I said about riding the stallion?"

13

Olivia

The music from the overhead speakers pours over me as I sink to my knees in front of the Beast. He's hurt so badly, and I'm sure he's going to die. I beg him not to leave me because I've found a home with him. I assure him he's going to live. I reach out to him, but his body is already still. No, it's not possible. The tears I've been trying to hold back slide down my cheeks. *No, don't leave me. Please.* I throw myself on his body and sob. He can't leave me because I love him. Silence descends. The hair on the back of my neck rises. A current of electricity swirls around me. A part of me is aware this is a musical, and I'm acting. Or am I?

I hold him tighter. My chest hurts, my limbs are numb, and every part of me is ready to die with him, when rose petals float down from above. The Beast stirs. The thick, scaly exterior which has covered his body fades away in front of my eyes. In front of me is a man. A handsome man. A man who is almost as large as the Beast in size. A broad chest, massive shoulders, a square jaw, and those pouty lips I'd recognize anywhere. I raise my gaze past that hooked nose to those gorgeous gray eyes, through which he regards me. There's a spark deep inside that hooks me and doesn't let go.

"*Stellina*," he reaches for me.

I jump back from him. "No. No, no, no. What are you doing here?"

"Don't you recognize me? I'm the one you fell in love with," he murmurs. That dark, rich voice sends shivers of need coursing up my spine.

It can't be. I stumble back and turn to leave, when something slams into me. The reverberations ricochet through my bones. I glance down to find blood spurting from my side. Blood? My blood?

I lurch forward, not sure what happened. Someone screams. I smell something burning, like charred flesh. A wisp of smoke arises from the wound. I touch the stain of black near it, and a burst of pain radiates from the contact. My head spins. My stomach churns. A numbness grips me. I stagger, then bump into the heavy dressing table with the mirror in which Belle had seen the image of her sick father and begged the Beast to release her. I stare at my reflection. My face is so pale. I reach out my palm to touch my reflection in the mirror, leaving a stain of red in my wake. *Huh? Do I have blood on my fingers?*

I glance at my palm, which fades in and out in front of me. Footsteps sound behind me. I half turn, lose my balance, and my knees give out from under me. I hurtle forward and my face smashes into the edge of the dressing table. Sparks explode behind my eyes, only to fade away, and darkness closes in on me. My last thought is, I shouldn't have lied to Massimo.

I float on a bed of white, light as a feather, tossed this way, then that. It's not unpleasant, just a bit confusing. I try to move my arms and legs, but they don't seem to obey me. I look down at myself and find the light pouring through me. How weird. I glance around, taking in the nothingness. It's not uncomfortable, just eerie. Not bad eerie; not a good eerie, either. It's just empty. A golden light comes into view. I glance at it, and my body moves toward it. Hey, this is cool. Apparently, I can use my thoughts to move my body. I glide toward it when something pushes me to glance over my shoulder. There's something... Someone's there. Someone's presence calls to me. I stay there, suspended, then turn back toward the light.

"*Stellina*," his voice echoes around the space. "Come back, Via."

I hesitate.

"I can't live without you. You're not leaving me, you hear me?"

I try to push toward the light, but this time, my body doesn't obey. I am sliding back, unable to stop myself. Fine, okay. If that's what you want. With a last glance at the light, I turn toward the voice.

"Via. Open your eyes."

My eyelids flutter open, and the harsh glare seems to burn my retinas. I moan and close my eyes again. Draw in a breath and my lungs hurt. Come to think of it, every part of me hurts.

"Via." There's an urgent tone to this voice now. Something warm squeezes my fingers. I crack my eyelids open again and glance down to where his fingers are wrapped around mine.

"Via!" His tone is more urgent. I raise my gaze to his, and it's almost not a shock when his gray eyes capture mine. "You're awake."

He places his other palm over mine, cradling my hand between both of his. "Thank *Santa Maria*, you are okay."

"Massimo?" I cough. " What are you doing here?"

He reaches for a bottle of water, then helps me up and supports me as I sip from the straw.

"Better?"

I nod, and he places the bottle back on the bed-stand.

"What happened? Why am I in the hospital?"

He lowers me back to the pillows and takes my hand in his again. "What do you remember last?" he asks softly.

"I was on stage for the opening night of the musical." I wrinkle my forehead, but even that gesture hurts. My entire face feels numb. I also have a bandage on my cheek. I bring my fingers up to feel its shape.

"Did I hurt myself?"

He nods, a gentle yet wary look in his eyes. Is he hiding something from me?

"Something hit me," I burst out. "I saw the blood on my chest, then I lost my balance and fell."

"You were shot, Via," he says in a soothing voice.

"Shot?" I blink rapidly. "What do you mean, shot?"

"A bullet—it grazed the side of your chest. Luckily, it was just a flesh wound, so you should heal soon."

"Thank God." A breath I hadn't been aware I was holding whooshes out of me. "So, I should be back on my feet very soon."

"That's right."

"So, I should be able to reprise my role again." Just my luck, considering I was the lead and Jeanne was my understudy. "I guess Jeanne will have to play the lead until I'm recovered."

Some of the tension leaves my muscles. I yawn suddenly, and my cheek throbs. I wince. "Is my face going to be okay?"

"You're beautiful, my Via."

Tears prick the backs of my eyes. A ball of something heavy clogs my throat. "I look terrible, don't I? That's the only reason you're showering me with compliments."

"You look perfect." He holds my gaze. "To me, you'll always be the most gorgeous woman in the world." He leans forward and rubs his thumb in circles over my wrist. A shiver trembles out from the point of contact. Damn, I am injured, and my body still can't help but respond to him.

"Massimo," I clear my throat. "How bad is it? You can tell me."

His lips firm, but his eyes are so soft, so tender. I instantly know he's trying to shield me. And I appreciate it. I do. But I also need to know the truth.

"Via—"

I shake my head. "Don't sugar coat it, Massimo, please. I need to know."

He nods, then twines his fingers through mine. "When you went down, you caught the edge of the dresser and hurt your cheek."

I frown. "I remember hitting it before I blacked out." I try to tug my hand from his, but he doesn't release it. "But it's going to be okay, right? It'll heal, and then I'll be able to get back on stage..."

"I'm not going to lie to you, *Stellina*. The doctor had to call in a plastic surgeon to consult on it."

"A plastic surgeon?" My stomach churns. Sweat beads my brow. "Wh-what do you mean, a plastic surgeon?"

"He tried to minimize the damage."

"Damage?" I gulp, "Minimize?" I tug my hand from his, and this time, he releases it. I bring it to the bandage again. "When... When does this thing come off?"

"In a few days. He told us you were lucky; the bullet didn't hit anything major, and you narrowly missed hitting your eye. All in all, you escaped without much harm."

"How can you say that? I hurt my face," I cry out.

"It'll heal," he says in a soft voice that sets my teeth on edge.

"It's going to scar, probably for life."

"It won't take away from your beauty."

"That's what you think. You're not a director. You don't know how tough the camera is on the face. The slightest imperfections are magnified."

"There have been lots of actors with less than perfect faces who went on to big things."

"Oh yeah? Name one."

"Tina Fey has a faint scar on her cheek. Joaquin Phoenix has a harelip. Seal has deep scars on his face due to lupus. I can go on."

I stare at him. "Have you been reading up on this?"

Color smears his cheeks.

"You *have* been reading up on this. So, you're convinced I'm going to scar, and this is your way of trying to tell me that it doesn't matter."

"That's not what I said."

"Then what is it you're trying to tell me?"

"That you were lucky to escape with your life, and this doesn't change anything."

"This changes everything." I squeeze my eyes shut. "You'll never understand. You haven't struggled the last few years to get to where I have. And I was there, on stage, in my first leading role, and this had to happen. I knew it was too good to be true when the director gave me the role in place of Jeanne..." I snap my eyelids open. "Oh, my god, was the bullet intended for her? Is that why I was shot at?"

He doesn't say anything, but the look on his face gives him away.

"I was right? The bullet was meant for her?"

"We think the same people who kidnapped her and Luca came after her again, but mistook you for her."

"But Jeanne's safe, right?" He nods and I sink back into the pillows and sigh.

"She is, and she and Penny want to see you, but I told them I'd take care of you and let them know when you're awake."

"How did you get in here, anyway?" The tiredness washes over me. The effects of whatever painkiller they gave me must also be receding because the wound in my side begins to hurt. My limbs feel too heavy, and my cheek throbs. A fuzzy sensation invades my brain, and I struggle to keep my eyes open.

"I told them I'm your fiancé."

My eyes pop open. "Wait, what? Why?"

"As soon as I heard what happened, I rushed to the hospital."

"Yeah, but why did you come?"

"Because I want to marry you, Via."

14

Massimo

Hold on. *What the hell are you doing?* I heard she was shot and rushed to the hospital to find Penny, Jeanne, and Luca in the waiting room. The doctor said Via wasn't in any danger, but he thought she was likely to scar. Jeanne and Penny had been extremely upset and wanted to stay. The doctor didn't think she'd wake up till the morning. I told them to go home and get some rest before they went on stage for the musical's performance. I promised them I'd call with an update.

Then I walked into Via's room, settled down in a chair by her side, and held her hand. She was so silent, so still, so pale. I wasn't able to take my gaze off of her. The doc said she was going to be fine, but my instincts wouldn't let me rest. I held her hand all night, willing her to awaken. For the first time in my life, I prayed. And when I couldn't pray anymore, I researched famous actors and actresses who went on to be successful, despite having scars on their faces. When she finally opened her eyes, I was so relieved. I'd had enough time to think in the dark hours of the night. Seeing her lying helpless in bed, everything else faded in importance. She's the only thing of consequence. The queen of my heart. The one thing I'd prioritize before anything or anyone else. The only thing that I want in my life. I need her with me, at my side. She's what I've been waiting for all this time.

So, when she asked me why I came, I wasn't able to stop myself. The pent-up hours of worry had loosened my mouth and the words had poured out. I hadn't meant to ask her to marry me… I have to admit, when I told the nurse I was her fiancé, it felt right. And when she woke up and asked me how I got in there, I couldn't help myself. I told her, and as soon as I did, I knew how much I wanted it. I want her to be my wife.

"Wh-what did you say?" She gapes.

"I want you to be my wife." I slide out of the chair and onto my knees, and brush my lips over her knuckles. "I've spent the last few hours watching over you and all I could think of was, I'd give anything to watch you look at me with your beautiful green eyes. I'd surrender all of my wealth to have you smile at me. To wrinkle your nose as if you're going to sneeze when you're thinking something through."

"I don't wrinkle my nose." She scowls, wrinkling up her nose at me. Then winces.

"You okay?"

"Yeah, it's this stupid bandage on my face. I can barely feel my nose, thanks to the painkillers they've pumped into me."

I open my mouth and she scowls. "Which is the only reason I tried to wrinkle my nose, by the way."

"Of course." I can't stop my lips from twitching.

Her frown deepens. "Either way, I can't marry you."

"Why not?"

"Because I don't know you. I only met you a few weeks ago."

"We met nearly a month ago, and we know each other well enough."

"I don't mean only on the physical level," she points out.

I allow my lips to curve in a smile. "It's a very important part of any relationship. We are combustible, Via, you and me. The chemistry between us is potent. Also, we get along well, and we can hold a conversation without boring each other. It's more than most couples have going for them."

"That's no reason to marry someone," she retorts.

"After what happened on stage, I'm going to do my best to keep you safe. If we were married, it would be so much easier to keep you safe."

"So, I should marry you to make it convenient for you?" She huffs.

I lean toward her, and below the smell of antiseptic, the scent of vanilla and coconut lingers—her scent. I draw it in and my heart stutters. Also, my cock instantly goes on alert. What witchcraft is this that I only have to smell her to turn into a yearning mass of need? "You should marry me, because—"

"Because?" She licks her lips.

My gaze lowers to her mouth, and when I raise it, her green eyes flicker. "Because you have feelings for me, but you don't want to admit it," I murmur.

"What are you, a mind-reader?" She scoffs.

"I can read you better than I can read myself." I bring her palm to my face and press it against my cheek. "Marry me, Via. Let me take care of you. Marry me because when I'm with you, I like what I become. I know you and I both wanted it to be a one-night stand, but that night was something so much more, and you know it. Marry me because you're the only woman I see myself spending the rest of my life with."

Her gaze widens. Her expression softens. She glances into my face and a small smile curves her lips. I'm sure she's going to agree, when something flickers in her eyes. She firms her lips, and tugs her hand from my face. I release it.

She presses her fingers together over the sheets, and turns her gaze away. "I can't marry you, Massimo."

"Why not?"

She swallows, then, without looking at me says, "I... I'm in love with someone else."

"What?" My heart seems to stop. The hospital room, the equipment, all of it fades away. My vision tunnels. "What did you say?"

Her chin trembles, then she seems to collect herself. "I'm in love with someone else."

"I don't believe it."

"Believe it." She bites the inside of her cheek.

"Look at me, Via. Look into my eyes and tell me that you don't have feelings for me, that you're not lying to me."

She hesitates, then slowly turns her face to stare at me. She holds my gaze, then tips up her chin. "I don't have feelings for you. I'm in love with someone else."

It feels like a ten-ton truck slammed into my chest. I rear back so suddenly I fall on my goddam ass. I stare up at her from my sprawled position on the floor. "It's not true. You're lying."

She shakes her head. "I'm not."

"You're with someone else, but you slept with me?"

"I don't have to explain myself to you."

"Like hell, you don't." I jump up to my feet and glare down to her. "Why did you lead me on if you were with someone else?"

"We, uh, had a fight, decided to separate temporarily. That's why I was at the bar that day locking for a hookup. I wanted to sleep with someone else to see if I could get him out of my mind."

"And you did."

She shakes her head. "I admit, the chemistry between us is off-the-charts, and the sex was above-average, but I told you even before we slept together that it was going to be a one-time thing. That I didn't want us to exchange names or contact details or anything. I emphasized that we were going to walk away the next day like nothing happened."

"But something did happen. That was more than sex, and you know that."

"Maybe." She raises her shoulder.

"And you fucked me again on the plane."

She glances away, then at me. "Only because you wouldn't take no for an answer," she mumbles.

"Bull-fucking-shit." My voice echoes around the room, and she pales.

"I'm sorry. I didn't mean to yell at you. I know you've been through a lot, and this is not the time to be having this conversation." I take a step toward her, but she cringes.

"Please leave."

I swallow thickly. "I can't, Via. I can't leave you like this."

"When I was floating in that space before coming awake, I thought I heard someone reach out to me. It's the reason I returned, why I woke up from my unconscious state. I heard a voice call out to me, and it wasn't you, Massimo. It was him. I love him."

I ball my fists at my sides. I squeeze my eyes shut, unable to understand how everything could have turned upside down in such a short period of time. I watched her sleep, and I was sure she was the one for me. I felt it in my bones, in the pit of my stomach, in my heart, in my head. Every part of me insisted… Still insists, that she's mine. How could she be in love with someone else when everything in me maintains that she belongs to me?

"Via..." I shake my head. "If you're lying—"

"I'm not." She firms her lips. "I'm not lying, Massimo. I told you I don't want to be with you. I told you I wanted to walk away without looking back. I told you to let me go, Massimo."

And I didn't. And now I'm paying the price.

Turning, I stalk to the door. With one foot over the threshold I stop, then turn to glance at her over my shoulder. "You're making a mistake."

15

Olivia

I made a mistake. He looked at me with so much emotion, so much *everything* in his eyes. He looked at me like I was his, and I told him the one thing I knew would make him hate me. It was the only way to get him to leave, to make him believe that I had feelings for someone else. How's that even possible, when all I can do is think of him? I was so sure he wouldn't believe me, but I must be a better actor than I thought. I met his gaze and I lied. Clearly, all those acting lessons paid off; he believed me. I looked into his eyes, and I lied convincingly enough for him to walk out of here hating me.

I lied to him and broke my heart—I mean, his heart, and now he hates me. That's the result I wanted, right? I close my eyes, and my head spins. The adrenaline recedes, leaving me shaking. A shiver grips me. *I'll never be warm again.* Not after what I did to him.

A doctor walks into the room, "Ms. Johansen, you're awake. Do you mind if I examine you?"

I nod my assent.

He approaches me, takes my pulse, then begins to examine me.

"How soon can I leave?"

He continues to listen to my heart with his stethoscope, then checks my eyes and proceeds to ask me a few more questions.

"Doctor, you didn't answer. How soon can I leave?"

He finally straightens. "Your vitals are looking good. I'd like to keep you for another night for observation."

"I'd like to leave right away," I choke out.

"Out of the question. We need to make sure there are no other complications from the wound. There shouldn't be, but it's a precaution."

"Tomorrow. I need to be out of here by tomorrow. I cannot stay another day."

"Eager to join your fiancé?" He smiles kindly.

"Who?"

"Your fiancé, Mr. Sovrano. He stayed with you throughout the night, refused to leave."

"He's gone now. I asked him to leave."

"Ah." He scans my features. "Everything okay?"

I nod. *No, I've made the biggest mistake of my life.*

I'd never be able to live with myself if I married a Mafia guy. Besides, Massimo has too powerful a personality. Too mesmerizing. If I were with him, I'd lose myself; I'd forget myself and the goals I set for myself. The promises I made to myself when I left home, and which I've fought so hard to fulfill. I can't give up on it. Not now. I owe it to myself to stay on track. To get back to pursuing my dream of becoming an actress. I'm going to get the kinds of roles I deserve, the kind I spent my life working toward. I couldn't give it all up for a man... *Could I?* Tears prick the backs of my eyes. I sniff, then close my eyelids so they don't spill.

"There, there." He pats my hand. "It's normal to feel woozy after what you've been through. If all goes well, we can discharge you tomorrow. Of course, you'll still need to take antibiotics to keep infection at bay, and make sure you take care of your dressings—"

"A phone. Can you get me a phone, please?"

"Of course. All of your belongings, including your phone, were delivered by Mr. Sovrano. We'll get everything to you."

The doctor turns to leave, and I stare out the window. He made sure I had everything I needed before he left. And I broke his heart. I didn't have a choice. *It's the right thing to do. It is.*

One of the nurses returns with my phone and my handbag, which I left in the dressing room in the theater. I probably won't know how bad the scar is until the bandage comes off. Meanwhile, I need to get out of here before Jeanne or Penny decides to visit. There's only one person who can help me.

I pick up my phone and dial Declan's number.

"You sure you're okay?" Karina helps me into the back of the SUV, then straightens.

"You sure you're okay helping me?" I retort.

She laughs. "What do you think, honey?" She addresses her words to the man behind the wheel of the SUV. "Are we okay coming to the rescue of Declan's friend?"

The man, who's wearing a suit that's been hand-tailored for him, meets her gaze in the rearview mirror and smiles. "We seem to be making it a habit. Good thing I had my jet on-hand."

"Umm, what do you mean 'making it a habit'? Has Declan asked you to help another of his friends before?"

"Not Declan." She shuts my door, then walks around to slide into the passenger seat upfront before she turns to face me. "But we got a similar SOS call to help out your friend Jeanne and her now-husband Luca when they were running from their kidnapper."

"You're the one who helped them?" I wriggle around, trying to make myself more comfortable. "I wondered how they managed to get back to Palermo in time for the rehearsal."

"My husband—" she places her hand on the man's sleeve "—loaned them his jet so they could fly to Palermo and make it in time for the rehearsal."

"And that's how you got here so fast? You used the jet?" I ask.

"What's the use of having your own plane if you can't use it when a friend needs help?" The man turns to me, a twinkle in his eyes. "I'm Arpad Beauchamp, by the way."

"You're Declan's brother." The family resemblance is unmistakable. Same broad shoulders, high cheekbones, that look of being trouble in their eyes.

"Indeed." He tilts his head. "And you are a friend of his from LA?"

"Indeed." I smile back.

He laughs. "Any friend of Declan's is a friend of ours. Thanks to you, I finally heard from him. He's been so busy, now that his movie is a big hit, it's been months since I last spoke to him."

"It's good to meet you—"

"Olivia Johansen." I shake his hand. "Thank you for helping me out."

"Couldn't refuse the chance of getting out of my office. Besides, this way, Karina and I get to visit Sicily. We've always wanted to come, haven't we?"

"We'd hoped to visit after we got married, but things have been so hectic of late." Karina leans over and plants a kiss on his cheek. He pushes a strand of hair behind her ear, and a heated look passes between them. Gosh, why do I get the feeling that I'm intruding? Clearly, they're in love and care for each other.

She leans back in her seat and Arpad guides the vehicle forward. After I'd called Declan and explained the situation to him, he'd told me to sit tight and that he'd reach out to me in a few hours.

"So, you live in London?" I ask the couple.

"I used to live in LA, where I still run my own security agency. But after we married, I moved to join my husband. Now we split time between both cities."

"And what do you do, Olivia?" Arpad asks.

"I'm a dancer, and the lead actor in—" I stop. "A dancer," I say firmly.

I'm not a lead actor anymore. I'm not going to be well enough to reprise my role in the musical anytime soon, and even if I were, would they accept me with a scar on my face? While I won't know how it's going to look until the bandages come off, fact is, I did hurt myself. Chances are, my face isn't going to look as flawless as it used to be. And I don't know what the hell that means for my career. I need a place to lie low and think through my options.

I'd have loved to leave Palermo, but the doctor discharged me on the condition that I check in with him over the next few weeks, until he's satisfied I'm healing properly. He knows my case, so it didn't make sense to return to London and start from scratch. Instead, I decided to find a place here and lie low. I can't go home to Penny, where she or Jeanne would easily find me. They're not going to forgive me for giving them the slip, but right now, I don't want to meet them or anyone I know and try to explain myself. How can I explain myself when I don't even understand? I just need space.

We drive in silence, for which I'm grateful. We head toward the outskirts of the city, more inland, away from the coast. After nearly an hour of driving, Arpad turns onto a narrow road that's bordered with trees on both sides. They meet in a canopy over the top, so sunlight dapples the windshield. We turn another corner and pull into the driveway of a two-story building. With white-washed walls and a wraparound porch, as well as the flowers that grow in profusion in the garden and span both sides of the driveway, it's gorgeous. Arpad brings the car to a stop. Karina gets out and opens my door. I slide out, and she hooks her arm with mine. "Come on, I'll show you around."

16

Massimo

I lift the barbell with the weights into the air, then bend my arms and lower it toward my chest. And again. I loaded on the weights, going higher than I normally would, in the hope it'd force me to focus my thoughts away from the woman who turned me down. That was a week ago, and I still haven't been able to get her out of my mind.

To a certain extent, it helped that I'd been busy helping Luca with his plan to lure Freddie—our father's one-time rival who kidnapped Luca and Jeanne—out into the open. Luca had faked his own death to do that. Jeanne had been devastated.

When she'd finally discovered he was still alive, she'd been livid, and rightly so. It didn't make sense, why he hadn't involved her in his plan. His excuse? He was trying to keep her safe. And I get why he'd want to do anything to protect her, but wouldn't it have been easier for all concerned if he'd simply shared his plan with her? *Maybe then, she wouldn't have played the part of the grieving widow so convincingly.* So he said. She'd been pissed with him, and he'd had to grovel to her and apologize before she came around.

Now, the two of them are back together. Another one of my brothers has found his soulmate. We're dropping like flies. I love my brothers, don't begrudge them their happiness, but if I were being honest, seeing how happy they are makes my chest hurt. Not out of jealousy—okay, there's a tinge of that—but because I thought I found my soulmate. Only, she didn't feel the same way.

How could I have not known she was in love with someone else?

I push the barbell and hold it above my chest.

My instincts are normally so bang-on when it comes to business. How had they failed me in the most important decision of my life? How could I have been attracted to her when she belongs to someone else?

Clearly, I'm losing my touch. I'd hoped to marry her and fulfill my promise to Nonna of finding a bride within a month of her passing, but obviously, that's out of the question. A part of me wanted to keep the PI on her case, to find out who she's in love with. But she doesn't want me. And nothing I say or do can change that.

Suffice to say, I don't take rejection very well. In fact, I can't recall the last time something was denied to me. I want something; I take it. It comes with the territory of belonging to the most powerful Mafia family on the continent. No one ever turned me down, until she came along. And I haven't been able to stop thinking about her. I've spent nights imagining how it would feel to be buried inside her again. All of which has to stop. She's gone. She doesn't need me. I have to let her go. It's time to move on.

My biceps tremble. The barbell slips from my palms. Before I can react, another pair of arms reaches over me, grabs the barbell and steadies it.

My youngest step-brother, Adrian's face appears above mine.

"Easy, *fratello*. If you get yourself killed by your own weights, then what will we say to your bride-to-be at the engagement?"

"I'd have straightened it myself. I don't need your help," I grumble.

"It's not weakness to accept assistance when you need it." He helps me lower the barbell onto its stand behind me, then steps back. I sit up, reach for my towel and mop my face with it.

"If you've come here to talk me out of the arranged marriage I agreed to, then you can fuck right off, *fratello*."

He raises his hands. "Except for the fact that I *do* think it's a really bad idea—"

"Zip it," I growl.

He comes around the bench and hands me my bottle of water. "You have to admit, it's too early for you to be considering a relationship of any kind, let alone, an arranged marriage."

"It's exactly the time I should be considering an arranged marriage." I tilt the bottle of water to my lips and drain it, then wipe the back of my hand across my mouth.

"I thought you said you met someone you want to marry?"

"I thought so, too." I squeeze the empty plastic bottle between my fingers, and it crumples. "But turns out, I'm not the person she wants. She loves someone else." I hurl the bottle across the floor. "And I'll deliver on the promise to Nonna."

"By opting for the arranged marriage with the *Camorra* princess?" His tone is dubious.

"It's the only way to bring peace between our clans. Also, I'm the only one in the position to do so."

"I'd have offered myself as the potential bridegroom, except—"

"Cass." I rise to my feet and begin to stretch. He's referring to Michael and Karma's housekeeper on whom he's had a crush on like forever.

"Cass." He blows out a breath. "Woman's disappeared off the face of the earth. I've had people looking for her, but they can't find her.

"Maybe you're not looking hard enough?" I offer as I stretch out my arms, then bend to the side.

"Neither are you—looking for your woman, I mean," he murmurs.

"The difference is, I don't care about her anymore," I retort.

"Keep telling yourself that."

"What did you say?" I scowl at him.

He covers his mouth and pretends to cough. "Me? Nothing."

"It's over before it even started. Whatever we had was a lie. She was in love with someone else when she slept with me. Clearly, I was too overcome by lust to notice it."

I kick out my leg, and lean my weight into my hamstrings. The muscles give and the tension slowly drains out of my limb.

"You can't blame yourself, Massimo. Haven't you heard the saying?"

I turn to him. "Which one?"

"Love is blind."

"In my case, it was also hard of hearing." *Which is why I didn't listen to the clues in what she was trying to tell me—that she would never be mine.*

17

Two weeks later

Olivia

Fuck them. Fuck all of them. Bet they're surprised I'm crashing the gathering. And honestly, I wouldn't give a damn about being here, or about any of them except, it's Solene's engagement day.

Since the day she was born, Solene has had my heart. I remember when Mamma placed her in my arms. A little bundle, wrapped up in baby clothes, with a shock of blonde hair peeking over the top. She opened her blue eyes and looked at me, and my heart stuttered. Something like love and a fierce need to protect wound its way around my heart. I rocked her to sleep that day, and swore I'd never let anyone, or anything harm her.

And she's getting engaged today... She texted me the address and begged me to come. She's excited about her upcoming nuptials, but she also wants me there to support her. She needs me, and I'm not going to let her down. I'll even face the ire of the rest of my family for her.

I spent the last two weeks recuperating and coming to terms with the fact that I'm going to wear the scar from my injury on my face for the foreseeable future.

It's going to fade with time, but the shadow of it will always be there on my cheek. The first time I saw my naked face in the mirror, I burst out crying.

I was alone by choice. I didn't want Jeanne or Penny with me. Jeanne would have felt guilty because I was shot instead of her. Penny would have felt obliged to spend time with me. And both of them are still starring in *Beauty and the Beast*, which just successfully completed its two-week run, and is now going to be extended for another two weeks. They need to focus on that, and I? I need to get my head back in the game and focus on rebuilding my career. But first, I have to get through Solene's engagement and this impromptu family reunion.

The scent of jasmine and roses surrounds me. I draw it into my lungs. Why is my heart beating so fast? They are only my family. So what if they hate me? I should be used to it by now, right? I take in the crowd in front of me. My uncle and cousins are dressed in black suits and ties. So, what's new? At least none of them are wearing their sunglasses indoors which, I shit you not, they have been known to do. The women have turned up in designer dresses, shoes, and bags. All bearing the labels of the most expensive couture, no doubt. That's one thing we in the *Camorra* do well—act as if every scene in our life is lifted from a Hollywood movie.

I plant my hand on my thrust-out hip and strike a pose at the entrance. Sooner or later, someone is going to notice me, and I can't wait to see the look on their face. One of my aunts turns in my direction. Her gaze passes over me, then swings back to rest on my face. Her features twist into an expression of dismay. It's comical, really. Ladies and gents, meet my dear blood family. More blood than family, really. My aunt nudges the woman next to her, and my mother turns her head. When she sees me, her mouth opens and shuts before she firms her lips. She takes a step in my direction.

Shit, best to make my presence known to the gathering before she marches over and tells me to leave. Not that I'm going to obey her. I just prefer to be the one taking the lead. Nothing like going on the offensive where my family is concerned. I toss my hair back, shove my leg, clad in sheer tights with nine-inch *Louboutin's* on my feet, through the slit in my dress, then paste a big-ass smile on my face. "Not happy to see me, *famiglia*?"

My mother takes another step in my direction. And I step toward her. And promptly stumble. *Fuck, fuck, fuck.* It has to be the heels. It has nothing to do with the shot of tequila. Okay, two… no, three shots I threw back to shore up my courage before I got here. My heart ricochets in my rib cage, and my pulse shoots through the roof. I squeeze my eyes shut, shoot my hands out in front of me, and brace myself to hit the floor, when my shoulders are gripped.

I hit something hard—not the floor—something wide and tall, clothed in a soft cashmere. Eyes still shut, I dig my fingers into the fabric, lean in until my nose connects with the wall… Not a wall—something steely, and ripped, and warm. So warm. Heat pours over me. Static electricity whips through my veins. The hair on my forearms stands on end. I drag in a deep breath, this one laced with darkness and musk and testosterone. An unmistakably male scent. One that I know.

Hot breath, hard fingers that had gripped my hips, the friction of his beard as he'd dragged it across my core. Goosebumps sprinkle my skin. My thighs clench. *No, no, no. It can't be. Not him. Please, not him. Not here. Not now.*

It's him. Here. Now.

"Open your eyes." His voice rumbles up his chest, sinks into my skin, and warms my blood. My nipples pebble. My scalp tingles and I shake my head.

"Open. Your. Eyes." He lowers his tone to a hush, and my nerve endings spark.

Only when his gray eyes hold mine, do I realize I've raised my eyelids. I take in those elevated cheekbones, so sharp they could, surely, cut my skin, those hollows under his eyes, more pronounced than I've seen them before, the thin, mean upper lip that hints at his sadistic streak, the one that speaks to the darkness inside me. That pouty lower lip, which I dug my teeth into and tasted blood. His jaw hardens. That square jaw, dusted with a five o'clock shadow, that I teased him about and which he confessed he made no effort to cultivate. That gorgeous neck, which I fell in love with even before I'd seen his features. Broad shoulders, so wide they block out the rest of the room, and for the moment, I'm grateful for that.

I need a second, a few seconds, to digest what's happening here. His grip on my shoulders tightens and I feel his touch all the way to my toes. My entire body is one mass of wanting, my stomach in knots, my chest so tight I can barely draw in a breath.

Massimo. Oh, Massimo. Where art thou, Massimo? Stop it, he's not your Romeo.

A trembling grips me, and my knees threaten to give out from under me again. His hold on me tightens.

"Via?" He frowns, calling me by the name that only he uses.

My heart aches for what he could have been to me. For what we once had. My guts twist, and my stomach churns. Darkness flickers around the corners of my vision, and I taste bile on my tongue.

"Via?" He drags his fingers down my biceps to hold me above my elbows. His fingertips dig into my skin. Pain shivers up my nerve endings, cutting through the noise in my head.

"What are you doing here?" His scowl deepens.

"What am *I* doing here?" Anger flushes my veins. "What are *you* doing here?"

He tilts his head, and the skin around his eyes tightens. "This is my engagement party."

The world tilts. "Your engagement party?" I glance past him to where my sister stands at the head of the crowd. She's wearing a simple white dress, so virginal, so pure. So everything I am not. A smile curves her lips, and she glances from me to her would-be fiancé. The man who is my ex-lover.

The one who asked me to marry him before I turned my back on him. The man who is now going to marry my sister.

A sense of inevitability grips me. Of course, it had to be this way. Of course, the man I fell for is the one my sister is promised to. My stomach chooses that moment to bottom out. The sickness boils up my gullet, my guts contract and I throw up all over his tailor-made jacket.

18

Massimo

"Oh, God, I'm so sorry." She raises stricken eyes to my face. Gorgeous green eyes that are burned into my brain. Her color is pale, and her cheekbones are prominent—more prominent than when I last saw them. She hadn't been this thin then. She also didn't have the scar that curves from eyebrow to cheek. A scar that only adds to her allure. She's the Queen of Sheba. She's Helen of Troy. Cleopatra herself, reborn to taunt my dreams and get under my skin and make my life a living hell.

I reach out my hand, wanting to touch the marred skin, but she turns her head. She wipes the back of her hand across her mouth, steps away, only to sway again. I tighten my grip on her arms and she shivers.

"Let me go," she says in a low voice.

"No."

"You need to clean up your jacket."

"Fuck that."

"You can't get engaged wearing my puke."

I firm my lips. She has a point there. I'm here for my engagement. To the *Camorra* princess, who is waiting for me to join her. I should release her and return to my future bride. A heavy sensation grips my chest. It has nothing to do with meeting this woman who turned my life upside down, then walked away from me.

"You never answered my question," I growl.

She tips up her chin. "Which one?"

"Why are you here, Via?"

"It's my sister's engagement party."

"Your sister?" I whip my head around to find my fiancée-to-be watching us with curious eyes. "She's your sister?"

"Yes, and I'm going to make sure you don't hurt her. If this is some ruse to get me back—"

"Get you back? You're the one who told me you were in love with another man." I turn around and glare at her. "Has that changed?"

She seems to grow even more pale. "No." She shakes her head. "That hasn't changed."

My chest feels like it's been split wide open. *Goddamn.* Granted, I barely knew her before I fell for her. It had been stupid of me to ask her to marry me when she was laid up in the hospital with the injury that scarred her. I should have waited for her to recover, but seeing her helpless in the hospital bed, and so dejected at the thought that she would be permanently disfigured, ignited something inside me. I wanted to go after the assholes who did this to her. I wanted to reassure her that nothing could ever detract from her beauty. I wanted to tell her she didn't have to worry about the scar because I'd always find her to be the most beautiful woman in the world. Instead, I asked her to marry me. I asked her to marry me, and she told me she was in love with another man.

I tighten my hold on her, then glance over my shoulder. My gaze connects with Adrian, who nods. He walks toward me, then turns around to face the crowd.

"We need a little time for Massimo to clean up."

A buzz of conversation instantly fills the air.

"Can we start the music again, please?" I hear him say. A second later, the strains of opera music, which had been streaming over the speakers before her interruption, fill the air.

I walk past her, pulling her along in my wake as I stalk out of the conservatory and down the corridor toward where I know there's a bathroom.

"What are you doing? Everyone will wonder what we're up to," she protests.

"Adrian will take care of it. Besides, all I'm doing is guiding my future sister-in-law to the bathroom so we can get cleaned up. It's the gentlemanly thing to do, after all."

"And everyone knows you're not one."

"Only with you, and only because it turned you on when I revealed my filthy side."

"Is that any way to talk to your sister-in-law?" she snaps back.

My guts clench. *Sister-in-law? What the fuck.*

"Future sister-in-law, and speaking of, when were you going to tell me that you were one of the *Camorra?*" I shoot back.

"Never?" She tries to drag her feet, but I compensate by half dragging her along, until she stumbles in my wake.

"Let go of me, you jerkass," she whisper-screams.

"Not a chance." I yank her along beside me.

She hurries to keep up. "I'm wearing heels, you asshole. I can't walk as fast as you."

I slow down just enough so she can keep pace.

"What is wrong with you?" she snarls.

"Save the injured party act." I reach the bathroom and shoulder my way in, then pull her in after me. I slam the door shut and lock it.

"Isn't that presumptuous of you? Should you be locking the door after us? If someone from my family were to come here—"

"They won't. Adrian will take care of it." I turn to her, then yank the tie off my collar. I fling it down, then throw my jacket on top. I brush past her, walk to the sink and flick open the tap. I cup my palms under the water and splash some on my face.

It's going to be okay. It has to be okay. I'll make it okay. I straighten, then stare at my slightly crazed eyes in the mirror. She does this to me. Every time I meet her, something in my orderly life falls apart.

Before I met her, I was sure I knew what I wanted. It's why I trained in finance. Numbers are my friends. They're black and white. They never lied to you. Never leave room for misinterpretation. It's why I'm the finance guy for the *Cosa Nostra.* I tripled our income from investments.

It's also why I'd been determined to find someone simple to settle down with. Someone who'd bear my children and be a pleasant wife. The kind who'd have dinner waiting for me when I came home in the evening. I'd hoped for a straight-forward life. Instead, I fell for a spitfire.

Someone who wouldn't hesitate to go toe-to-toe with me and tell me off, and basically, be a giant pain in the backside. Which is why I was intrigued by her. I wanted her as soon as I saw her. And she wanted me. We wanted each other that first night we met, and I was sure she'd never leave my bed again.

Only, she did. She ensured I'd leave, and never try to see her again. I certainly didn't expect to see her on my engagement day.

My engagement day. *What a clusterfuck.*

I close the tap, grab a towel and dry my face, then turn to her. She's leaning against the door, a hand pressed to her stomach.

My guts twist, and the heaviness in my chest intensifies. I cross the floor toward her and grasp her shoulders.

"What's wrong?"

"Uh, I may have had a little too much tequila before I left home."

"You were drinking before noon?"

"Hey, it's happy hour somewhere in the world, isn't it?" She lowers her arm to her side.

"Really, that's your rationale for turning up drunk in front of your own family?"

She huffs, "Relax, there's nothing wrong with me. Nothing some painkillers won't fix."

"You need to drink some water, rehydrate." I grab her arm and pull her along with me to the sink, then snatch a glass and hold it under the tap before I shove it under her nose. "Drink."

"Fine, stop worrying!" She takes a mouthful of water, gargles and spits it out once, twice, before tipping the glass back and drinking from it. She drains the glass and sets it down with a snap on the counter. "There, happy?"

I'll be happy when I have you under me, in my bed, writhing around my cock.

I glare at her and she bites down on her lower lip. Of course, I feel the tug all the way to the crown of my dick. Un-fucking-believable. I'm supposed to marry her sister, and here I am, getting turned on by her. And it's not like we've kissed or I've held her inappropriately… Recently.

Her chest rises and falls. The air between us thrums with that chemistry that's so overpowering when the two of us are together.

Hell, even when we're not. I haven't stopped thinking of how it feels to mold her body to mine, to hold her hips against mine, to squeeze her breasts and pinch her nipples, and tweak so hard, she curves her back and cries out, and when I reach between her legs, she's soaking wet, her cum trickling down her inner thigh. She's ready and waiting, the pink lips of her pussy swollen from the need to have my shaft buried balls deep inside her. The crown of my cock stabbing into that secret place of hers which drives her crazy. I tilt my hips and drive into her over and over again. With her, the hunger that gripped me is like nothing I've experienced before. The scent of her hair, the taste of her skin, the feel of her breath on my lips as I kiss her and plunge my tongue inside her honeyed mouth and drink from her, even as I empty my load inside her.

She blinks, then takes a step forward, "Massimo, I—"

"Don't." I hold up my hand. "Whatever it is, don't say it."

"Right." She glances away. "You're right. I shouldn't be talking to you like that. It's not appropriate." She squeezes her eyes shut. "Look, I didn't mean to barge in like that and turn your engagement upside down."

"You didn't," I say through gritted teeth. "Things will proceed as planned."

She snaps her eyes open and turns to me. "You're still going to marry her, despite what happened between us?"

19

Olivia

"Nothing happened. We had a casual fling, we parted. End of story." He pulls himself up to his full height. "It happened. I moved on. Just like you did."

I gasp. It's like someone took a hot knife and stabbed it into my chest. I can't blame him, though. I'm the one who told him I was in love with someone else. And I was right in doing so. *He's the Mafia, remember? And you swore not to have anything to do with the likes of him.* Not to mention, I was disfigured by the accident. One bullet and my entire life fell apart. I went from being the leading lady of a musical headed for the West End, to someone who had to start all over again. Story of my life. I always seem to take two steps forward and one step back, to end up where I started. I need time to figure out what I'm going to do next.

"I'm sorry, I didn't mean for it to come out that way." He reaches for me, and I evade his grasp.

"It's fine. We both moved on. I just didn't expect to see you engaged to my sister. Do you even love her?" *Fuck. Fuck. Fuck. Why did I ask that? Do I even want to know the answer? And why my sister? Of all the people in the world, why her?* "Do you?" I turn to him.

"It's an arranged marriage, decided by the heads of the *Camorra* and the *Cosa Nostra*," he murmurs.

"And you went along with it?"

He tilts his head.

"Bullshit. You're not the type to fall in line with someone else's plan."

"You're right." He rakes those piercing gray eyes of his across my features. "I wouldn't normally agree to have my destiny decided by someone else, unless it were Nonna."

"Your grandmother? What does she have to do with it?"

"She wanted all of us brothers to be married within a month of her death. Also, it was her dying wish to settle the feud between the *Camorra* and the *Cosa Nostra*."

"So, you offered yourself up as a candidate?"

"Little did I know, when I proposed to you, I was potentially fulfilling both of her wishes." He takes a step forward into my space, forcing me to tilt my head further back.

Good God, I'd forgotten how big he is, how imposing. How his shoulders block out everything else. How the heat radiates off of his big body and slams down on my chest and pins me in place. How that earthy, musky scent of his, mixed with the spicy notes of his cologne, goes to my head when I draw in a breath in his presence. I press myself into the counter of the sink behind me, not that it helps. He's not touching me, but he may as well be, the way he drags his gaze down my body, alighting upon every nook and cranny and curve and dip, like he's remembering how he touched me with those rough fingers of his.

"What are you doing?" I gasp.

"Nothing. Yet." He shakes his head. "You go to my head, you know that? I only have to see you to forget about my responsibilities... Who I am. What I want out of life. You make me want to throw you down and rut into you until you're screaming my name over and over again."

"Massimo, please don't." His name on my lips conjures up visions of dark nights, heated glances, sordid whispers and the filthy things he could do to my body, which would shred me from the inside out.

He notches his knuckles under my chin and lifts it, so I have no choice but to meet his gaze. His soul-stirring, thigh-clenching, toe-curling gaze.

A current runs up my body, lighting up each cell under my skin. The hairs on the back of my neck stand on end. My breasts ache, and my chest hurts. Every muscle in my body goes on alert.

"Massimo," I whisper as he lowers his mouth to mine.

Don't do this. Don't do this. You let him go, and he's marrying your sister now.

His breath mingles with mine. He positions his lips so close, our eyelashes tangle, but he still doesn't kiss me. He stays there, peering deeply into my eyes, into my soul, seeing the secrets I hadn't had time to reveal to him. The past I was running from. The future I had wanted with so much passion; all gone. In one single second. And now, all I have is broken dreams. And shattered memories. And maybe… maybe this one last kiss. *Fuck it.* I lean in, when there's a knock on the door.

We break apart so quickly, I almost fall over. I grab hold of the counter at the last second and stare at him. His chest rises and falls, but otherwise, he seems unaffected by the intrusion. A pulse beats at his temple, the only sign that something just happened. But then, nothing did.

"Nothing happened." I square my shoulders. "Nothing. Happened," I repeat again.

"You trying to convince yourself or me?"

"Both of us." I tuck my elbows into my sides. "Nothing. Happened."

"If you say so."

More banging on the door, then, "Massimo? You guys in there?" a man's voice calls out. Probably Adrian, come in search of us.

Massimo draws in a breath.

"This—" I wave a hand at the space between us. "This can't happen again."

His lips twist. Then he spins around and walks to the door and flings it open. "What?" he snaps.

"They're all waiting."

"Fuck that."

"You know that's not possible. You committed to this marriage. We're about to solemnize the engagement. Both families are gathered here. You have to go through with it, *fratello*."

"Fucking fuck!" Massimo roars.

I turn to take a look at the mirror and wince. The scar stands out like a slash of red against my pale skin. My eyes are always drawn there first, as are everyone else's, I'm sure. The doctor had suggested plastic surgery, but in a fit of defiance, I'd turned it down. It's only a scar.

On a man, it would be called dashing. On a woman? It's something to be pitied, the cause of whispered conversations whenever I walk into a room. Well, fuck that. It *is* only a scar. Soldiers have come out of war with far worse wounds and carried on with their lives.

Surely, I can move on after what happened to me? I'm still in one piece, physically. Mentally, it's another matter altogether. I have PTSD from the incident when that asshole shot at me, which is to be expected. What I hadn't realized was how difficult it would be to actually engage myself with life and do the things I once found exciting. I wanted to be an actress, and now, the thought of facing a camera with this face makes me break out in a cold sweat. And the thought of appearing on stage again? I can't even fathom that.

So instead, here I am, wearing the most outrageous dress in my closet, and acting out my frustrations on my family. Who deserve it, by the way. No question. Still, what was I thinking, flouncing in here, ready to take them on? Or maybe, I wasn't thinking at all. I simply wanted to be there for my sister. I hadn't intended to steal her fiancé.

Her fiancé.

He's going to be her fiancé.

And I almost kissed him again. A trembling grips me. I press my fingers into the edge of the sink. He's going to marry her. And I'm going to spend the rest of my life watching the two of them together. *Fuck!*

Footsteps approach and Massimo's face fills the mirror.

I lock my gaze with his. "Did you know you were going to marry her when we—"

"When we fucked?" He searches my features. "What do you think?"

"I'm asking you, aren't I?"

"Do you think I'd have slept with you if I knew that I was going to get married?"

"You tell me."

His jaw hardens, his lips flatten and a coldness enters his features. "The answer is no. I resisted the idea of an arranged marriage, hoping to find someone of my choosing. And I did. Only she's in love with someone else, isn't that right?"

I swallow, hesitate, then nod. "That's right."

He narrows his gaze. "Which is why I moved ahead with the arranged marriage."

"Within days of our breaking up?" Not that we'd been together. A one-night stand does not a relationship make. I curse myself for saying that aloud. Jesus, how insecure do I sound? But I can't help it. The scar on my cheek is not even properly healed, and he's moved on.

It hurts; I admit, it hurts. I thought when I forced him to walk away from me it was heart-breaking. That's nothing compared to the claws that have dug their hooks into my soul and are playing merry havoc. It's like my insides have been put through a wood-chipper, and mutilated beyond recognition.

"You told me you didn't love me." His shoulders flex and he steels himself. "And my family needed one of us to go through with the arranged marriage. Considering Adrian, here, is nursing a not-so-secret crush on Michael's house-keeper, it seemed I was the person for the job. Besides, I needed to get over you fast."

A nerve pops at his temple. His silver eyes are so light they are like colorless pools of glass. Yet, his stance is relaxed, as if he fought an internal battle with himself and won it. As if he's moved on already.

"And, are you over me?" I hold his gaze in the mirror.

He tilts his head, a serious look in his eyes. "Yes."

20

Massimo

Liar. What a fucking liar I am.

And what else could I say? Of course, I'm over her. I have to be; I'm getting married to her sister. This is the only way forward. I allowed myself to feel for her. In my entire life, I never made a spontaneous decision, except with her, and where did that get me? She sent me packing, for another man. A man she's still in love with. She was never mine. She always belonged to another. It's time to accept that and move on.

I transfer the chain with the horseshoe pendant from my shirt to the pocket of my pants, then wipe down my shoes. After a quick wash, I change into the clothes Adrian brought me.

When I re-enter the conservatory, the group turns to watch me approach. My younger brother, Seb and his wife Elsa, have their arms around each other. My other brother, Axel, leans against a windowsill, his wife Theresa pressed into his side. Christian and his wife Aurora, who is also the doctor for the *Cosa Nostra,* are talking in low tones to each other, and the newlyweds Luca and Jeanne? They're holding hands and gazing at each other with a nauseatingly 'in love' look on their faces.

These are the Sovrano Seven? The men who run the *Cosa Nostra* and who are feared for their violent pasts? The fuck happened to us? Falling in love and finding women turned us into pussy-whipped motherfuckers.

On the other side of the room, I sense the *Camorra* watching me with as much interest. My fiancée-to-be is seated in a chair on the far end. She looks like she wants to approach me, but knowing how the Mafia ingrain correct protocol into their women, she probably won't. Thank fuck for that. I have to face Via, no doubt, just not yet.

Michael, my oldest brother and the Don of the *Cosa Nostra,* stands next to a seated woman. His wife, Karma, has her hands over her belly. She's nearly three months along and beginning to show. Michael grips the chair behind her head, his stance protective. They both watch me as I close the distance between us.

"You okay?" Karma asks softly.

"I will be." I tilt my head.

"You don't have to do this, or at the very least, we can push back the engagement a few more days to give you some time."

Next to her, Michael shifts his feet. He and I both know it sends the wrong message to the *Camorra* if we ask for more time. Between Mafia clans, honor is everything, and saving face is why we do most things. To bring both families together, only to push things back, would be taken as an insult. It would escalate the tension between us and leave us vulnerable to possible attacks.

"It's too late." I widen my stance. "My mind is made up."

"She's right, though." Michael scans my features. "Better to call off the engagement if you're unsure, than to take it all the way to the altar, only to find you can't go through with the wedding."

"That won't happen." I set my jaw. "I want this marriage."

"Didn't seem that way when you rushed out earlier, dragging her sister along."

"I didn't know they were related. Had no idea she was part of the *Camorra*." I thrust my hand in my pocket.

"Where did you meet her?" Karma asks.

"At a bar."

"And you knew she was the one?"

I lower my chin to my chest. "She's in love with someone else."

"Ah." Karma's expression grows sympathetic. The heaviness in my chest intensifies. *Fuck, will it ever get easier to say that? Will it ever be possible to think about her without my stomach folding in on itself?*

"That's too bad, I was going to suggest you simply marry her instead," Karma murmurs.

Michael and I train our gazes on her.

"What?" She looks between us. "She's *Camorra;* you're *Cosa Nostra.* If you marry her, there's an alliance between the two clans."

"I'm supposed to get engaged to her sister."

"Things change." She raises her shoulder.

"She's in love with someone else."

"Are you sure?" She purses her lips. "What if she told you that simply because she was upset with you?"

I scowl. "I was there. I didn't imagine it when she told me in no uncertain terms that she wasn't in love with me."

"You're not in love with your wife to-be," she points out.

"It's an arranged marriage."

She raises a shoulder. "So, make this one, too."

I stare at her. It can't be that simple, can it?

"What are you getting at?" I finally force the words out.

"Ask her to marry you."

"I already did," I point out.

"Ask her again."

I straighten to my full height. "No. She's made up her mind, and so have I."

"Are you sure?" Michael rocks back on his heels. "This is your last chance to back out if you have any doubts."

I hold up my hand. "I don't. I'm going through with this."

He holds my gaze for a beat, another, then nods. "So be it."

A ripple runs through the assembled crowd, and I know she's entered the room. I resist the urge to turn. I hear her footsteps on the tiled floor as she passes me and heads for the front of the room. I can't resist peeking from the corner of my eyes as she walks over to her sister. Olivia sits down next to her and the two embrace before they speak in low voices.

I wrench my gaze away from her, and turn to Michael. "I'm ready."

21

———————

Olivia

I am not ready for this. So not ready for this. After that run-in with Massimo in the bathroom of their Don's house, I made it back to the conservatory, managed to walk past the rest of my family to my sister, and stood by her side as my one-time lover slipped an engagement ring on her finger. I stood by as pictures were taken of the newly engaged couple. They hadn't held hands or anything, thank God. In fact, Massimo didn't do much, except stand next to her stiffly, as his family and mine congratulated the two of them. Then, thankfully, everyone moved to the formal dining room for lunch.

There were two tables in the room—one for my family and one for the *Cosa Nostra*. Whoever had been in charge of the seating arrangements had been farsighted enough to realize that, while the two families are being joined in marriage, it doesn't mean they get along very well together yet. My sister is seated opposite me. Normally, she'd have been seated at the *Cosa Nostra* table, since she is now engaged into the family, but she opted to sit with us, and the Sovranos had not demurred. My family didn't protest, either, which was unusual considering how much of a stickler for tradition they are. Maybe they're just happy to have their daughter with them a while longer?

The back of my neck prickles and I know he's staring at me from across the room. I refuse to acknowledge it, though, and keep my gaze riveted on the plate in front of me as I play with my food.

"You need to eat, Livvy; you're fading away." My mother scoops up a spoon of the risotto and brings it to her lips. I've told her so many times, I hate being called Livvy, but does she listen? Of course not.

"The food's not bad, eh?" my aunt pipes up from my other side. Yep, the two maneuvered me so I'm seated between them.

"You'd think, since we're lunching at the house of the Don of the *Cosa Nostra* he'd, at least, have provided for a five-course, if not a seven-course meal." My mother sniffs.

"I think the food's tasty," my younger cousin pipes up.

"Don't interrupt when the adults are taking," my aunt scolds her.

"I'm almost eighteen," she points out.

"You're not yet eighteen," my aunt shoots back.

"And when I am, I'll be gone," she says triumphantly.

"That's what they all say; then look what happens." My aunt glances at me in a not-so-subtle manner.

I blow out a breath. "If you want to say something, you can do so to my face."

"Oh, it's not my place." She scoops up more of the food. "I'm only your aunt, after all."

"I, on the other hand, have no such compunctions," my mother announces. She turns to me, but I refuse to meet her gaze. I know what's coming. More of the same ol' same ol'. She doesn't disappoint. "You've had your shot at doing what you wanted. I'm glad you finally came to your senses and returned home."

"I haven't returned home. I'm merely here because Solene wanted me to attend her engagement."

"And now that you're here, it's time you think of getting married." There you go. That didn't take too long, did it?

"I've told you many times, I'm not getting married."

"Oh, pfft." My ma waves her hand in the air in a gesture she's used so many times with me in the past. The gesture that indicates what I think doesn't matter. That she'll have her say, and I have no choice but to listen. I raise the glass of water to my lips and steel myself, but even I'm shocked when the next thing she says is, "Of course, with that scar, no one's going to want to marry you now."

Ladies and gentlemen, presenting exhibit A: my mother, who never pulls any punches. I choke on the water and burst out coughing.

"There, there." Mamma pats my back. "I know it's a tough thing to hear, but maybe it's God's way of telling you your career is no longer worth pursing and it's time for you to come home and get married to a good Catholic boy."

"I thought you just said no one will marry me?" I say when I've stopped spitting all over my food.

"I meant, no one of good prospects. On the other hand, there are enough men in the community who'd be happy to marry you, for a good dowry, of course."

"Of course," I say through gritted teeth.

"Good thing you're still of childbearing age, though it would be too much to assume that you're still a virgin."

"You know I'm not, Mamma; you caught Raoul leaving my room when I was sixteen," I shoot back.

My mother touches her pearls. "Please, Livvy, must you bring up such unsavory topics while we are eating?"

"You brought it up first," I point out.

She blows out a breath. "Is that any way to talk to your mother? I only have your happiness at heart. You know that."

Guilt twists my insides. "I know. It's just... I'm not going to get married."

"Why, is there someone else?" my sister asks from across the table.

I shoot her a glance. "And if there were?"

"I knew it." She leans forward with her elbows on the table. "Who is he?"

"No one you know." I glance away in Massimo's direction, only to catch him staring at me. *Fuck. Fuck. Fuck.* I look away, keeping my gaze trained on my sister.

"Did you meet him in LA?"

"Maybe."

"Not in LA, then. Closer to home? In this city?"

"I'm not saying anything."

"So that's how you managed to make it to my engagement. You were already in the city."

"I'd have come from wherever I was; you know that."

Her face cracks in a wide smile. "I do. And I'm so pleased you're here." She flicks a coy glance in Massimo's direction, then back at me. "I think I'm going to be so very happy with him."

"How do you know? You just met him."

"When you know, you know," she says in a soft voice. "There's something about him that I find very reassuring."

"Wait until you get to know him better," I say under my breath.

"What was that?" My mom shoots me a dirty glance. "It's bad enough you're not ready to get married; don't scare off your sister who's doing the right thing."

"Fine." I raise my hands. "I didn't mean anything, okay? It's just—" I turn to Celia. "How can you marry someone you don't love?"

"Love, shmove." My mother huffs. "You young people put too much importance on what's essentially a fleeting emotion."

"What else is it about?" I frown.

"Security? Protection? Someone who can take care of you and make sure you never want for anything material?"

I gape. "What about everything emotional?"

"That's why you have children, and sisters, and girlfriends—"

"And aunts," my aunt pipes up.

"So, according to you, the only reason someone needs to get married is for money, and then for sperm donation."

"Do you always have to be this gross?" My mother eyes me with disgust.

"Just repeating what you told me, Mamma," I drawl.

"I thought, at least, now that you've learned your lesson, you'd be more amenable to settling down. Seems I was wrong."

"Why, because I'm scared because you think no one will want me now? Is that why?"

My mom pales. "You know I didn't mean to hurt you by saying that. I was simply pointing out the obvious."

"Gee, thanks. Like I don't get enough of it every time I look at myself in the mirror."

"Livvy." She sets down her spoon and turns to me. "You know you'll always be beautiful to me."

"You have a funny way of showing it, Mom."

"I am your mother; it's why I have to watch out for you. I only want to see you settled."

"And *I* don't want to be settled. There are a lot of things I want to do to prove myself first, Mamma."

My mother wrings her hands. "I should have never allowed you to leave home. I should have married you off the first chance I got."

"Like I would have allowed you."

"It's not too late." A cunning look comes into her eyes. "There's this man—"

"No, absolutely not." I allow my fork to fall from my hands with a clatter. Silence sweeps across the table. My brother looks up from where he's been speaking to my uncle from the other side of the table.

"Can you leave her alone, Mamma?" He scowls at her. "Olivia's old enough to figure out what's best for her."

I narrow my gaze on him. "And why are you coming to my defense, *fratellino?*"

"I'm your brother." He scowls.

"Yeah, that's why I ask. Like the rest of the Mafia guys, all you care about is seizing more power. If you think you can get it by marrying me off to some other clan, you can think again." I glance at my sister, who's been watching the exchange in silence. "No offense."

"None taken." She shoves her hair over her shoulder. "But you should know, I was happy to go in for this arranged marriage. I'm not doing this against my will."

"Something I don't understand at all," I retort.

My mother scowls at that, but I ignore her. "You have so much going for you, Solene. You're smart, talented, beautiful; you can have any man you want. You don't have to sacrifice your future for the sake of the family."

She glances away, then back at me. "I really don't mind marrying the man my family has chosen for me," she says softly.

A cold hand grips my heart.

I walked away from Massimo, by choice. I knew I needed time to find myself again, to figure out my shit and where I'm going with what I've become. And I couldn't do it if I allowed him into my life. I needed space to breathe, to be myself, and I could never do that if I plunged straight into a relationship with him. Also, I admit, I was insecure. I have a scar on my face, and he's the most gorgeous, most lethally attractive man I've ever met. Of course, I couldn't allow him to tie himself to me. Not when he could have anyone else. I needed time to think, and figured it would help to put distance between us. That's why I told him that lie. I didn't think it would hurt him so much that he'd go straight into an arranged marriage. With my sister! And now, it's too late. Surely, now, I can't step in between them. Not if she's set on marrying him. There's only one way out. I need to, somehow, get away from here.

"Excuse me." I dab at my mouth with my napkin. "I'm late for my rehearsal." Ah, how easily the lies come from my lips. I rise to my feet, my movements precise. If I make any swift movements, I might shatter.

"You're leaving? So soon?" Solene cries out.

"Sorry, sis, I wouldn't if it weren't so important. But I really do have to go. I'll come visit."

"We're staying in a house loaned to us by the Don, so we'll be in the same city," my sister says excitedly.

"You will?" My family lives in Naples, the heart of the region controlled by the *Camorra*. I'd hoped they would return home after the engagement party. Not because I don't like them… Okay, that's not the complete truth, either. I do love my mother, but having her too close, for too long, is like being circled by birds of prey who are just waiting for a chance to attack.

"Diego thinks the wedding should take place sooner than later," my sister adds.

Of course he does. Marriages of this nature take place very quickly after the engagement. It's partially to make sure the brides and grooms don't change their minds, but also because the heads of the clans want to proceed with the business transactions that often accompany such arrangements.

"Wh-when do you think it'll take place?" I force myself to ask.

"In a few weeks." My brother rises to his feet. "I'll see you out."

I wave him off. "Relax, stay back. I know you're dying for a chance to speak to the *Cosa Nostra*." I jerk my chin in the direction of the Sovranos, and the man who I know, even now, is watching me from under hooded eyes. "No doubt, you have business negotiations to finalize as a result of this arranged marriage."

The guilty look in Diego's eyes confirms my words.

I bend and kiss my mother's cheek. "I love you, Mamma." And I really do. Despite the fact that she's never understood me, she's still my flesh and blood, and I believe her when she says she has my best interests at heart.

I blow a kiss at my cousin, touch my aunt's shoulder in farewell. Then I push back my chair and walk out of there—past the Sovrano table, past the man who has his head turned away from me, but who I know is tracking my every move—out of the conservatory, down the hallway, out the front door, then down the steps, and toward my car as fast as my shaky legs will carry me.

Footsteps sound on the stairs behind me, then, "Olivia!"

Damn, and I almost made it, too. I pause, then fix a smile on my face and turn to face one of my best friends. "Jeanne."

I hold out a hand, but Jeanne ignores it and throws her arms around me instead. "You look good Olivia," she murmurs.

"You mean, despite the scar on my cheek?"

She leans back in the circle of my arms and scowls at me. "Don't put yourself down, you know better than that."

Color flushes my cheeks, and I glance away. "I'm sorry. I didn't mean that."

"It's all right. I know how rough things must have been for you. Where have you been, woman? You moved out of the apartment without informing Penny, and you haven't returned any of our calls, either. Do you know how worried we've been about you?"

My guts twist. *Shit, shit, shit.* Of course, they've been worried about me. They're my best friends.

"I'm sorry, Jeanne. It's just... You know, there was so much happening. It was all too much. It's not every day one is shot at on stage and ends up getting scarred, you know?"

"Oh, Olivia, I wish you'd given me and Penny a chance to be there for you. We'd have done anything to share your pain, babe."

The band around my chest tightens. Tears press down at the backs of my eyes and I blink them away. "I'm a bad friend. I shouldn't have left the way I did, I know. I'm so sorry, Jeanne."

"No more keeping secrets from us now Olivia, okay?"

I nod.

"And that includes whatever is going on between you and Massimo."

"There's nothing between me and—"

She shakes her head. "I know he proposed to you and you turned him down," she interjects.

My gaze widens. "How do you—your husband... Luca told you?"

Jeanne nods. I glance away, then back at her. "There's nothing more to tell you. I told him I wasn't going to marry him, and now, he's engaged to my sister." My chin wobbles, belying my protest.

"Oh, Olivia, honey..." Jeanne takes a step in my direction, but I put up a hand. "I really have to go, Jeanne." I swallow down my tears. "I promise, I'll call you."

The door at the top of the steps opens. I glance up just as Massimo steps out. My heart slams into my ribcage. My guts churn. I turn to my friend. "I'm sorry, Jeanne. I really have to go."

Tearing off my heels, I race past the other cars and reach my own. Luckily for me, I'm in a good position to get out of there quickly, since I arrived last. As I open the door, I hear Massimo calling my name. I ignore him as I get into my car, slam the door, and peel out.

22

Massimo

Let her go, let her the fuck go. What are you doing following her? I saw her leave and rose to my feet. Michael stared at me, and I knew he wasn't pleased. But I risked a glance at her face as she'd passed and saw the glimmer of tears on her cheeks. My heart contracted, and my stomach tied itself in knots. I had to follow her to make sure she got to where she was going safely.

Maybe she's going to meet her boyfriend, the one she's in love with.

Jealousy sliced through my veins, and I nearly unbalanced my chair as I pushed it back. I needed to see where she went, and if that meant I was acting like an unbalanced stalker, so be it. Once I made sure she reached her destination safely, I'd leave. I'd return home, to my life, to my fiancée. I wince.

Fuck. I haven't spoken a single word to her. Couldn't bring myself to look her in the face. Not when my mind is filled with thoughts of her sister. Something I needed to purge myself of before I upset everything. The eyes of everyone in that room were on me as I walked out. Not that anyone would stop me.

I'm the soon-to-be son-in-law for the *Camorra*, after all. The key to them acquiring a lot more power overnight. My actions won't be questioned by them. And if my fiancée thinks it's strange, she'll keep her thoughts to herself. No, it's my brothers whose disapproval I felt keenly as I walked out of there and to my bike, just in time to see her vehicle disappear down the driveway. I managed to follow her without losing sight of her Porsche. The woman has style and guts, and she drives bloody fast.

I accelerate, and my Harley leaps forward. It was a last-minute thought to jump on my bike today. Probably the thought of being chained to a woman—one I don't know at all—for life prompted it. Either way, now it serves me well as I weave in between the cars, keeping her in my sights. I'm sure she's spotted me, but fuck that. She knows I'm pissed at her and I need to—have to—settle whatever it is between us so I can move on with my fucking life.

She drives through the town and keeps going until she reaches a bar at the edge of the city. I frown as she parks the car and strides in. What the hell is she doing here? Doesn't she know it's dangerous for her to be here alone?

I park my bike, hook my helmet on the handle—no motherfucker would dare touch what belongs to the *Cosa Nostra*, not even here—and walk inside the establishment.

The smell of alcohol, sweat, and stale, unwashed bodies fills the air. It's gloomy, and at this time of the afternoon, not crowded. My gaze alights on her instantly. She's a flash of light, a beacon in the dark sky, my very own Bat-Signal calling to me as she leans into the bar and orders a drink. I stalk over to the bar, making sure to keep enough distance between us. I order a whiskey, nurse it as she knocks back a shot of tequila, and another. She reaches for the third, and finally slows. She places the small bag dangling from her wrist on the bar and bows her head. If she's waiting for someone, I can't tell. If she knows I'm here, she's doing a hell of a job hiding it. I watch her as she stares into the depths of her glass.

A man slides onto the stool next to her. He tries to talk to her, but she turns away and tosses back her drink. Orders another. And she was already tipsy when I met her in the morning. He continues to try to get her attention, and I squeeze my fingers around my glass. She turns her back on him, so he reaches out and touches her shoulder. My vision tunnels. Adrenaline laces my blood. The glass cracks, the whiskey spilling over my hand, and I stalk toward the *stronzo*. I reach for him as he crumples to the floor holding his crotch. I glance up to find her glowering at me.

"I can take care of myself," she snaps.

"You kneed him?" My balls shrink at the thought.

"I know how to fight. Took self-defense courses for a character I was auditioning for. A part I didn't get," she laughs bitterly, "but guess it had its uses." She turns back to the counter and reaches for her glass again. I sidestep the guy on the ground who's curled up on his side, and snatch the glass from her.

"Hey, what the fuck are you doing?" she protests.

"You've had enough," I say through gritted teeth.

"You're not my keeper," she snaps back.

"I am marrying your sister. I have the responsibility for taking care of the rest of her family." The words burst out of me and—*fuck, fuck, fuck, I didn't mean for it to come out that way.* Or maybe I did, for her features crumple. Maybe I wanted to see some reaction from her. Maybe I wanted to find out if she's hurting as much as I am inside.

She tugs on her arm, and this time, I release her. We stare at each other, then she seems to pull herself together.

"That's right." She glances away. "You are marrying my sister, and it's best for both of us to remember that."

"This isn't how I wanted to see you again. I had no idea you were part of the *Camorra*."

"Not something I go about shouting from the rooftops." She folds her arms around her waist.

"And your accent..." I shake my head. "You have an American accent. How do you have an American accent when you grew up in Italy?"

"I went to the American school." She rolls her eyes. "Why are we even talking about my accent?"

"You're right, let's talk about how you lied to me when you said you were in love with someone else," I snap.

"I did not." She tips up her chin.

"Oh, yeah?" I prop my hands on my hips. "Where is he, this man you claim to be in a relationship with?"

She blinks, then firms her lips. "None of your business."

"Everything about you is my business."

"As you said, you're marrying my sister, so you don't have to worry about who I'm with."

"Look Via—"

"The name's Olivia," she snaps.

"Via—" I firm my lips. "I already told you that the only reason I agreed to an arranged marriage with your sister is so I could fulfill the promise made to my Nonna. Also, she was keen we make our peace with the *Camorra*."

"How convenient for you," she snaps.

"You're upset." I sigh. "Listen, you're part of the *Camorra*, and now you're one of the family. I can't have you risking our reputation by going off and fucking any random man."

"But you can?"

I want to tell her she's not some random woman I fucked, but she beats me to the punch.

She tucks her elbows into her sides then tips up her chin. "He's not a random man; he's my fiancé."

Olivia

His jaw hardens and he lowers his gaze to my left hand. "I don't see a fucking ring."

"It was, ah… too big for me, so he had to have it resized." I blink rapidly. Jeez, and I thought I was such a good liar. Surely, he's able to see through me right away. "But I do have a ring."

He looks me up and down. "If you're engaged, where is this fiancé of yours?

"Uh, he, ah, is not in the country."

"He's not in the country," he deadpans. "Couldn't you get a little more creative with your lies?" He snorts.

"It's not a lie." I draw myself up to my full height, which still means I'm at the level of his chest. Damn, this man is huge, like the biggest guy I have ever come across. He's so tall that I have to tilt my head all the way back to look at him.

His eyebrows draw down, and the tendons of his throat are so taut, I'm sure they're going to snap any second. He looks pissed-off, and honestly, I don't know why. It's not my fault I turned up at my sister's engagement party to find he's her future bridegroom. So what, I didn't tell him I have more in common with him than he realized? Why would I, when I was so sure I wanted him to turn his back on me and never want to see me again?

"Another lie?" He leans forward on the balls of his feet. That dark testosterone-laden scent of his laps at my senses. My belly flip-flops. He's so close, I can make out the fine lines that radiate out of the corners of his eyes. So close that I can see the silver sparks in his eyes. In this light, they seem more green, like a stormy sea just before the clouds open up and the rain pours down. He's unpredictable that way. You'd think he was calm and serious on the surface, but look below that mask he wears to the world, and the tightly leashed emotions are there, waiting to burst out. Waiting to lash me, and sear me, and mark me, and brand me. The more time I spend with him, the more I'm liable to forget what he's going to be soon—*married to my sister.* As part of the arrangement between the two families. I need to convince him that I won't have anything to do with him.

"It's not a lie." I tip up my chin. "My fiancé is an actor, a very well-known actor, actually. He travels often for work. It's why I haven't seen him in a while." *And the lies keep coming.*

"Where was he when you were injured and lying in the hospital? Where was he when you woke up and found yourself injured?" His gaze lowers to the scar on my cheek. "Does he know what happened to you? What you've been through?"

"What's it to you?" I retort. And *why do I keep digging myself deeper and deeper into this lie?*

"Answer the question, Via. Has he seen you since the incident?"

I wince, but don't glance away. "I've FaceTimed him," I snap. Which is not *untrue.* The person I'm hoping will help me out of this situation I've trapped myself in—as if that's even possible—is someone I FaceTimed with not long after the accident.

"FaceTimed?" A pulse pops at Massimo's temple. "You need someone with you all the time, especially at night, when you're bound to have nightmares from the incident."

"Nightmares..." I open and shut my mouth. "How did you—" I shove my hair back from my face. "Doesn't matter. I don't have nightmares."

"Bull-fucking-shit!" He peers at me closely. "You have dark circles under your eyes, and under that pancake you've slapped on your face, your skin is pale. How long has it been since you had a full night's sleep?"

"Too long." I glower up at him. "You're crossing a line. It's not good for us to be seen together. You shouldn't have followed me out of the house. You left your own engagement party. Do you know how awful that looks?"

"No one questions me."

"That may be the case. But remember, this is an arranged marriage between two of the most influential Mafia families in Italy who have been bitter rivals forever. You can't afford to screw it up. Also, it doesn't feel right meeting like this. You're marrying my sister."

"Not yet," he says in a hard voice.

"A technicality. The deed is as well as done."

"I don't have to go through with it." His features take on a determined set. "You could marry me instead. It would still mean the two families are united. I'd be marrying a different sister."

"And what about Solene?"

"What about her?"

"How would she feel about this? Have you thought about that?"

"She'll find someone who's actually in love with her."

"But she wants to marry you," I burst out.

"Only because she hasn't looked at other options. Only because it's been drilled into her that she needs to do what's best for her family."

"You marrying Solene is what's best for our families." My heart stutters, and a tsunami seems to build in my chest. *What am I doing? Why am I pushing him toward her? Why am I turning my back on him again? He's right, this is my chance to take what I really want. Him.*

And give up the chance to figure out what I want to do with myself? I need to reinvent myself, find my focus, and I can't do that if I plunge straight into a marriage with him. It's why I turned him down in the first place. "I don't want your pity." I curl my fingers into fists. "I don't need you marrying me because of what happened to my face."

"*Gesù Cristo*, is that what you think? That I proposed to you because I feel sorry for you?"

"I know you did."

"That's not true."

"Can you look me in the eyes and tell me it didn't cross your mind even once that you marrying me would solve a lot of my problems?"

He hesitates.

"That's what I thought."

"You're twisting my words. I wanted to marry you so I could protect you, so I could ensure something like this never happened to you again."

"I don't need your protection. I've already been hurt, so it's not likely it's going to happen again, and the only reason they came after me is because they thought I was Jeanne." I square my shoulders. "Besides, you're fulfilling the promise made to your Nonna. You're going to marry my sister."

His lips firm, and a pulse thuds at the base of his throat. Those golden sparks in his eyes seem to recede so they turn into chips of ice. A shiver crawls up my spine. Jesus, he looks so angry, so mean. He squeezes his fingers at his sides, and his biceps bulge. His shoulders seem to grow bigger, until it feels like I'm surrounded by him.

"Don't do this. Don't throw away this opportunity."

"All I see is the man who's supposed to marry my sister, making a fool of himself," I say lightly.

Anger leaps off of him. The planes of his chest seem to swell, until his jacket is straining at the seams.

"You are going to regret this," he growls.

"The only thing I regret is meeting you again. Now, if you'll excuse me..." I brush past him, take a step, another, putting distance between us. The tension begins to drain out of me when something hard circles my wrist.

"I'm not done with you."

23

———————

Massimo

I should let her go. This is supposed to be when I allow her to walk away from me and never look at her again. Instead, I circle her wrist with my fingers, and tug on it, so she unbalances and falls against me.

"What the—" She yelps as I twist her arm behind her back, so her breasts are flattened against my chest.

"You don't get to walk out on me like that," I snap. If I sound desperate, it's because I am. If I let her go, I'm not sure when I'm going to see her again, and I can't bear that thought. If I let her leave, she might turn her back on me and disappear again, and I can't allow that.

"It's best we don't see each other. Surely, you realize that?" she says in a low voice. "Whatever we had was over before it even started. I'm not the person you met, Massimo. I've changed."

I push aside the strand of hair that's fallen across her forehead. "You're even more of a woman than when I met you. More courageous. More fearless. Pluckier. More resilient. More everything." I draw my fingers across the scar on her cheek, and she winces.

"And I'm not yours."

My guts twist. Anger slices through my veins. The blood pounds at my temples as I take in the stubborn set to her jaw. I need to leave her, forget what I felt for her. Forget that she's the one woman who'd have made me happy. I try to pull back my arm, but goddammit, I can't. I wind my fingers around the nape of her neck and pull her close.

"Say that again," I say through gritted teeth.

"I. Am. Not—" I haul her to me, so my lips are poised over hers. Our noses almost bump, and our eyelashes nearly entwine. I glare at her and she shivers.

"I want to kiss you. I want to close my mouth over yours, and absorb the little moans you make. I want to nip your lower lip, and when you open your mouth, I want to suck on your tongue and deepen the kiss, until it feels like I am drinking from you."

"Massimo, don't," she whispers.

"I want to drag you up to your tiptoes, spread my legs to take your weight, then plant my other hand on your butt and pull you into the space between my thighs, so you're aware of what you do to me."

A trembling runs down her body. Her chest rises and falls.

"I want to feast on your mouth, and drink from you until my entire body is one large aching throb."

The buzzing grows insistent; something vibrates in my pocket. Another sound of buzzing joins the first, this time from the bag dangling from her wrist. I ignore it all as I hold her gaze.

"I want to ravage your mouth and draw your scent deep into my lungs and hold it there, hoping to carry some part of you with me always."

"Massimo." Her features take on a stricken expression. "Please don't do this. It's not right and you know it."

But it could be.

Fucking fuck.

Of course, I know that. But damn, if I'm not tempted to throw caution to the wind and take what is mine.

The buzzing increases in intensity from my pocket, and from her handbag. She pushes at my shoulders, and we break apart, staring at each other. Her pupils are dilated, her cheeks flushed. Her lips are swollen, even though I haven't kissed her. The blood rushes to my groin. My thighs harden, but my chest feels like someone has stabbed a burning sword into my heart.

Without taking my gaze off of her, I pull my cellphone from my pocket as she flips open her purse and pulls out her device.

"*Pronto,*" I growl the Italian word for hello into the phone.

"Hello," she says into hers.

"Massimo, where the fuck are you?" Adrian's angry voice comes down the line. "Do you know the kind of shit show you've left behind? The *Camorra* are asking for the wedding to be pulled forward, after that stunt you pulled."

"What?" I straighten.

The voice at the other end of her phone squawks, the tone as angry as Adrian's.

She pales, backs away as she listens.

"What do you mean, pulled forward?" I snap.

"Exactly that. They're pissed-off that you left your engagement early, and rightly so. What were you thinking, running out of the house leaving everything behind? It's good we managed the situation so they think you had to leave because of a work-related emergency which only you could handle, and it had nothing to do with you chasing after her sister. At least, I think we managed it without their noticing the true reason you left and—"

"And if that is the reason I left?" I widen my stance.

There's silence, then Adrian clears his throat, "Don't do this, *fratello*. You're making everything very complicated."

"What's life if you can't follow your instincts, eh?" I drawl.

He blows out a breath. "And what does this instinct tell you? No, don't tell me. I don't want to know. You need to get your ass back here and explain it to Michael, and I'm warning you, it's not going to be pretty."

"I can't right now—"

"You've stretched the good will of the Don already. Don't push it further, brother." He disconnects.

Fuck, fuck. F-u-c-k. I drop the phone into my pocket, glance up to find she, too, has disconnected the call.

"I really do need to go."

I step back and hold out my arm, indicating for her to precede me. I follow her out to her car. She beeps it open, then slides into the driver's seat. She goes to close the door, but I plant my foot in her way, so she has no choice but to leave it open.

"This is not over," I warn.

"It is." She stares straight ahead.

"You haven't seen the last of me," I retort.

"This has to be the last we see of each other. My fiancé is, uh, expected in town soon, and he wouldn't like it if he saw us together."

"Why don't we meet, the four of us?"

"Eh?" She darts her gaze up in my direction. "You mean—"

"You and me, and the people we're engaged to? Why don't we go out for dinner together?"

"You're joking, right?"

"You are family, after all, so it's not unusual to ask to meet the man you're engaged to." My chest hurts, but I push the sensations aside. If she's hellbent on holding on to this farce, then I am going to dig in until I unearth the truth of the situation. "Unless—" I peer into her eyes "—you're not engaged, in which case—"

"I *am* engaged." She tips up her chin. "And fine, I'll arrange for you to meet my fiancé."

"I'll text you the details," I reply.

She pulls the door shut, and I step back barely in time to avoid the door smashing into my leg. A smile curves my lips as she steps on the accelerator and the car leaps forward. She makes a turn and peels out of the parking lot.

Why the hell do I find her temper so attractive? She has more personality in the tip of her little finger than any woman I've ever met. That includes her sister. Not that there's anything wrong with her. She's just not Olivia.

And I'm trapped in this god-awful mess, where I'm engaged to a woman who I have no interest in marrying. Except to fulfill my promise to Nonna—which I have every intention of keeping. But first, I need to figure a way out of this quandary, and face the music with my brothers.

I grab my helmet, swing my leg over my bike, and drive out of the lot.

Half an hour later, I park my bike outside my oldest brother Michael's home and head for the entrance. Before I can ring the doorbell, the door swings open. Adrian scowls at me. "Took you long enough to get here."

"I came as soon as I could. Had some business to finish."

"And did that business have anything to do with the sister of your fiancée?"

"Vaffanculo." Fuck off. I brush past him and head down the corridor with Adrian at my heels.

"He's pissed at you," Adrian murmurs.

"Won't be the first time." With the death of our father, Michael took over as head of the *Cosa Nostra.* He's also spearheading the plans to legalize our businesses, an initiative I whole-heartedly support, and one which my brother Luca hadn't been in favor of until he fell in love and married Jeanne, Olivia's friend. The two women are still friends, although Olivia has managed to cease all communication since the incident. If it hadn't been for her sister's engagement, I might never have run into her again. And now that I have, I'm going to find a way to keep her. No way am I letting her out of my sight again.

I walk up the hallway and into Michael's study, not surprised to find the rest of my brothers scattered around the space. The floor-to-ceiling bookshelves on opposite walls look down on the wide desk against which Michael leans. Seb and Axel are talking in one corner near the window. Luca is sprawled out in a chair, with Christian on the settee. All of them turn to watch me walk in.

They track me as I cross the floor and fling myself onto the settee.

They don't take their gazes off of me as Adrian shuts the door behind him and walks over to the bar. The silence stretches as he pours out a healthy measure of Macallan into two glasses and brings one over to me. I take a glass from him and throw back the liquor. It burns its way down my gullet and hits my stomach, sparking off a steady heat. I place the glass back on the coffee table, then lean back and watch them watch me. Finally, I throw my arm over the back of the settee and fold one leg over the other.

"Out with it," I snap through gritted teeth.

Still, no one says anything. The tension in the room ratchets up. A bead of sweat slides down my shoulder blades. Not that I'm nervous. I've known these men my entire life. Been with them as each of them navigated the perils of having an abusive father at home, then helped them as they fell in love and overcame challenges to marry their wives. All except Adrian, who's in love with Michael's housekeeper but hasn't found the balls to propose to her yet.

"Anyone care to tell me why I've been summoned?"

The men look at each other, then stay silent.

"If you have nothing to say to me, then I might as well leave."

I start to rise when Michael stops me. "Sit down," he says in a deceptively soft voice.

I take in the determined set of his jaw and sink back. "I know what you're going to say, so you may as well save your breath."

"Do you, now?" He leans forward on the balls of his feet. "Have you any idea how serious the situation is?" His gaze narrows on me. "You walked out of your own engagement. Your. Own. Engagement."

"I did go through with it, didn't I?"

"That's not the point. This is your future we're talking about. You left your fiancée without acknowledging her or speaking a word to her. Worse, you ran out after her own sister. Do you know how grievous that is?"

"Nothing that hasn't been done before." I raise a shoulder. "Men cheat on their fiancées and wives all the time."

"Not the Sovranos. Not anymore," Michael says through gritted teeth. "And anyone who's not a Sovrano does it *after* they're married. They don't flagrantly ignore their fiancée, and declare to the world they prefer her sister, and—"

"You and Adrian handled it though, they don't suspect the real reason I left."

"—You insulted the *Camorra*. You showed them no respect. If you think Diego didn't notice that you walked out and chased after the wrong sister, you're mistaken. He may be weak, but he's not a fool. They are pissed at us, and upset enough to start a clan war, and they'd be justified in doing so. It's why they asked to push forward the wedding and—"

"No," I snap out.

"—*I have agreed*," Michael completes his statement.

"I don't." I keep all expression off my face as I face down my oldest brother.

"I don't think I heard you right," Michael says in a dangerously calm voice.

"It's my marriage—"

"It's a marriage between two clans," Michael points out.

"Things have changed." I cross my arms across my chest.

"You knew when you agreed to the arrangement that you couldn't back out of it."

"All I'm asking for is a little time."

"You lost your right to ask for anything when you took off right after the engagement. What's wrong with you?" Michael looks me up and down. "You are the most responsible of all of us. It's not like you to act without thinking, unlike our brother here." He jerks his chin in Luca's direction. "No offense."

"None taken." Luca smirks. "Perhaps we should ask him what prompted such an action?"

Michael straightens to his full height. "We've been over this. I told you if you wanted to back out, it had to be done before the engagement was solemnized. At that time, you were confident you wanted to go through with the arrangement."

"I still do." *Just not with the intended bride.* "Look—" I lean forward in my seat. "I understand the importance of this alliance, and that I'm the only one amongst us who can go through with this marriage arrangement. All I'm saying is that I need a little time to sort my shit out."

"And what are you going to do during this time?" Michael crosses his arms across his chest. "If she were going to marry you, she'd have agreed to it by now. She's not interested in it."

"I need a little time to convince her."

"It's only because I understand how it is to fall in love with someone and want to spend the rest of your life with that person that I'm agreeing to this." He shakes his head. "How long do you need?"

I release a breath. "A week."

"You have two days, and if she doesn't agree to marry you at the end of it, you're going through with the wedding as planned. With her sister."

24

Olivia

I had almost allowed him to kiss me. If he'd touched his lips to mine, I'd have been a goner. I'd have kissed him back, then probably thrown myself at his feet and asked him to fuck me. *Jesus, what's wrong with me?*

He's going to marry my sister, and I told him I want nothing to do with him. I made that clear to him. But he hasn't gotten the memo. And if I'm being honest, neither has my body. When I walked into the conservatory and stumbled into him, every part of me came alive. My pulse rate went into overdrive, and it still hasn't calmed down. My stomach is tied up in knots and my clit throbs. I want his face between my legs, his cock inside my channel, and his tongue in my mouth as he fucks me. My pussy clenches, and my core dampens further. The constant need under my skin to have him has only grown more insistent in the past few hours.

I'd managed to put him behind me and focus on starting my life again, and now he's swept in and turned everything upside down. *Fuck.* I park outside the house where my family is staying and stomp up the path to the door. I ring the doorbell and wait, drumming my fingers on my dress-covered thigh. Maybe I should have changed before coming here... but fuck that. They know who I am. They know I'm not going to change. Besides, they already saw the dress, so it's not going to be a surprise to them.

The door is flung open, and my sister stands there.

"Livvy." My sister throws her arms around my shoulders. She's the only one I've tolerated calling me by that nickname.

I pull Solene close and bury my nose in her fragrant hair. "Are you okay?"

"Are you?" She pulls back and scans my features. "You left so suddenly."

"I had some business to take care of," I murmur. I take her hands in mine. "I am so sorry I interrupted your engagement."

"Oh pfft." She waves me off. "It doesn't matter. Besides, because the engagement was interrupted, Diego demanded the Sovranos to push the date of the marriage forward."

My heart leapfrogs into my throat. A massive weight seems to have parked itself on my chest. I force out the words, "They… They have?" I glance away, then back at her. "How do you feel about it?"

She raises a shoulder. "Guess I'm okay with it."

"You don't sound very convinced."

"I'm fine with it… I suppose." She blows out a breath. "To be honest, I don't think I have too much of an opinion about it."

"It's your wedding, your engagement… your life, Solene." I squeeze her fingers. "You need to expect more from it."

She scans my features. "That's why I've always envied you. You've always known what you want, Livvy. And you've gone after it. The only thing I've loved is singing."

"And I've told you, you could make it professionally, if you wanted. You just need to—"

"Leave home and try my luck in LA, I know." She shuffles her feet. "I've never had the self-confidence you have. I don't think I'd survive out there on my own."

"You wouldn't be alone; you'd have me," I point out.

"I wouldn't want to cramp your style." She bites the inside of her cheek. "Remember when we were younger, how I'd always tag along behind you and try to imitate you?"

"And I loved it."

She narrows her gaze on me.

I release her hands. "Okay, not always. You could be a pain sometimes, but I enjoyed having you along."

She half-smiles. "You're a wonderful sister, and now you're going to become a famous actress."

I laugh weakly. "Somehow, I don't think so." I raise my hand to touch the scar on my cheek, then lower it to my side.

"It doesn't take away from your beauty. It only adds to your mystique, you know?"

"If you say so." I scan her features. "I just came to make sure you're okay."

"I am," she says in a soft voice.

"You sure?"

She nods.

"I didn't mean for him to follow me out like that... I'm not sure why he did it."

She frowns up at me. "I guess he was being a gentleman and making sure you were okay?"

I tilt my head. Is that what she chooses to believe? Was the tension between me and Massimo not that obvious? Maybe I'm the only one who noticed it? Should I put her right? And what would I say?

"Olivia, is that you?" my brother calls out from inside the house. "Come in and visit with us, will you?"

Thank God for the distraction. Not that I want to see my brother, or anyone else in my family. I back away from the door. "I have to get going, uh... another thing that I need to be at."

I hear my brother's footsteps and he appears behind Solene. "Come in and have dinner with us. You owe us that much, after the stunt you pulled earlier."

A-n-d that's Diego for you. If he'd said he missed me, I'd have gladly joined them, but he had to turn this into a negotiation, as if I owe him something. If he could achieve something by threatening me or making it transactional, he would, when the straightforward route would work much better with me. He spins around and walks off, leaving Solene to look apologetically at me. "You know he doesn't mean to be this abrasive. He loves you, Livvy."

"He has a funny way of showing it." I blow out a breath. "Come on, let's join them before he bellows again."

"So, how did you meet Massimo?" Diego asks.

I stop with my spoon halfway to my mouth. The only reason I accepted the invitation for dinner is the food. God, I've missed the food. My mom can be a bitch, but her cooking is still the best I've ever tasted. And she doesn't even make too much of an effort. She seems to put the ingredients together without any measuring or tasting, and the dishes just take shape. I, clearly, didn't inherit that flair from her, but then, I hope I am not a total shrew like her, either.

I bring the fork to my mouth and taste the pasta. The tangy taste of tomatoes, the acidic bite of garlic, the slightly sour flavor of the mozzarella cheese—all of it combines to explode on my palate. Not even the fact that I have to face the conversation I've been dreading takes away from the taste of the food. I swallow down the portion, then place my spoon back on my plate.

"He was at my friend Jeanne's wedding to his brother, Luca."

"Clearly, the two of you got to know each other well," Diego murmurs.

Next to him, my mother opens her mouth as if to say something, but thinks better of it.

I whip my gaze in Diego's direction. "What are you insinuating?"

"Just that it's useful you're already acquainted with him, since he's going to be part of the family." He glances up and meets my gaze. "As long as it doesn't interfere with your sister's wedding."

That familiar anger knots my guts. A pressure builds behind my eyes. "Why don't you come out and say what's really on your mind?" I lock my fingers together in my lap.

He places his fork in his plate and blows out a breath. "Whatever happened between the two of you is of no consequence to me. Men like to fool around with women, but when they marry, they want to settle down with someone who is untouched and who can bear them children and keep their home—"

"All of which I am not. That's what you're implying, right?"

"You said it." Diego tilts his head. "You knew the road you were embarking on when you left home and decided to become an actress. I warned you it wouldn't be easy. I warned you once you left, you couldn't return to the fold. That the career you'd chosen would only bring you grief. And especially after what happened to your face—"

I resist the urge to touch the scar on my cheek.

"—it's clear that your choices aren't going to serve you well."

"But they were my choices. My mistakes and my successes, all of which I'm perfectly happy to contend with."

"Oh, you'll have to do more than that. Life isn't as simple as you think it is. You were sheltered in the family. Treated like a princess. Your every whim catered to. Our father spoilt you; he was lenient toward you. If it were me, I'd have never let you leave home in the first place."

"Good thing you're not my father." *Oh, Papa, you're the only one who understood me.* "If he were still alive, he'd have never agreed to this arranged marriage with the *Cosa Nostra.*"

"It's because he was so lenient in his affairs and allowed his own clan to swindle him that I had to make this arrangement with the *Cosa Nostra.* It's the only way to strengthen our position and ensure that our future is taken care of."

"So, you'd barter our sister for that? You'd allow her to be treated as a piece of merchandise so that *your* future is secure?" I shoot back.

"I wonder if you'd be protesting so much if it were you who was the bride-to-be."

The blood drains from my face. "What are you insinuating, Diego?"

"If you feel so badly for your sister, why don't you marry him instead?"

"Diego!" I lean forward in my seat. "You can't treat us like commodities to shift around at will. Solene's engaged to the man. You can't go around making these kinds of statements. It's not being fair to her."

"And you running out of the engagement, only to be followed by Massimo, is?" Diego steeples his fingers together. He narrows his gaze on me and there's something in his expression that indicates he knows I had a relationship with Massimo.

I curl my fingers, so my nails dig into the palm of my hand. "Whatever there was between me and Massimo is over."

A silence descends on the table. My mother draws in a breath. I sense my sister stiffen, but don't turn my head to look at her.

"There's nothing between us now."

"So, you admit you had a relationship with him?" Diego taps his fingertips together.

I glance away. "It wasn't a relationship. It was… nothing."

"It was something, considering how he rushed after you," Diego points out.

"It doesn't mean anything. He was probably just being gentlemanly. That's all," I lie out of desperation. "It's not my fault he chose to come after me to make sure I was okay. I don't want anything to do with him, okay?" *What is wrong with me?*

The silence at the table intensifies. I glance toward my mother, who's watching me with disappointment on her face. Yeah, yeah, so what's new? I've never managed to live up to her expectations. I wasn't the demure, girly daughter she longed for. That's my sister.

Me? I never did what I was told. I rebelled. I asked questions. I could never accept the status quo. It's why I left home to pursue my dreams. I left my sister behind. And while my father and mother loved her, she never had a chance to find out what she wanted to make of herself.

No doubt, they indoctrinated her in the ways of the Mafia and convinced her that her future was that as wife to a Mafioso. If I had stayed behind, I might have encouraged her to think otherwise. On the other hand, if she's going to marry anyone in the Mafia, it might as well be Massimo. This way, I'm sure she'll be taken care of. If she were to marry anyone else, there'd be no guarantee of how he'd treat her. I was selfish and left her behind, and now I have to make it right. For all our sakes, I have to give up Massimo... For her.

I glance around the table, then declare, "I have a fiancé."

25

———————

Olivia

How have I managed to land myself in this situation? *Oh, what a tangled web we weave. When first we practice to deceive.* Walter Scott's words have never rung truer. Unfortunately, I never did take to any of his other poems. But this particular line has always stuck in my mind.

I glance at myself in the mirror. Tug on the sleeve of my dress. It's a shift dress, with netting for sleeves which run down to my wrists. The hem hits below my knees. It does have a slit that runs up the side so the dress parts when I walk. And the neckline may be a little more daring than usual, but still, totally acceptable. Combined with my favorite Ferragamo's—which were another impulse purchase—I feel more confident in facing the upcoming evening.

I should have totally turned down the invitation, but when Massimo threw it down as a challenge, I wasn't able to refuse. And then I had to go open my big mouth and tell my family I'm engaged.

I wasn't even able to apologize to my sister about the fact that I hadn't come clean to her about my prior interactions with Massimo. I mean, what would I tell her? That I slept with her future husband, once—okay, twice—before I had any idea that he would be the person with whom her marriage was going to be arranged. And that to cover it up, I lied to him, and then to my family. *Oh, my god!* I squeeze the bridge of my nose. This is such a mess. Only bright spot is, I have someone I think can be persuaded to back up my story. At least, I hope he will.

The doorbell to my flat rings. I rented this place with Penny, and another actor friend, who moved back to London after the musical finished its run. I extended the lease by another week, just until I can see this mess through. All I have to do is convince Massimo I've moved on, and convince my family I don't want anything to do with Massimo. Oh, yea, and I have to convince myself, too. No biggie.

I march to the door and throw it open.

The tall man in the doorway blocks my view with his broad shoulders. His dark hair is slightly long, his jaw unshaven. His blue eyes crinkle at the corners as he takes me in. "Whoa, Olly, you sure do clean up well."

He notices the scar on my cheek, though it shouldn't be a shock, since I've FaceTimed him a few times already.

"Shut up." I grab him by his tie and pull him in for a peck on his cheek. "Good to see you, too, Declan. Thanks for coming."

"How could I refuse? Also, I was in the South of France which isn't that far off."

"You were on the *Riviera*?" I step back and beckon him to enter. He follows me inside. I shut the door, then watch as he prowls around the apartment. He's so large that the space, which is normally enough for me, seems much too small with him in it. "If I'd known you were on holiday, I wouldn't have interrupted you."

"It was work." He raises a shoulder. "Or rather, networking with other producers and actors. Deathly boring. You know how it is." He throws me a glance over his shoulder.

I do know. I was one of them. A struggling actress who made the rounds of parties, lunches, more auditions, all in search of that one elusive role that would get me noticed. I'd landed a few bit parts, but nothing big, until the role in *Beauty and the Beast* had come along. It had been as the understudy, of course, but it was regular pay. And it meant returning to Italy, which I'd had mixed feelings about. Not that I had a choice. When a role comes your way, you take it.

"I really do appreciate you coming down here on such short notice."

"Anything for you, Olly, you know that." He turns to face me. "You look good, babe."

"You mean, despite the scar on my face?" I gesture toward my cheek with my hand.

"It's honestly not that noticeable."

"Noticeable enough to have been ditched by my agent."

His gaze widens, then he scowls. "You needed a new agent, anyway."

I chuckle. "You're probably right." I walk past him to the kitchen. "And I know you're right about the scarring. It's not a big deal, except when the camera zooms in for a close-up, and then it's right there."

He stares at me.

"I know. I mean, I know it shouldn't stop me. At most, maybe it should just temporarily slow me down. It's just, it makes my job even more difficult. It's tough enough landing an audition, never mind when they find out you have a scar on your cheek."

"And when have you ever let a challenge stop you?" He leans a hip against the counter.

"Wait until you find out about the one that I'm faced with now," I grumble as I pull a beer from the refrigerator and offer it to him. Then, I head over to where I have a bottle of tequila stowed away at the back of a shelf. I pull it out, and turn to find a glass.

He arches an eyebrow. "That much of a challenge?"

"Worse." I pour myself a shot of the alcohol, then toss it back. I cough, then grab a glass, fill it with water and drink from it. When I've finally composed myself, I turn to find him watching me with an amused glint.

"It can't be that bad."

"You have no idea." I proceed to tell him everything, and when I'm done, he bursts out laughing. He laughs so hard that the bottle in his hand tilts, and some of the liquid spills over the side.

"Watch it." I mop up the liquid and toss the paper napkin in the waste disposal basket. "It's also not that funny." I scowl.

"It's hilarious. In fact, it reads like a comedy of errors." He chortles.

"Hmph." I cross my arms across my chest and lean against the counter. "So, will you come with me to dinner tonight? I couldn't think of anyone else who could play the role of my fake fiancé."

"You sure this mobster beau of yours won't shoot me for it?"

"He's not my beau." I shuffle my feet. "I slept with him, once." I think about lying, but the least I can do is be honest with the person here to help me. "Okay, twice."

"Well, clearly, you made an impression on him, if he hasn't forgotten you."

I bite the inside of my cheek. To be fair, I haven't forgotten him, either. I remember every touch, every kiss, every stroke of his palm on my hip, every brush of his fingers over my clit, every breath of his on my cheek, every nudge of his lips against mine, seducing me to open my mouth for him, part my legs for his invasion, press my aching breasts against his chest. The humor in his eyes, which occasionally surfaced when he thought I didn't notice, the softness in his features whenever he pulled me into his side. The banter which we traded, the way he seemed to tolerate my flashes of temper. God, there's no one else with whom I've ever felt this comfortable, yet this turned on. The intensity of our connection was something I've never experienced before. And I may never experience again. I grip the edge of the counter and blink against the telltale pressure that crowds the backs of my eyes.

"You're in love with him," he states.

I jerk my chin in his direction. "What, no. What gave you that idea?"

"The fact that you look like you lost your best friend?"

My features crumple. He walks over and pulls me into a hug. "Didn't mean to upset you."

"You didn't. Well, it wasn't only you. I've been such an ass. And I barely know the man, so how can I feel so much for him? Also, I can't just give in and marry him, you know. I need to figure out what I really want first." I press my face into his shoulder. Draw in his scent... which is male, but strange. Nothing like the darkness and testosterone that is Massimo. *Jesus, why am I so hung up on him?* I made my decision to walk away from him. Why can't I stick to it now? "I'm so confused." I swallow.

He pats my shoulder as I compose myself.

"I'm fine now." I push away and he steps back.

"Come on, have a seat." He pulls me over to sit at the table. Then refills the glass of water and sets it in front of me.

I take a sip, and another. "I'm good." I place the glass back on the table as he drops down in the chair across from me.

"The way I see it, you have three choices now."

I tilt my head.

"Either you can come clean to your family that you love him and tell them you want to marry him."

"Never," I say with finality.

"Or you can tell him you love him, and accept his proposal to get married."

I scowl. "And the third option?"

He lowers his chin to his chest. "I don't have a third option."

26

Olivia

Talking it out with Declan confirmed one thing. Basically, I'm fucked, any which way I look at it. The best option is to get through this dinner and split town. Leave and return to waitressing, and to the endless rounds of auditions. Neither of which appeal to me. What the hell has happened to me? Surely, I'm not going to let the fact that I'm scarred hold me back from embracing my ambitions?

Declan promised to put me in touch with his manager, who he thinks would be a great fit for me, but even that doesn't make me as excited as I should be. It seems, along with scarring my face, I've scarred the dreams I may have once had for myself. Maybe hurting my face ripped off the mask hiding the shallowness of the industry I'd wanted to belong to.

Massimo texted me the address for the restaurant, and I pause in front of it now. It was a business-like text. The address and time of the dinner reservation, that's all. This is just a dinner. I have to go in, eat, leave… Weather Massimo's glower, and his anger, which will surely be directed at me. Not to mention, all the unsaid conversations lurking between me and my sister. This is going to be fun… not. I hunch my shoulders.

"Hey, you're going to be great." Declan presses his palm into the small of my back. "You look amazing, and remember, you're an actress. You can pull this off without effort."

I chuckle. "Yea, I'm a professional liar. It's easier to act on screen than in real life, know what I mean?"

"Not if you put on your movie star persona before you flounce in there. That's acting 101, or have you forgotten?"

It's true. If you walk the walk, and talk the talk, you become the talk. Or so someone said. I draw in a breath, snap back my shoulders, and take a step forward with Declan on my heels. The hostess ushers us to a table at the far end of the restaurant—a Michelin-starred one. Nothing but the best for him, of course.

As I approach, I notice Massimo has his head bent over Solene's. My sister's fair, blonde looks, set off his dark, swarthy ones to perfection. He's dressed in a dark jacket and black shirt that stretch across his wide shoulders. She has her hair coiffured to perfection and is wearing a pale pink dress with a demure neckline. She places her pink-tipped fingers on his shoulder, and he laughs at something she says.

My heart twists, and my stomach churns. I pause so suddenly, Declan bumps into me from behind. "Steady," he whispers in my ear. He wraps his fingers around my wrist and walks forward. As he approaches the table, Massimo looks up. His gaze clashes with mine—storm clouds looming on the horizon, waves rising up to drag me down. I'm drowning. Sinking fast, and not sure how to save myself.

Then my sister jumps up. "Livvy, you look beautiful," she bursts out.

"And you look angelic." I move around, and taking my sister by her shoulders, kiss her on both cheeks.

"This must be your sister," Declan says from behind me.

I take a step back, and still holding my sister's hand, turn to him. "This is my sister Solene. Solene, this is Declan, my—"

"You're Declan Beauchamp, the movie star. Livvy, why didn't you tell me your fiancé was someone famous?" She tugs her hand from mine, and holds it out in his direction.

He takes her hand in his, his gaze riveted by her features.

Solene's features flush. She swallows and stares at him like she can't believe he's really standing in front of her.

Declan chuckles, then kisses her fingers. "At your service."

Solene blushes. Declan's gaze intensifies.

I clear my throat and she blinks. Declan releases her hand with reluctance, then turns to Massimo.

"You must be the lucky man."

Massimo ignores his proffered hand. "I still don't see a ring." He directs the comment to me.

I nudge Declan, who tears his gaze off of Solene with great reluctance. "Uh, yeah, we don't believe in a ring to be engaged, do we now, darling?" he murmurs.

Massimo's gaze narrows. "I thought you said your ring was being resized?"

"Eh?" Declan blinks rapidly.

I nudge him with my elbow and he coughs. "That's what I meant. The ring is being resized. But whether she's wearing a ring or not is not the point. We don't need it to proclaim the veracity of our love, do we now, darlin'?"

"Exactly what I meant, darling." I wrap my hand around Declan's bicep, then meet Massimo's gaze.

Massimo glances down at where I clutch at Declan. His jaw hardens. He looks up at me and his blue-gray eyes darken until they resemble black holes of anger. Meanwhile, my sister hasn't taken her gaze off Declan, who, by the way, is sneaking a sideways glance at her, as well. Oh shoot, this wasn't a good idea, was it?

I gesture toward the chairs. "Let's all sit down, shall we?"

**

Twenty minutes later, I know for a fact this was a bad idea. Since we arrived, Massimo hasn't spoken a word, except to glower in my direction. Solene hasn't stopped staring and Declan, who seems to have forgotten all about me, is focused on Solene. He's topped up her wine, ordered her food, and snarled at a waiter who came too close to her while setting down her plate.

As for me, I gave up trying to hold a one-sided conversion with the rest of them and have my attention focused on the food, which might be delicious, but I wouldn't know because I haven't tasted a morsel. I've managed to swallow a few mouthfuls. I reach for the wine and drain it. A waiter appears next to my elbow to refill it. Massimo glares at him. He pales, places the bottle on the table, and backs away. Massimo grabs the bottle and fills my glass. I pick it up and drain half the contents. The liquor hits my stomach and sends a warm buzz pulsing through my veins.

"You need to slow down," he says through gritted teeth.

I glance at him, then raise the glass in his direction. "You need to remove the stick up your ass."

His jaw hardens. A vein pulses at his temple.

"If you grit your teeth any harder, you might crack your molars," I whisper.

"Do you care?" he shoots back.

I glance down at my drink then back up at him. "And if I say I do?"

"I won't believe you."

I raise my shoulder. "I know this entire situation is tricky—"

"Tricky?" He grips his tumbler so hard, the skin across his knuckles stretches with it. "Negotiating a contract is tricky. Evading your enemy in a car chase is tricky. This—" He leans forward in his seat. "Is a goddamn catastrophe."

His voice cuts through the noise, and both Solene and Declan fall silent.

Declan glances between us. He seems to finally remember me, the traitor, and places his arm around my shoulder. "Everything okay?"

Massimo glares at him like he's going to leap across the table any moment, grab his tie, and yank him across to his side. Or worse. The tendons of his throat flex like he wants to say something but is holding back. His shoulders swell. He must grip his glass even tighter because it splinters. The smell of alcohol laces the air. Blood drips from a cut in his palm and stains the white cloth on the table.

He shoves his chair back and springs up. "Excuse me." He pivots and walks off in the direction of what I assume is the restroom.

I jump up, as well. "I… Just need to make sure he's okay." Without glancing at the two of them at the table, I take off after him. I reach the corridor and spot him entering the men's room. I walk toward it and enter, to find he's alone. I shut the door behind me and lock it, then lean against it.

He holds his hand under the tap for a few seconds before straightening and grabbing a fresh towel from the holder and wrapping it around his palm. He glances at my reflection in the mirror. Anger radiates off of him. His eyes flash as he meets my gaze.

"Massimo, I'm—"

"Get out of here. If you don't, I won't be responsible for what happens next."

I rub my sweaty palms on the fabric covering my thighs. "I'm sorry. So sorry."

"For lying to me? For trying to pass off someone with whom you don't have a shred of chemistry with as your fiancé?"

I hunch my shoulders. "Is it that obvious?"

He glowers at me in the mirror. "Get out of here, Olivia. Else, I swear, I'll say or do something that both of us will regret for a long time."

The air in the space grows thick with unspoken words. He continues to hold my gaze, and my insides turn to smoke. Every pore in my body seems to pop. An electric current seems to stretch from him to me and I can't stop myself from taking a step forward, then another. He stalks me with a brooding look as I draw level with him. I can't break the connection between our gazes. Can't stop myself from reaching out and placing my palm at the small of his back.

He squeezes his eyes shut. A shudder runs up his spine. He brings his unhurt hand down to the edge of the counter and squeezes it. "Fuck. F-u-c-k, Via, don't do this."

I slide my arms about his waist and flatten my cheek against his broad back. The muscles jump under his skin. The wings of his back pull back toward each other. Nervous tension thrums from him. That dark, testosterone-filled scent of his teases my senses. My nipples tighten, and my core clenches. I'm going to hell for this. I shouldn't be doing this, but he feels so damn good.

"Step away, Olivia, please." His voice is tortured. "I won't be able to contain myself any longer."

I swallow. I should say something. Ask him to not react. Ask him to stay where he is. Ask him to turn me around, bend me over the counter and fuck me. And then what? How will I face my sister again? She may be attracted to another man, based on her reaction to Declan. It doesn't change the fact that she's engaged to my— To Massimo.

I lower my arms to my sides and spin around to take a step away, when he grabs my wrist, turns me around and pushes me up against the counter. "The hell you playing at? Have you any idea how much you've complicated all of our lives?" He glares at me, and I can't stop the shivers that ladder up my back. Little zings of fire spark off from where he's touching me.

I open my mouth to speak, but no words emerge. I want to say I am sorry, but that doesn't seem enough. I peer into his face, and we stand there breathing each other's air, not touching, except for where he's gripped my wrist. My chest rises and falls. My breathing grows shallow. The scent of him bats against my senses, pulling at me. Tugging on me. Moisture laces my core, and I sway closer to him. I fix my gaze on his lips. I'm going to kiss him now. That's it, damn everything that happened. Fuck the engagement to my sister. *I want him. I need him. I—*

He releases me and steps back so quickly that I stumble. He doesn't right me, though, and I miss him already.

"You made your point. You're engaged and so am I." He takes another step back. "It's best we keep our distance from now on."

Someone jiggles the handle, then bangs on the door. "Olivia, are you in there?" Declan calls out. I sink back against the counter as Massimo heads to the door and flings it open.

"See her home safely. If something happens to her, I'll shoot you in the face."

He brushes past Declan and leaves.

27

Massimo

Leaving her is the hardest thing I've ever done. She looked at me with her big, green eyes, and my resolve had almost crumbled. I wanted to close the distance between us, wrap my arms around her, pull her to me and kiss her scar, and tell her she didn't have to worry about anything. All she had to do was trust me, to lean on me for a little while, and let me take care of her while she sorts out whatever it is she needs to get right in her head. But doing so would have meant being rebuffed by her. Again.

I have less than forty-eight hours to convince her to break off her engagement, if I can even call it that, and marry me instead. And her engagement *is* a sham. Declan and Solene haven't been able to keep their eyes off of one another. In fact, he barely spoke with Olivia over lunch. Clearly, he's attracted to Olivia's sister. Not to mention, there's not a shred of chemistry between Declan and Via. Nope, it's all a front. Something she's concocted in the hope of throwing me off track. No way am I buying it. I am going to convince her that I'm the man for her. That I'm the only one who can make her happy. And the way to do that is to show her what she's missing. I need to put distance between us, and hope she comes to me. I'm gambling on the belief that not having me around will show her how much she needs me, and not that asshole Beauchamp, with his pretty-boy features and suave manner.

Is that what she likes? A man who faces the camera and worries about his looks for a living? Someone who probably spends all his time in the gym, and puts more cosmetics on his face than she ever would. She doesn't need anything artificial to enhance her looks.

Olivia is the most beautiful, most gorgeous woman I've ever met, inside and out. She's also the most stubborn. And no one will ever compare with her. It's her or nobody else for me. If only she'd see that.

"Massimo?" Solene calls out from the seat beside me.

I force my attention back to her. "Solene," I say politely.

"You don't want to marry me," she states.

I tense. I don't want to hurt her, and I don't want to lie to her. On the other hand, if I admit that I'm not in favor of our engagement, before I can change her sister's mind, the consequences for my clan would be serious.

"It's okay, I know you have feelings for my sister."

I firm my lips. Is this a trap? Is she saying it just to get me to admit my feelings aloud so she can use it against me?

"My brother's the head of the *Camorra*. I'm one of them, too, but I'm not a Mafioso. I don't want anything to do with the politics between the clans. Unfortunately, as a woman, I don't have that luxury. So, I find myself in this situation where I'm, apparently, engaged to a man who doesn't want anything to do with me, and who would do anything for my sister."

I wince. She's right, though. What can I say to that? I certainly can't deny it.

"When my father was the head of the *Camorra*, he was strictly against arranged marriages. He was fiercely proud and was ready to fight for his clan, even take on the *Cosa Nostra* if needed, to keep his independence. Then he died, and my brother took over. He's more ambitious, more power-hungry, and he wants an alliance with your clan. When he asked me if I was open to an arranged marriage with you, I agreed."

She looks down at her lap. "You see, until then, I'd been drifting along, happy for others to make decisions for me. I didn't have any opinions of my own. The one thing I've always wanted is to be a singer, but I was never ambitious enough to go for it. I didn't think I had the courage it takes to go out into the world and try my luck, so I've been content to sing for myself and for my family. To do what was needed to make them happy. To play my part as a dutiful daughter and sister, so I could help secure their futures..."

"Not anymore." I turn to face her.

"No." She shakes her head. "I thought I could find happiness in their happiness. I was perfectly content to coast along until—"

"You met him."

She swallows. "I... I know it's sudden. I know I have nothing to base my decision on, except my instinct—"

"It's all we ever have, after all," I retort.

"People might call me crazy for making up my mind in a split second, but when you know—"

"You know." I half-smile.

"Is that how it was for you with my sister?" she asks.

I draw in a breath. "Meeting Via was explosive. Volatile. Incendiary. Combustible." I shake my head. "She blew my mind, and now I can't think of anything or anyone else."

She laughs. "You definitely have feelings for her."

I allow my shoulders to relax.

"So why don't you marry her instead?" she asks.

"I would, but she turned me down." I rub the back of my neck. "She claims she's in love with that *stronzo*, Declan."

Solene scoffs. "She's not. She had eyes only for you."

"And Declan couldn't take his gaze off of you." I roll my shoulders. "Olivia also said she needs time to figure out what to do with her life. The scarring on her face hasn't been easy for her. I understand, but I wish she'd let me help."

"I think she's scared of her feelings for you. Maybe what she needs is a little push."

I narrow my gaze. "You don't want to go through with this wedding, I take it?"

"Not anymore, I don't." She glances to the side then back at me. "I have a reason to fight now."

"Hmm..." I drum my fingers on my thigh. "Maybe we can help each other."

28

Olivia

Declan dropped me back at my place. We didn't speak much on the way back, both of us lost in our thoughts. He walked me up to my apartment, and asked me if my sister wanted to go through with the wedding. I saw the hope on his face, which faded when I told him she seemed content with the arrangement the last time I asked her. Of course, I noticed she couldn't keep her eyes off of him at dinner and hung on his every word, but I didn't want to get his hopes up. His features clouded before he set his jaw, a glint of resolution shining in his eyes. Something I knew meant trouble. An instinct which was confirmed when he asked me for the address to where Solene was staying.

I didn't have the energy to tell him it was a bad idea to visit her and he shouldn't go through with whatever it was he was thinking about doing. Instead, I bid him good-night, locked the door behind me, and collapsed on my bed.

I barely slept all night—plagued by thoughts of how Massimo hadn't taken his eyes off of me all through dinner, how he'd been so distraught that he'd broken his glass, how he'd wanted to touch me, yet held himself back. And then, he'd walked away. He'd been right to do that. After all, he's engaged. And he'd managed to not compromise his values. I have to respect him for that.

There's nothing stopping him from touching my sister, though. When Declan and I returned to the table, they both were gone. No doubt, he was dropping her back home. Would he touch her, hold her, kiss her, caress her?

Images of the two of them together occupied my mind all night. Every time I shut my eyes, I saw them together. My entire body tensed, my muscles locking with tension, and I honestly thought I would throw up. I finally dozed off, and woke up close to noon with a raging headache, which had nothing to do with the wine I drank last night, and everything to do with the images I tortured myself with.

I glance at myself in the mirror and winced—dark circles under my eyes, hollowed cheeks, and the scar, which stands out even more against my skin. Not only have I lost my looks, but I'm also dangerously close to losing my mind. I squeeze the edge of the sink and take stock. I can't go on like this. I need to get away from here. At least I've already heard back from Declan's agent, who's happy to take me on and wants to meet me right away in London. It's best I move to London, and if all goes well, to LA.

Given how much I enjoy live performance, I should focus on becoming a stage actress, but being shot during my first performance as a lead actress has, somehow, cured me of the urge to go on stage again. Not that I'm looking forward to facing a camera with the scar on my face. But between the two, I know which one I'd pick. And with a new agent who seems to believe in me, I have a better chance at getting roles.

It's time to move on with my life and leave the past—and him—behind. My stomach churns, and my chest hurts. I breathe into the pain, but it doesn't help. The helplessness builds inside of me, fills my cells, and pushes up against my skin until it feels too tight for me. I need to relieve this pressure, but how? I glance around, and grab the knife I left on the counter. Then pull up the hem of my nightshirt and drag the blade across my thigh.

The blood drips down my leg, and instantly, some of the pressure inside of me releases. I know what I'm doing is wrong... but I'm not hurting anyone, am I? Except me, of course. I started doing it recently... after I was shot. I'll stop soon, I promise. It's just to cope with the pressure of everything. It's not easy facing the camera, and even less so, now that my face is not like it used to be. But I can do it. I have to. I can't give up, not now. I grab the antiseptic, dab it on the wound, then wince when the burn radiates up my hip. I grab the bottle of ibuprofen, shake some out into my palm, and swallow it with water. By the time I've showered and dressed, I feel better. I need to get out of this town. But first, I need to say goodbye to my sister. She's the only one in my family I still want to see, but once she marries Massimo... I squeeze my eyes shut. My heartbeat ratchets up. My pulse pounds at my temples. Why is the thought of the two of them together so unbearable? I need to leave before the wedding, and then try not to see her again. Ever. That's the only way out.

Half an hour later, I stare at the black Maserati parked outside the house where my family is staying. It's Massimo's car. Is he in there with my sister? I glance at the house, then hesitate. Do I have the courage to go in there? Do I leave without seeing my sister one last time? A ball of emotion crowds my throat. I try to breathe, but my lungs burn. Oh, my god, I'm going to burst into tears and embarrass myself. No way can I go in there, I can't. I turn to leave. I've taken only a couple of steps when I hear her.

"Livvy!" Solene's voice calls out from behind me.

I cringe, but don't dare turn.

"Livvy, where are you going?" I hear footsteps behind me, and like a coward, I begin to walk faster.

"Livvy, stop!" My sister's footsteps sound behind me and she draws abreast. "Livvy, where are you going?" She steps in front of me, forcing me to stop. Her face is flushed, her blonde hair flowing around her shoulders. "Were you going to leave without coming inside?"

"I—" I blink away my tears. "I... uh, forgot something."

"Did you really?" She peers into my face. "Or are you lying to me again?"

"Again? What do you mean again?"

"You aren't happy about my marrying Massimo, are you?"

"That's not true." I draw myself up to my full height. "I fully support your decision to go through with the wedding."

"Do you? I thought you said I could do better. That I didn't have to sacrifice my future for the family?"

"I... I did say that. But if your heart is set on it, then..." I raise a shoulder.

"So, you're not unhappy that I'm marrying him?"

"No." I glance away.

"You're not upset that he'll be married to someone else?"

That ball of emotion in my throat drops to my chest, and it's like a massive weight is pressing down on my lungs. Specks of black flicker at the corners of my eyes. I sway a little, and she grips my arm.

"Are you okay?"

I nod, not trusting myself to speak.

"Did you eat anything today?"

I shake my head.

"Come on, have lunch with us."

"But—"

"No buts." She leans in closer. "I know you, Livvy. I know how upset you are. I know you have feelings for him."

"What? No." I try to pull away, but she tightens her grip on my arm. "You don't have to hide it from me. I saw your emotions all over your face last night."

"And I saw how you looked at Declan."

She flushes, but doesn't let go of me. "So, you understand why this engagement cannot happen."

"Solene." I stare. Not that I dispute what she's saying, but a Mafia engagement between two clans cannot be broken—not without serious consequences. The band around my chest loosens, and I draw in a breath. Have I been that upset about the upcoming nuptials? Apparently, so.

One side of her lips kicks up. "I know what you're thinking, but there's a plan."

29

Massimo

"So, fifty percent of the overland routes through South Europe for running guns would belong to the *Camorra*?" Diego's tone is steady but there is an underlying thread of excitement running through it. Since I got here, the man's quizzed me about the benefits of the upcoming partnership, which he can't wait to enjoy. I raise the glass of whiskey to my lips and sip from it. It's not even lunch time, but the only way I could get through this meeting is with alcohol for company. It was a meeting I asked for. The only way to ensure I could see her again.

"Massimo?" Diego prompts me. "The gun routes?"

"Yes, the *Cosa Nostra* would hand the routes over once the nuptials are complete," I murmur.

"That's good; that's very good." He sips from his own glass… of bourbon. Never trust a man who prefers bourbon over whiskey, or so my father would say. Not that I'd trust the *stronzo* with much else, but it's proved to be a warning sign countless times

His features light up. He doesn't even bother hiding his glee at my confirmation. "*Salute.*" He raises his glass. I drain mine without bothering to clink glasses with him.

His jaw hardens, but he doesn't admonish me. That's what happens when you want something with so much desperation; you'll put up with the insult to get it. He drains his own glass and sets it aside.

"And the routes which are with the Bratva—"

"Stay with them. And our prior arrangements with the Kane company stay, as well. They are our allies, which also makes them your allies. Don't forget that."

He draws in a breath. "I don't trust either of them."

"You don't have a choice in the matter. It's the cost of doing business with the *Cosa Nostra*."

I hear a noise at the door, but continue to focus on the *pezzo di merda* who jerks his chin. "You should know, I'm pursuing an alliance with the Mexicans for my remaining sister."

I scowl. "Your remaining sister?" *Is there another one?* His words don't quite compute. Who is he talking about? It can't be, surely, can it?

His gaze turns canny. "For Olivia."

I curl my fingers around the bandage that's wrapped around my right palm. "The Mexicans are ruthless. They're into slave trading, and have been known to sell off their own daughters for money. You'd arrange to send your own sister into that?"

"I'm sure once she is married to the Don, they'll treat her differently."

I glance past him to where a pale-faced Olivia stands by the door next to Solene, who's looking at her brother with a horrified expression on her face.

"The Don?" I glare at Diego. "He's a piece of shit, notorious for his sadistic tendencies. He's been married thrice already, and none of his wives have survived, so far."

"Maybe my sister will be the one to get lucky, huh? Besides, she's scarred. Her prospects for marriage to anyone else are close to nil."

I sense Olivia shuffle her feet. I flick my gaze in her direction, and shake my head faintly to gesture she shouldn't interfere. Anger pours off of her, but she doesn't say a word. *Thank fuck.* I focus my attention on the *testa di cazzo* who offers to top up my glass. When I cover my glass with my palm, he places the bottle aside.

"Olivia has a fiancé," I snap.

"And you believe her?"

I stay silent.

"That's what I thought." He cracks his neck. "It's time to get her settled, and the Mexicans are more than happy with the alliance."

"And what about what Olivia wants?"

"What *about* her?" He turns to me. "She'll do as she's told. She's had her fun, trying to become an actress. Given the condition of her face, there's no future for her in it." He pours more bourbon into his glass. "This is the best solution. She gets a husband out of it, and I ensure the future of our clan. Given you are now family, you'd benefit from it, too."

"The *Cosa Nostra* never has and never shall trade people, nor do we associate with those who do. The Mexicans deserve to be shot, every last one of them."

"Surely, you're not so archaic in your beliefs. It's business."

"So is this." I pull out my gun, aim it at his forehead, and fire.

There's a scream from the doorway. I pocket my gun and turn in time to find Solene crumple. Olivia catches her sister, then lowers her to the floor, her gaze still on me. I walk toward them, then sink to my feet next to Solene, unable to tear my gaze off Olivia's face.

"I couldn't allow him to hurt you."

She takes in my features, then reaches out and wipes something off my cheek. "Blood," she says in a steady voice.

"Ah." I tilt my head. "Are you upset?"

"I don't know." She searches my eyes. "I understand why you did it, but that was my brother."

"I couldn't let him go through with his plan for you. I had to protect you, at all costs."

Solene moans, and she darts her gaze down to her sister's face. "Honey, are you okay?"

Solene glances from her to me, then pulls away. "Take me away from him, please." Her voice wavers.

"Sweetheart, you don't have to be scared of Massimo."

"I can't stand to see him." Solene's chin wobbles.

I hear footsteps, then see Adrian approaching. When he sees me crouched on the floor in the doorway, he growls, "*Fratello*, what the hell happened?"

Declan, who arrived shortly after I did, under the pretext of seeing me, follows closely behind. He takes in the scene, then squats down next to us. "Solene, are you okay?"

She pulls off her engagement ring and holds it out in my direction. Without meeting my eyes she says, "I can't marry you."

I accept the ring.

She turns to Declan and holds out her hand. "Please, take me away from here."

30

Olivia

"He shot him, point-blank." Solene hiccups from the bed.

"He did it to protect me." I, too, should be hyperventilating, but somehow, when he shot my brother, then turned to me with the blood splatters on his face and pocketed his gun, a calm had descended on me. I'm not sure if it's shock, but I don't think so. It's more like a certainty I had to be there at that point in time to hear what my brother said, and to see Massimo defend my honor. I'd seen his nostrils flare as my brother had told him about his plans to marry me off to the much older Mafia head of a rival clan. I'd sensed the anger pouring off of him, seen his shoulders bulge, his biceps twitch, and I'd known what he was going to do a second before he whipped out his gun and shot Diego.

Do I mourn Diego? Yes. He was my brother. I have memories of us playing together when we were little. As we grew, so did our differences. I'd seen through his bluster, his tall claims, his constant need to prove himself to our father, while not always succeeding; his jealousy when my father had seemed to favor me over him, even though he was the man of the family. He hadn't been in favor of my leaving home to pursue my dream. And he hadn't waited an hour after my father's passing to declare himself the new head of the *Camorra*. But he was still my brother, so yes, I was sad to lose him. Even though, the truth is, I lost my brother a long time ago.

Declan carried Solene to bed, where she refused to let go of him. It's hard to believe they met only once. She seems to trust him in a way she hasn't trusted me for a long time. He held her while she cried, and when she finally subsided, he left her in my care as he headed off to confer with Massimo and Adrian.

I haven't seen my mother yet, although I'm sure she heard the gunshot, and by now, she must know what happened. I'll have to go to her, but first, I want to make sure Solene's okay.

"I'm sorry I wasn't there for you more growing up." I push the hair off of her forehead. "I'm sorry I wasn't there to protect you from Diego. I left to follow my dream, and let you bear the brunt of his need to prove himself in the eyes of the world."

"Livvy, don't be so hard on yourself." Solene sits up in bed and reaches for her glass of water. I place it in her hand, and she sips from it. "He wasn't too bad as a brother."

"He was only concerned with growing his power and consolidating his position as the head of the *Camorra*," I retort.

"He wasn't abusive."

"Only manipulative, and ready to offer up his sisters to rival clans without a thought for their happiness."

"He didn't deserve to die."

"It was only a matter of time before he was shot. You know as well as I do, when you pursue the path he did, you meet your end by the same means."

Solene's features crumpled. She places her glass on the bedside table and buries her face in her hands.

"Oh, sweetie." I throw my arms around her and allow myself to mourn the boy my brother once was. "He was going to marry me off. He'd have held me here and done so, whether I agreed or not."

Solene doesn't refute me. She knows I'm right.

"But shoot him?" she says in a small voice. "Did he have to do that?"

"In this business, you don't leave loose ends. You can't. There was no other way Massimo could have stopped him."

She lowers her hands and stares at me. "So, you're on his side?"

"I—" I pause, not sure what to say. Truth is, I was never not on his side. I may have pushed him away over and over again, but I've always believed in him. I've trusted him and rooted for him. I've never stopped wanting him. It's just, I can't afford to let myself get lost in him while I'm trying to figure out what my new reality is going to be.

"You are, aren't you?" She peers into my eyes. "He still loves you, you know."

"What's that got to do with anything?"

"You keep pushing him away, yet he's always there, waiting for you. He's not taking 'no' for an answer. He's being persistent because he feels something genuine for you. I wouldn't treat it so lightly. If you take him for granted, one day he'll be gone, and then you'll really miss him."

"Like how you already miss Declan, even though you just met him?" I tease.

Her cheeks flush. "I'm not sure what there is between Declan and me. All I can say is that I feel safe with him. I don't know him very well, but I'd trust him with my life."

"Whoa." I sit back in my chair. "I didn't think you'd fall this deep, this fast."

"Neither did I." She twists her fingers together in front of her. "I don't think I've ever felt this connected to anyone before."

"I know the feeling." I shake my hair back from my head. "Looks like both of us are goners, eh?" I chuckle. "Who'd have thought this could happen."

"You know I can't marry him, right? Not that there was ever a doubt that he was going to marry anyone other than you."

I rise to my feet and begin to pace. "I can't marry him, Solene. I really can't. If I do, I'll get distracted. I'll lose myself in him and not be able to focus on what I need to do."

"And what is it you need to do?"

"I need to figure out what I want. Whether I still want to be an actor. Whether I want to do something else with my life, and if so, what that is. I left home with a promise to myself, never to become a Mafia bride." I spin around and face her.

"Umm, Livvy?" Solene interrupts me, but I ignore her.

"I told myself I'd never be dependent on a Mafia guy, that I'd make something of myself before I settled down. Yet here I am, in the one situation I've been trying to avoid. I can't do this."

"Livvy, stop," Solene says urgently.

"I can't. I need to get this out. It's been eating away at me." I throw up my hands. "If I married him now, I'd be untrue to myself. I'd turn into the very woman I've wanted to avoid becoming, know what I mean?"

"I do." She blows out a breath. "And now, so does he."

"What?"

She glances past me. I turn to find Massimo at the doorway. Heat suffuses my face. Oh hell, I hadn't meant for him to hear me ranting like a lunatic.

"I tried to warn you." Solene twists her fingers together. She keeps her gaze averted from Massimo.

The silence stretches for a few seconds, then Massimo leans a hip against the doorframe. "Can I talk to you, Via?"

Ugh, not exactly what I want to do right now. I squeeze the bridge of my nose.

"Livvy? I think you need to speak with him," Solene whispers.

I lower my arm and search her features. "Are you going to be okay?"

"I'm fine," she smiles a teary smile. "A little in shock, but I'm okay. I'm not sure about you, though."

"Me?" I shake my hair back from my shoulders. "I'll survive. It's all going to work out, Sol, you'll see."

She holds my gaze for a second, then nods. "Okay."

"Okay." I lean forward and kiss her cheek, then rise to my feet and make it to the doorway. I brush past him and down the corridor to one of the guest rooms, aware he's on my heels. I walk toward the window and glance out.

He stands in the doorway. "Think she'll ever forgive me for what I did?" he asks.

"Probably not."

"Will you forgive me for what I did?"

"There's nothing to forgive. If you hadn't shot him, he'd have married me off to that Mexican Mafia lord." A shudder grips me. "Nothing I could say or do would have stopped him. He'd have probably made me a prisoner in my own home, and if I had escaped, he'd have found me and brought me back." I turn toward him. "You saved me from a future worse than death, so really, there's nothing to forgive."

A pleased look flashes across his face. "Now that we have that out of the way —" He steps inside the room and shuts the door behind him, then locks it. "Let's talk."

31

Massimo

The plan had been for me to negotiate with Diego. To hand over the *Cosa Nostra's* overland routes through Southern Europe to him, in exchange for my marrying Olivia, leaving Solene free to be with Declan. But the moment he said Olivia's name, referred to her as being scarred, then said he was going to marry her to that Mexican *stronzo*, he signed his own death warrant.

I'd asked Solene to set up a meeting with him. Not that he'd have refused if I'd asked him directly; he wouldn't dare. But if the request came through Solene, it would seem like I was accepting the idea of the marriage to her, and it would put him more at ease. It definitely loosened his tongue as he began to accept me as part of the *famiglia*. Enough to confide the plan he had for Olivia, and thank Santa Maria, I was able to nip that in the bud.

While Declan carried Solene, and Olivia accompanied them to ensure her sister was okay, I left Adrian to make some calls and take care of Diego's fallen body. I marched out of Diego's office just as Olivia's mother was heading toward it. I asked her to follow me, rounded up the rest of the family and household staff, and informed them of what had happened. Their mother collapsed crying. She'd lost a son, and while I have no doubt it was a shock, I couldn't delay letting her know that they're now under the protection of the *Cosa Nostra*. Leaving her sister and niece to look after her, I walked back to find Declan waiting for me.

He told me the truth of his non-engagement with Olivia. Then he looked me in the eye and told me, in no uncertain terms, that he wanted to take Solene with him to LA. I told him that was up to her. If she was willing, I had no objections. Then I stalked out in search of Olivia.

When I overheard her outburst, I knew, it was time. Time to settle this thing between us. Time to take matters into my own hands. Time to make her mine.

Now I lean back against the door and take in her features.

Her cheeks are flushed, and her hair mussed around her shoulders. Her chest rises and falls, and she darts her tongue out to wet her lips. Oh, she's nervous, even though she's trying not to show it. My queen straightens her spine, then tips up her chin and holds my gaze.

"Wh-why did you lock the door?" Her tone is breathless.

I allow a small smile to play on my lips. "Why do you think?"

"You don't scare me." She squares her shoulders.

"Maybe it's time I did." I plant my hands on my hips.

She scoffs, then shoves her hair back from her face. "What did you want to talk about, anyway?"

"How about we begin with why you turned down my proposal in the first place? Then, why did you lead me to believe you were engaged to someone else, when clearly you were not?" I take a step forward and her flush deepens. I take another step, and she shuffles back until the backs of her knees hit the bed, and she sits down.

"You know why I turned you down." She lowers her chin to her chest. "I, uh, I was engaged to Declan."

"Is that right?" I walk over to her, and her gaze widens. I come to a halt in front of her and she tilts her head back to meet my gaze.

I survey her features, then drag my knuckles down her cheek. "How long are you going to lie to me, Via?"

She swallows, then the fight seems to go out of her. She sags a little and shudders. "I'm pathetic, aren't I? I'm so afraid of losing myself, I can't take a risk on us."

I sink down next to her and gather her in my arms. She struggles, but I wrap my arm around her shoulders and pull her to my chest. "Shh, let me hold you, okay?"

She starts to struggle again, then stops. I tuck her head under my chin and hold her until the tension begins to drain out of her limbs. Until her muscles unwind, her shoulders relax, and she leans into me. I comb my fingers down her hair from root to end, and again. She sighs and leans more of her weight into me. Such a prickly little thing. She finds it so difficult to trust.

"Who hurt you, Via?" I murmur.

She blows out a breath. "I think I hurt myself," she whispers. "My childhood wasn't unhappy, but it wasn't very happy, either. Mainly, because I was so independent. I always wanted to be free, to live my life the way I wanted. I hated being told to conform to the role expected of women in a Mafia clan; they're seen as pawns, or as childbearing vessels. I wanted to break away and build my own future. It didn't help that I wanted to be an actress. When I told my family, my mother practically had a nervous breakdown, and my brother was vehemently against it. My father was the only one who supported me, much to Diego's ire." She rubs her cheek against my shirt.

"You and your brother always had a tumultuous relationship, eh?"

"Diego was eight years older than me, but he may as well have been a third parent. And it didn't come from a place of protectiveness, either. He steeped himself in Mafia culture, and wanted to take over as the head of the *Camorra* from a very young age. He thought my father was too soft in his dealings and was always challenging him. When I left home at eighteen, he bitterly opposed it, but my father was having none of it. My father died of a heart attack before I finished drama school. He never did get to see me on stage, or in any of the films I've appeared in."

"Have you been in any movies I know of?"

"Probably not. I've been lucky to get a few seconds of screen time. Mostly, my parts have ended up being cut. But that's the risk you take with acting. You have to keep moving on. Keep believing in yourself."

"I believe in you."

She grows still.

"I've believed in you from the moment I set eyes on you."

She tips up her chin and glances at me. "Why? Why would you say a thing like that?"

"Because it's true." I cup her cheek. "Can't you see my world begins and ends with you? Without you, I'm only half complete. You are what makes my life worth living. Your words complete my sentences. Your voice filters through my dreams. Your laughter is the soundtrack to my life."

She opens and shuts her mouth. "You don't mean it."

"You know I do."

She pushes away from me, then jumps to her feet. "No, no, take it back. Take all of it back. You're spoiling everything. This is not how it's supposed to be."

She begins to pace back and forth. "I know we're attracted to each other. I know there's chemistry between us. You think I don't feel it? The difference is, I refuse to give in to it."

She turns to face me. "I can't sleep with you again. If I do, I'll lose myself. And I can't afford that. I need to focus on my career, or what's left of it. I need to return to London and figure out where my next role is coming from, find out what opportunities are available for me. And I can't do that if all I am thinking about is your face and your—"

She firms her lips.

"My?"

She shakes her head.

"Say it." I rise to my feet. She slides back. "Complete the sentence, Via." I narrow my gaze. "Right fucking now."

She pales, then squeezes her fingers together in front of her. "Your cock. Okay? Your beautiful, gorgeous, monster cock that's spoilt me for anyone else."

32

Olivia

Argh! Why the hell did I say that? Clearly, watching him shoot my brother shocked me so much I can't stop spewing out the first thing that comes into my head. The one thing I haven't been able to forget since the time he fucked me. The feel of his cock inside me as he plowed into me and brought me to orgasm so quickly; I came thrice before he finally emptied himself in me.

He moves toward me, and I refuse to skitter away. I am not some shy virginal scaredy-cat who's not able to hold her own against an alpha male like him.

"Took you long enough to admit it." He smirks.

Asshole levels that gorgeous smirk of his at me and my insides flutter. My ovaries sit up and take notice, and my panties have definitely combusted.

"See?" I stab my finger in his chest. "This is what I mean. You distract me. All you have to do is look at me, and all of my thoughts twist in on themselves. You touch me, and I want to pant. You glance at my body, and my breasts hurt. My nipples become so tight, they feel like they're going to poke out of my shirt. When you glare at me, all of my pores seem to pop, and then you scowl, and my ovaries seem to become egg machines, ready to open shop."

He stares at me, then begins to laugh. Deep rumbling waves that seem to roll up from somewhere low in his belly. It's so sexy, so hot. Goddamn. Is there anything he does that could put me off? Probably not. He's a walking, talking lust machine who'll always strike right to the core of me... And I don't mean only the one between my legs. There's something primal about him that appeals to the baser side of me. Something real about him that strikes a chord in my heart. Something very alluring about him that ties me up in knots and catches my attention and has me riveted and wanting to find out everything about him.

"I'm so fucked." I bury my face in my hands and shake my head. "Fucked, fucked, fucked."

"Hey." He's instantly there, trying to get me to move my hands from my face, but I turn away from him.

"Why did you have to come into my life when you did? Why couldn't you have waited until I was more established as an actress? And why the hell did I have to hurt my face, making it all so much worse for myself?"

"Via, look at me." I hear him walk around to stand in front of me. He grips my wrists and tugs. I lower my arms, but refuse to meet his gaze.

"Via." He pinches my chin so I have no choice but to raise my eyes to his face.

"What?" I huff.

He chuckles. "You're cute when you pout."

"I am not pouting. And I'm not cute."

"You are, too." His lips kick up in a smile. "You're beautiful, Via, and nothing can take away from that. You know that, right?"

"You're sounding less like a scary Mafia guy and more like a Hallmark card."

"Never been called that before, but—" He raises a shoulder. "I've never felt so connected to someone else before, either."

"You can't say things like that. I thought guys found it difficult to share their feelings?"

"Guess I'm the exception to the rule. Besides, you make it easy for me to speak my mind. Life is short, Via." He peers between my eyes. "And I want to ensure I make the most of every second of it."

"That's why you pounced on me as soon as you saw me?"

"It's fair to say it was mutual, don't you think?" His lips quirk, and of course, my core instantly clenches. Clearly, my body didn't get the memo that I'm not ready to be in a relationship.

"Fine, I'll grant you that, but I thought it was a one-night stand. I didn't expect to meet you again on the flight to Jeanne and Luca's wedding. And definitely didn't think you'd turn up as my sister's arranged fiancé. I mean, what are the chances?"

"It's nature trying to send us a sign that we're meant for each other."

"Argh! Please don't say these things. You're making it very difficult for me to resist you."

"So don't resist." He chuckles again. The rich sound shivers over my skin and sinks into my blood, arrowing straight to my traitorous pussy, which laps it up and pants for more.

"Easy for you to say. You don't have to prove yourself to the world. You didn't have to fight off the possibility of an arranged marriage. You—" I shut up. Of course, he did agree to an arranged marriage, didn't he?

I scowl.

He smirks. "Yep, exactly. We aren't that different. You're trying to forge your future as an actress. I'm reorienting myself to take on the role of a COO when the *Cosa Nostra*'s businesses turn legit."

"What's COO?"

"Chief Operating Officer. Kind of like a CEO, but with more day-to-day responsibilities for the running of a company."

"Oh." I bite the inside of my cheek. "That's going to be a big change."

"It's what we think is right, now that most of us are settling down. It's also why it was important to form a blood alliance with the *Camorra*. This way, the danger to our families is considerably reduced. It's also why I agreed to an arranged marriage, for the sake of my clan. And also, because you'd made it clear that you had someone else in your life, and never wanted to see me again." He raises one eyebrow and gives me a disapproving look.

"So, you'd have gone through with the marriage if I hadn't turned up that day?"

He tilts his head. "Maybe. Maybe not. But we'll never know now, will we? We were meant to be together, Via. One way or the other, I'd have found my way back to you."

He sounds so certain. So confident of himself. He almost convinces me— almost. But that's his superpower, to screw with my head until it feels like his thoughts are my own.

"No, no, I am not letting you talk me into this."

"Into what?"

"Into whatever it is you're trying to convince me to do."

"How do you know it's not something that you'd want to agree to anyway?" he murmurs.

"Because I know I won't."

"I think it's in your best interest to listen to what I have to say." He tilts his head, and a sly look comes into his eyes.

"Uh-oh, why do I get the feeling I'm not going to like whatever it is you're about to say?"

He merely gestures to the bed. "Take a seat."

I scowl. I'm definitely not going to sit on the bed, not with him next to me.

It'd only lead somewhere I don't want to be. *Yea, keep telling yourself that.* I brush past him to the table with two chairs by the window. I sit down on one.

He follows me without comment, then lowers his bulk into the other chair.

He drums his fingers on the table as he surveys me.

"What?" I growl.

"With your brother dead, the *Camorra* is under the protection of the *Cosa Nostra*. That is, if I decide to take on that responsibility."

"Why would you take on that responsibility? With my father and my brother gone, the next person in line for the role of the head of the clan—"

"Would be your uncle, and then his sons, all of whom have said they are not interested in taking charge."

Of course they aren't. They'll be happy enough to have their needs looked after by the *Cosa Nostra* and coast through life. "Why am I not surprised?"

"Of course, I could decide not to take on that duty," he adds.

I stiffen. "If you decide not to take on the safeguarding of my clan, then—"

"You leave your family wide open to threats from other Mafia gangs."

I stare at him in horror.

"Like the Mexicans, the Albanians, the Chinese, all of whom would love to move in and take on the very lucrative routes that your family's business now owns. And then..." He leans forward. "Who knows what could happen to your family? None of these groups are known for their empathy or their capacity to be merciful."

I swallow. "You wouldn't do that."

"Wouldn't I?" He drums his fingers on the table. "You'd be effectively signing the death warrant of your extended family members. Unless..."

My heart begins to pound into my rib cage. My throat goes wrong. Oh, he wouldn't go there with this, would he? "What—" I clear my throat. "What is it you want?"

"For you to marry me."

I cross my arms around my waist. "I've already said I won't do that."

"If you don't, I can't guarantee your family's safety."

"Knew it." I stab my finger in his direction. "I knew, under all that emotional bullshit you threw at me, you're a Mafia asshole at heart."

He tilts his head. "What do you say?"

"If you think I'm going to sleep with you after this stunt you've pulled, you're sadly mistaken."

"Who said anything about fucking you?" His lips curve.

"You mean... You don't want to fuck me?"

"Not unless you ask me to."

"Which is never going to happen." I lean back in my seat. "And isn't that why you want to marry me?"

"I want to marry you to keep my promise to Nonna of getting married within a month of her passing away. It's not necessary for us to consummate the marriage, not unless—" He drags his thumb across his lower lip. "Well, not unless you want it, as well."

33

Massimo

"So, she agreed to marry you?" Adrian pours a measure of the Macallan into my glass and slides it across the bar counter. We're in Michael's home in his study, waiting for him and the rest of our brothers to join us. I toss back the whiskey, then hold out my glass.

He raises his eyebrows, but tops me up anyway.

When I drain the glass and set it down, he frowns. "Go easy, will you?"

I reach for the bottle of whiskey and top up my glass, then take a sip.

"I assume the reason you're ecstatic with joy is because you had to coerce her into saying yes?"

"Yes," I snap.

"And what was your negotiating tool?"

I blow out a breath. "I told her I wouldn't take on protecting her family unless she agreed to marry me."

He narrows his gaze on me. "You know she's going to hate you for this, right?"

"Not more than she already does."

"Why is it that you, and every one of our other brothers, seem to screw up when it comes to pursuing the woman of your dreams?"

He's talking about Michael, who kidnapped Karma before marrying her;

Christian, who held Aurora captive until she agreed to marry him; followed by Axel, who agreed to marry Theresa to spy on the Sovranos; then Seb, who married Elsa with the promise that he'd find a way to help her get custody of her daughter, which he did; and Luca, who coerced Jeanne to marry him by promising to get her back home after they were kidnapped.

"And all of them are well-settled now," I point out.

"After rough starts to the relationship," he retorts.

I raise a shoulder. "It's the result that matters."

"Sometimes the journey is the destination," he shoots back.

"Is that Confucius, or one of those shithead philosophers you love quoting so much?" I scowl.

"No, that's just me pointing out the obvious." He smirks

"Is that why you've held off from speaking what's on your mind to Cass?" I take another sip of my whisky.

"I'll do it when the time is right."

"And when's that? When she's decided she's tired of waiting and decides to see someone else?"

He straightens. "Is she seeing someone else?"

"Relax, I'm kidding."

"That wasn't funny, *stronzo*." He pours out a glass of whiskey and takes a healthy gulp.

"If the thought of losing her is so stressful, why don't you move in on her and lock her down?"

"Like you did?"

"Exactly." I lean my elbow on the bar counter. "She may hate me now, but she's bound to come around, and when she does, I'll be waiting for her."

"And if she doesn't?"

"Of course, she will."

"What if she's so pissed at you, she never comes around?"

"She will, I'll make sure of it. Once we're married, I'll figure out a way to win her over. She wants to pursue her career as an actress, and I'm all for it."

"You sure that's wise?"

"It's her entire life, her passion. I'd never stop her."

"If you're fine with it, then…" He raises a shoulder. "When's this wedding going to be anyway?"

"As soon as I speak with Michael about it."

"I've been receiving calls from our associates and partners, asking what guarantee they have that they won't be shot point-blank at their next meeting with us." My oldest brother's voice sounds from behind me.

I raise my glass to my lips and drain the rest of the liquid before I place it on the counter. I turn to face him. "You can tell them not to worry. None of them are Diego Sabatini, the leader of the *Camorra*, who was planning to trade his oldest sister to the head of the Mexican Mafia in return for additional trading routes."

His jaw tightens. "He was going to arrange for Olivia to marry Alvaro Garcia?"

"He'd already decided. He was planning to force her into it, one way or another," I growl.

"That's why you shot him?"

I hold his gaze.

He searches my features, then blows out a breath. "I understand why you did it, but it's not going to help our case. On the one hand, we claim we're legalizing our businesses. On the other, you shot the guy. Oh, and not just any guy, by the way." He holds up a finger. "The head of our rival clan, the one whose sister you're going to marry, so he's practically family. Fuck, Massimo, of all of us, I wouldn't have expected you to turn everything into such a shit show."

"It's always the quiet ones who turn out to be the most unpredictable," Luca drawls as he walks in the door. "I say good riddance. Diego was a *pezzo di merda*, and you know it, Michael." He approaches the bar, then ignores the whiskey to lean over and grab a bottle of grappa. "I'd say this calls for a celebration."

Michael firms his lips. "This is a fucking pain in the rear end, Massimo." He folds his arms across his chest. "Are you going to arrange for the burial?"

"It's already taken care of. And the cops have been paid off, too."

We may be going legit, but some things aren't going to change. The *Cosa Nostra* own this town, and everything and everyone in it, and it's going to stay that way for a long time.

"Ease up, *fratellino*, these things happen," Adrian murmurs.

"I assume you're marrying Olivia now, instead of the younger sister?" Michael snaps.

"Just so you're aware, she's found her own beau, so breaking that particular marriage contract isn't all on me."

"Well, Nonna still gets her wish. A *Cosa Nostra-Camorra* alliance," Seb, my other brother, pipes up from the doorway. He prowls in, followed by Christian and Axel. They head for the bar, each of them accepting a glass of grappa from Luca.

"What are we celebrating?" Axel asks.

"Seems one more of us has seen the light and is getting married… And to a woman of his choice," Adrian murmurs.

Everyone turns to stare at him.

"What?" he snaps.

"It's your turn next." Axel smirks.

"Not any time soon. I'm not rushing into anything." He tosses back the whiskey, then slaps the glass back on the table before reaching for the grappa.

"Remember our promise to Nonna?" Christian asks.

"There is that," Adrian frowns into his glass. "I'm sure Nonna also wanted us to be happy. There's only one woman I'd marry and right now she's being elusive to track down. Once I find Cass though—" He raises a shoulder.

"You ever miss those days when it was us seven, with nothing to worry about except Mafia business?" Luca asks.

"Do you?" Seb narrows his gaze on Luca.

"Fuck no." He raises his glass. "I propose a toast to the women who've made us better versions of ourselves."

Adrian scoffs, "*Gesù Cristo*, never thought I'd see the day when hot-headed Luca is singing the praises of someone other than himself."

"That's because I found someone worth living for. Apparently, there's more pleasure in giving, more satisfaction in protecting someone who means more to you than all the wealth and all the power in the world, more fulfillment in returning home to the one who, today, is more precious than all of my tomorrows."

Silence descends. He looks up from his glass and takes in our faces. "What?" He frowns.

"You going to tell him, or should I?" Axel says out of the corner of his mouth.

"This one is all yours," Seb replies.

"What is it?" Luca growls.

"I am sorry to inform you that you are absolutely and completely pussy-whipped," Axel drawls.

"As are you," Luca shoots back.

"And I don't regret it one bit," Axel confesses.

"It's never going to happen to me. No way am I going to go around spouting flowery odes like motherfucking Luca here," I declare.

Adrian coughs.

"What?" I snap.

Adrian tries to speak, then chokes. His face turns purple, and he clutches his stomach.

I stare. "*Che cazzo?* What's wrong with you?"

"You— I—" Adrian wheezes, "You—" His shoulders shake.

"The fuck is he trying to say?" I growl.

"He's trying to say it's too late for that," Axel informs me.

"Eh?" I look between my already married brothers. "You going to tell me that it's inevitable?"

"Yes," Seb replies.

"That I can fight it, but nothing's going to stop my eventual downfall?"

"I'd say, in your case, you're already there." Adrian stops choking long enough to reply.

I stare at him, and he promptly begins to wheeze again.

"Hope that's a sign that you're having a coronary," I turn away disgusted. "You guys should know, it's nothing further from the truth. In fact, we're not even going to live together after we get married."

"No?" Seb rocks back on his heels. "It's a good plan, but it's not going to work out."

"Why the fuck not? She has a career in London, and she wants to pursue it. As she must. And I need to stay here to help with the transition of the businesses to the legal entities."

"You can work from anywhere, in this day and age." Axel smirks. He turns to Christian. "Who bets that within a couple of days of her leaving, he's going to follow her to London?"

"You're being too charitable. I'd give him six hours, if that," Christian replies.

"Twenty-four," Axel retorts.

"Twelve," Luca holds out his palm, face up.

"Done." Axel slaps it.

"Hold on a second, did you all bet on me?" I snap.

"Seems that way, *stronzo*." Luca laughs.

"If I were a betting man, I'd say the *Cosa Nostra* is losing its edge," a new voice sounds from the doorway.

"You?" My fingers itch to reach for my gun again, but I ignore it. "What are you doing here?"

"Don't even think about it," Michael orders.

I brush my fingers against the butt of the gun outlined at my hip. Maybe it's the leftover adrenaline from the earlier shooting, but my nerves are still on edge.

"Massimo," Michael warns.

I look from him to JJ Kane, our one-time rival, now our partner in Trinity Enterprises, a company with three-way holdings between the *Cosa Nostra*, the Kane company, and the Bratva.

"It's all right, bro." Seb closes the distance to JJ and holds out his hand. "Wasn't expecting you until tomorrow."

"Things change," JJ says in his clipped British accent. He glowers at me. "You set up a meeting with your ally, then shot him in his face. Why?"

"Who are you to question me?" I growl.

JJ stiffens. He looks me up and down. "I was picking off twits like you with my gun when you were still in short pants, young man."

I blink. "You Brits have strange insults."

"Should I call you *testa di cazzo* instead?" JJ remarks.

I glower at him.

"Thought not. What's your excuse, motherfucker?" He takes a step forward, but Seb plants his body between us.

"Not a time to fight, guys. The hard-won truce is important to both our businesses. Let's see this through with a calm head, shall we?"

JJ glares at me. I crack my neck, then raise my hands to show they are empty.

Some of the tension in the room dissipates.

JJ doesn't take his gaze off me. "Well? What's your excuse?" he asks.

"The *stronzo* was looking to barter his sister, my future wife, with the head of the Mexican cartel."

JJ seems taken aback. Then, "Fuck." He rubs the back of his neck. "The last thing we need is to give those bastards an entry point into Europe. And to think, he'd do that to his own sister. I knew Diego was a slime ball, but this is remorseless, even for him."

"Ergo…" I whip out my gun and aim it in JJ's direction.

JJ freezes. So does everyone else in the room. Silence cloaks us while nervous tension bleeds into every available corner of the space.

"Massimo," Michael growls.

"Just demonstrating how I shot that *testa di cazzo*, which you are not, JJ. So, you have nothing to worry about, do you?" I flip the gun over and slide it back into my waistband.

"Motherfucker." Seb releases a breath. "You're losing it *stronzo*."

"Asshole." Axel runs his fingers through his hair.

"Watch it, *fratello*," Luca says in a mild voice. "You're changing, and not that I don't appreciate it—it's good not to be the only spontaneous one in the room— still, a little bit of warning before pulling such a trick next time?"

Adrian shuffles his feet next to me. He stays silent, but his displeasure pours off of him.

Only JJ stays silent, then he bursts out laughing. "You have some balls, motherfucker, I'll give you that. And as much as I hate to admit it, I admire your courage and conviction. You did what it took to keep your woman safe, I respect that." He walks over and holds out his hand. I shake it.

He jerks his chin in my direction, then turns to Michael. "We need to talk."

34

Olivia

"We need to talk." Solene pulls her knees close to her chest. We're in one of the guest rooms of their temporary home, which I have taken over as a dressing space. She's huddled on the window seat watching me as I get dressed. In my wedding dress. Or what I've chosen as my wedding dress. At least, it's a dress. For which that asshole should be grateful. Not that it makes a difference to him. As long as I turn up in front of the priest and say my vows and wear his stupid ring on my finger, he'll have fulfilled his role as a faithful grandson who kept his promise to his Nonna, and then everything will be okay. My family will be safe, and I'll finally be able to pursue my dream. I run my palms down the fabric of my dress. It hugs my waist and flows in an A-line to my ankles. There are slits that run up each side, so my thighs flash with every step I take. If he doesn't like it, then too fucking bad. He chose a tigress, not a lamb, and he'd better be able to deal with it. Or not. More fun if he can't. He should know from the time I scratched his back the first time he fucked me that my nails are sharper than they seem, and I'm not above using them to get my way.

I glance at my black-tipped nails, then lean closer to the mirror to apply the dark red to my lips. So what if it makes my skin appear chalkier and the scar on my cheek stand out even more? He knew what he was getting, and lest he forget, I'm going to remind him.

"Are you really going to wear that?" My mother breezes into my room. She's wearing a black dress that flows to her ankles. Her features are pale, her eyes are swollen like she's been crying, but the expression on her face is one of horror. "Surely not," she continues without waiting for an answer. Yep, that's my ma. She can hold a conversation with herself without much effort. And that includes asking questions and supplying multiple possible answers to them, all by herself.

She walks closer and looks me over again. "You look like a whore."

"Gee, thanks, *madre mia," mother mine*, I say lightly.

"You're marrying into the *Cosa Nostra*—"

"Don't remind me."

"You need to dress the part."

"Or not. My husband-to-be doesn't care. Neither do I." I finish touching up my lips and bring them together in a pout. "Nor should you. As long as I turn up for the wedding on time and do the deed, everything will be fine. You, Zia and her worthless husband, and my cousins will all be taken care of. None of you will ever have to worry about money, or anyone else trying to mess with you. So, the least you can do is allow me to dress the way I want."

My mother's forehead creases. She purses her lips, and I steel myself. Here we go—another tirade of how she knows better than I know myself, how I'm going to regret this, et cetera, et cetera.

"You hate me," she finally says.

"Eh?" This is something new. Normally, I'm the one using that dialogue. "You may be right. That feeling has, more or less, been on the top of my mind for me in connection with you for a long time," I retort.

She looks taken aback, then laughs. "You never did mince your words. It's something I've always admired that about you."

"You have?" Now she's complimenting me? That can't be right. "Why are you here?"

"My daughter is getting married."

"To the man who killed your son," I remind her.

She pales, then seems to sway a little.

"Mamma!" I move toward her, but she evades me and walks over to the chair in the corner of the room and sinks into it.

"I'm sorry, I shouldn't have said that," I take another step in her direction.

She raises a hand. "You're right. He did kill your brother." She takes a breath and seems to compose herself. "Are you wondering why I'm not more upset about you marrying him? Why I'm, in fact, encouraging you to marry Massimo?"

I nod, unable to find any other words to speak.

"I'm not a fool, child. I'm fully aware that he threatened to leave us without protection if you didn't marry him."

"You… you knew that?"

"I guessed it. Look, from the time you walked into that conservatory and he got a good look at you, he hasn't had eyes for anyone else. It was clear he was fixated on you. Diego should have called off the engagement with Solene right away, but he didn't. He was too greedy for power. He wanted the liaison with the *Cosa Nostra* to get access to their business, and then he wanted to marry you to the Mexican crime lord." Her features wear a haunted look. "I forbade him to do so. I told him if he went ahead with it, I'd never forgive him. But none of that made a difference. He was dead set on it, and I wouldn't have been able to stop it."

"I… I wouldn't have let him marry me off."

She laughs. "You live in another world, child. You forget, within the *Camorra*, the head's word holds sway. He would have kidnapped you and kept you captive until he married you off."

A shiver squeezes up my spine. "He… he told you that?"

"He left me with no doubt about his intentions. I was powerless to stop him. My own child, who emerged from my womb. I couldn't believe he would go to such lengths to satisfy his greed." She shakes her head. "So, while I mourn his loss, I feel like I lost him a long time ago, and I'm relieved he's no longer around to see his plan through."

"Mamma." I shake my head. "I… I don't know what to say."

"You don't have to say anything." A crafty look enters her eyes. "You can, however, show your gratitude by listening to me."

I scowl in her direction. "I know what you're going to say, but—"

"I know you think I'm flighty and a nag, but the one thing I have on you is years of experience when it comes to men," she proclaims.

I exchange a glance with Solene, who's watching us with rapt attention.

This is something new. I never heard Mamma talk about men, or anything remotely related to relationships, in all the years I was at home.

"Umm, I'm not sure what you're trying to say?"

"I assume you're going to stay married to this man for the foreseeable future, yes?"

"I guess." I meet her gaze in the mirror.

"And for better or worse, he's the man you're going to spend some part of your life with.' Interesting, my ma didn't say 'the rest of your life,' or use definitive words like 'forever,' or anything indicating an expectation of a long future together.

"Where are you going with this?"

"For the time that you are going to be with him—"

"We'll probably be in different cities," I interject.

"Which makes it all the more important that the times you meet him face-to-face, you make an impression on him."

"And this—" I wave a hand at my dress "—doesn't cut it?"

"Men are simple creatures. They like to know they're getting their money's worth—"

"I am not a transaction."

"Or good sex—"

I gasp. "You didn't just say that, Mamma!"

"How do you think you and your siblings were born?" She scoffs.

"Yes, I know, but still—" I shake my head. "You've never spoken about this to us before."

"That's because the situation never arose before where I needed to have this talk."

"A little late for the-birds-and-the-bees discussion, don't you think?" I shuffle my feet. "And really, we don't have to do this. I know everything there is to know—"

"Not about marriage, you don't. And you probably won't heed the advice I'm going to give you, but I'm going to say it anyway."

Of course she is. I blow out a breath, but don't react. If I do, it'll only make it worse. Best to hear her out on this.

"You want your Mafia guy to see you as the epitome of beauty, as everything he respects and wants to take home to protect. You want him to be proud of you—"

"I don't care what he thinks of me, actually."

"—so you can use it to your advantage and negotiate with him."

I hold her gaze in the mirror. "Negotiate? As in, press my advantage?"

"Marriage is a bargain, a contract from which both of you will benefit. You bring some strengths, and so does he. The two of you fulfill your roles, trying to cancel out the other's weaknesses and build upon each other's strengths. And gain benefit from your mutual agreement."

"You make it sound so coldhearted."

"The best relationships are. Don't be fooled by what you see from the outside. Every good marriage has, at its heart, a negotiation. Lines have to be drawn, and rules have to be adhered to. If any one of you doesn't do your part, the connection suffers," she says with emphasis.

"You talk about it like it's a business contract," Solene says as she walks over to join us. "But you forget, this is about hearts, and emotions, and love."

"Love?" My mother laughs. "You girls are so naive. Love is a concept made up by poets, filmmakers, and authors, to fool people. When real life intrudes, love goes out the window. When your child cries at night, it's not love that wakes up and feeds it. When wrinkles crease your skin, and your body sags under the weight of having breastfed your kids, and your husband decides to keep younger women on the side, it's not love that comforts you then."

"Wait, hold on." I spin around to face her. "Are you telling us that our father had mistresses on the side?"

"He was a good father, and I'd go so far as to say he never shirked his duties as a husband, but he wasn't a saint, either."

"B-but..." Solene shifts her weight from foot to foot. "Didn't the two of you have a love match?"

"And that's why you should never fall in love." She glances from me to my sister. "To think you have found your soulmate, only to have him betray your trust, is as disappointing as having your children think the worst of you."

I flush a little. Guess I deserve that. But I'm not making excuses. My mother may have had her fair share of issues to deal with, but it doesn't negate the fact that she was an absolute bitch to me growing up.

"You see, love is a mirage, and I'm trying my best to save the two of you from future disappointment."

"That's why you wanted us to have arranged marriages?" I lower my chin to my chest.

She nods. "This way, you walk in with your eyes open and no illusions, and if your husband does fall in love with you, it's a welcome surprise. And if he doesn't, you still have the money, the prestige, the security of a marriage, and later, children. It's all you need."

"That's such a pessimistic point of view. What's there in life if you don't have love?" Solene tips up her chin.

"What is there in life when you're betrayed by love?" My mother draws in a breath. "I know you don't want to believe me. You think I'm saying all of this because I'm envious that you're only now starting your lives. But really, I only want to save you from heartbreak."

"You don't have to worry about me, because I'm not marrying for love."

"Aren't you?" My mother glances at me with a funny look on her face.

"Of course not. It's an arrangement. He needs to marry to fulfill his promise to his grandmother and I—" I press my lips together. "As you're well aware, I'm marrying to keep our family safe. So, no, it's not love."

"If you say so," my mother murmurs.

"I, on the other hand, have no intention of marrying yet, and when I do so, it *will* be for love.' Solene draws herself up to her full height. "It's why I'm going to LA with Declan."

"You're going to LA?" my mother and I both say at the same time. We glance at each other, then back at Solene.

"Are you marrying him?" my mother asks.

She laughs. "Of course not. I just met the man. But he's promised to help introduce me to agents and help kick start my singing career."

"That's wonderful. I'm so happy to see you giving this a shot."

"You're not marrying him, but you're going to stay with him?" My mother's tone is censorious.

My sister raises a shoulder. "I have nowhere else to stay. And he's told me he has a spare bedroom, and I can use it until I get on my feet."

"Why don't you marry him? That way you'll have some security, at least."

"Ma, please. I don't know him at all." She scoffs.

"But you're going to LA with him," she points out.

"Yes, but that's only because he has connections in the industry."

"And you're attracted to him." I narrow my gaze on her. "I'm not going to stop you from following your dream. Far from it, but I do want to ask you to be careful."

"Will the two of you stop treating me like a child?"

"You just turned eighteen, Solene, you're still a teenager," I say gently.

"And I can decide what I want to do with my life. I'm done with letting other people make my decisions for me," she says through gritted teeth.

I bite the inside of my cheek. "I'm glad you recognize there's more to life than getting married and having babies. Not that it's not something I don't want for you, or for myself, but it helps to live a little and figure out what you want first."

"Right now, I want to pursue my career as a singer and—" She glances away then back at me. "I admit, I want to see where this thing with Declan goes."

"Have you slept with him?" I ask.

My mother draws in a breath, but doesn't say anything. Considering she was a virgin, which is why my brother chose her for the arranged marriage proposition.... Let's just say, virginity is still highly-prized in our clan. Thankfully, though, no one has that expectation of me.

"Have you slept with Massimo?" Solene shoots back.

"Eh?" Heat sears my cheeks. I'm not shy about the fact that I've slept with men in the past. That I have a healthy sexual appetite. That I enjoy sex—in fact, more than enjoyed the explosive encounter with Massimo the night we met. But I'll be damned, if I am going to admit that to my sister and mother.

"None of your business," I snap.

One side of Solene's lips twists in a smile. "Exactly."

"You are so annoying." I throw up my hands. "I'm just looking out for you."

"As I am for you," Mamma retorts.

"I have a dress for the bride. One in which I guarantee she's going to look ah-ma-zing!" a new voice singsongs from the doorway.

I turn to find someone who looks familiar walking in. I think I saw her at Solene's engagement. Her dress hints at her pregnant stomach and she's holding a garment bag that says: Karma's Creations. Oh, that's right. The bridesmaid dresses. And I thought she might be Massimo's woman.

"Hi. Karma, right? We got our bridesmaids' gowns for Jeanne's wedding from you." I smile.

"Correct on all accounts. I'm also Michael Sovrano's wife. I took the liberty of creating a wedding dress for you. This here is an original Karma Creation, and I'd be honored if you wore it."

35

———————

Olivia

At least the wedding isn't in a church or at City Hall—two logical venues, both of which I wanted to avoid. He seems to have understood that; Karma told me that the wedding would take place in their conservatory. The same place where I had walked in on Solene's engagement party.

And yes, the wedding is real, but if I pretend I'm playing a role in a movie, I'll be able to get through this with more ease. At least, that's what I'm telling myself. I'm filling a role; that's all there is to it. I'm not getting married to the man who's occupied my dreams, my every waking thought, and who I had masturbated to almost every night since meeting him. Nope. Of course not. I rub my palms down the satin of the dress I am wearing.

Karma Sovrano insisted that I accept the dress. I refused, of course, and told her I was happy with what I had on, but she was so persuasive. She told me it had become a bit of a tradition in the Sovrano household for her to design the wedding dress of the bride. She did it for most of the weddings of Michael's brothers, and she said she would be so grateful if I accepted the dress from her. She was so humble, so sincere, I couldn't turn her down.

Also, she's the Don's wife. Not that she used her position to get me to agree, but I was conscious of the fact that my family is now at the mercy of the *Cosa Nostra,* and I don't want to upset that balance in any way.

She's my future sister-in-law, and while I can be stubborn, I'm not dumb. I'm marrying into the Sovrano family, after all. And believe it or not, my mother's words made an impact. She was trying to tell me that I need to start this relationship on the right footing, by giving it the kind of respect it deserves. And while I'm not a romantic, by any stretch of the imagination, this is probably the only time in my life I'm going to get married, because neither the *Cosa Nostra* nor the *Camorra* believe in divorce.

I have to admit, I didn't want to appear at my ceremony looking less than stellar. And when Karma revealed the dress, I couldn't deny, it was beautiful. I saw the dress and immediately knew I wanted to wear it. And when I saw myself in the mirror, a shiver had skimmed through me. A simple sheath made of a liquid, metallic material that made it seem like the dress had been poured over me and then sewed to my curves, it hugged me in a warm embrace without restricting my movements. It shifted and slithered over my skin and across my thighs, and as I moved, little flickers of static electricity ran under my skin. I looked beautiful, elegant, sophisticated. I looked like I was ready for the starring role in my own life. I had to wear that dress. I thanked Karma, and when I finished getting dressed, she accompanied me down to the waiting car driven by Adrian. My sister and mother followed in another car.

We drove to the Don's house, and now I wait in the room just up the corridor. Soon, I'll walk down the aisle.

Solene and Karma are speaking quietly in one corner of the room. I decided not to have any bridesmaids or have my mother walk me down the aisle. I'd rather get through this as quickly and as painlessly as possible. The door opens and Penny and Jeanne walk in.

Penny breaks into a run and comes over to stand in front of me. Her fingers are squeezed together, and she takes me in with a dreamy expression on her face. "You look so beautiful." Her voice is choked. She takes my hand and squeezes it. "I can't believe you're getting married," she gushes.

"Me neither," I drawl.

"I'm the only one left unmarried. Can you believe that?" She purses her lips.

Jeanne draws abreast. She scans me from head to toe. "Wow, that's some dress."

"Thanks to Karma," I jerk my chin in Karma's direction.

"I thought I spotted Karma's trademark touch." She shoots a smile in her sister-in-law's direction. Jeanne is married to Luca, Massimo's brother, which makes us—

"Shit, we're going to be family," I exclaim.

"Y-e-p." She smiles widely. "How cool is that?"

"Too bad there isn't another Sovrano brother for me to hook up with," Penny mutters.

"There's only Adrian left, and I'm afraid his heart is already taken," Karma says as she walks over to join us. "I'm so happy to welcome you to the family, Olivia. I'd kiss your cheek, but I don't want to risk spoiling your makeup." She places her hand on her stomach. "I'm feeling a bit exhausted, so I'm going to go sit down in the conservatory."

"Are you okay?"

"Of course." She waves off my concern. "Sometimes I just forget I'm pregnant, so I overdo it. I'll be fine." She smiles at me again. "See you on the other side. It's going to be amazing."

She walks past us and to the door.

Jeanne turns to me. "You sure you want to do this?"

Eh? "Why do you ask that?"

"I know how overwhelming the Sovrano men can be. If you don't want to get married, let me know and I'll get Luca's help in telling Massimo off."

"You'd do that for me? You'd ask your Mafia Capo husband to tell his brother to get lost if I didn't want to go through with the wedding?"

"Of course I would." She looks offended. "Didn't you, me, and Penny decide we were the three musketeers who'd always have each other's backs?"

I glance from her to Penny, then back at her. "We did."

"So tell me, is he forcing you to get married to him?"

"Did Luca force you?" I shoot back.

"Umm..." She chews on her lower lip. "As you know, we didn't exactly meet in the most normal of circumstances. And yeah, he did strike a bargain with me —getting married in exchange for him getting me back to the premier of the musical. So, he didn't force me, but I wasn't exactly overly enthused about getting married to him, either. But things changed. And we figured stuff out, and found out we love each other. And I'm not saying that isn't possible for you. Just... If you need me to back you up in something, then you should know I'm here for you."

"And me, too." Penny tightens her hold on my hand.

I'd held it together when I'd discovered Massimo was getting engaged to my sister. I'd kept my wits about me when things had turned on their heads, and I'd realized I was the one marrying Massimo, after all. I'd been shocked, but I hadn't broken down when he'd taken out my brother. But hearing my friends declare their loyalty to me, somehow, tips me over the edge. A burning sensation builds behind my eyes, and a big knot of emotions seems to lodge itself in my throat. "You guys are going to make me cry," I choke out.

"Aww, honey, I didn't mean for you to get all teary-eyed. I only wanted you to know you have options." Jeanne grips my free hand, and I bring our palms together—mine, Jeanne's, and Penny's—so I can hold their palms between both of mine.

"I want you both to know how much I appreciate knowing you are in my corner." I look between them. "Also, no one is forcing me to get married. At least, not in the strict sense of the word."

Jeanne frowns. "What does that mean?"

"Meaning, much like Luca struck up a bargain with you, so has Massimo."

I'm not going to tell her the details of it. I don't believe Massimo would actually harm my family if, for some reason, I backed out of the marriage, but I don't want to test that theory. Also, as much as it's reassuring to know Jeanne could get Luca to confront Massimo, I don't relish the idea of pitting brother against brother. Massimo would be pissed. He'd probably react negatively, taking it out on either me or my family, and again, I don't want to put either of us in that situation. Besides, if, after all that, we still went through with the wedding, I'd have a very angry groom on my hands, and Lord knows where that would lead. Nope, this is good. I'll marry him, then I'll move to London, where Declan's agent has offered to meet me. Bye-bye, Massimo. Bye, Italy. I'll focus my efforts on my career as an actress, without worrying about my family back home. It's a good deal for both of us.

"And you're fine with the deal?" Jeanne searches my features. "You can tell me if you're not."

"Are you doubting me?" I hold her gaze.

She looks deeply into my eyes, then nods. "I was, but not anymore. I didn't realize you had feelings for the guy."

"Oh, please. This marriage really is an arrangement, one that benefits both of us."

"Hey, who am I to say otherwise?" Jeanne quirks her lips. "If you're happy, I'm happy."

"I'm… not sad about walking down the aisle, if that's what you're asking."

"I'm—"

There's a knock on the door, then a blonde-haired woman—Elsa, if I remember correctly from earlier introductions—pops her head around the corner. "They're ready for you."

36

Massimo

"You ready for this?" Adrian asks from near my elbow.

I should be more nervous. I've seen my brothers get nervous at their weddings. I saw them shuffle their feet and roll their shoulders to relieve tension as they waited for their brides to walk up the aisle. I had to calm them, joke with them, until they settled down.

I should be more than nervous. I should be petrified at the thought of joining myself willingly in matrimony to a woman who, clearly, doesn't want to marry me. A woman who doesn't feel the same way I do. A woman who, possibly, hates me for how I manipulated her into marrying me. A woman who's going to find every opportunity to avoid me and stay in a different country after she marries me.

I should be angry with her for having tried to pass off someone else as her fiancé, but I'm not. All that heartache and struggle, and trying to figure out a way to bind her to me, was worth it because she's marrying me now. And once she's mine, I'll never let her go. Something she's going to find out soon enough.

"I'm good," I reply.

He shuffles his feet and I side-eye him. "What is it? You seem more nervous than me."

He peers about the gathered crowd and his face falls.

"She's not here, is she?" I murmur.

"Don't know what you're talking about," he snaps.

"Sure you do. You're looking for Cass, and you're disappointed she's not back for my wedding."

"This is her family. She's loyal to all of us. I'd have thought she wouldn't miss your wedding."

"She probably doesn't know about the wedding, and even if she did find out about it, maybe she's too far away to get here from wherever she is. It's not like I gave anyone enough notice to prepare for the wedding."

"Maybe." He locks his hands behind his back. "Still, I can't believe she'd leave without having a way to keep in touch with what's happening back home. She's loyal to the Sovranos."

"Maybe she doesn't want to come. Maybe she wants you to go to her. Have you thought of that?"

He raises a shoulder. His expression giving nothing away.

"You need to figure out your shit before it's too late, *fratello*," I advise.

"You mean like you did, by coercing Olivia to marry you?"

"The ends justify the means. She's marrying me; the rest will fall into place."

"I'll remind you of that when you're wondering what the hell hit you. If your wife's not happy with you, trust me, your marriage can turn to hell very quickly."

"And you have experience with that?"

"Maybe not personally, but I've seen enough marriages turn to shit when the missus is fed up."

"That's not going to happen in my case," I say. At least, I think not. *I hope not.* "Once we're married, I'll be sure to make it up to her."

"And if she doesn't give you the chance?"

"I'll make sure she does. I—"

A shimmer of electricity runs up my back. The hair on the nape of my neck rise. I don't realize I've turned to glance down the aisle until I see her. She stands there at the entrance to the conservatory in a shimmering steel gray-blue gown that dips just enough in the front to hint at her cleavage before nipping in at the waist and flowing down to her feet.

The music starts and she glides forward. The gold threads through the fabric shimmer and undulate with every step she takes forward. The full-length sleeves only accentuate the dip of her waist, the flare of her hips, the perfectly guitar-shaped figure of hers that caught my attention the first time I ever saw her.

I didn't realize I'm someone who prefers curvy hips until I saw her. But one sight of her glorious behind, and I was a goner. In her hands, she carries a spray of white flowers. Her hair is twisted up, and she wears a gray-blue netted veil that flows down to cover her eyes. She looks ethereal yet earthy, gorgeous yet natural, aloof yet so filled with passion. She looks like she was made for me. Like she wore that dress only for me. Like her gaze is only on me.

The rustling of clothes, the sound of someone coughing, of shuffling feet—all of it fades as she draws near. When she reaches me, she turns to face me, her lips adorned in a transparent lip color which, along with the netting that falls over her eyes, makes her look mysterious, and secretive, and so very seductive.

The officiant, who was roped in to preside over the ceremony, clears his throat. I barely listen to him as he recites the necessary words. I can't take my gaze off of her face as she says, "I do."

I make the appropriate noises when it's my turn, then slide the ring I purchased onto her finger. I hold out my hand for her to slip the wedding band onto mine. When he pronounces us husband and wife, I close the distance to her and raise the veil over her eyes. Her green gaze holds mine. Her eyes are clear, and her lips part as I lower my head to hers. I brush my mouth over the scar on her cheek, and she shivers. A noise escapes the back of her throat, and every cell in my body shifts into high alert. I drag my lips down to hers and kiss her firmly. Her mouth trembles under mine, and sensations unlike anything I've ever experienced course through my veins. Ownership, possession, wanting to protect her from the world, to hold and to cherish her, to show her every possible joy, to shield her from hurt, to ensure I give her everything she needs. To love her, to keep her happy, to satisfy all of her desires, to teach her just how good it can be between us. To show her what it means to be desired by me. To be mine. Only mine.

I raise my head and glance at her through half-closed eyelids. Her own are heavy with lust, her cheeks flushed with color. She's staring at me as if she's only now realizing what she agreed to do, and she's unable to wrap her head around it, unable to comprehend exactly what it means to be married to me. If I'm being honest, that expression of surprise gladdens me. Best to keep her a little off-kilter. At least, until she develops feelings for me.

"You okay?" I tuck a strand of hair that's come loose behind her ear.

She draws in a sharp breath, her gaze still fixed on mine.

"Via?" I whisper my knuckles across her cheek, and she blinks. Then nods.

"I'm good."

"Good." I allow my lips to twist in a smile as I lower my hand and twine my fingers with hers.

We walk forward, and her friend Jeanne is the first one to rush forward to congratulate us. She throws her arms around Via and congratulates her as Adrian shakes my hand.

"You did it, man."

"It's your turn next." I bump his shoulder with my fist.

He chuckles without comment, then steps back as my other brothers surround us.

An hour later, I glance to my right where my wife is sipping prosecco from her flute. She laughs at something her friend Penny says. She hasn't said a word to me since that exchange right after I kissed her. Clearly, she's avoiding me. Perhaps she's still reconciling herself with the change in her status. The ceremony was mercifully short, at least. Now, we just need to get through this dinner.

Given the choice, I'd have returned home with her, but no way would my brothers allow us to leave without partaking in the feast. Karma mentioned to me that Nonna's old chef, Gino, had pulled it together specifically for us. So, I led Via to the dining room, made sure she was seated, and took the chair next to her. All of which was accomplished without her so much as meeting my eyes. She can avoid me all she likes, but both she and I know we'll have to talk soon. There's time for that, though.

For now, I glance around the table. To my right is Adrian. My other brothers and their wives sit in the other chairs. On one end, Solene and Declan sit next to each other. There's enough space between them that they don't touch. They're not looking at each other, and not talking to the people next to them. They seem to be focused on staring straight forward, as if trying to avoid each other's eyes. That should be an interesting relationship.

Olivia's mother congratulated both of us, but opted not to stay for dinner. Not that I'm complaining. Besides, she's in mourning, which was obvious to me as soon as I saw her dressed all in black. I don't regret what I did to Diego, but it stands to reason that his mother's pissed-off at me. Although if she is, she didn't let on when she came face-to-face with me. Either she silently agrees with what I did and recognizes it was the only way to save her daughter from the unimaginable fate her brother intended for her, or she knows how to hide her true feelings. Either way, I admit, I wasn't too sad when she left with Olivia's aunt, uncle, and cousins right after the wedding.

As for Solene, I doubt she has forgiven me, but she's here for Olivia, and that's what matters.

The staff serves us our starters, tops off our flutes, and steps back.

Michael rises to his feet. He raises his flute, and everyone quiets down. "I am truly happy to have our entire family together today. We have been through a lot in the last few months, and my heart is full seeing my entire family in my home, at my table." He glances around the space, until his gaze alights on me. "I want to start by wishing Massimo and Olivia the very best in the journey they are starting together. May you find happiness and discover the joys of a true partnership."

"Hear, hear," Christian raises his glass.

"I also want to, once more, welcome Jeanne, Elsa, Theresa, and Aurora to our family. You have all been a welcome addition to the lives of my brothers and have changed the energy of this family to one of hope, joy, and anticipation for the future. You've given all of us a reason to come home safely at the end of the day, and for that, I'll always be thankful to you."

Jeanne smiles, Elsa chuckles, Theresa nods. Aurora tilts her head in Michael's direction. She's a doctor, and we relied on her father, and then on her to nurse us through various wounds at the time when we were more actively engaged in the traditional *Cosa Nostra* business. As my brothers married, the realization that we couldn't continue to risk our lives, and that of our loved ones, dawned on us. Which is why we're in the process of legalizing our businesses—something that's taking longer than expected, given the vast number of enterprises we're involved in. The intricacies of this switch have kept me busy, but I hope we'll see the end of it very soon. It's a shift that I'm glad to make, and I'm confident it will prove to be seamless.

"I also want to toast my wife, Karma. You're the most incredible woman I have ever met. I'm lucky to have you in my life and I can't wait for our child to arrive so we can be a family."

He bends down to kiss her lips. He deepens the kiss to choruses of "ooh," and "get a room, guys."

They continue kissing, and Luca throws a roll at Michael's head. It misses, barely—which is intentional, as Luca is the best shot I know—and Michael straightens with a smirk on his face.

Karma leans back in her seat, her features slightly paler than usual. The pregnancy has been hard on her, and Michael has seldom left her side since she announced her pregnancy.

Michael glances around the table again, and his features sober. "I also want to take a moment to remember those who are not with us anymore: our brother, Xander and Nonna."

"Xander?" Olivia turns to me. "Couldn't he make it today?'

I shake my head. "Xander was Christian and Axel's triplet. He died in a car bomb explosion rigged by our father."

She gasps. "Oh, my god, that's awful. I had no idea." She places her palm over my hand, and her touch travels straight down my arm, down my waist, to my groin. *Fuck.* At this rate, I'm going to throw her down and rut into her in front of everyone, and while that picture is highly appealing, it's not how I want to start our marriage. Not that I don't want to consummate our relationship, but it has to be when she's ready for it. I draw in a breath and her scent, that elixir of vanilla and coconut, fills my senses. My cock throbs, and goddamn, she better be ready to consummate this marriage soon. There's no telling how long I'll be able to hold out.

I pull my hand out from under hers, then raise my glass. "I'd like to propose a toast."

37

Olivia

He rises to his feet and raises his glass of prosecco. I keep my gaze facing forward. I will not look at him; I will not. I tried to console him—why the hell did I do that?—and he pulled his hand out from under my palm. *What the hell?* Clearly, he doesn't want my touch anymore. Hard to believe, after the way he responded to me the first time we met. Then, he was all over me, commanding me, demanding of me, asking me to dig my nails into his back so he could feel them. He claimed that it had turned him on even more. Or when he fucked me on the plane, when he wanted me to hold on to him as he hauled me up with his palms under my butt and shoved me into the wall and claimed me.

"I'd like to raise a toast to my wife." His dark voice tugs at my nerve endings. My belly flip-flops. Butterflies take flight in my chest.

"You fought well, darling, but I have you now, and I'm never going to let you go."

I huff, and refuse to glance up at him.

"The first time I saw you, I knew you were going to turn my life upside down. I just underestimated how much. If I'd known the merry chase you were going to lead me on, I might've walked away from you right then."

I jerk my chin up to find him smirking at me. *Jerk.* I glower at him, and his smile only grows wider. His gaze, though, is sharp as he watches me closely.

"Thankfully, I didn't... And I'll never forgive you for what came after."

I tense. Is he going to lay out the intricacies of our relationship thus far for everyone to see?

"You plowed your way into my heart and have never left. I know we've had our differences. I know you decided that, maybe, I wasn't the person for you. But we're together now, for better or for worse, in sickness and in health." He reaches over and takes my hand in his. "I promise to always take care of you, to protect you, to ensure you never want for anything. I promise to wipe away your tears, and always provide for you."

My chin trembles, and pressure builds behind my eyes. *What the hell is he doing? Why is he putting on this act? Why is he pretending he genuinely has feelings for me?*

"I promise, you'll forget what life was like with your fake ex-fiancé."

A-n-d there he is. That was a direct dig at Declan. I shoot a glance in his direction, but he's too busy staring at Solene, who's watching the two of us with wide eyes. Fine friend he is. I asked him to stand in as my fiancé, but he seems to have acquired a legitimate future fiancée instead.

"I promise to make you so happy, you'll never want to be anywhere else but by my side."

"We'll see."

Laughter rings out from those at the table.

Oops, did I say that aloud? Sorry... Not sorry.

I raise my own glass of prosecco. He clinks his with mine. I take a sip, watching him over the rim. He sits down without breaking our connection. That's how it's always been with us. Our eyes have always conducted their own dialogue, without either of us saying a word. Somehow, we've always known what the other wants, especially in bed, and outside... Well, I screwed things up by falling for him so fast and so quickly. I tried to leave him, gone so far as producing a fake fiancé as a deterrent, but that didn't stop him. He managed to find a way to marry me, anyway. And I'm still not sure how I feel about that.

Dealing with the scar on my face is stressful enough. Add to that, the fact that I have to reinvent my career, and now, apparently, I've acquired a husband. It's enough to send me straight back to bed, hoping to wake up and discover it was all a dream.

He leans over and pinches my arm.

"Hey." I pull away from him and place my prosecco flute back on the table. "What was that for?"

"To show you you're not dreaming."

I stare at him. He couldn't have guessed my thoughts from my face, could he?

He drags his hand down my arm and twines his fingers with mine. "I'm never letting you go, *Stellina*."

"Don't call me that."

"I'll call you what I want, when I want."

"So that's how this is going to be, huh? I thought you said I'd be free to pursue my career."

"You are."

"I want to leave for London tomorrow."

"Fine."

I blink. "What, no protesting?"

"Why should I? I'm coming with you."

"No, you're not." I try to tug my hand from his, but he holds on. "You promised I could continue to audition for roles and follow my dream of becoming an actress."

"And you will, with me by your side."

"That's not part of our bargain."

"It is now." He releases me and folds his fingers together. "I can conduct my business from anywhere, and I choose to do it from London for the time-being."

"I don't want you with me."

"You're my wife; we're married. We'll stay together."

"You needed to marry to keep your promise to Nonna, and you've done that. Why can't you let me do my own thing now?"

"And make a mockery of Nonna's intentions?" He shakes his head. "When she asked us to get married, it wasn't about just exchanging rings and paying lip service to our vows. She meant having a marriage, in the real sense of the word."

"If you mean sex, I already told you, I'm not sleeping with you."

"Yet." The *bastardo* smirks.

"Make that never."

"Never say never, *Stellina*."

"I wish you wouldn't call me that. I am not exactly little, in case you haven't noticed."

He drags his gaze down my chest, my waist, my hips, then back to my face. Color flushes my cheeks. "You are exquisite. Your curves are a siren call that haunts my every waking moment. Your ass, your tits, the way your waist flares to meet your hips is the harmony of my life."

"Oh." My flush deepens. My heart stutters. Pinpricks of heat stab my skin. *No, no, no. I can't allow myself to soften toward him.* This is how he's going to wear me down. This is how he's going to seduce me. With words that arrow straight to my heart and cause me to forget my promise of putting my career first. Everything else pales in significance. I stare into his gray eyes, and a shudder wraps around my chest.

I turn away, grab my flute and throw back the rest of the prosecco. "I think we should leave for London tonight."

38

Massimo

I glance across the aisle to where my wife is fast asleep. She had thrown down the gauntlet by asking to leave for London right after dinner. Bet she hadn't expected me to accept it.

We wrapped up dinner in the next half an hour, bid everyone goodbye, and then I ushered her out to the waiting car which took us back to her place. I told her to pack, and she was surprised, but recovered quickly. Meanwhile, I called the caretakers of my place in London and let them know to expect us. I didn't need to pack, considering I have a completely functional home and wardrobe there. We swung by my place to pick up my passport, and then we drove to the airport. We boarded the plane, and she decided to sit separately from me. I didn't stop her. She tried her best not to meet my gaze. The few times I caught her glancing at me, she blushed. No doubt, she's recalling what happened the last time we boarded my private plane.

She fell asleep soon after. I asked for a blanket and covered her up. She snuggled into it with a mewling noise, and my dick instantly hardened. I stood over her, watching her sleep. Cheeks flushed, hair mused around her shoulders, her face pillowed on her palm. The same palm on which she wears my wedding ring on her finger. She belongs to me, whether she accepts it or not.

Right now, she sees our marriage as an irritant. A condition she had to accept to enable her to lead the kind of life she's been preparing for her whole life. I have to make her see it's possible to have both—a career and a family. Assuming she wants a family.

To see her pregnant with my child, to have the kind of life I've seen my brothers embrace—I would do anything to have that. To have her. I married her… Now, all I have to do is make sure she realizes I meant every word of the vows and of the toast I made earlier. I'm not into romantic gestures, but it felt important to me that she understand I'm going to take this marriage seriously. She'll come around. She has to. I walked over to my seat on the other side of the aisle, and I'm not ashamed to say, I haven't taken my gaze off her face since.

When I told my brothers of my decision to move to be with her, they weren't surprised. Although it probably killed him, Michael didn't take credit for putting the thought in my head. And my dumbass brothers avoided exchanging their bet money in my presence. Instead, like adults, we decided to work as seamlessly as possible by being in touch every day via video conferencing. It remains to be seen whether the arrangement will work, but I'm optimistic. Michael told me he reached out to our partner, JJ Kane, who's based in London. JJ will be meeting with me to work out the details of our partnership in Trinity Enterprises, the company we co-own with the Kane company and the Bratva. So being based in London has its uses, after all. It seems like a win for everyone…

Except, I still didn't have her trust and her love. Soon enough. I'll have to bide my time. Surely, my actions will show her I don't intend to come in the way of her dreams. And if I push things along to help her, well, that's what a good husband does, after all. He makes sure that his wife lacks for nothing.

I lean my head back into the seat, and this time, when I close my eyes, sleep overcomes me. The scent of vanilla and coconut teases my senses. A soft brush across my lips, the touch of her knuckles over my cheek, the sweep of her hair against my chest. I crack open my eyes to find her moving away.

"Not so fast." I grab her wrist and tug. She overbalances and tumbles into my lap.

"Let me go," she hisses.

"Not a chance." I twist her arm behind her, forcing her to jut out her chest. Her nipples are outlined through the layers of her bra and her dress. I raise my gaze to find her watching me with an angry look on her face.

"We have a deal. No sex," she hisses.

"This is not sex, it's merely… A husband wishing his wife a good morning."

"It's not yet morning."

"It is somewhere in the world."

She huffs. "We need to establish some rules if we're going to cohabitate."

"Rules, eh?"

She nods. "No touching, no kissing, no brushing against each other. Nothing remotely romantic can take place between us."

"So, it's okay for you to kiss me while I am sleeping, but I can't do the same to you?"

"I didn't kiss you," she snaps.

"Oh, come on, *Stellina*, I felt you kiss me. I smelled you as you whispered your knuckles across my chin."

Her cheeks flush. "You must be imagining things."

"And was I imagining things when I saw you move away from me?"

"I was merely going to find the stewardess to get something to drink."

I peer into her features and take in the dark circles under her eyes.

"The wound in your side, does it hurt?"

She shakes her head. "It really was only a flesh wound. It healed quickly."

I reach out to touch the scar on her face, and she flinches. I lower my hand. "And this? Does it still hurt?"

She glances away, shakes her head, then nods. "Sometimes. When I least expect it, it twinges, kind of like a phantom pain. But otherwise, no, it healed very quickly."

"And what do the doctors say about the scarring?"

She pulls on her hand, and I release her. She twists her fingers together in front. "That it will fade in time, but there'll always be a mark of some kind."

"You are beautiful, *Stellina*, inside and out. No one can take that away from you."

She flushes a little, and her forehead creases. "I don't want to talk about it."

"You should. I think you should see a therapist."

She jerks her chin in my direction. "What? No. I don't need to see a shrink."

"Have you spoken to anyone else about the experience? Are you sure you're not suffering from PTSD related to what happened?"

She tries to pull away from me, but I wrap my arm around her and hold her in place. "Have you been sleeping well? How have you been eating since you were shot at?"

Her breath heaves. She shoves her fingers into her ears. "La-la-la-la. I can't hear you."

I grip her arms and wrench them away from her face. "Too disturbing for you to hear what happened to you, eh?"

"Stop it." She turns and pushes her face into mine. "Stop trying to psychoanalyze me."

"Then get analyzed by a professional."

"No." She firms her lips.

"You know, you're going to have to face what happened to you, don't you?"

"Maybe I don't want to." She sighs and turns her head away. "I'm not stupid. I know what happened to me is life-changing. And I will face it. Just not yet, okay? I just need to figure out how to salvage my career first."

"Maybe the way to reclaim your career is by first reclaiming yourself."

She stills, then a reluctant chuckle spills from her lips. "When did you get so wise?"

"When did you get so stupid?"

"A-n-d there he is, the asshole I met at the bar."

"Alphahole actually."

She scoffs. "That's so trite, I'm going to pretend you didn't say it."

"Even though you agree?"

"That you're alpha enough to kill the man who might have pushed me into the kind of life I'd have little hope of escaping... and thereby, saving me? Yes, you are. Only, you spoiled it by manipulating me into marrying you."

"And I would do it again."

She searches my features. "Does it mean that much to you to have me in your life?"

"Yes."

Only, it's more than that. I can't function without having her connected to me. The thought of her with any other man makes me want to commit murder. And I don't want bloodshed on my hands. Not more than necessary, that is. And killing Diego had been a necessity. I have zero regrets on that. Doesn't mean I want to go around killing others, but if any other man touches her, I'll do so without a second thought.

Something of my thoughts must reflect on my face, for her gaze widens. Her breathing grows rough. She looks between my eyes, then shakes her head.

"I don't belong to anyone."

"You belong to me."

"I belong to myself," she argues.

"And you're mine."

39

Olivia

Mine, mine, mine.

It shouldn't affect me when he says that word, but I would be lying to myself if I said it doesn't. He's so confident about it. He has been from the moment I met him. If only I could allow myself to feel the same way. Because there's no doubt, I'm attracted to him. The sex with him is explosive, and when I'm with him, I definitely feel protected... And all of it is a reminder of why I cannot allow myself to be dependent on him. If I open myself up to him, I'll lose myself, and then, how will I be able to focus on making something of myself?

I glance out of the window at the raindrops that patter against the pane. We moved into a townhouse on Primrose Hill. Why am I not surprised he has a place in Primrose Hill? I wanted to refuse to stay with him because it didn't feel right. He's rich enough to afford prime real estate in this city, and I'm just a struggling actress. Don't I completely fit the role of eye-candy on the arm of a rich prick?

I press my fingers against the glass, allowing the coolness to filter through them. Am I in danger of becoming a cliché? I press my forehead against the pane and peer through the rain-soaked sheet of glass. We've been here forty-eight hours, during which time I have, thankfully, seen little of my husband.

We landed in London a few hours after that conversation. A town car was waiting for us, and we were ushered to this house. I walked into the living room, and something about the wood flooring, the wide French windows that let the light pour in, the fireplace, the carpet, the deep leather settee, had made me relax my shoulders. Then, I walked into the adjoining room, discovered the library with the floor-to-ceiling bookcases stacked with books, and I literally salivated.

There's a fireplace there, as well as a big comfortable armchair with a throw over it. I wanted to grab a few books, throw myself down in it, and not move. I lingered there, running my fingers over the spines of the books, trying not to give away how excited I was. When I tore myself away, he showed me the kitchen—a big, square space with doors that open into the back garden. The room itself is airy, with an island in the center and stools scattered around it. A double refrigerator, a gleaming oven, and utensils that hang off hooks on one side give it a homey feel. Best of all, it doesn't join the living room, which means it's completely separate, so you can cook and bake without having to worry about the food smell invading the rest of the house. I went to the door, glanced out at the deck, and he invited me to walk out. I walked to the railing and took in the wide sweep of the slope of the hill beyond the garden. To the side was an infinity pool, which seemed to join with the horizon.

"Wow," I breathed. "This is gorgeous."

"It is, isn't it?"

I glanced sideways to see him staring at me, and oh, my god, I felt his look all the way to the tips of my toes. I stood there, caught in the intensity of the moment, unable to take my gaze off of him, unable to blink, unable to breathe. It felt like there was a cord stretched between us, something that linked us—something overflowing with unsaid words, and pulsating emotions, and hopes, and dreams, and yearning. So much yearning. Something so tangible, I could reach out, touch it, and taste it if I wanted to.

I took a step forward, and so did he. His gaze narrowed, and his shoulders seemed to grow larger. His dominance thrummed in the space between us. His presence seemed to absorb all of the oxygen in the vicinity. The force of his personality slammed into my chest, making it difficult to breathe. The pores on my skin popped, heat flushed my chest, and every cell in my body seemed to be open, and throbbing, and needing him. Only him. And I hadn't even touched him.

I remembered enough of how that night between us had been. He had consumed me. I'd come so close to opening myself up completely to him, to giving him everything. I'd have been left with nothing.

He took another step in my direction, and I turned and ran inside, away from him. I ran up the stairs, avoiding the double doors at the end of the corridor that, clearly, led to the main bedroom. I chose one of the other rooms, a guest room, and slammed the door behind me. I crawled into bed, curled into myself, and fell asleep. When I woke up the next morning, I found my bags placed next to the door leading into the walk-in closet. Did he set them here? Did he watch me sleep? I also found a key fob on my nightstand, with a note from him indicating they were for my car, which was parked in the garage.

At least he doesn't mean for me to be a prisoner in this house, so... That's something, I suppose.

I showered and went downstairs to find his housekeeper in the kitchen, cooking. She informed me she comes in daily, whenever someone is in the house, to take care of chores and cook for us. She also told me he'd eaten breakfast and left for the day.

I haven't seen him since.

Now, I turn back to the makeshift office I set up on the table pushed up against the window. I've been on the phone with Declan's agent, who seems positive he can get me into auditions in both London and in LA. I've spent the last day revamping my website and putting out feelers for the voice-over work I'd already begun doing, which actually pays quite well. Only, it isn't what inspires me. I don't want to hide behind my voice. I want to show my face on screen, on stage, to people. Massimo's wrong. I don't need therapy. I've faced my fears by putting myself forward for roles. Haven't I? Nope, I'm fine.

An incoming call on my phone vibrates. I swipe the screen, and Penny's face appears.

"Hey, hey, hey, look at you; already glowing with happiness. How's the honeymoon going?" she chirps.

"No honeymoon. I came here to work, remember?" I sink into my seat and place the phone in its stand next to my computer.

"How boring. You only get married once… Or at least, for the first time once. Shouldn't you be making the most of this time and bouncing on his dick and other parts of him, as well?"

I yawn. "Already done that. Next?"

She blinks, then bursts out laughing. "You cow. You didn't. So, you slept with him before you got married, didn't you?"

I hesitate. No harm admitting it now, is there? "And if I did?"

"And he was so enraptured by your pussy, he had to have you, to the extent that he abandoned his fiancée to-be, made you abandon your fiancé in-name-only, then killed your brother, who'd have married you off elsewhere, and married you."

When she puts it like that… It does sound excessive. I tip up my chin. "What are you trying to say?"

She sobers. "I know you're pissed off at what happened to your face, but you can't let it hold you back.

"It's not holding me back. Do I look like it's holding me back?" I gesture to myself. I'm dressed in slacks and a sweater, my hair tied up in a ponytail. Also, I've worn enough makeup to minimize the scar without looking like I want to hide it. I definitely don't resemble someone with PTSD from having been shot at. Or like someone who cuts herself. My fingers tremble and I press them into the desk. "Well?" I scowl at her. "How do I look?"

"You look great," she says sincerely. "You always look great, Olivia, but you know I'm not talking about that. Sometimes, the people who look the most put together on the outside are the ones falling apart on the inside."

I stiffen. A ball of discomfort tightens my guts. "I'm not falling apart inside."

"I didn't say you were. All I meant was, if you need help—"

"I don't need help. Why does everyone around me think I need help? This is me, more focused than I've been in my entire life."

"Maybe too focused."

I begin to protest, but she holds up her palm to cut me off.

"I know you'll deny it, and that's fine. You can hide from yourself, but not from your friends."

"Or from my husband, apparently," I grumble.

"What was that?"

"All I'm saying is, I'm tired of the lot of you trying to tell me how to live my life, you know?"

"It's only because we care about you. What you went through is nothing to joke about. It's only been a few weeks after the incident, and already you're back on your feet and super-focused on your career."

"Ergo, I'm ready to put it behind me and go after the one thing I've always wanted."

"Things change. Our hopes and aspirations broaden as we get older," she murmurs.

"Not mine. I'm going to become a well-known actress. I want the fame, and the recognition that goes with it. I'm good at what I do, and I want the world to know it."

"And they will. It may not be on the timetable you want it on, but I'm sure you'll get everything you deserve."

I blink. "That's a very nice thing to say."

"I truly believe it." She smiles widely.

"I wish I were more like you, Penny."

"What do you mean?" She frowns.

"You're always so optimistic about the future. So cheery, sometimes disgustingly so. And you don't take anything too seriously."

"Not even my career, you mean?" she remarks in a self-deprecating tone.

I raise my hands, palms face up. "You're definitely easygoing about it, and I like that. I feel relaxed around you because of it. Jeanne and I, we're the more competitive ones. I wish I could be more like you, but something in me always pushes me forward. It forces me to achieve, to keep moving forward, know what I mean?"

"It's what I admire you for—your single-minded focus. I wish I had more of that," she says in a soft voice.

"Yeah, well, I'm going to need all of it to find new roles." I rotate my neck, trying to ease the tension in my shoulders. "Much as people like to say they don't discriminate on the basis of looks, you know we do. I mean, bias is inherent in how we survey people who look out of the ordinary, like having a scar on their face, for example. And that's even more true in the world of acting."

"If anyone can break through those barriers, it's you."

"I agree, and I have every confidence that you can do it, too." Hands wrap around my shoulders and begin to massage. A shudder runs down my back. I glance at the screen of my phone and spot Massimo's reflection staring back at me.

"I gotta go, Penny!" I wave at my friend.

"But—"

I cut her off, then stare up at my husband.

"What are you doing here?" I demand.

40

Massimo

"Can't I come by and see how my wife is doing?"

Her cheeks flush. She glances away, then back at me. "Why do I get the feeling your intentions are not that innocent?"

"You're doubting me?" I widen my gaze.

She snorts. "Don't act so innocent. Why are you really here?"

"Just wanted to make sure you weren't overworking yourself."

"I'm not."

"Have you taken your meds?"

"Yes, Dad." She rolls her eyes.

"You sassing me, *Stellina*?"

"Like I would ever dare to do that."

"Oh, you would, all right. Other than my brothers, you're the first person I've met who's not afraid of me. It's a fucking turn-on when you stand up to me, you know that?"

She swallows. "I wish you wouldn't say things like that."

"Like what?"

"Like you mean it," she whispers.

"But I do, Via. I have, from the first moment I met you."

"Don't." She jumps to her feet, and I lower my arms to my sides. She darts out from the front of her chair and begins to pace.

"Why do you always have to make everything so difficult? Why do you always have to say the right things?"

"Because I'm right?"

She spins around to face me and plants her palms on her hips. "See, that right there? That, I can take. I prefer you to be smug, and egoistical, and full-of-your-self, and difficult to like—"

"Because that would make it easy for you to rationalize turning me down?"

"I didn't turn you down. I married you," she points out.

"In name only."

"That was our deal," she huffs.

"That was your understanding of the deal." I close the distance between us, and she doesn't move back.

She tips up her chin. "You got what you wanted. Why are you still bothering me? Why did you have to come with me? Why couldn't you have let me leave and pursue my career on my own?"

"Because I take my vows seriously." I lower my face to hers, until our noses bump. "I swore to protect you, to cherish you, to take care of you, and nothing will stop me from delivering on my promises."

Her pupils dilate. "Are you always this conscientious?"

"Only when it comes to you." I twine my fingers with hers so our rings brush against each other's. "Are you done with work today?"

She holds my gaze, a slightly dazed look in her eyes. Good. As long as I can keep her off-kilter, I might be able to convince her to unbend enough to give me a chance. A-n-d, I can't believe I'm here, coaxing my wife to take a chance on me, when I've never in my life had to coax a woman for anything. Normally, I'm the one saying no. I admit, I'm enjoying this challenge of trying to get her to do my bidding.

"Via?" I ask again.

She blinks. "Eh, what did you say?"

I suppress my chuckle. "I asked if you were done with your work for the day?"

"I am."

"Good, I have a surprise for you."

Forty-five minutes later, we walk into a restaurant on the top floor of *The Heron*. The hostess leads us to a table at the far end. Halfway across the floor, Via tugs her hand from my grasp. She walks over to the floor-to-ceiling windows and glances out. "This view is incredible."

"This is the highest restaurant in London," I confirm.

"It's mind-blowing," she murmurs.

You are mind-blowing. I glance down at her profile.

She shuffles her feet. "I wish I'd worn something more formal."

"You look great."

She scowls at me over her shoulder. "I'm wearing slacks and a sweater, and have barely any makeup on—"

"You look like yourself, and I love that."

She glances away. "Don't do that."

"Do what?"

"Be all nice to me. It confuses me."

"You'd rather I command you to do what I want, is that it?"

Her scowl deepens. "I'd like you to try that, asshole."

I wrap my arm around her waist and draw her up against me. "I have a feeling you might enjoy it entirely too much. Is that your kink, *Stellina*? Would you rather I not give you a choice and take what I want?"

Her breath hitches. She opens and shuts her mouth, but no words come out. I bring my other arm up to wind it around her neck. "If I touched you between your thighs right now, would I find you wet and aching for me?"

"Of course not," she claims. Her chin trembles. The scent of vanilla deepens. Goddamn, she really is turned on. The blood drains to my groin. My pants feel too tight. She must sense the evidence of my arousal stabbing into her ass, for she stiffens. A trembling runs down her body, and my thighs tighten. If I stand here a second longer, I'm liable to turn her around and kiss her, right before I throw her down, tear off her panties, and bury myself inside of her. And that won't do. Not when I'm trying to behave. Not when I'm trying to show her she can trust me enough to be patient. That I'll let her come to me of her own volition. I release her, then brush the hair off the back of her neck and kiss her nape. She shivers.

"Come on, let's feed you."

I step back, then twine my fingers with hers and tug on her. She turns and follows me. I lead her over to our table—the best in the house, tucked away at the back of the restaurant, with a panorama of the city spread out before us. I make sure she's seated before pushing her chair in, then walk over to take mine. The waiter materializes almost instantly. I order our drinks, whiskey for me, a tequila-based cocktail for her. When the waiter leaves, she turns to me.

"Presumptuous of you to assume you know what I like."

"Presumptuous of you not to realize that I know exactly what you like. I also know that you only eat gluten-free food."

"How do you know I eat only gluten-free? Also—" she narrows her gaze "—is this how you're going to be all evening?"

"To answer your first question, I made sure to acquaint myself with your tastes. As for the second question, like how?"

"Like someone who's going to anticipate my every move?"

"How am I doing so far?" I smirk.

She shakes her head, and a reluctant smile curves her lips. "If I say anything, it'll only go to your already swollen head."

I raise my hand. "I solemnly swear that… I'm up to no good."

She blinks. "You quoted *Harry Potter*?"

"Why are you so surprised?"

"You don't look like the kind to enjoy *Harry Potter*?"

"What do you think I'd enjoy instead?" I ask.

"Let's see," she pretends to count. "Sacrificing baby goats? Scaring those who dare cross you? Shooting down people?" Her face falls. "Sorry, I didn't mean to say that."

"No, I'm glad you brought it up. I'm sorry you had to see that, *Stellina*. That, on top of you being shot? God knows, your mind must be reeling from it."

"You forget, I grew up in the Mafia. Violence is not new to me."

"But you must have hated it. Isn't that why you ran from it?" A second waiter materializes with a carafe of water. I hold out my hand and take it from him, then fill her glass. I push it toward her. "Drink."

She tilts her head.

"You need to drink at least a liter of water a day."

"How do you know I don't?"

"You were locked up in your room all day, and I didn't see any water on your desk, either. I'll ask the staff to ensure you have water in your room."

"Have you always been this bossy?"

"What do you think?" I smirk.

"That you love getting your own way?"

I reach for my own glass of water and take a sip.

"And when you don't, you manipulate things until they fall in exactly the pattern you like."

"The only pattern I like is the one where you are at the center of it. Preferably without any clothes."

She draws in a sharp breath.

I lean forward in my seat. "And spread-eagled and tied so that you can't move an inch as I tear into your pussy."

Color flushes her skin. She squeezes her fingers around her water glass. "Jesus." She swallows. "I thought you didn't want to consummate the marriage."

"My exact words, if you will recall, were that we don't have to consummate the marriage; not unless you want to."

She firms her lips. "And I told you, I don't want to."

"Only, I don't believe you."

41

Olivia

"Better believe it." I squeeze my thighs together. If I look down at my sweater, I'm sure I'll find my nipples outlined through the fabric. I am not going to sleep with him again. No. It's just, when I'm sitting opposite him, in this gorgeous place, with his gaze fixed on me, and those seductive words coming out of his mouth, I'm not sure about anything anymore.

Maybe I should say fuck it and fuck him. And then what? Consummate the marriage and walk into his trap? That's exactly what he wants. It's why he didn't push me about the sleeping together part before we got married. It's why he came to London with me. He knew, once we were together, under the same roof —under his roof—he'd find a way to seduce me. And he doesn't have to do much, except sit there and smolder at me. All he has to do is narrow his gaze on me, and I'm a goner. And once he starts talking dirty, I have no chance. But I am going to fight this attraction to him. I am not going to give in to him.

I drain my glass of water and place it on the table with a thump.

"Thirsty?" His smile grows wider.

Asshole knows exactly the kind of effect he has on me.

"Aren't you?" I ask sweetly.

As if I've summoned him, the waiter arrives with our drink orders. Thank God. I grab the cocktail, thankful I have something to hold on to.

Massimo raises his tumbler of whiskey. *"Salute,"* he drawls. "To our future together."

"May the best person win." I clink our glasses together.

"I always win," he replies with complete authority.

"You've never competed with me before," I scoff.

"You're here, aren't you?" he reminds me.

I toss my hair over my shoulder. "I won't let anything stand between me and my dreams."

"I promised you I wouldn't get in the way of your dreams, but I won't let anything stand between the two of us."

I firm my chin, then take a hefty swallow of my cocktail. And cough. The alcohol content in my drink is so high, I can taste the acidic bite of the liquor on my palate. The taste of elderflower chases it down. I take another sip and roll the liquid across my tongue. The sting of ginger, the softness of thyme, the distinctive peppery taste of rosemary, and beneath it all, the mellow purpleness of vanilla coats my tongue. He must see the expression on my face, for he tilts his head. "Good?"

I swallow, then nod. "It's the best cocktail I've had in, like, ever."

"Good." He smirks.

The waiter arrives again. Massimo orders a roasted cod fillet with sea vegetables for himself, and a wild mushroom risotto with shaved black truffle for me.

When the waiter leaves, I scowl at him. "I can order for myself."

"And I wanted to order for you."

"That's really chauvinistic of you," I say through gritted teeth.

"Maybe I want to take care of my wife."

"And no doubt, keep her at home, barefoot and pregnant," I mutter.

His gaze heats. "I'd love to see you barefoot and pregnant. However, I also know how much it means to you to pursue your career, and I've already told you, repeatedly, I'll never stop you from owning your dream."

My cheeks flush. I play with my cutlery and arrange them parallel to each other on either side of the plate. Our every conversation ends with him, somehow, gaining the upper hand. He's always come across as fair in our discussions, except for how he maneuvered me into marrying him, that is. But he saved me from my brother's plans for me, so I can't even stay angry at him for that, I suppose. It's my damn ambition that's getting in the way. I've always taken pride in being a feminist and in being independent. How can I reconcile that part of me with the lust that fills me every time I think of him owning me, caressing me, fucking me in every filthy way he's promised? How can I allow that to happen and not become dependent on him?

"Via, look at me."

I refuse to raise my gaze.

"Via."

There's a note of warning in his voice that sends a thrill through my veins. Somehow, I like it when he gets upset. I like seeing this commanding, unyielding part of him—that alphahole core of him which he seems to have cloaked under this understanding man whenever he's near me. I know myself well enough to realize that I'm not one of those women who wants to be treated like a lady in bed. Which is why the night we had together was so hot. He was rough and demanding. He pushed me to open myself up, but he was also generous in how he took care of my needs. He was the epitome of what I want from a lover. And now, he's my husband. *Mine.*

I reach for my cocktail and drain the rest of it. The alcohol hits my stomach, setting off a pleasant buzz under my skin. I slide my leg under the table until I reach the inside of his ankle, then drag my foot up the inside of his pants.

He stiffens, and his eyes flash. He holds my gaze as I rub my foot up and down his calf, as much as I can reach it, that is.

One side of his lips twists. "You're playing a dangerous game, Via." His tone drops an octave, and every cell in my body seems to pant. My ovaries seem to vibrate in anticipation. I reach over for his glass and slide it over to my side of the table, then turn it around until I fix my lips to the very space he sipped from. I tilt the glass back and take a sip. When I raise my gaze to his, his shoulders are tense. His jaw is hard. A pulse thuds at his temple. I didn't realize how much power I hold over him, until right now.

"Massimo, I—"

"Sovrano," a man's voice intrudes.

Both of us start. I lower my leg to the ground, then both of us turn our heads to watch the man who approaches us. He's tall—not as tall as Massimo, but he makes up for it with his powerful physique. His dark hair is cut short at the sides, slightly longer on top. His dark eyes sweep over me with a look that is part assessing and part slimy. A shiver runs down my spine.

Massimo rises to his feet and steps in front of me, effectively cutting me off from the stranger's line of sight. "Who are you?"

"The man to whom she was first pledged."

42

Massimo

"The fuck? What are you talking about? Who are you?" I widen my stance, making sure this asshole can see no part of my wife.

"I'm Alvaro Garcia—"

"Head of the Mexican cartel." I plant my palms on my hips.

"Diego promised me her hand in return for paying off his debts." His eyes gleam.

"Debts?" I scowl.

"Debts?" She jumps up from her chair, and I thrust my hand out to keep her behind me and away from this *stronzo's* view.

"He owed money to the cartel. A lot of money, actually. Money he'd never have been able to pay off in this lifetime. I agreed to write off the sum in return for her hand."

"She's my wife now." I lower my chin to my chest. "She's mine."

"I'm not anybody's possession. I—"

"Keep quiet." I glare at her over my shoulder.

She huffs at me, then slowly presses her lips together and scowls at me. I ignore her and turn back to Alvaro.

"How much did he owe you?"

"You sure you want to know?"

"How much?" I snap.

One side of his mouth kicks up. "A billion dollars."

"What? How is that even possible? How can anyone run up such a big amount in debt?" She tries to pop her head from around me, and I turn and glare at her.

"Will you keep quiet and sit down?"

She opens her mouth to protest.

"Please?" I soften my voice. "Please, *Stellina*, do this for me, will you?"

She tips up her chin, but to my relief, she sinks down into the chair. I turn to Alvaro. "I assume you have the requisite paperwork to back this up?"

His grin widens. "Of course. You do realize what happens if you don't pay this back?"

I close my fingers into fists. "Touch one hair on her head, and I'll kill you."

He laughs. "If you don't return my money within forty-eight hours, I will collect what is owed to me."

She jumps up and brushes past me. "If you think I'm going to let myself be treated like baggage that can be passed around, you are sadly mistaken." She points a finger at him. "I didn't belong to my brother." She stabs a thumb over her shoulder. "I don't belong to him." Her tone drips with derision, "And I definitely don't belong to you."

He arches an eyebrow at me. "On the other hand, I hope you don't pay." He turns his attention back to her and traces his finger down her cheek. "Apparently—and despite the disfigurement—she's interesting enough that I might let her warm my bed."

Anger twists my guts, and blood thuds at my temples. *How dare he touch her?* Adrenaline laces my blood. I push her behind me, then grab his wrist. I yank him forward with enough force that he crashes face down into the table. I bend and place my mouth next to his ear. "Be very careful about how you talk about my wife."

A woman screams from a nearby table, and I hear the sound of footsteps as people move away.

I slap his hand down on the table, then pull out my gun and shoot him through his forefinger. The same finger he used to caress my *Stellina's* cheek.

He howls in pain. I snatch up a napkin and shove it inside his mouth.

"In fact, don't fucking talk about her at all, you *pezzo di merda*. If you dare lay eyes on her again, I'll pull them out of your sockets and feed them to the birds. After I've smashed your head in, *capisce*?"

I pull him up to his feet, then release him. He staggers forward, tears the napkin out of his mouth with his uninjured hand, then turns to me.

"You've made an enemy today, Sovrano. I won't forget what you did."

"Get out of my sight," I snap

"The money, or her. You have forty-eight hours." He pivots and leaves.

"Anyone tell you that you have a flair for theatrics?" She turns on me. "And how dare you speak to me like that? I am *not* an asset. I am *not* something to be handed over, I am *not*—"

I lean forward and clap my fingers around the nape of her neck. "You are my property. Mine. Mine to fuck, if I want. Mine to own. Mine to control. Mine to do with as I want, and I am not letting anyone take you away from me, you feel me?"

Her green eyes dart sparks at me. Her features are flushed. A pulse flutters at her throat. With her hands curled into fists at her sides, and with strands of hair framing her face, she looks like an avenging angel. My angel.

"Fuck you, Massimo," she says in a tight voice.

"I intend to." I grab her hand and haul her across the floor and toward the service doors in the far corner.

"Where are you taking me? The elevators are the other way."

"And he just went that way."

"Oh, right." She shuts up, thank fuck, and allows me to lead her through the double doors, past the sous-chefs in the kitchen, past the chef yelling at another sous-chef, and past the dishwasher, who gives us a curious look. We make it out the back door, then into another passageway, and to the service elevator. I slap the button, still holding her hand as we wait. She tries to pull her arm from my grasp, and I glare at her.

"Can you stop fidgeting?"

"Can you stop acting like a dog with a hurt paw?"

"What?"

"You're acting really stupid and overly possessive."

The car arrives and the doors open. I step inside, pull her in after me, and stab the button for the ground floor. "I'm the one acting stupid? Do you realize how completely foolish you were in there? Have you forgotten where you come from? Do you understand how much danger you put yourself in when you yelled at him?"

"I'm not afraid of anything."

"And that's what got you in this position." I jerk my chin at her scar.

She pales. "H-how dare you? It's not my fault someone shot at me."

"It's your fault that you stepped up on that stage. Your fault you decided to become an actress."

"How dare you say such a thing?" she cries out.

"Why couldn't you have stayed home and quietly married whoever your family chose for you?" I close the distance between us, and she skitters back until her back hits the wall of the elevator car. "That way, I wouldn't have met you. I wouldn't have slept with you. I wouldn't have become obsessed with you. Since I met you, my entire world has been turned upside down."

"You're making no sense." She plants her palms on my chest and tries to push me away. The touch of her hands slides under my skin and arrows straight to my groin.

"You know what doesn't make sense? How I could kill a guy—and your own brother, at that—for you, and not feel a shred of emotion. All I felt was relief. Then, that asshole dared look at you, and all I could think of was that I'd take pleasure in tearing him limb from limb. I am going to tear his heart out and cut him into little pieces so his blood stains the ground. Then, I'm going to throw you down in it, pry your thighs apart, and fuck you until you come."

She swallows. Her pupils expand until there's only a circle of green left at the edges of her irises.

"You're crazy," she whispers.

"Fucking crazy about you. Crazy enough to want to marry you as soon as I saw you in that bar. Crazy enough to want to hide you away until this danger has passed." A hot sensation coils in my chest. I glance between her eyes. "Crazy enough to conceal you from all prying eyes, and fuck you until you know your place."

"What?" She blinks rapidly. "Are you even hearing yourself?"

"Crazy enough..." I bend my knees and peer into her eyes. "To start right now." I slide the gun into the waistband at the small of my back, then lean over and slap the stop button on the elevator.

43

Olivia

The elevator jerks to a stop. The vibrations travel through the walls of the car and up my spine. I glance up at the indicator to find we've stopped on the tenth floor.

"What the hell are you doing?" I try to push him off of me, but he's so damned solid, he doesn't move. Not an inch. He simply stands there with a slightly crazed look in his eyes.

"M-Massimo?" I gulp. "You're scaring me."

"Good." He plants his palm on the wall of the elevator next to my head and I jump.

"What are you doing?"

"Deciding which hole I want to take first—your mouth, your pussy, or your ass. And you know how much I enjoy your ass, *Stellina*."

I gape at him. "You've completely lost it."

"I have."

"Guess all that talk of giving me my space and allowing me to decide when I wanted to sleep with you was just that. You never meant it."

"I did. I do. Only, I overestimated the extent of my patience." He lowers his head and runs his nose up the length of my throat. "You smell like vanilla and coconut. Like an exotic dessert I want to eat up and ask for more."

"It… it's my shampoo. Tropical delight. It has essence of vanilla and a touch of coconut; also, passion fruit and mango and—"

He buries his nose in my hair and draws in a long whiff. A moan spills from my lips. Oh, my god, that was… so erotic. No one has smelled me like that. Like he wants to eat me alive. He drags his nose down my neck to the curve of my shoulder. He bites the skin there and I shiver. He licks the skin he's marked, and my knees almost give way from under me.

"You do it purposely, don't you? Dress in this way that covers so much of you, it makes me yearn to get another glimpse of you. Makes me want to tear your clothes off and mark every creamy inch of you. Makes me want to squeeze your curves and bite your breasts, then slap your ass until my palm prints are imprinted on your behind."

"Oh my god," I bite down on my lower lip. A pulse flares to life between my thighs, mirroring the frantic beating of my heart. "Massimo, please."

He plants his massive thigh between mine. I yelp. He grabs my hips and pulls me forward, then back, so I'm riding his leg. Through the layers of my clothes, my already sensitive clit rubs against the unyielding bulk of his thigh. Sensations zing out from the point of contact. Sparks of heat flush my skin, and moisture laces my core. He continues to rock me against his thigh, and I hook my fingers into his shirt and hold on. He glares into my eyes. I'm enraptured, captured, unable to look away, unable to remind myself not to fall head-over-heels into the depths of those eyes of his, which are so clear they, once more, resemble sheets of ice.

His hot breath sears my lips. I can't stop the whine that slips out. One side of his mouth twists, and he intensifies his actions, pushing me into his thigh and hauling me back and forth until the sensations zing up my spine. The tightness at the base of my spine crowds in on itself. The trembling starts somewhere deep inside of me, then shivers out to my extremities. My back bows. I tug on the front of his shirt as the climax grips me. He peers deeply into my eyes, watching me closely as the orgasm gathers speed. He increases the intensity of his movements, tugging me toward him, then away, again and again… and again. My climax rips through me and I cry out. I throw my head back, and I'm dimly aware that he releases his hand on my hip, only to shove it behind my head, so I slap into it instead of the hard wall. Then my orgasm splinters behind my eyes and I come. Moisture laces my core, and my pussy flutters, seeking something more. I want more. *More. More. More.* I slump, and he catches me and pulls me into his chest. My hold on his shirt loosens and I lay there, my heart thumping in my chest, my blood pumping through my veins. I sense his heartbeat echoing mine, feel the heat of his body sinking through mine. He runs his hand down my hair, then, in soothing gestures, over my back.

I burrow into him further. I turn my head into the strip of skin visible between the lapels of his shirt and inhale deeply. Dark pine. Citrus. Woodsmoke. All of it plays havoc with my senses. He lowers his leg, holds me until I find my balance, then he steps back and runs his hands over my hair, righting my sweater. When he's satisfied, he punches the button on the elevator and steps back, twining his fingers with mine.

When the doors open, he leads me out and toward his car. He walks quickly, scanning the area. I almost have to run to keep up with him. He beeps the key fob as we approach the car, then opens the passenger door and guides me inside, before he rounds the car and gets into the driver's seat. He eases it out of the parking space and instructs his phone to dial JJ Kane. When JJ answers, he says we're coming over and we need his help, then disconnects before the other guy can say anything.

"We're going to his house?" I ask.

Massimo looks in either direction, then pulls out of the parking lot.

"Why are we going to his house?" I turn to him. His jaw is set, his gaze narrowed, and it's not because he's driving. He's angry about something.

"Are you pissed off with me?" I burst out.

No answer.

"Are you upset because that guy approached us?"

"He's not just any guy; he's the head of the Mexican cartel. If you think Michael is ruthless, you should meet Alvaro. If you thought your brother was a *testa di cazzo*, Alvaro is far worse."

"And you shot off his finger and pissed him off even more."

"He touched what was mine. He dare lay a finger on you, *Stellina*. He had it coming."

My heart crashes into my chest. Pinpricks of heat arrow down to my core and my clit throbs in tandem to the pulse that beats at my temples. I shouldn't find what he did a turn on, but the sheer vehemence, the brutality and the ease with which he hadn't hesitated to punish Alvaro for what he did is so hot. When I remember how Alvaro eyed me, how his weaselly gaze made my skin crawl. A shiver runs up my spine... I'm glad he did it.

I lock my fingers in my lap, "He's lying. Diego couldn't owe him a billion dollars. It's not possible." I drag my fingers through my hair.

"What's right or wrong doesn't matter anymore. That's the sum Alvaro has put on your safety."

I shudder. A million—make that a billion—bugs seem to crawl under my skin at once. I wrap my arms around myself, then stare forward.

He must sense my disquiet, for he shoots me a sideways glance. "You don't have to worry about anything; I'll take care of it."

"You do realize, I'm used to taking care of myself?"

"That was before you were my wife," he retorts.

"See, this is what I hate about you Mafioso. You get so macho, so possessive. You forget that we women are individuals with the ability to choose for ourselves."

"And I don't doubt that. I'm aware that you're a career woman, someone who is strong-willed enough to make it on her own in the cutthroat world of acting. But this is beyond your capabilities."

Anger twists my guts. I whip my head around to face him. "How can you say that? I grew up in this world. I know how it works."

"Then you also know that being a woman makes you more vulnerable. Especially when you consider the fact that your brother bartered you—"

"Like you took me as collateral for the safety of my family."

"It's not the same thing, and you know it," he says through gritted teeth.

"How isn't it the same thing? That *stronzo* wants me for just one thing. And you want me for the *same* thing."

He slams on his brakes in the middle of the road. The sound of brakes screeching reaches us, then a chorus of horns sound.

"How dare you compare what we have to what that *faccia di merda* threatened you with?" He turns on me. "You're my wife, goddammit," he growls.

"With no say in how I get to live my life, apparently."

"I'm letting you pursue your career, aren't I?" he snaps.

"And I'm supposed to be grateful for that? Men can do what they want, when they want, even after they're married, and no one questions it. Whereas, we women have to justify what we want, explain why we want it, beg some man to allow us to do things. Why, almost every director who puts out a casting call is a man. Do you know women constitute about ten-percent of film directors in the world today? That's it. About ten-percent. And PS, I still have to bow and scrape to a man to get a role. Not to mention, maybe having to sleep with him."

"You are *not* going to sleep with anyone else, you hear me?" he growls. "You're my wife. It should go without saying, I expect you to be completely faithful to me."

Behind us, someone hits their horn again.

"You're blocking traffic." I glance over my shoulder, then back at him. "Can you keep the car moving, please?"

"You're not going to sleep with anyone to get a role. Not now; not ever."

I throw up my hands. "Of course, I'm not going to do that. I've never done it, and I never will. I have more self-respect than that. I was saying that's how things work in the film world. How did we even get onto this topic?"

The litany of horns grows more insistent.

"Please, can you move the car?"

"And you will obey me when it comes to matters of your safety. You will not do anything foolish to endanger yourself again."

"Oh, so you do believe it's my fault I was shot?" I fume.

"I didn't say that."

"Then what did you mean by that?"

"All I meant was you need to do as I tell you so I can ensure your safety until we deal with this new threat."

"And if I don't?"

"If you don't, I'll—" There's a banging on his window.

44

Massimo

I whip my head around to find a stranger peering through the window. He's gesticulating and saying something. I roll down my window.

"—what the hell, dude? Why are you parked in the middle of the road? If you're having an argument, why don't you go home and—"

I shoot my hand out through the window, grab his collar and jerk his face forward. "You were saying?" I snap.

His eyes bug out, he opens and shuts his mouth, then shakes his head. I thrust him away from the car, then roll up my window and release the brake. This time, we drive in silence.

How could she compare what we have to what that *figlio di puttana* threatened her with? How could she compare me to him? I hadn't meant to pull my gun on him, but when he touched her, I lost control. It's only the fact that killing him would have led to a full-out gang war that stopped me. I'm trying to keep her safe, and all she does is resist me. I thought we were safe in London. With Diego dead, and the last of our enemies killed by Luca when he saved Jeanne, I was lulled into complacency. No more. I'm going to ensure we have round-the-clock security, and eyes on her at all times. Hell, I'm going to make sure I don't take my gaze off of her. Going to make sure I'm always in her vicinity, until I've dealt with that *bastardo*, Alvaro.

We reach Hyde Park, turn onto another street, then a side road that leads to a set of gates which open as we approach. I drive onto a secluded driveway, and guide the car forward under the canopy of trees, then pull up in front of a large Queen Anne-style Victorian home. It's three stories tall, and made of painted brick with church-like roof finials on the steely pitched roofs. On either end of the house is a rounded tower with a turret that draws the eye upward. In the gathering darkness, it seems medieval, with the mist rolling in from the park to wreath the top of the roof.

I round the car to find she's already stepped out.

"This is JJ Kane's home?" She glances up at the imposing house.

"One of them."

"Huh. Does he live here alone?"

"I think his son and daughter used to live with him, but they've moved out now."

She purses her lips. "It's not very welcoming, is it?"

"Doesn't matter either way." I walk up the steps and toward the massive door. When it swings open, JJ Kane stands silhouetted in the doorway.

I close the distance between us, until we face each other. Our gazes meet, connect. For a few seconds, neither of us move. Then, he holds out his hand.

"Alvaro is here in London?" JJ straightens in his chair. He brought us straight to his study, a massive room with floor-to-ceiling bookshelves that cover one wall, stacked with books. Olivia left us to go browse amongst them, for which I'm grateful. If I'd asked her to leave us so we could talk, she'd have made sure to stay. Of course, she can see me from across the room, but hopefully she's out of earshot. While I have nothing to hide from her, I prefer to have this conversation with JJ on my own, so she won't see just how worried I really am.

"Motherfucker walked up to me in the restaurant, in front of a roomful of people, and threatened me." I reach for the glass of whiskey he poured me. He ushered me, not to the comfortable arm chairs in front of the fire, but to the antique desk in front of the window in the far corner. He took the armchair behind it, leaving me to slide into the chair opposite. If he's trying to intimidate me, he's going to be disappointed. I'll take his *Lock, Stock and Two Smoking Barrels* and raise him *Goodfellas*.

"I'm going to kill him." I raise the glass to my lips and toss back the alcohol.

"What does he want?" JJ asks.

"A billion dollars."

He tilts his head. "Which you can arrange for, no doubt. So why did you come to me?"

"You need him out of this city as much as I do."

"Do I?" JJ's lips draw up in the semblance of a smile, which makes him resemble a shark.

"Stop fucking around." I lean forward in my seat. "The last thing you need are the Mexicans moving in on this city."

"Haven't you heard? Like the *Cosa Nostra*, the Kane company is going legal with its businesses," he murmurs.

"All the more reason you want to see him gone. You can't have him set up operations here, and upset the balance of power."

He surveys my features, then glances toward Via. I follow his gaze to find her reaching up on her tiptoes to pull out a book.

"You love her?" he asks.

I watch as she walks over to an armchair by the window and sinks into it. She snaps open the book, then pulls her legs up and under her as she begins to read.

"Do you?" JJ prompts.

I turn to face him. "I married her, didn't I?"

"So, you do love her?"

"What's that got to do with anything?"

"What would you give to see her safe?"

"My life," I say simply.

He searches my features, then jerks his chin "What do you need from me?"

"Security. I want to have someone on her twenty-four-seven, I want our home protected, and I need your help tracking down Alvaro. I want eyes on him. I want to know if he so much as takes a piss."

"Your brother, Axel, is not only an ex-cop, but also runs his own security agency—"

"He's in Palermo," I interrupt him. "I need help right now to keep her safe."

He tilts his head. "And what do I get in return?"

I drum my fingers on the table. "First, you wouldn't have known Alvaro was in your city unless I'd mentioned it to you. Secondly—" I plant my palm flat on the table "—you help me, and the *Cosa Nostra* will become your loyal allies."

"Which you already are."

"We have a business alliance in Trinity Enterprises. With this, you cross over to becoming a loyal partner."

He pulls out a cigar, offers me one, then lights them for both of us. He blows out a puff of smoke, then trains his gaze on me. "Partners, huh? I assume you have the authority to deliver on this?"

"You doubting me?" I glare at him.

He laughs. "Just making sure you can keep your word, ol' chap."

"You make sure your security doesn't let her out of their sight. Leave the rest to me."

"If you think I'm going to put up with someone following me all the time, you're sadly mistaken." Her voice reaches me from across the length of the room. I'd hoped she couldn't hear what we'd been discussing.

JJ chuckles. "You really have your hands full, don't you?"

"You have no idea." I shoot her a glance to find she's staring at me over the top of her book. I hold her gaze. She flushes, then rises to her feet, and drops the book on the chair, before walking over to us.

"This isn't the dark ages, where you men think you have to protect us women from your work talk. I'm aware that both of you are discussing how to deal with Alvaro."

I hold out my hand, and she hesitates, then takes it. I pull her close and wrap my arm about her waist. To my surprise, she doesn't shrug it off.

"I'm told you're a powerful man, Mr. Kane." She tips up her chin.

"JJ." He half-smiles. "Call me JJ."

"JJ," she corrects herself. "Are you going to help my husband track him down?"

It's the first time she's called me her husband. Is she aware of that? Heat coils in my chest. My dick, which has been in a state of excitement since I made her come in the elevator, hardens further. She's the only woman who's appealed to my heart and to my cock, at the same time.

"Is that what you wish?" JJ leans back in his seat.

"It is definitely what I wish." She inches closer to me.

"Consider it done." His smile widens.

"And you don't put men on me," she says in a casual tone.

He laughs. "I'm afraid I'll have to defer to your husband on that."

She blows out a breath. "It was worth a try."

Forty-five minutes later, I glance through the window of my room to find JJ's men taking up position outside the gates of our home. I'd gone over and introduced myself to Peter, the team leader, earlier, and reviewed the security arrangements with him.

After that catch up with JJ, which went better than expected, we drove home in relative silence. I excused myself to head to the study, where I caught up with my brothers and updated them about the latest incident with Alvaro, and the deal I struck with JJ. I told them JJ would step in with security arrangements until Axel's security firm was able to get on the case.

Michael was insistent about sending some of our own men down to shore up the security and I agreed. There could never be too much security, as far as I was concerned. I also told him to liquidate half of my share of the assets in the family businesses to raise the billion dollars. With luck, that's all I'll need to raise the money. He told me he understood why I had to do it, and promised to help me facilitate it.

I agreed to update him on how things went, then hung up. By the time I came up the stairs, the door to her room was shut. No doubt, she retired for the night. I walked over to the door of her room, raised my hand to knock, then changed my mind. Instead, I went to my room, stripped off my clothes, and flung myself on the bed.

The radiators sigh as the heating kicks in. March in London feels like December in Italy. Fucking weather here is as piss-poor as the attitude of its citizens. At least the English countryside had redeeming qualities to it. Unlike this goddamn city, which takes itself way too seriously. Except when they get 'pissed.' No wonder the Brits have nearly a hundred ways to say 'drunk' in English. Or so goes a popular song.

I pull up the sheet and close my eyes, then turn on my side. I already checked in with the men around the perimeter of the house, and provided them with enough coffee to ensure they'll be alert through the night. Just having them visible should prove a deterrent for Alvaro and his men. I hope.

I also checked every door and window, to make sure we were secure before I went to bed. I turn on my back, then fling my arm behind my neck. I close my eyes, and images of how she came apart in the elevator fill my mind. How the scent of her intensified, she thrust out her chest, and bowed her back, and I knew she was close. I continued to rock her against my leg, and even through the layers of cloth that separated us, I felt her pussy flutter.

My cock extends, and blood drains to my groin. *Cazzo!* I'll never be able to go to sleep now. I fling off the sheet, pad toward the bathroom, and switch on the shower.

45

Olivia

I turn over on my side, kick off the covers, then pull them on again. The heating kicked in, and the room is warm. Maybe too warm? Or maybe it's me? The events of the evening crowd in on me—Alvaro's threat, then my coming apart as Massimo made me ride his leg. I never knew that was possible. Since the last time he fucked me—in the aircraft bathroom—I've been horny. I came then, but it wasn't enough. And now, being forced to see him day and night, it's agony. Being near him, being under the same roof as him, seeing him, and smelling him, and wanting to be close to him, when I know it's all wrong for me, is torture. I didn't expect this. I didn't think I'd miss his touch, but the way he looks at me, like I'm at the center of his universe, how he'll do anything to protect me... It's all so overwhelming. And I heard his reply when JJ asked him what he'd give to keep me safe. He replied, his life. Without any hesitation. I'm sure he didn't think I could hear him from across the room, which is why he said that, but still... It means something.

He hasn't admitted he loves me... Although, somewhere inside, I can't help but think he does. I mean, he must feel something for me. It's why he shot my brother, why he manipulated me into marrying him. Why he wants to make sure I'm protected day and night... That last part, though, I can do without. I can take care of myself. I've been doing so all these years on my own, after all. Not that I want to give Alvaro a chance to get to me. That man's pure evil. I've seen Mafia men in the course of growing up with the *Camorra,* and none of the men my father interacted with came across as being as much of a monster as this guy, and Massimo agreed to pay him.

Shit, he's going to pay him a billion dollars. To keep me safe. He didn't have to think twice; he agreed right away. Not that he can't afford it. He's a wealthy man, but still. Bet if Alvaro had asked for more money, he'd have agreed to that, too. He'll do anything to keep me safe. He will. A funny sensation tickles my nose. I sniff. Why does he have to be so handsome, so sexy, so possessive... and so caring, whenever he lets down his guard? Why couldn't he have been ugly and fat and obnoxious? And why does every action of his confuse me further? My chest hurts, and my stomach clenches. Shit, I'm never going to sleep this way. I need to figure out what's happening here. I need time and space away from him to unravel exactly what I feel for him.

I shove the covers off, swing my legs over the side of the bed, and rise to my feet. At this rate, I'm never going to fall asleep. Maybe if I get something to drink, it'll help. I walk out of my room, down the corridor, and past Massimo's room. The door is slightly open. I hesitate. I should keep going, go to the kitchen as planned. I take a step forward, but in the direction of the door. Fuck it, I'm just going to peek in, and see if he's awake. Maybe he'll want to talk to me, or watch a movie or something?

I pop my head around the door, only to find the bed is empty. Hmmm. Light flows out from the bathroom, and sounds of the shower reach me. OMG, he's in there, under the shower, with water running down the demarcation of his pecs, down his sculpted abs, over his crotch and his monster cock. Is he erect? I brushed up against the column in his crotch when he pulled me up on his thigh in the elevator. And he didn't come. He would have left there with a big ol' hard-on. Is he still engorged?

Leave now, turn, and just go back to bed. Or I can go to his bed? I take a step forward, then another, until I'm standing at the foot of his bed. I glance at the mussed-up sheets. The duvet is hanging off the end, and one of the pillows has fallen to the floor. Apparently, he hasn't been able to get to sleep, either.

The shower shuts off. Silence descends. *Shit, shit, shit.* I turn to leave, when a noise reaches me. A *whack-whack-whack* of flesh meeting flesh. It can't be... Is it? Is he in there taking care of himself? Maybe I can help him... I move toward the door, then stop. *You walk in there and everything changes, you know that, right? Oh hell!* I squeeze my thighs and my fingers ball into fists at my sides. *Leave now, and nothing will change. You can continue to focus on your career.* And he... is going to pay up the money to save me. He's going to do his best to protect me. And he's my husband. It's his duty, isn't it? And my duty as his wife, is what? To ensure he doesn't have to suffer?

Not my problem. I only married him to keep my family safe. I don't really feel anything for him, do I? I don't consider him my husband. Not really. Best to get out of here.

I take another step toward the exit when a groan reaches me. The hair on my forearms rises. My scalp tingles. *Don't turn, don't.* I spin around and walk on the wooden floor, my bare feet making no sound, and draw abreast with the open bathroom door. I push it open further, and spot him leaning his forehead against the shower cubicle, completely naked. He has one hand pressed onto the tile above his head. The fingers of his other hand are wrapped around his cock.

Guess he just finished his shower, but there's no steam, so... He took a... cold shower? And when that didn't help, he decided to help himself?

Water clings to his shoulders and slides down his back to the valley between his firm ass cheeks. And that is one fine ass. I felt it up that night in the room above the bar, but seeing him like this is another thing altogether, let me tell you. Is it crazy that I want to go over there and bite it? His glutes are a work of art. They need to be memorialized in marble, and I'll be the first in line to bid for it, and spend every penny of my earnings buying it to keep it on my bed-stand.

Only, I don't need to do that because he's here, standing in front of me. The muscles of his forearms flex, his biceps tense, and the planes of his shoulders draw back as he swipes himself from crown to base. The wet sound of flesh hitting flesh fills the space. My mouth waters. My fingers tremble. Wetness squeezes out from between my legs as he continues to massage himself. His actions are vicious, almost violent, and there's a strength to them I'd never be able to replicate. He swipes himself again, and a grunt leaves his lips. Jesus, that's such a male sound—thick with pleasure, and filled with pain, and so much more I can't put into words. His breath comes in pants, and his movements increase in intensity. His forearm almost blurs as he speeds up. His entire body shudders. A nerve throbs at his temple. He grits his teeth, and squeezes his eyes shut as he slams his forehead into the wall. He opens his mouth and moans my name. "Via," he gasps. "*Gesu Cristo*, Olivia, you're killing me."

A whine bleeds from my lips. I slap my palm to my mouth, but he's already whipped his head around in my direction.

"What the—" he growls. His gray eyes are almost blue... and I know it means he's equal parts turned-on and angry-as-fuck—

"Don't stop." I lower my arms to my sides. "Please, don't stop."

He looks me up and down, his chest heaving. "Touch yourself."

"Eh?"

"Now," he snaps.

His voice seems to have a direct connection to my brain, for I slide my fingers under the waistband of my sleep shorts—I'm only wearing that and my camisole —and my fingertips brush my already throbbing clit. A moan wells up.

"Stuff your fingers inside your cunt; bring yourself to orgasm."

He slows his speed, drags his palm from head to base leisurely as he continues to stroke himself. He lowers his gaze to my crotch, I slide two fingers inside myself and gasp as shivers of heat burst from the point of contact.

"In and out, Via; repeat with me."

I hold his gaze. "In," I breathe, as I slide my fingers inside my channel. "Out."

"In," we say in tandem, as he swipes himself from tip to base.

"Out," we chant as I pull my fingers to the edge of my slit, and "in." I add a third finger inside and gasp when the breadth stretches me.

"Out." He drags his hand to the crown of his dick.

"Faster," he says through gritted teeth. His ministrations pick up speed, and so do mine. I bring my hand up to squeeze my nipple as I keep pace with him.

"In," he growls.

"Out," I gasp.

"In," he snaps.

"Out," I whine as a trembling grips me. My entire body shudders as the pressure builds at the base of my spine.

"Stay with me, Via," he says in a hard voice.

A bead of sweat slides down my temple. I pant, gasp, and weave my fingers in and out of myself. In and out. The pressure squeezes in on itself. I moan, shake my head. "I'm coming."

"Don't you dare."

His eyes grow fierce, and his jaw clenches. The fingers he holds above his head clench into a fist. His movements grow frantic; the slap of wet flesh against flesh increases in momentum.

The orgasm rocks against my core, sending shudders of liquid heat spurting up my spine. "I can't. I can't."

"You can." He bares his teeth, and holds my gaze.

His spine bends, and my back curves. Every part of me cries out for release. His shoulders seem to swell, his biceps bend, and his forearms grow so tight, I can see every individual vein outlined under his skin. Then finally, finally, he growls, "Come with me," and with a cry, my orgasm sweeps through me.

46

Massimo

She throws her head back and cries as she comes. I lower my free hand to hold it under my cock and spill myself into my palm. I come and come, and she pants, watching me from under her hooded eyes.

"Take off your top," I snap.

She blinks then, with a trembling hand, pulls off her camisole and drops it to the floor.

"Come here, *Stellina*."

Without hesitation, she walks forward, coming to a halt in front of me.

The aftershocks of my climax jolt through me and I raise my palm full of my cum and smear it over her breasts. Her breath catches, and her gaze grows wide. She watches as I massage the gooey mess into her tits, her nipples growing so hard they resemble bullets. I bend to suck on one of them, and she moans. I bring my other hand up to fondle her other breast. I pinch her nipple, and she cries out, then grabs hold of my shoulders as I suckle at her breast. I release the nipple with a pop, then turn my attention to the other breast. I squeeze the first one, then swirl my tongue around the nipple of the other. Her spine curve, and she pushes her breast into my mouth. I grip her under her butt and haul her up, she wraps her legs around my waist.

"Do you want me, Via? Do you want this?"

She tips up her chin, then nods.

"Are you sure?"

Her lips curve. "Can you shut up and fuck me already?"

I crash my mouth into hers and she gasps, then parts her lips. I thrust my tongue in between them, drag them over her teeth. She winds her fingers about my neck, plasters herself to me. Her breasts flatten against my chest and her entire body shudders. I lick inside her mouth, and she moans. I walk out of the bathroom toward my bed, then throw her down on the mattress. She bounces once, her hair in a cloud about her shoulders. I bend down, grab the waistband of her sleep shorts and pull them off. She shivers, then parts her legs, showing off the pink flesh between her thighs. Completely bare, just as I remember her. Just how I like it.

I slide my palms under her and squeeze her butt. I tilt her up, and press my nose into her pussy. I draw in a deep breath, she moans. She's every bit as aromatic as I remember.

I lick her from rear to clit, and she mewls.

I swirl my tongue around her clit, and she pushes her pelvis up, chasing the feel of my mouth.

I lift her higher, leaving only her shoulders and head on the bed, then stab my tongue inside her pussy.

"Massimo, you're killing me."

"I haven't even started." I straighten, then flip her over.

"Wha—?" Eyes wide, she stares over her shoulder. "What are you doing?" Her voice is high.

I grip her hips and urge her up so she thrusts out her butt. Then flatten my palm on her back, encouraging her to push her face into her mattress.

"Massimo, are you going to—"

"Fuck your ass? You bet." I hold her gaze. "Unless you'd rather I not."

She bites down on her lower lip.

"What's it to be, Via? Yes, or no?"

She hesitates, then nods.

"Good girl."

I walk around her to the drawer in the nightstand, and pull out a tube and a vibrator.

"What is that?" Her tone is tinged with worry.

"Shh." I walk over and place the items near her knees.

Her gaze widens, "Is that a vibrator? Why do you need a vibrator?"

"You'll see."

"Did you buy those, anticipating I'd be here with you, in your room?"

"What do you think?"

She firms her lips. "Very confident of yourself, aren't you?"

"You're here, aren't you?"

"I think I should leav—"

I spank her butt.

She yells, "What the hell! Why did you do that?"

I slap her other butt cheek, then go back to the first, then the other. I alternate between her ass cheeks and she whines, then moans. She digs her fingers into the mattress, and thrusts out her butt even further. I slide my fingers between her pussy lips and groan.

"*Gesù Cristo,* you're soaking."

"I don't know why, when I hate it when you spank me," she snaps.

"And we both know, that's not true." I place a knee on the mattress. " Slide your knees further apart, baby."

She complies, and goddamn, much as she may protest, her body craves the kind of pleasure only I can give her. Only I know what she wants. Only I can bring her to the edge of arousal and hold her there while I continue to wring pleasure from her body, so when she finally comes it will be more intense than any orgasm she's ever had before.

I snatch up the lube and trail it between her butt cheeks.

She shivers.

"Is it cold?" I ask.

"N… no… I'm just nervous."

"Don't be. I promise, I'll make you come so hard, it'll be worth it."

I brush my fingers across the knot of nerves between her butt cheeks. She clenches, and I bend and kiss the curve of her butt.

"Relax." I slide my hand around to play with her clit. She draws in a sharp breath, then the tension seems to leave her muscles. She curves her tailbone into my touch, and I slip a finger inside her backhole. I weave it in and out of her as I strum her pussy lips. She moans, and moisture beads her core. A fat bead of her cum slides down her inner thigh. I continue to pleasure her enough that she relaxes further. I slide another finger inside her. I curl my digits, and she shivers. Her clit engorges and I slip my other fingers into her cunt. I press my thumb into her clit, and rub her. She clamps down on my fingers.

"Massimo please," she huffs. "Please, Massimo."

I pull my fingers out of her, then grab the vibrator. The buzz of the device fills the space. Her gaze widens. She opens her mouth to protest, but before she can speak, I hold the wand to her clit.

"Jesus," she moans. The skin over her knuckles stretches white, her eyelids draw down.

I position my cock against her back opening, then slide the vibrator inside her pussy.

Instantly her back curves, and her shoulder shudders. She begins to ride the device, and I slide into her. I brush up against the rim of her sphincter, and she freezes. I bend over and cup her breast. I squeeze her nipple, slide the gadget deep inside her, and she whimpers. I grind my heel into her clit and her entire body seems to vibrate. She opens up for me and I slip through the tight ring of muscle to sink inside her.

She groans. "Oh, my god, it's too much. I can't take it. I can't."

"You can, *Stellina*. You will do this."

I move the vibrator in and out of her, then continue to pluck on her nipple, giving her time to adjust to my size. Bit by bit, her body relaxes, and the tension drains out of her butt muscles. I release her breast, hold her hip, and begin to move.

47

Olivia

I've always refused anal with anyone else, but with Massimo he went right there the first time we met. I knew he'd prep me first. I knew he'd make it good for me. And he had. But this? Oh, my god! I never imagined how intense it would be, how confident his touch. How he'd play my body like it was one of his guns. How he'd use the vibrator to drive me to the edge and back.

The combination of the heat of his body at my back, the toy in my pussy, and his dick in my ass as he fucks me, is too much. The climax sweeps through me. My pussy spasms, my breasts swell, the quivering streams out from my core up my spine, and I shatter. He lets the vibrator fall to the bed, then hauls me up and holds me as my body convulses in the aftermath.

He turns my head and kisses me. It's a deep, drugging, meeting of our lips. His taste of mint and something darker sinks into my tongue. His mouth covers mine, and his tongue slides over mine. His scent envelops me, and my head spins. I bring my arms up and around his neck. Still kissing me, he holds my hips and begins to move. He pulls his dick out until it's balanced at the rim of my back entrance, then he pushes forward. He sinks inside me, and his balls slap against the backs of my thighs.

I'm spread around his cock, stretched until it feels like I can't breathe. I gasp, and he swallows the sound. He brings his hand to my soaking cunt and begins to finger fuck me. The next time he stuffs his dick inside, he bottoms out and… It's too much for me. My body trembles, and my pussy flutters around his fingers. He adds a third and a fourth, and dear God, I'm surrounded by him.

He's consuming me, surrounding me, engulfing me. This is what I was afraid of—losing myself so completely that I'll never be able to recover from it. I open my mouth and he deepens the kiss even further. He's eating me up and there's nothing I can do to stop him. He thrusts his fingers inside me, and slams into me with such force the entire bed shakes. The headboard slaps against the wall and he tears his mouth from mine. He holds my gaze, the medley of confused feelings inside me mirrored on his features. His eyebrows draw down as he brushes my lips with his… gently, so gently. A tear squeezes out from the corner of my eye. He darts down, licks it up, then twists his fingers inside me. This time, the climax rolls up from where we are connected. He fucks me again, and his dick thickens inside me until I'm sure he's going to cleave me in half.

"Come for me," he whispers, and together we hurtle over the edge.

When I open my eyes next, I'm curled up on his chest, his thick arm pinning me to him. *Thud-thud-thud;* the drumbeat of his heart mirrors mine. Good to know I'm not the only one shaken by what just happened. Speaking of, I need to get away from him to salvage what little of my brain power is still left. I begin to pull away, but he doesn't release me.

I glance up to find he's watching me with angry eyes.

"What?" I yawn. "What's wrong?"

His gaze intensifies. A nerve throbs at his temple. There's a furrow between his eyebrows, and I reach up to smooth it. He pulls away.

I blink.

"What is it, Massimo?" I ask cautiously.

"When were you going to tell me?"

I frown, "Tell you what?"

"Don't pretend you don't know what I'm talking about."

"But I don't know what you're talking about." I half-smile, but he glares at me, and the smile drops from my face. "I really have no idea what you're talking about," I confess.

"Oh?" He rubs his fingers over the now healed cuts on my thigh.

I shrink away, but he grips my hip and holds me in place.

"How long have you been cutting yourself, Via?"

"Cutting myself? I don't cut myself. I just fell and hurt myself. I—"

"Don't bullshit me." His eyebrows slash down. "Is it the incident with the shooter that prompted this? Is it the pressure of rebuilding your career from scratch? How long has this been happening?"

I blow out a breath. "Not long, okay? And it's only a few cuts, in a place where no one else can see—"

"I can see it." He peers into my eyes. "You're hurting, Via. What you've been through is not easy. It's understandable that a part of you is still trying to cope with it. Also, you forget something."

"Oh?" I tip up my chin. "And what is it that I'm forgetting?"

"This body is mine, Via. Mine. You can't cut it, or scar it, or do anything intentionally to hurt it, because it belongs to me, Via. You feel me?"

I swallow. A pressure builds at the backs of my eyes. Something huge seems to have dug itself into my chest and refuses to let go. "You're a jerkass, you know that? How dare you talk about my body like it's your possession."

"Because it is. Your every breath, every thought, every emotion is owned by me. When you hurt yourself, you hurt me; you are a part of me, Via. And I will not let you harm what is mine."

A hot sensation grips my chest. My nose stings. My cheeks hurt. I blink away the tears that threaten to trickle out and set my jaw. "You're crazy."

"And you're going to see a psychologist about this."

"Am not." I jut out my chin. "It's a phase. It'll pass; that's all it is, I promise."

"I understand why you cut yourself. I understand how you feel better when you do it, but the release is temporary. It's going to harm you more in the long term, and I won't let you do that to yourself, Via."

Of course he's right and I know it, but couldn't he have let me keep this secret a little longer? I squeeze my eyes shut.

"Fine, I'll see a psychologist," I mumble.

"Besides, now that we've started fucking again, that should relieve most of the pressure. I plan to make you orgasm so hard and so often that the rush of endorphins from the climaxes I grant you will ensure that you don't miss the high from the cutting."

I pop open my eyelids and gape. "You sure have an ego the size of the budget of a Marvel movie."

He blinks. "You say the weirdest things."

"I'm an actress; deal with my version of pop culture references, will you?" I try to shift away from him, but he doesn't release me. "Let me go." I scowl.

"Why?" he shoots back.

"I want to head back to my room."

"No way. You're sleeping with me tonight."

"I don't want to sleep with you."

"Liar." He digs his fingers into my side and I cackle.

"Hey, not fair." I wriggle around, trying to get out of his reach, but he follows me. He tickles me under my arm and down my torso, and laughter wells up my throat. "Please don't," I gasp. "Please, please don't."

He intensifies his efforts and soon I am rolling in his grasp, laughing until tears slide down my cheeks. He turns me over, then fits himself to me, spooning me. Oh my god, I'd forgotten how good he is at this. The warmth of his body surrounds me, and his arm around my middle holds me close. His body faithfully follows ever line of mine, and it feels like I am wearing him like a big, luscious, warm overcoat. I really should try to get away from him, but maybe I can close my eyes for just a few minutes first?

When I wake up next, early morning light shines through the gap between the curtains. We're still in the same position, only he's covered us both with a blanket. The warmth is like a drugging cocoon, pulling me in, inviting me to fall asleep again. I manage to turn in the circle of his arm to face him. His eyes are shut, and his dark hair falls over his forehead, tousled by my fingers, no doubt. His cheeks are slightly flushed, and his jaw holds none of the tension that characterizes his every waking moment. His mouth, that luscious mouth, is right there. All I have to do is lean forward and press my lips to his, and savor the feel of his firm lips against mine. And if I do, I'll never be able to get him out of my head. I edge back carefully, until his arm slips off of me. I manage to slide off of the bed without waking him up. I creep around the bed, grab my sleep shorts and pull them on, then walk into the bathroom to retrieve my camisole. I shrug it on, then with one last look at his massive figure sprawled on the bed, I leave.

I go to my room, have a shower and get dressed. I need to get out of here. I need a little time to clear my head. I glance out the window at the security personnel outside. One of them stands outside the gate. And there's a car on the opposite side of the road. I can't be sure, but it looks like the men in there are asleep. Doesn't matter. I'm sure they're going to follow me when I leave.

48

———————

Massimo

The phone buzzing on my nightstand penetrates my sleep. I snap open my eyes, turning to find the space next to me on the bed is empty. Huh? I reach for my phone and answer it. "This had better be urgent."

"We lost her. I'm so sorry. One minute she was there; the next she was gone." Peter's voice is toneless.

The hair on the back of my neck rises. *The fuck?* I jerk my head back in the direction of the empty space next to me on the bed. Rake my gaze around the room and find the sleep shorts I tore off her are also gone. *Fuck, fuck, fuck.* How could I have not woken up when she left the bed?

"Where did she go? What do you mean you lost her?" I growl.

"She drove to the mall, and we followed her in. She walked into a store, and never came out.'

"Why didn't you stop her from leaving the house?"

"Those were not our instructions, Sir."

He's right. I hadn't intended for her to be a prisoner. I merely wanted her to be protected, and for her to be followed everywhere.

"Have you tried her number?"

"She's not picking up," the man says warily.

"And you call yourself trained personnel? I'm going to have your head!" I lower the phone and take a deep breath. It won't help to blame these men. I need their help. I need to find her before that *pezzo di merda* Alvaro gets to her.

I raise the phone to my ear. "Get back to my house; I'll meet you downstairs."

I disconnect and try her number, but it goes to voicemail. *Fuck!* I raise my phone, ready to throw it across the room, then catch myself. Keep it together, *stronzo*, you need to stay calm and figure out what to do to ensure she's safe.

I call her once more, not surprised when she doesn't pick up. I hang up and call JJ Kane next. He listens to my update and promises he'll be here as soon as possible. I call Michael next, and when he answers I tell him Olivia is missing. Michael's not very complimentary about the fact that we lost her; he also assures me that he has additional men on their way to me already. Then, he tells me to be vigilant, before hanging up.

I toss the phone aside and take a quick shower. By the time I'm dressed and headed downstairs, the doorbell rings. I open it and JJ stands there, a scowl on his face.

"Jesus, Sovrano, didn't you tell your woman how important it was not to stray from her security detail?"

"And you think she'd listen to me?"

"You should have tied her up and kept her here until we found Alvaro."

"And have her hate me?"

"At least she would've been safe." He brushes past me and walks inside.

"Have you ever been in love?" I call after him.

"Are you kidding me?" He glances over his shoulder. "The only four-letter words in my life don't begin with L."

"Wait until you meet someone you fall for. Then you'll know how difficult it is to straddle that line between doing what's best for them, but not dictate their every action."

"That will never happen," his lips twist, "I've passed the age where I'm looking for love."

"That's when it always finds you."

He looks at me like I have gone crazy. "You okay, ol' chap?"

I shake my head. "Not really, no. I woke up to find my wife gone, and your men lost her." I stab a finger in his direction. "If anything happens to her—"

"Hold on." He gestures toward the living room. "It's still early, but you look like you could do with a drink."

"I don't need you to manage me."

His brows draw down. "It would help if you'd calm down, so we can decide what to do next."

"I'm going to kill the men who let her out of their sight."

"And how is that going to help us find her? She knew she was under threat.

She was there when Alvaro came over and threatened her. And yet, she chose to give her bodyguards the slip. Why is that?"

"How the hell am I supposed to know what goes on in her mind?" I drag my fingers through my hair. That drink was starting to sound very good right now.

"She's your wife, isn't she? Surely, you must know why she decided to leave home and run away?"

"Fuck!" I stomp through the living room and to the bar in the far corner. I pour the whiskey into a glass and chug it down. The alcohol bursts in my stomach, releasing a trail of warmth in its wake. I set the glass down and turn to him. "Maybe she wasn't very happy about the marriage?" Fuck knows why I'm saying that aloud, and to JJ. He's not family, but given my brothers are not here at the moment, he's the closest I have to a sounding board. Considering he used to be our rival once upon a time… It's strange that I have come to rely on him so much since getting here.

He tilts his head. "So, she didn't want to get married, I take it?"

"Something like that."

"But she did marry you anyway…"

"I didn't give her a choice," I squeeze the bridge of my nose, "I told her if she didn't marry me, we wouldn't extend our protection to her family."

"Leaving them vulnerable to all of their enemies." He whistles. "No wonder she's pissed at you."

"No way was I walking away from her. I did what I had to do to ensure she became mine."

"Yet, you didn't lock her down to prevent her from walking out on you."

"Things had improved between us since the wedding. I thought she was coming around to the idea of being my wife. I thought I wouldn't force her into doing anything else she didn't want to do, as a show of good faith."

He walks over to the bar and tops up my glass, then pulls out a glass for himself and pours whiskey into it. "You should realize there are no half-measures here, my friend. You started the ball rolling in a certain direction when you maneuvered her into marrying you. It's best you keep to that path until you've tied down her loyalty completely."

"How do I do that?"

He raises his glass in my direction. "Get her pregnant. Bind her to you in such an irreversible fashion that she's too preoccupied to think of escaping, and even if she wanted to, she wouldn't, for the good of the child."

I stare at him. "That would mean making it even more difficult for her to pursue her career as an actress."

"There are actresses who've had children," he points out.

"That profession is so fickle, and having children means she'd have to devote time to them, time that would take her away from following her dream."

"She's deferring it, not giving it up."

I scowl at him. "You sound like you've given this some thought."

"Unlike you, I don't have a heart." He tosses back the whiskey and places his glass on the table with a thunk. "And no, I've never been in a situation where I needed to strategize to keep a woman tied to me. All I did was think it through logically."

"Is that what you would do if you were in my situation?"

His lips twist. "Your woman is the most important thing to you, above anything else, right?"

I nod.

"You value her life more than her career, more than her right to choose, am I right?"

I glance away. *Do I?* She already hates me. Would I risk alienating her completely by binding her to me in this fashion? And then, she'll always be safe. And she'll be happy. I'll make sure she's happy.

I turn to JJ. "What do we do next?"

49

Olivia

I found a mall that opened early in London and made it there with my security in tow. Thank God for early morning shoppers. You would think seven a.m. was a little too early to buy clothes and shoes, but apparently not, for there was enough traffic in the hallways of the mall to help me in my quest. I snuck into a clothes shop, ducked behind a display, grabbed a few T-shirts and headed for the changing rooms at the back. There was no one there, so I ducked into the employees' exit and took the service elevator down. Then I ran to my car and peeled out of the parking lot.

Now, I race the car down the motorway that leads out of London. I watch the side mirror, but I can't see the car that followed me to the mall. Some of the tension drains out of my shoulders. I did it. I gave them the slip. Also, I'm not too worried because Alvaro gave Massimo forty-eight hours to pay the money. That should buy me enough time to, at least, begin to figure things out. I hope.

I fiddle with the radio, find a station that plays rock tunes, then make sure to keep under the speed limit. The last thing I need is a speeding ticket. With every mile that I leave the city behind, the rigidity in my body eases. I sing along to a classic rock anthem, *"Smooth Up in Ya"* by the Bullet Boys—a song my brother introduced me to. It's one of the few things we bonded over. He loved rock anthems, and I loved to listen to them with him. This was before he grew up and decided he was going to become a typical Mafia man, right down to his attitude toward women.

And is my husband any different? Massimo isn't Diego, that's for sure. He's not as uncaring, or as heartless. Oh, he is as much of a Mafioso, but he'd never barter a woman to the likes of Alvaro. No, he only engineered things so he could force me to marry him. And I can't help but feel that he did it because he wanted me so much. Even if I'm still angry with him about it, maybe I should have told him I needed some space. But would he ever have allowed me to drive out on my own? Of course, not. He's so possessive; and I admit, I do find it hot. But it also worries me that I like it so much. He told me he doesn't want me to hurt myself because it'd be like hurting him, because I'm a part of him, and while that's probably the most romantic thing anyone has ever told me, it's also alarming. I don't want to get swallowed up by his dominance. I don't want to be so dazzled by his charisma that I forget who I am and what I want out of life, what I've sacrificed to get this far.

No, I did the right thing. I just need space and time to think. To figure things out. And I can't do that when I'm with him or under his roof, surrounded by reminders of his presence. I need some perspective on everything that's happened.

I also need to figure out birth control. He's been using condoms, but it's best to be doubly protected. If I become pregnant now... I shake my head. Having Massimo's baby, a boy or girl who looks like both of us? Am I ready to be a mother, when I haven't even managed to get my career off the ground?

It would have been so much easier if he hadn't gotten engaged to my sister. If I'd met him again, under different circumstances... I still wouldn't have been able to stop myself from sleeping with him. And then... I would have forced myself to walk away from him. No wonder he made sure I married him.

If only I weren't so angry with him. If only I weren't already in love with him.

My foot slips off the gas and the car slows down. The car behind me honks, then veers around and drives past, the driver not looking very pleased. I keep my speed at half of what it was. I'm in love with *him*?

I'm in *love* with him.

Maybe a part of me always knew it, but didn't want to accept it. And it's not just about the sex, either. Although that last performance by him most certainly deserves an Oscar. I snicker. Ugh, bad pun, but you know what I mean.

Perhaps I fell for him that first night, when I heard his voice at the bar, even before I saw him, as he growled, *you've had enough*. The first time I smelled that spice and citrus and smoky firewood scent of his. The first time he ordered me to call out his name when I came. When he compared my muscles to liquid gold. When I walked into Solene's engagement party and tripped into him, after being sure I'd never see him again. When I was injured and half-conscious, with the painkillers still in my system, and I heard his voice asking me to come back to him. Later, when I woke up in the hospital, and the first thing I saw was his features.

When he believed I could still be an actress, despite the scar on my face. When he saved me from the fate my brother had planned for me. When I walked down the aisle toward him... Or maybe, when he moved countries to be with me?

He's shown me he's the kind of husband my father never could be for my mother. He's been in my corner, every step of the way. And I keep coming back to the fact that he shot my brother, who'd have married me off to a monster, then maimed said monster, who dared to touch me; it endeared him to me further.

But really, before all of that, I was his the first time I set eyes on him. Only, I've been fighting him every step of the way. Does love-at-first-sight even exist? Because it sure as hell feels like I'm living it. I reach over, turn off the radio, and keep driving.

How can I feel so strongly for him, yet not want to acknowledge it? Are my prejudices about the Mafia so ingrained that I'd risk running into those who could harm me, rather than staying with the one man who'd give his life to protect me? Am I so focused on holding onto my independence that I'm willing to compromise my safety for it? This... It makes no sense. I make no sense.

My phone rings. I glance at the dash, and Massimo's name pops up. I ignore it. This is the third time he's called me. To be honest, I'm surprised he hasn't been calling nonstop. The call disconnects, then starts ringing again. Oh hell, I'm going to have to answer his call at some point, right? He must be worried sick; I owe him that much. I press the button on the side of the steering wheel, and the call picks up.

"Massimo?"

I glance at the side mirror to find a new car falling behind me. Hmm.

There's silence for a beat, another, then, "You're safe, Via?" His voice is so calm, the tone so even, I gulp. This is not good. He's pissed at me. His anger all but leaps out at me from the call. *Shit. Shit. Shit. Of course he's angry, what else did you expect?* Still, realizing he's angry, hearing him when he's angry, and knowing I'm going to have to face him when he's angry, is another thing altogether.

"Via?" A note of impatience enters his tone. "You okay?"

"Of course I am." I draw in a breath. Why am I acting like such a bitch? I'm angry with myself for behaving the way I did, so why am I taking my anger out on him?

"Massimo, I—"

He interrupts me,. "I'm in a car en route to you. I know where you are, Via."

"You do?" I frown.

"Your car and your phone are both—"

"Tagged?" I burst out. "You're tracking me?"

"You didn't think I'd let you go anywhere without making sure I know exactly where you are, did you? The Mexican cartel is after you."

Goddamn! I slap the steering wheel. Of course he knows where I am.

"You're joking, right?" I gape.

See? This is what happens. Every time I want to act rationally around him, he goes and does something so alphaholish, so presumptuous, that I want to smack him on the head, or better still, on that perfectly tight ass of his.

"Do you think I'm joking?" he growls.

Asshole. "Well, since you know where I am, you can follow me on whichever app you're using to track me." I reach for the button to disconnect the call when—

"I'm sorry, Via," his tone lowers in pitch. The emotion in his words is unmistakable.

A-n-d, there he is. That sensitive, caring man I know, who exists under that jerkface exterior he likes to present to the world.

"You... you have nothing to be sorry about, I—"

"I do. I'm not sorry for killing your brother, but I am sorry I manipulated you into marrying me. I wish I could have gone about it differently, but I had to work with the hand I was dealt. I couldn't let go of you, Via." I hear him swallow. "*You* didn't want me to let go of you."

"Ha, that's what you'd like to think." I glance in the side mirror to find the car I'd spotted earlier drawing closer.

"This is strange," I mutter.

"What's strange?"

"Eh, nothing, just this car that's been following me and—"

Another car speeds up until it's abreast, then zooms forward into my lane, forcing me to stop.

"What the hell!" I yell as I slam on the brakes. Fear is a sharp, pungent taste in my mouth. Adrenaline laces my blood.

"Via, what the hell is happening?" His voice is tight, like he's reined in all of his emotions. His strength pours through the airwaves, and I hold onto it.

"There's a car in front of me, one behind me, and they've forced me to stop." My voice wavers and I swallow down the uncertainty bubbling up. "Someone... No, two men have gotten out of the car in front. They're coming toward me. Oh my god! They're armed, Massimo," I cry out.

"Listen to me, Via. Don't panic. Don't show them any fear. I'm on my way, and I have JJ tracking down Alvaro, as we speak. I will make sure you're safe, baby, you get me?"

"Y-yes." I squeeze my fingers around the steering wheel. "I'm sorry I evaded the bodyguards the way I did. I'm so stupid, Massimo. I wasn't thinking. I just didn't want to lose myself to you completely. I wanted to keep a part of me for myself. I wanted to hold onto something that would help me stay focused on my career. It means a lot to me to be an actress, know what I mean?"

"I know, baby, and you will, I promise." His voice softens, and oh, god, hearing him call me baby, my heart seems to melt into mush. My arms and legs tremble. I've been so, so stupid. Such an idiot. I only have myself to blame for landing in this situation.

"I'm so sorry for running from you. So sorry for eluding my security detail. I wasn't thinking clearly; I felt so overwhelmed. I needed space to figure everything out, you know?"

"You'll be fine Via, I promise."

The men reach the car door. One of them points a gun at me.

"They're going to shoot me, Massimo," I cry out.

"No, they won't. You're more valuable to them alive. You stay calm, and don't try anything stupid. I'm going to find you, you hear me?"

One of the men points to my door with his gun and indicates I should open it.

"I… I love you, Massimo." I unlock the door and the man pulls it open.

He raises the butt of his gun.

"No!" I scream, as he brings it down toward me.

50

—————

Massimo

"No!" she screams.

"Via! Via!" I yell as I hear the sounds of a scuffle, the unmistakable sound of someone being hit.

"Via!" My heart leaps into my throat. I clutch at my phone with such force that my fingers hurt.

I hear her gasp of pain. A car door slams shut, then... Nothing. I lower the handset and glance at the two unmoving dots on the screen. Her car and her phone. "*Goddammit,* they have her." I squeeze my fingers around my phone so hard, the case cracks.

JJ, who's driving the car, shoots me a sideways glance. "Get a hold of yourself, ol' chap, we'll find her."

"I am going to kill the *bastardo*!" Anger twists my guts. My heart seems to have dropped to my stomach. My fingers are trembling as I lower them to my sides. "If he thinks he can antagonize us and get away with it, he's so fucking wrong."

"My guess is, he is not going to harm her. He's taken her, simply to make a point."

"Well, he's fucking with the wrong man." I slide my hand into my pocket and my fingers brush up against the pendant. Perhaps this idea of Michael's to legalize the *Cosa Nostra* businesses is all wrong. What's the point in doing that, if I'm not going to be able to take care of what's mine? I pull my hand out of my pocket and pat the trusty weight at the small of my back. As long as I have my gun, I'll be able to protect her, no matter what the future of the *Cosa Nostra*.

"We know where Alvaro is. We'll get to her in time, I promise," JJ says in a hard voice.

I drag my fingers through my hair and stare out the window. How had I not anticipated something like this happening? Why hadn't I been better prepared? I'm used to being on high alert at all times, but something about being with her has lowered my defenses. Making love to her last night—and it was that; it most definitely was not fucking—connecting me with her in a way I had with no one else, changed something inside me. I fell into a deep, dreamless sleep, and wasn't aware of anything else. And I'm the one who put her in this spot. I should have killed him when I had the chance. But I didn't. And now he's taken her.

JJ's phone rings, and he puts it on speaker.

"We're at Alvaro's place; no movement here yet," one of his men says.

"Keep a lookout, and let me know when they bring her there," JJ orders them before he cuts the call.

"How long?" I glance at the blue dot on the screen.

"Fifty minutes—an hour, tops."

"Get us there in thirty," I growl.

He shoots me a sideways glance, then steps on the accelerator. The car leaps forward.

My phone rings again. I glance at the screen, and it says *Unknown number*. *Motherfucker!* I answer the call and growl, "Where is she?"

A chuckle comes down the line. "You saw her only an hour ago. What's the hurry?" By the accent, it's clear it's Alvaro.

"I am going to kill you for this, you *testa di cazzo!*"

He merely laughs. Anger shoots up my spine and adrenaline laces my blood. I lean forward and dig my heels into the floor of the car. "Don't you fucking hurt her, you hear me?!"

"Two billion dollars," he murmurs, "or you'll never see her again. But first, maybe I'll shoot off her finger like you did mine."

"You *carogna*, you motherfucking *figlio di puttana*—"

The line goes dead. My heart slams into my ribcage. My stomach folds in on itself. I taste bile in my mouth and swallow down the taste of fear. She'll be fine; she has to be fine.

Drawing his own conclusions from the call, JJ steps on the accelerator so the car speeds up even more. The countryside whizzes by. I dial Michael's number.

"*Pronto!*" he answers on the first ring.

"He doubled the amount. I need to do whatever it takes to get that money," I say through gritted teeth.

"It's going to take a while to get this together," Michael says in an even tone.

"I don't have time." I roll my shoulders. "Do whatever it takes. Liquidate all of my assets, if necessary."

In the silence that follows, I sense him nod. Then, "I'm on it. Wait for my message." The line goes dead.

Twenty minutes later, we ease onto a side road and park next to the cars already there. Through the trees, the red-bricked Victorian building is visible. JJ busted all of the speed limits getting here. No doubt, we set off a lot of speed cameras on the way. And no doubt, he has enough clout with the cops to take care of it, too.

I get out of the vehicle and JJ follows. Peter walks over to join us. He's the one who called to let us know when Alvaro's men brought Via to the house.

"They still in there?" JJ asks.

The other man nods.

"We need to go in." I turn to head toward the house, but JJ steps in front of me.

"We need to think this through," he insists.

"That's the problem with you Brits, you think too much," I growl.

"And you Italians are so intent on shooting from the hip, you don't care if you end up hurting yourselves in the process," JJ retorts. "We need to figure out a plan to go in, or else we're putting ourselves at risk."

"She's at risk inside there. I can't stand around doing nothing while that bastard is doing god-knows-what to her."

"And if you end up getting hurt, you won't be able to help her at all."

I glance in the direction of the house, then back at him. He's right, of course. I jerk my chin. "You have two minutes."

"There are two exits, front and back, both guarded. Guards around the perimeter, snipers watching the approach. He's sewn down tight," Peter confirms.

"Are you saying there's no way in there without being noticed?"

He hesitates. "It doesn't seem likely, no," he finally says.

"Fuck." I turn away to glance at the house again. "I'm going in through the front door."

"That's suicide," Peter says flatly.

I slide my fingers inside my pocket and brush my fingers over the horseshoe pendant on her chain. "Better than hanging around here while he has her in his possession," I growl.

JJ glances between me and Peter. "Maybe we could use the situation to our advantage?"

51

Olivia

The pain at the back of my eyeballs cuts through my sleep. It feels like someone is hammering the inside of my head. I open my eyes, and the light slices straight to my brain. I swallow and my tongue feels like it's too swollen to fill my mouth.

I move my arms and legs, and realize I'm slumped forward in a chair. At least I'm not tied up or anything. My forehead throbs. I touch my fingers to it, and they come away wet. I glance at my hand and see blood, then wince. It could've been worse; they could've shot me. A shiver grips me. But I'm fine, and except for the wound on my forehead, no other part of me seems to be hurt. I groan, then press the heels of my palms into my eyes.

I stay like that for a few seconds, until the drumming in my head seems to decrease in intensity. I lower my arms and glance around the room. It's empty, save for another chair opposite me. The bay windows let in enough light to illuminate the corners of the room. I rise to my feet, pleased to see my legs are steady, then walk over to the window and peer out. I'm on the ground floor, facing a rolling lawn, at the edge of which are big evergreens. Everything looks peaceful, like a postcard of a classic British countryside.

How long have I been out? Half an hour, maybe? My head throbs again. I wince. Hopefully the wound will heal without leaving a mark to compete with the scar on my cheek. Asshole hit me with his gun. I lower my arm to my side.

Goddamn, how could I have been so stupid? I never should have left the house this morning and given my security the slip. I can't even imagine how pissed Massimo must be with me. He called me 'baby' over the phone… It was probably only his concern speaking, but it felt so good. He cares; he really does. I mean, I knew that, of course, but haven't wanted to acknowledge it. Nothing like being taken away from everything you hold dear to put things in perspective, eh?

The door behind me opens, and I spin around to find a man silhouetted in the doorway. He walks over to stand behind the chair facing me. Dark hair, swarthy features, lifeless eyes, it's the same guy who threatened me at the restaurant. It's Alvaro. He has a bandage across his forehead, and another wrapped around his left palm, which is now missing his forefinger. Massimo should have shot him dead when he had the chance.

"What do you want?" I set my jaw.

"Why don't you have a seat?" he says in an affable voice. A voice I don't trust. Not one bit.

When I don't move, he blows out a breath, then uses his uninjured arm to turn the chair around. He straddles it. "Please, I'm not going to hurt you."

"Why did you bring me here?"

"Have a seat first, and I'll answer your questions."

I hesitate, then walk over to sink into the chair. I keep my spine erect, and shove away the pain that drums at my temples. "Massimo agreed to pay you already."

"Indeed. And he's going to pay even more to see you safe."

"You've been in touch with him?" I lean forward in my seat.

"If I'm not mistaken, he'll be here very soon."

Thank God! A spurt of satisfaction fills my chest. "You needn't have brought me here. You could have called him up and struck a bargain with him on the phone."

"Maybe." He raises his shoulder. "But you're my leverage, and I'm a business man. I saw an opportunity to make even more money from the transaction, and I took it."

He drags his gaze down my body, and my flesh crawls.

"Of course, considering I lost a finger in the process, I should keep you for myself as compensation for what you put me through," he muses.

My heart jumps into my throat, and my ribcage contracts. I tip up my chin, and force myself to stay calm. "But you're not going to do that. You don't want to make enemies of the *Cosa Nostra*, do you?" I fold my hands in my lap.

"Smart, as well as good-looking; except for that scar." He touches his cheek.

I stiffen.

"How did it feel taking the hit for your friend? She got to live her happily ever after and become the star of a musical. A role which should have been yours."

"It was never meant to be mine. I was always the understudy."

"You got elevated to the part of the lead. The director believed in you."

I scowl. "How do you know all of this?"

"I have my sources." He kicks out his legs. "With the scar, your roles are very limited. You must be aware of that."

"I'll take my chances." I firm my lips.

"The good thing about Hollywood is, it provides a great channel to funnel my money into."

I tilt my head. "I have no idea what you mean."

"You're a smart woman; you know how it works. Movies need money, a lot of money, to get made. And the kinds of films that make it to the wide screen in today's world need double that, in some cases."

"So?" I shuffle my feet. "What's that got to do with me?"

"Come with me, and I'll make you the lead in the latest movie from a very prominent studio, with a three-time Oscar-winning director at the helm. It also costars a Golden Globe and BAFTA-nominated lead, who is the next big thing in Hollywood. The script had a bidding war before the studio acquired it. All indications are, it's the next franchise-spawning blockbuster."

"Let me get this right. If I come with you of my own free will, you'll make me a star?"

"Your face will be on billboards in all of the biggest movie watching countries in the world. You may be scarred, but your reputation is that of a solid actress. Do your job, and you'll be the one who walks away with the awards."

"And in return, I'll be your slave, I suppose?"

"Among other things. You'll be the investment that earns me many times the money I put in."

"You're crazy." I glance away.

"Is it because you feel something for your husband? Is that what's stopping you from taking me up on this offer?"

I open my mouth to answer, and he holds up his hand.

"Think carefully before you turn me down. This is your chance to achieve the dream you've always wanted."

"You don't know what my dreams are," I snap.

"Don't I? Your husband shot your brother, and you didn't do anything about it."

"My brother was a misguided man who was hell-bent on selling me to you. My husband saved me."

"And the only reason you married him was to ensure the safety of your family."

I peer into his face. "What? How do you know all this?"

"News travels fast within the organized crime community. Much like Hollywood, we, too, have the gossips who carry news from one clan to the other." Alvaro chuckles.

"You're kidding me, right?"

"Ask your husband."

"And if I refuse you?"

"I might take what I want from you anyway. Especially since your husband is now in my grasp."

"What?" I jump up so quickly my chair overturns. "What are you talking about?"

He snaps his fingers, and the door opens. Massimo walks in. He has his hands raised. Behind him, are two more men with their guns pointed at him.

52

Massimo

Olivia's gaze widens. Her features are pale, and dried blood clings to a cut in her forehead. Every muscle in my body tenses. A hot sensation stabs my chest. The bastard hurt her. The blood punches into my temples. I am going to kill him. I take a step forward, and the cold barrel of a gun presses against my rib cage.

At the same time, Alvaro pulls out a gun and aims it at Via. She freezes, the color fading from her cheeks.

Alvaro rises slowly to his feet. He turns to me, his gun still trained on Via. "If I were you, I wouldn't do anything rash."

"Let her go," I say through gritted teeth.

"No can do, I have plans for her. As for you? I can't decide if it's stupidity that made you come through the door unarmed, or is it true love that made you walk in here? You're making my revenge plan seem ridiculously easy."

I force myself to relax. I need to keep my wits about me if I want to save her. I square my shoulders. "You have me. You can use me to get to my brothers. The Don will give you anything you ask for in exchange. I'm the one you need; she's of no value to you."

"But she is… to you."

My guts twist, and the hot sensation in my chest intensifies until it feels like it's consuming me from the inside. The muscles in my forearms spasm. I curl my fingers into fists, and the barrel of the gun in my side is shoved deeper, until pain radiates out from the point of contact.

His lips kick up, he closes the distance to her, and I growl. "Don't you fucking touch her," I say through gritted teeth.

His grin widens. He wraps his arm around her waist, yanks her to him, then places the gun at her temple.

"One wrong move, and I'll shoot her," he drawls.

Her throat moves as she swallows, her gaze locked on mine. A bead of sweat slides down her temple, but she manages to keep the terror she must be experiencing off her face.

Good girl. Hang in there, baby. Just a little while longer. I won't let anything happen to you, I promise.

With my eyes, I try to convey my thoughts to her. I must succeed, for her forehead smoothes out. She stands perfectly still.

With a last look at her, I raise my gaze to Alvaro. "Why don't you put down the gun so we can fight this out? One on one."

He tilts his head. "Not falling for that," he says in a pleasant voice.

"Scared I'll get the better of you? Clearly, I'm in better shape than you. And now that you've lost a finger, you must know that you have no chance of winning in hand-to-hand combat."

His jaw hardens. "I am well aware this is a delaying tactic. No doubt, you have reinforcements on the way? You should know that, as we speak, my men are moving in on yours. Not only do we have the element of surprise on our side, but your team is sadly outnumbered."

Motherfucker! My leg muscles tighten, my fingers tingle, and what I wouldn't give to bury my fist in his face. If only I could get him to engage with me. If I could get his attention away from her. If I could get him to agree to a fight and buy more time for our plan to be set in motion.

"In which case, you have nothing to lose by agreeing to a fight. Not only would your men overpower mine, but you'd have the satisfaction of defeating me."

"Oh, I have no doubt of that. Even injured as I am, I could defeat you, with ease," he boasts.

"Then lower your gun and let's spar. If you defeat me, I won't resist you again."

She draws in a sharp breath. Tension radiates off of her body. I avoid looking at her, because if I do, I'll be lost. If I take in the expression in those green eyes, I'll never be able to go through with what I have in mind. Worse, I won't be able to contain my anger anymore. More than likely, I'll make a move which will end with the two of us getting hurt. No, I need to steel myself and see this through.

"What do you say? If I lose, you get to keep her."

Her gaze bores into me, but I refuse to meet her eyes.

His lips curl. "I already have her."

"And you'll have the satisfaction of having beaten me, as well."

He hesitates.

"Three rounds, that's all I'm asking for."

He appears to think for a few seconds, then jerks his chin. The man behind me lowers his gun and steps back.

Alvaro releases her. He walks over to the chair where he'd been sitting, and places his gun on it.

"Ask your men to move away," I say in a casual tone.

He raises his hand, and his men comply. They step back and place themselves at the perimeter of the room with their backs to the walls.

"Ask them to lower their guns, as well."

He scowls. "Not happening."

"What are you afraid of? They're your men. One command from you and they'll train their guns on me and shoot. Unless, of course, you think I'm going to overpower you and all of them, at the same time?" I infuse a thread of smugness through my voice.

His scowl deepens, then he gestures to the men. "Lower your guns."

One of them glowers back. "But—" he begins to protest.

Alvaro points his finger at the man. "Do as you're told," he snaps.

The man firms his lips, then lowers his gun.

Alvaro turns to me "Now, where were we?"

"I want Olivia to stand back at a safe distance, too."

"Why, are you afraid I might touch her again?" He moves in her direction, and that's when I charge him.

"Get out of the way," I yell at Olivia. She jumps aside, and I lower my head and ram into his chest. The speed of my impact carries us past her, toward the wall. His men leap aside, and Alvaro crashes into the wall. The vibrations from the collision shudder through me. I rear back, then grab his head and smash my forehead into his. Pain explodes behind my eyes, and I shove it aside. He groans, and I fully expect him to slump, but he seems to recover almost instantly. He grabs my throat and begins to choke me. I dig my fingers into his upper arms, try to pull his hands off of me, but he tightens his grip on my neck and begins to squeeze. Spots of black flicker at the edges of my vision. The sounds around me begin to fade. Behind me, I'm aware of movement, of someone screaming my name.

"Massimo, fight back!" Her voice slices through the silence in my head. The room swings back into focus.

I raise my knee and bury it in his groin. He yells, and his hold loosens. I draw in a breath, and oxygen fills my lungs. I pull away, then smash my fist into his stomach, and again, then follow up with an upper cut to his chin. His head snaps back, and blood sprays from his mouth. I raise my fist again and land it at his temple. The back of his head connects with the wall. I pause, panting, my breaths coming in gasps, sweat pouring down my throat. The back of my shirt sticks to my sweat slicked skin. I weave on my feet. He straightens, and with a howl, plows into me.

He throws his arms around my waist and leans his full weight on me. I stumble back, the momentum carrying me backward until I hit the chair on which he sat earlier. The chair tumbles over. The gun hits the floor and skitters away. I crash into the floor with Alvaro on top of me. He pushes up, straddles me, and begins to pound my face. Left-right-left.

Each time he smashes his fist into my cheek, stars explode behind my eyes. I taste blood on my tongue, and my vision goes hazy. Pain sparks my nerve endings and fills my blood. My breath catches in my throat, and once again, dark spots dance across my line of sight. *Fuck, fuck, fuck. I need to finish this off right now, before I lose consciousness.* I reach up wrap my fingers around his throat, and squeeze and squeeze.

His next blow barely grazes my cheek. The one after that misses me completely. I grip his neck and increase the pressure until his eyes bulge, and then he overbalances and falls to the side. I follow, refusing to release him, until finally, his eyes close. I remove my fingers, before joining them together and pulling them over my head. And quickly swoop down, bringing my joined-up fists down on his forehead. His body jerks, then he slumps.

I hear the clatter of footsteps, and realize his men are approaching us. I reach over to grab the gun from where it fell earlier, cock it, and train it at them. "Back off," I growl.

They pause, then one of them begins to squeeze the trigger. I fire the gun. The bullet slams into his chest. The gun slips from his fingers, and he slumps to the floor.

In a flash, Olivia is on him. She snatches up the gun and aims it at the nearest man. "You heard Massimo, back the fuck off," she snaps.

I almost laugh with relief. That's my woman. She's badass that way. I push up to standing. My knees threaten to give way from under me, and I press the heels of my booted feet into the ground for purchase. The scene sways in front of my eyes, and I shake my head to clear it.

"Move back, right the fuck now," my voice rings out. The men hesitate, then another man takes a step forward. A gunshot rings out, and he collapses to the ground. I glance sideways to find Olivia has both of her hands on the gun and her white-knuckled finger around the trigger. The gun wavers a little as she lowers it.

I stagger forward until I'm shoulder-to-shoulder with her. "You okay, baby?" I murmur.

A shudder runs down her body and she nods. Her gaze is frozen on the man she shot.

"You did the right thing, Via. It was either him or me."

She tears her gaze from the fallen man and glances around the faces of the others. "I won't hesitate to do it again."

I grip her shoulder, my gun still trained on the men, and urge her to follow me as I begin to inch toward the door. The men stay where they are, their guns trained on us, their gazes following our every step. We're halfway to the door, when a movement catches my attention. I glance down to find Alvaro stirring. I shoot at him, but he rolls over, and I miss him.

He grabs a gun from the hip holster of one of his men and fires it at her. I step in front of her, and pain explodes at my side. *Shit.* I raise my gun and depress the trigger. A perfectly round hole appears between his eyes. Smoke wafts from it. His gaze widens and his arm wavers. Then, the gun slips from his fingers, and he collapses on the floor. For a second, there's silence. Then I grab her hand and pull her toward the door. The wood on the frame explodes. *Fuck, they're shooting at us.* I yank her through the doorway, slam the door shut behind us, and haul her to the side. Just in time, for the next second, the door explodes as bullets rain through.

Pain screeches up my side, and sparks flicker behind my eyes. I grit my teeth as I pull her up the corridor and toward the main exit.

"You're hurt," she gasps.

"Keep moving," I order. I focus on putting one foot in front of the other. I have to make it out of here. Have to. I increase my pace, break into a run, and she stumbles to keep up with me. I reach the main door, fling it open just as a bullet slams into the door frame next to my head.

"Porca miseria!" I shove her forward, then turn, depressing the trigger on my gun. The hollow click reverberates in the corridor. "Fuck!" I let the gun fall from my fingers, and hold up my arms.

The man who defied Alvaro earlier raises his gun and his lips kick up.

"How much money do you want? Name a figure and I'll double it," I snap.

He chuckles. "No amount of money can equal the respect I'll command when I kill you and take this bitch as mine."

Behind me, Olivia stiffens. I sense her moving forward. She has a gun, but if she steps around me, he's going to shoot her. He's going to hurt her, and no way can I let that happen.

"Stay back, Via," I order in a low voice. But does she obey me? Of course not. My woman tries to step around me, and I thrust out my arm to stop her.

"Let her go; it's me you want."

"On the contrary..." He walks forward. "It's she who cost Alvaro his life. It makes her much more valuable right now."

More men appear, guns raised as they follow him. Shit, this is not good, not good at all.

"Run, Olivia, I'll hold them back."

"And die in the process, no doubt? You think I'm going to let that happen?" she shoots back.

"Leave, Olivia. If they get their hands on you, I'll never forgive myself."

"And if I leave you behind, I'll never forgive myself."

"Give me the gun and get out of here, woman," I say impatiently.

"No way am I going to let you pull this macho shit on me anymore. If you die, I die with you."

"This isn't one of your movies. This is real life, baby. You need to leave while you still can."

"Don't you know? Real life is often stranger than reel life, baby." She begins to step around me, gun aimed at the advancing men. I snatch the gun from her, and shove her out the front door. "Sorry, *Stellina*, I can't let anything happen to you."

"What the—? Massimo, you—" I slam the door in her face, then turn and fire.

53

Olivia

I try to wrench open the door when shots ring out on the other side. I drop to the floor and bullets tear through the door above me. "No, no, no, Massimo!" I throw myself to the side and huddle there as more bullets rip through the door. Fragments of wood rain down on me, I throw my arms over my head to shield myself. The shooting seems to go on and on. My pulse thuds at my temples, the blood pumps in my ears, and my heart beats against my rib cage like a bird caught in a net. *Massimo, Massimo. You can't die on me. Don't you dare leave me, you hear me?* I squeeze my fingers together, close my eyes and pray.

Then, the shooting cuts out, and all I can hear is the ringing in my ears. The pounding within me continues. A chunk of wood from the frame hits the ground with a thud, then the entire middle section of the door crumples into pieces. I squeeze my eyes shut, curl myself into as small a ball as possible, and tremble. Suddenly aware of the stillness pressing down on me, I snap my eyes open, and rise to my feet. My knees threaten to give out from under me.

I lean against the wall, panting like I've run a marathon. My heartbeat is still so loud, I hear it pounding in my ears, feel my pulse thudding under my skin. I slide toward the edge of the door and peek inside. The corridor is littered with fallen bodies, and there on the floor, with his arm flung toward the door, is Massimo. Everything around me fades. There's only him.

"No!" I jump forward and sink to my knees beside him. Blood stains the side of his shirt. The skin surrounding one eye is discolored. His eyelids are shut, the eyelashes a dark semicircle against his cheeks. His features are pale, and he's so still. *Oh my god!* My breath catches on a sob. Is he even breathing?

No, it's not possible. The tears I've been trying to hold back slide down my cheeks. *No, don't leave me. Please.* I throw myself on his body and sob. He can't leave me because I love him

I hold him tighter. My chest hurts, my limbs are numb, and every part of me is ready to die with him. My man. My beast, with his broad chest, massive shoulders, a square jaw, and those pouty lips I'd recognize anywhere. He can't leave me. He can't.

Massimo! I fling my arms around him and press my lips to his. I kiss him fervently, lick his unresponsive mouth, and nibble on his lower lip. "Massimo. Massimo," I murmur. His lips part, and I slide my tongue inside. He sucks on my tongue, and I deepen the kiss, then pause. I raise my gaze past that hooked nose to those gorgeous gray eyes, through which he regards me. There's a spark deep inside; it snares me and won't let go.

"Massimo, you're alive!" I cry.

"You didn't think I was going to leave you that easily, did you?"

"You scared me!" I lower my mouth to his and kiss him again. He wraps his arms around me, hauls me closer, then gasps in pain.

"Sorry, sorry, you're hurt." I try to pull away from him, but he doesn't let go. "Massimo, you're hurt."

"Fuck that." He digs his fingers in my hair and pulls me close, then fits his mouth to mine. He tilts his head, thrusts his tongue between my lips, and kisses me passionately. I inhale his scent, draw his smell into my lungs, and allow his taste to sink into my blood, as I kiss him right back.

I don't hear the footsteps until they are almost on us. Massimo must hear it at the same time, for he pushes me to the side and raises his gun.

"We both know there are no bullets left in that," JJ drawls.

"What took you so long?" Massimo growls.

"Don't you mean, I'm just in time? If it weren't for me, you'd be dead." JJ holds out his hand to help me up. "You owe me."

An hour later, I glance toward the door of the examination room in the hospital. On the heels of JJ reaching us, an ambulance had drawn up. The paramedics had attended to Massimo right away. They had tried to take me aside to take care of my wounds, but I'd insisted on staying with Massimo.

He was hurt, but didn't fully lose consciousness. He held my hand the whole time, refusing to let me go, much to the chagrin of the first responders. One of them tried to separate us, and he growled at them. JJ finally intervened and told them to keep us together.

The cops arrived soon after, and JJ stayed back to deal with them while the ambulance rushed us to hospital. En route, Massimo answered my unasked question and assured me JJ would take care of everything. I didn't probe more, but I'm no fool. Given my own background with the *Camorra*, I know it means JJ has enough clout within the police force and the justice system to neutralize any consequences from what happened.

Once we reached the hospital, the doctors took Massimo away. When I protested, one of them explained they needed to take him into surgery right away to deal with the gunshot wound in his side. The full impact of what had happened finally sank in, and I confess, I almost fainted then. I allowed the nurses to take care of my wounds, but refused any painkillers. I wanted to stay awake for news on Massimo. The last I'd heard was that it was a minor surgery they'd had to perform on him, but he was okay and resting. They'd promised to send someone to take me to his room, which was on the floor above me, but so far, no one has arrived.

I slide off of the examination table. Except for the bump on my head from where I was hit by the butt of the gun, I haven't suffered any injuries. The nurses insisted I strip and wear the hospital gown so they could examine me thoroughly. I pull the slit in the gown closed to make sure I don't flash anyone by mistake, before I head to the door. I peek out and find there's a man on guard outside.

"Who're you?" I frown.

"Peter. I'm one of JJ's team."

"Are you?" I frown.

"Massimo was clear that he wants you watched twenty-four-seven."

"Hmm, how do I know you are who you say you are?"

Peter smiles. "It's good to be cautious." He pulls out his phone, dials a number, then hands it over to me.

"Who did you call?"

"Why don't you talk to JJ? He'll confirm what I told you."

Without taking my gaze off of him, I accept the phone.

"Hello?" JJ's voice comes on the line.

"It's Olivia," I reply.

"Ah, how are you feeling?" he asks.

"I'd feel a lot better if I could be with Massimo."

JJ chuckles. "Young love." A smile laces his tone.

"You're not that old," I retort.

"Too old to fall in love," he insists.

"Careful. You know what they say: when you're least looking for it, love finds you."

"As for me? The only four-letter word I'm acquainted with doesn't begin with an L, I assure you," he counters.

"Moving on swiftly." I cough. "I assume this Peter guy is one of yours?"

"Indeed. And I have guards posted outside Massimo's door, too. Peter will take you there. Hand the phone over to him, will you?"

"Thanks for everything, JJ." I hand the phone over to Peter who listens to whatever JJ has to say, then nods.

He disconnects the call and indicates I should precede him. He walks me to the elevator, takes me one floor up, and guides me down the corridor to Massimo's room.

I push the door open and peek inside to find him stretched out on the bed. His eyes are shut, his color pale. The darkness of his skin contrasts with the white sheets that surround him. I slip inside the room, ensuring the door closes quietly behind me. I pad over to the bed and survey him. His chest rises and falls, and the white of a bandage peeps around the hospital gown they've draped over him. On the other side, the black ink of his tattoo is visible from under the neckline. I pull over a chair and lower myself into it, then take his hand in mine. I place my head on the pillow next to his. The next thing I know, a whispered touch on my cheek has me snapping my eyes open.

His gray eyes—now almost colorless again—hold mine. I stare into their depths, allowing myself to get lost in the brilliance there.

"Hey." He cups my cheek.

"Hey..." I clear my throat. "How are you feeling?"

"How are *you* feeling?" he counters.

I can't stop the smile that curves my lips. "I guess you must be fine if you're answering my question with a question."

His lips twitch. "Seriously, though, are you okay?"

I glance down to where my fingers are still twined with his. "Never better. But when I saw you lying on the floor, I freaked out for a second."

"Sorry about that." He drags his thumb across the underside of my mouth. "JJ came just in time. I pushed you out the door, then turned, with every intention of firing and getting shot, but before I could pull my trigger, JJ burst in from the other side with his team. They took down every single man, except for that bastard who was leading them. I pumped every last bullet of mine into him, but that took the last of my strength, and my legs gave out from under me. I must have lost consciousness for a few minutes."

"If anything had happened to you—" my voice breaks. I clear my throat and try again, "If anything had happened to you, I'm not sure how I could have gone on. I wouldn't have been able to bear it, Massimo, truly. I thought I had lost you." A ball of emotion clogs my throat, and my heart somersaults in my chest. A heavy anchor weighs down my belly. "I can't live without you, Massimo. I can't."

He places his finger over my lips. "Shh, I'm here, baby. I am not going anywhere. From the moment I saw you, I knew our futures were intertwined. I knew you were exactly what I needed in my life. Knew, without a doubt, that you were my today and all of my tomorrows. That my yesterdays were nothing more than a blur of darkness until I met you."

"Oh." Heat sears my cheeks. "That is… so romantic."

He chuckles. "I'm only just getting started." He pulls me even closer. I lean my weight on him, and he groans.

"Oh, god, sorry, you're hurt. I shouldn't have—" I try to move away, but he holds me in place.

"You absolutely should." He peers deeply into my eyes. "Surely, it's the entire universe that conspired for us to meet. When I'm with you is the only time I feel like myself. When I'm with you, I love what I become. I love you."

54

Massimo

"What?" She blinks. "What did you say?"

"I love you, Olivia. My wife, my heart, my true self. Meeting you made me realize what I was missing in my life. You're a mirror for my desires, the book of my passions written to bring my deepest yearning to life... The reflection of everything I was seeking, only I wasn't aware of it, until I met you. What I feel for you is bigger than myself, more significant than anything I've encountered before, or will encounter again. I saw you and realized every step I've taken in my life was a step closer to finding you. Everything I've done so far has pushed me toward you. You were my true north, and I didn't even realize it."

Her face pales. "What are you saying?"

"That you are magnificent. You were created for me. Since I met you, there hasn't been a time when I'm not thinking of you. I love you, and everything about you. I love your fiery nature, your ambition, your focus on making something of yourself, how you're loyal to your family, despite the fact they've never recognized your talents, how you'd do anything to protect your sister, even turn your back on your true love."

"You don't mean it." Her chest rises and falls.

"I do." I bring her fingers to my lips and kiss them. "You are my every hope and dream, every thought I've ever had. I *am* because of you, Via."

"Stop." She tries to pull away, and this time, I release her. She jumps up and begins to pace. "You're confusing me, Massimo."

"Confusing you?" I sit up straight. My side protests, and my shoulder screams in pain, but I ignore it. "I thought I was being very clear when I said that I love you, Via. I am in love with you, I—"

"Stop." She slaps her palms over her ears. "Please stop." She turns away from me. Her body language is stiff, her muscles tense. She folds her fingers into fists, tucks her elbows into her sides. I can't see her features.

"What is it, Via? I thought you felt the same way about me?"

"I—" She shakes her head. "I do. I love you so much, Massimo. And when I saw you collapsed on the ground, my heart almost stopped. I was sure I was going to die. I thought I'd lost you. It felt like someone had reached right into me and pulled out all of my insides." She turns on me. "And then, when you kissed me—" she wrings her hands together "—I was so relieved, I thought I was going to die all over again. I'm not sure I could take another one of these incidents. If something were to happen to you again, I'm not sure I'd survive it."

I open my mouth to protest, but she stops me.

"And it could happen again." She squeezes her fingers together. "Don't deny it. You're a Mafioso. You'll never really be free of what it means to be part of an organized crime syndicate."

"Maybe; maybe not. Either way, we're going to try. We have enough clout to ensure that our futures, and that of our offspring, are free of the shadow of our past deeds."

She hunches her shoulders. "What if that's not enough? What if, each time you try to move forward, a shadow from your past—from our past—crawls out to confront us? What if—" she raises her palms and stares at them "—despite your best attempts, we're put in situations where we're forced to make split-second decisions, the consequences of which we're going to have to live with for the rest of our lives?"

I flinch, then square my shoulders. "Being part of the Mafia is in my blood, and it's in yours. It's not something we can ever get rid of completely. It's not something we should hesitate to talk about. In fact, to move forward, it's important we come to grips with it and confront it," I retort.

"And no doubt, kill if needed," she says in a low voice.

My heart twists, and my guts churn. "I'm sorry you were put in a situation where you had to do that. But I'm not sorry that you did it."

She shakes her head. "Neither am I."

I frown. "So, what's the problem, Via?"

"Can't you see?" She tips up her chin. "That is the problem. This—" She gestures between us. "All of this—you being hurt, me not hesitating to shoot someone to protect the both of us, you killing my brother to safeguard my future. The fact that I'm not even upset about that, or that I had to shoot someone to protect us. It's not normal. It's not how ordinary people would react, Massimo."

"But we're not ordinary, Via. We live on the edges of society. We see the things that other people refuse to see. We do the things that other people won't do. We're the kind who constantly push the boundaries of what's right to survive."

She scoffs. "You might, but that's not what I want for myself."

"Like it or not, our legacy defines us. We were born into it, and try as we might, we can't walk away from it. It's what we were born into."

"But it's not something I chose as my lifestyle. I don't want that. It's why I left… Not only to pursue my passion, but also so I could find a life separate from what it means to be part of the Mafia. Then you came along; and here I am, right back where I didn't want to be."

My heart begins to race. My pulse thrums in my stomach. A drift of snow seems to localize in my chest, and I ignore it. "I thought you cared about me, Via," I say carefully. "I thought you had feelings for me."

"I do." She locks her fingers together. "It's what makes this so much more difficult to say."

The hair on the back of my neck rises. "Don't." I keep my voice level, but every muscle in my body tenses. Even before she opens her mouth, I know what she's going to say. It still doesn't prepare me for the shock when she turns her face sideways.

"I need some time apart, Massimo."

"No," I growl.

"Yes." She shuffles her feet. "Please understand, I just need to figure out where I am at with all of this."

"With all of what?" I snap.

"With you, me, this wedding, with what happened... How you almost died."

"But I'm alive." I swing my legs over the side of the bed and she starts.

"Please, don't get out of bed, you need to rest."

"And watch as you walk away from me? You want me to lie back and allow you to talk yourself into some bullshit explanation for why you need some space from me?"

"I do need space, and it's not bullshit. I simply need to hear myself think. I need to figure out what I want."

"I know what you want. I'm the only one who knows what you need. Thinking of you is what keeps me awake. Dreaming of you is the only reason I allow myself to sleep. Wanting you is the one good thing I've done in my life, and you want to take that away from me?" It feels like someone has wrapped their hands around my neck and is squeezing the life out of me.

I push up to my feet. My knees wobble, but the damn things hold, thank fuck. I take a step forward, and fuck, maybe I spoke too soon, because my thighs spasm. "*Che cazzo!*" I thrust out a hand to grab the edge of the bed, but she rushes over and grabs it instead.

"Massimo, please." She squeezes my arm, and pinpricks of heat shiver out from the point of contact. Every cell in my body seems to come alive. This woman. Why can't she understand how much she means to me?

I wind my arm around her waist and draw her close. "Look into my eyes, Via."

She shakes her head.

"Via, please, baby, give me this, at least."

She bites down on her lower lip, and my dick twitches. She tips up her chin, then finally raises her gaze to mine. Watery green eyes, smudges in the hollows under her eyes, skin that reminds me of the finest gossamer, and the scar that curls across her cheek toward the corner of her eyes.

"You are so beautiful."

A teardrop squeezes out from the corner of her eye. "Don't," she whispers.

I bend and lick the trail of moisture down her cheek. She shivers. I press tiny kisses down to the corner of her mouth, and a moan bleeds from her lips. I brush my mouth over hers, and a sigh breezes out from her.

"I wish I could turn back the clock. I wish I'd found you sooner, so I could love you longer."

Another tear rolls down her cheek. "Massimo, please don't make this so difficult for me."

I peer between her eyes and I see pain, pleading, and something else, something I dare not put a name to. An emotion so very much like love. She loves me; she's just not ready to admit it. Maybe what she needs is time… and space.

I tilt my head and capture her mouth with mine. I thrust my tongue between her lips and drag it across her teeth. I suck on her tongue and kiss her, trying to convey all of the love I feel for her, then release her so suddenly, she stumbles a little. I step back, and the cool air rushes between us. She stands there, blinking.

"Go." I jerk my chin toward the doorway. "Go, please... before I change my mind."

55

Massimo

"So, you let her leave?" JJ leans forward in his chair. The same chair she was seated in less than an hour ago. I asked her to leave and she hesitated. When I didn't say anything more, she conveyed her thanks with her eyes, then pivoted and walked quickly through the door. I sagged back onto the bed and fell asleep almost immediately. When I woke up again, it was to find JJ in my room. I'd be lying if I said I wasn't disappointed to find him instead of her.

"She asked you to let her go, and you did?" he asks again.

"What choice did I have?"

"You always have a choice." He drums his fingers on the arm of the chair.

"So what, I should have restrained her and prevented her from leaving?"

"It's an idea." He raises a shoulder.

"You've never been in love, have you?" I scoff.

"As I told you before, The only four-letter word I'm acquainted with doesn't begin with an L."

"Never say never." I move around to find a more comfortable position on the bed. "I was just like you. Then, I met her, and my world tilted on its axis. I didn't think it was possible to feel anything as remotely intense as what I feel for her. I met her, and now, she's the last thought in my mind before I drift off to sleep, and the first thought when I wake up each morning. When I'm not with her, I want to be with her, and when I am with her, I want to never let go of her."

He watches me with a curious look in his eyes. "It sounds… painful."

I chuckle. "It's… energizing, and strangely, life-affirming. Apparently, life is all about living it for someone else. Who knew, eh?"

"That's how I felt when I had my children. I took one look at them and knew my life had changed irrevocably. I knew I'd do anything for them. But feeling that way for a woman…?" He shakes his head. "I confess, I've never had such thoughts for a woman. And hopefully, I never will."

"I never wanted to have kids. But then, I met her, and the thought of seeing her pregnant with my child brings out a part of me that I didn't even know existed."

His gaze narrows. "And yet, you let her go?"

"That's part of being in love with someone. I've already made her marry me without giving her a choice… Making her fall in love with me isn't as easy. Giving her the space she needs so she can not only acknowledge her feelings for me, but also act on them? That's something I can't force. It's something she's going to have to realize on her own.

"And if she doesn't? What if she never arrives at that conclusion on her own?"

My chest hurts, my shoulder muscles tense. The pain in my side turns up a notch, and I squeeze my fingers into a fist. "Oh, she told me she loves me. Now, she has to find the courage to act on her emotions. To accept that I am the only one for her. She knows it deep inside, too. She just needs a little space to accept it, is all."

"You're a brave man," a new voice announces from the doorway. Both JJ and I turn to find Michael leaning against the doorframe.

"How long have you been standing there?" I press my fingertips together.

"Long enough." He prowls inside the room. He's followed by Seb, Adrian, Luca, and Christian.

"What's this? An intervention?" I scowl.

The men wander around the room before Seb props a hip against the window frame. Christian stops at the foot of the bed, Luca positions himself on the side of the bed opposite to JJ, and Axel stays just inside the door. It might look casual to an outsider, but I know they're positioning themselves to be ready in case of an attack. They're also carrying firearms, as evidenced by the slight bulge under each of their jackets. No doubt, thanks to JJ's influence, they weren't stopped.

"Heard you took a hit?" Michael nods toward the bandage which peeks out from under my hospital gown.

"You should see the other men," I say lightly.

Michael fixes me with his gaze. "It was a foolhardy thing you did, walking in there unarmed."

"I assume JJ here gave you the background about what happened?"

Michael nods.

"You should know then, that I was never in any trouble. We had planned for JJ to come in with his men."

"Which took longer than expected." Michael folds his arms across his chest. "Ergo, here you are, laid up with another bullet wound."

"Hopefully the last one." I tilt my head.

Michael holds my gaze, then blows out a breath. "I've accelerated the process of legitimizing our businesses. It's taking more time than expected, due to the complexities involved, as you well know."

"It needs to happen faster, Michael. The faster we go legit, the less chance we have of running up against more characters like Alvaro. We can't risk our families being exposed to the likes of him again."

"I am aware." His forehead creases. "Speaking of, wherever Olivia is, I assume you have eyes on her?"

I glare at him. He raises his hands. "Just asking. Giving her time alone to think things through is very mature of you, not something I'd have been able to agree to if I had been in your place."

"Time alone?" Seb asks.

"So much has happened in the last few days. She needs to sort things out in her head."

There's silence in the room, then Christian nods. "It's a good thing. Best to get the thinking out of the way, once and for all."

"Peter's been instructed to never let her out of his sight. He'll drop her wherever she wants to go, then make sure to keep himself out of sight," JJ offers.

Michael turns to him. "Thank you for helping out my brother." He extends his arm. "I will not forget how you stepped in when the rest of us couldn't make it in time to help."

JJ shakes his hand. "It's my pleasure, but you do realize it's going to cost you, right?"

Michael's lips kick up. "A bigger stake in Trinity Enterprises, I assume?"

JJ tilts his head. "Actually, I want you to invest in a private members' club that I'm opening in London."

"A members' club? Is that a euphemism for a sex club?" Luca pipes up.

"It's a members' club in Mayfair, and it's not a euphemism for a sex club. Although there will be a space in the club for that purpose, too, yes. And, of course, all of you will get VIP membership to the space."

"Naturally." Christian nods.

"Aren't there enough exclusive clubs in London?" Adrian murmurs.

"None like this. None where the entry will be restricted to billionaires… and those I deem fit to be given membership."

"You mean we, don't you?" Michael drawls.

"If you invest, you'll get a say, but the final decision will belong to me."

"And what's in it for me?" Michael demands.

"This place will be a meeting ground for those who are the most influential, most powerful, and most exceptional. Membership will be based, not only on how much money you have, but also on what value you've contributed to the world. A veritable roster of who's who, this will be the place to unwind without being worried about the media. A place to entertain and be entertained. A time-less combination of comfort, glamour, and intimacy, where what's said and done in the club will stay in the club. In short, this will be the place to meet and network among the tastemakers, the influencers, those whose every choice has a ripple effect on the decisions of millions."

"Sounds intriguing," Seb offers.

JJ rises to his feet. "What do you say? Are you in, then?

"You helped my brother. It goes without saying I'm with you in whatever venture you want me to support." Michael shakes his proffered hand. "As for you…" He turns to face me. "Once the doctor gives you the all-clear, how about we get you home?"

56

One week later

Olivia

The hair on the back of my neck prickles. I glance over my shoulder, but nope, nothing seems out of the ordinary—just the flower stand at the corner, the coffee shop next to it with a bunch of teenagers hanging around the exit, a take-out delivery guy strapping his bag to his back—nope, there's no one else. Definitely no one watching me.

So why do I feel like someone is following me? I shake my head. Probably just my overactive imagination. After the doctor discharged me from the hospital, Peter drove me to Massimo's home. He told me they were arranging for me to move to a service apartment where I could stay on my own and figure out what to do next. I hadn't wanted to accept Massimo's generosity, partly because this meant he'd know where I was going to be, but who was I kidding? With JJ's help, he wouldn't have any trouble tracking me down in London, anyway.

Also, if I turned him down, I wouldn't have anywhere else to stay in London. I gave up my flat before moving to Palermo to be part of the musical there. It would take me time to find another place to rent. Meanwhile, if I wanted space, then I had no choice but to accept Massimo's plan and move to the apartment. Which I did. Peter dropped me off with my bags, and since then, I haven't seen or heard from any of them. I keep glancing at my phone, but it has stayed silent. Guess Massimo took me at my word and decided to leave me alone.

I spent my days following up with Declan's agent Kimberly, who already put me up for an audition for an indie film. It's a small budget production, but the role is exciting. It's where I was earlier today, and for once, I'm actually satisfied with my performance at the audition, too. The people at the audition didn't seem surprised to see my scar. Best of all, the role doesn't call for a character with a scar, either, and they still agreed to audition me. Which means, the crew behind this production is more open-minded than the people I normally meet in this industry. Which is good, right? I wrapped up the audition and took the tube home. The whole time, I felt as if someone was tailing me, but each time I looked over my shoulder, nothing seemed amiss. If someone is following me, they're very skilled.

I stop off at the supermarket to buy a bottle of wine and some frozen pizza, because I feel like I earned it and because, unlike Massimo, I don't have staff to cook for me. As a result, my diet has gone to the dogs but… At least, my career is looking up. I walk up the steps to my first-floor apartment and let myself in. I drop my handbag on the sofa and head to the kitchen, where I turn on the oven and slide the pizza inside. Then, I open the bottle of wine, pour myself a glass, and walk back into the living room. A buzzing sound from my bag reaches me. I sink down into the sofa, pull out my phone, and accept the FaceTime call.

"Helloooo!" Penny sing-songs. "How are you doing?"

"I'm good, now that I have a glass of wine in hand." I raise my glass, and Penny shows her own glass of wine to me.

"*Salute!*" she chirps.

We both sip from our glasses of wine.

I roll the wine around my tongue before swallowing it. "Mm, that's good."

"How did the audition go?" she asks. I messaged her to let her know about it before I headed off earlier.

"I think it went well. I told you I sent in my audition clips earlier, right? They loved them and asked me to read in person, which is what I did today, and guess what? The casting director was very enthusiastic about it. He gave me positive feedback on the spot."

"How unusual," she exclaims.

"Right?" I laugh. "I mean, usually they barely acknowledge you, and here, he pretty much told me he loved me and that I might need to come back for the second round to audition with the director."

"No way," she cries. "That's such good news."

"I still can't believe it." I shake my head, "Apparently, I found the one unicorn director and casting team which doesn't care about the scar on my cheek."

I touch the offending mark on my face, feeling the slightly puckered skin against my fingertips.

"To be honest, it doesn't look that bad. If anything, it adds to your personality. It makes you stand out, actually."

"I'm not sure that's a good thing—"

"It is a good thing." She leans forward. "It really is. It makes your face unforgettable."

"But how many people will want to see a scarred woman playing a lead role in a film?" I shift around in my seat.

"Don't go second-guessing yourself. If the casting director believes in you, surely, they see something in you that others will, too."

I bite the inside of my cheek. "We'll see. It's too early to be worrying about that, anyway. I have yet to audition with the director."

"And you are going to ace it, I'm sure."

I laugh. "I wish I were half as confident as you."

"You are enormously talented, Olivia, I've seen you work so hard at your craft. And you've been so proactive, so hungry for every opportunity that has come your way. And you didn't allow what happened to you to hold you down. Anyone else would have taken the scarring as a sign to move away from trying to make a career out of acting, but not you. You were even more determined to prove your prowess as an actress. You deserve the successful audition. You deserve to get this role."

A pressure builds at the backs of my eyes. "You're going to make me cry," I sniff.

"Aww, don't, babe, I was only stating the truth. If only I had half the drive you do." She laughs. "But I'm too easygoing for my own good sometimes."

"And I wish I were half as carefree as you. I wish I had the patience to let things unfold, instead of always trying to push my way forward, you know?"

We smile at each other.

"It's what makes us so good for each other." She chuckles. "Now, Jeanne, though, she's somewhere in between. She knows when to push and when to take it easy."

"The three musketeers. No wonder the three of us get along so well. How is she doing, anyway? I bet the two of you killed the performances in the musical."

"You know my part was minor, but Jeanne, she was amazing as Belle. She stole the show. No doubt, finding her own beast in real life had something to do with it, too." She peers closely into the screen. "Have you forgiven her for taking the role from you?"

"Given I was injured, and she was my understudy, it's not like she had a choice. Also, if you remember, originally, I was the understudy, and she was the main actress. So, the role did, in effect, belong to her."

"But the director wanted you to play the main role instead."

"Only because Jeanne missed a very important rehearsal. Because she had been kidnapped. I never felt completely comfortable about how I got it, anyway. It all worked out for her, though. If she hadn't been taken, she wouldn't have met Luca. If they hadn't met in that cell, they wouldn't be married now," I remind her.

"And if you hadn't made it to your sister's engagement, you wouldn't be married now," she murmurs.

My stomach ties itself in knots. My chest feels like someone stabbed a hot sword through it. Something of my emotions must show on my face, for her gaze widens.

"Oh, sweetie, I didn't mean to upset you."

"You didn't." I swallow the ball of emotion clogging my throat. "I mean, you did, but I know you didn't mean to."

"Are you going to tell me what's happening between the two of you?"

Yeah, I've told her everything work-related, but talking about what's happening between Massimo and me? Nope. I'm not sure I want to tell anyone about it. I mean, what am I going to say? I realized I loved him, then shot a man for him, then asked him for time apart to figure things out? It sounds confusing, even to me.

"It's okay to share, you know?" Penny says softly, "Of the three of us, you've always been the most closed-off when it comes to your feelings."

"Well, not all of us can be like you, wearing our heart on our sleeves," I sniff, then slap my palm to my forehead. "Shit, didn't mean for that to come out like that, I promise."

She chuckles. "It's true, though. I wake up every morning, convinced today is going to be the best day of my life. And I'm never able to keep my emotions from showing on my face. So, you're right, I can come across as annoyingly chirpy and all sunshine-and-rainbows, and sometimes people think it's all an act, but it's not. It's just how I am."

"I know." I half-smile. "It's why I like you so much. Although I confess, there are days when I look at you and think, how can anyone be so cheerful all the time? But then I remind myself it's you. It's how you've always been. And it does perk me up. It's a good foil to all that intensity that Jeanne and I bring to our friendship."

"A-n-d, you're not fooling me, missy. You can't get away with changing the subject that easily."

"What?" I widen my gaze. "What did I do?"

"It's what you didn't do. You still haven't told me what happened with Massimo. I assume you're not staying with him anymore?"

"How did you guess?"

"You've been texting me nonstop and have time to take my calls, which means, you have time to think of me, which means, you're not with him because if you were, no way would he not have monopolized all your time."

I scowl at her. "You make me sound like a bad friend."

"And you're guzzling that wine like it's going out fashion."

I glance down at my wine glass to find I've drained it completely. "Shit."

"Yep." She presses a finger to her cheek. "So, what happened? Did you two guys fight or something?"

I slump into the sofa. "Or something," I grouse.

"Did you move out of his home?"

I remain silent.

"Holy shit, you did move out of his house. What, you guys broke up already?"

"We're, uh, taking a short break, is all."

"A short break?" Her frown deepens.

"It was my idea."

"Your idea?" She gapes. "What the—? What do you mean, it was your idea?"

"Just that. I told him I needed a little bit of time to get my head around everything that happened."

"And what happened? What are you not telling me, Olivia?"

I blow out a breath. "I need more wine for this conversation." I take the phone with me and walk back to the kitchen, where I pour myself more wine, then balance the phone against the wine bottle.

"Don't freak out, but remember my brother promised me to be married to some other Mafia guy?"

"I do recall you mentioning that," she replies slowly.

"Well, apparently, my brother not being on the scene didn't matter. He made a deal and the other guy wanted to collect."

"W-h-a-t?" she exclaims.

"Yep. Alvaro—that was his name—decided to come to London and he may have, uh, briefly kidnapped me."

"Excuse me? He kidnapped you? Do you mean he took you, like that Freddie character did with Jeanne?"

I nod.

"What the—!" The phone shakes a little, then she disappears from the screen.

"Hey, Penny, you okay? Are you okay?"

"Yes, of course I am," she says crossly. "Just thought I should be sitting down while you tell me the rest of this story."

I hear her moving around, then she comes back into focus again. "Had to refill my wine glass again, as well."

"So, he took you, but here you are, talking to me, so I assume Massimo found you and rescued you?"

I nod. "He did, with the help of some colleagues of his. I admit, it did get hairy, and there may have been some shooting involved."

"Oh my gosh, they shot at you?"

"They ended up knocking me out, actually," I reply.

She peers into my face. "They knocked you out?"

"Yeah, uh, you can't see the wound now," I gesture to my forehead. "Makeup, and it wasn't serious, so it's been fading quickly. Thank God. Can you imagine how it would've looked if I turned up for the audition with not one, but two scars?" I joke.

She frowns. "Seriously, though, you're okay?"

I nod.

"And Massimo?"

"He, uh, was hurt. That's what caused this issue."

"He was shot?" she asks slowly.

I nod.

"And then what happened?"

I shuffle my feet, take another big gulp of the wine. "I saw him collapsed on the floor and thought he was gone. I had a mini-meltdown, and then I found out he was alive and lost my mind." *So, it was a full-on losing-my-shit kind of breakdown, but whatever.*

"I don't understand." Penny blinks rapidly, "You lost your shit because you found out he was alive?"

"I lost it because I thought I'd lost him. Then, I discovered he was fine and lost it even more."

She shakes her head. "Okay, explain it to me. I get that you freaked out when you thought the bullet had gotten him. Then, you discovered he was alive, and you freaked out some more?"

"You don't understand." I jump up to my feet and begin to pace. "When I saw him lying on the floor, I thought I'd lost him. I think my heart stopped beating. I mean, my entire body went cold. I couldn't feel my hands or legs. I tried to wake him up, but he was so still. Then, he opened his eyes and… I looked into them and knew things would never be the same again."

"So, you discovered you love him."

"Well, I realized I loved him just before Alvaro's men kidnapped me. But when I thought I'd lost Massimo, I—" I swallow. "I realized I couldn't live without him." I stop in front of the phone screen. "Do you see how that changes everything? Now I'll want to be with him, probably follow him wherever he goes, maybe move back to Palermo—" I shudder. "Then, I'll probably end up getting pregnant very soon, and then, goodbye career."

"Would that be so bad?" Penny asks softly. "Don't you want to find a man and get married and have kids?"

"Of course I do. But I promised myself when I ran from my family that I wouldn't waste the opportunity I'd been given. So many women never get the chance to pursue their dreams. I have this chance and don't want to waste it, you know?"

"Don't you think you can have both? Why does it have to be one or the other?"

"Is it really possible to have both? I think of having Massimo in my life and I lose sight of everything else. When I'm in his presence, he's all-consuming. All I can think of is being with him, wanting him, holding him… He overpowers all of my thoughts, his personality subsumes me, and I worry about losing myself and losing sight of my dreams. And as for kids…" I shake my head. "I can't even think about it. I know I'm not supposed to say that. As a woman, motherhood is supposed to be the most important thing I can accomplish, but right now, I can't even think of children. I'm too busy trying to figure out myself, you know, and what I become when I'm with him."

"You're afraid of how he makes you feel?"

"I'm afraid of…" I glance away. "…of what I feel when I'm with him. Everything is too intense, too real. It's too much."

"So, you decided to run away?"

"I decided to take a short break," I correct her.

"You sure about that? You sure this is not a tactic to break things off completely?" She scowls at me.

"No, of course not." I stare at her in horror. "I... I don't want to not be married to him."

"From where I am, it seems you don't want to be married to him, either."

"I…" I shake my head. "I know I don't not want to have him."

"You said you don't want to not be married to him." She shakes her head. "You're confusing me, babe."

"I'm confusing myself." I twist my fingers together. "It's just, realizing the depth of what I feel for him, and then having him tell me he loves me—"

"Wait, he told you he loves you?" she screeches.

I wince. "Stop that godawful sound, and yes, when I went to see him in his hospital room, he told me he loves me." A small smile curves my lips. "Most eloquently, actually. I'd have never thought that big, bad Mafiahole would have such a, a... lyrical vocabulary when it came to declarations of his feelings."

"So, he told you he loves you, and you responded by telling him you needed some time apart from him?"

I wince. "Pretty much."

"And he let you go?"

I glance into the depths of my glass. "Reluctantly, but he did."

"Wow, I wouldn't have expected that."

"Me neither. It would have been easier if he hadn't, you know? It would have given me a reason to doubt his declaration. But not only did he control himself, but he also didn't try to stop me. He just agreed to my wishes, and that... only made me look at him differently. I mean, clearly, the man has it in him to respect what I want. He gave me space when it was the last thing he wanted to do. In fact, he hasn't called me since I left his hospital room."

"You don't sound happy about it."

"I'm not," I confess.

"Isn't that what you wanted? Space and time to think."

"Yes, but..." I drain my glass, then place it back on the table. "I mean, he could have, at least, called or texted to check on me. It doesn't feel right, you know, for him to give in to my wishes like this. It's not like him to agree to what I want without wielding some form of control over the proceedings."

"So, what, you think he's watching you or something?" She laughs.

I stare at her. "That's it. I bet he's having me shadowed by someone, or maybe, he's doing it himself... No, he's probably not fully recovered yet for that. I'll bet he has someone following me around. That's why I've felt like I was being watched. That's why he hasn't called me. He doesn't need to. He knows where I am, because he had one of JJ's men drop me at this apartment, which belongs to him, by the way." I glance around the space. "Wanna bet he has cameras on me in this apartment, too?"

"Ooh—" She perks up. "So he's watching you sleep and stuff?"

"And stuff." I look around the room, take in the corners of the ceilings, the paintings on the wall. There are so many places where he could have hidden a camera. I stiffen. Yes, that's it. He's probably watching me, even now, as we speak. "Jerkass," I growl.

"You know, if he's watching you, you can use it to your advantage."

I swivel my head to face her. "What do you mean?"

"If he's watching you—" a sly look comes into her eyes "—you can show him what he's missing."

57

Massimo

"What the—?" I stare at the window on my phone. The window that's linked to the app which monitors Via's apartment. So, I hadn't been completely truthful with her when I said I'd give her space. I mean, technically, I gave her space. I let her leave and I'm not with her physically. In fact, I haven't been in the same room as her since she'd left the hospital room.

I was relieved when she agreed to move into the apartment Peter suggested for her. Of course, if she decided to move elsewhere, I'd have found a way to bug that, too, so I could have eyes on her. And it has nothing to do with the fact that I love watching her when she's home. And when she's out, Peter has her in his line of sight all the time.

Technically, now that Alvaro's dead, she shouldn't be in any danger. But I underestimated the kind of security she'd need the last time, which is how Alvaro got that close to her. I don't intend to allow that to happen again. Hence, the level of security I've maintained around her. Of course, the fact that I always know where she is means I can keep her safe. Only, it hasn't prepared me for what she's up to right now.

I watch as she walks out of her closet wearing a skimpy robe made of a material that's so diaphanous I can see right through it. I can make out the bra and panties she's wearing, and fishnets that are held up by... It can't be, can it? Fuck me, she's wearing a garter belt. The blood drains to my groin.

Who the hell is she dressing up for? Herself? Me?

She walks toward the bed, picks up the package she placed on the nightstand earlier, then slides onto the bed. She leans back against the pillows, parts her legs just enough to give me a glimpse of the pink-colored panties she's wearing underneath. *Che cazzo!* Does she want to kill me?

I walk over to the armchair near the window of my bedroom and sit down. Thankfully, my brothers left a few days ago. They brought me home, made sure I was settled, then stayed to make sure I didn't need help around the house. It was only after JJ promised that he'd look in on me—as if I'm an invalid—and they ensured that my household staff were equipped to take care of me, that my brothers had finally taken their leave. Oh, and after Michael had, once more, warned me that while he didn't approve of my watching over Olivia, he understood why I had to do it this way.

I wonder if he realizes the extent to which I've taken the stalking, though.

Now, I watch as she places the box next to her on the bed. She tips up her chin and stares directly at me. Her green eyes gleam with intent.

Fuck me, but she definitely knows I am watching her.

How did she figure out where the camera's placed, though? The mirror's right opposite her bed, so perhaps she's watching herself in it. Yes, that's probably it. Just my luck that the camera's mounted on the top edge of its frame. She licks her lips and a shiver ripples down my spine. She slides her robe down her shoulders and it pools around her body. She spreads her legs wider, then slides her fingers into the waistband of her panties.

Heat coils in my belly, and my thighs stiffen. She begins to move her fingers inside her panties, the back-and-forth movements leaving me in no doubt that she's weaving her digits in and out of her cunt. My cock lengthens. The crotch of my jeans is uncomfortably tight, and I have no choice but to adjust myself. I shove my legs apart. My fingers tingle to touch myself and I resist. I really shouldn't masturbate, not when I'm watching her. That would be too stalkerish, wouldn't it? I curl my fingers into fists and dig my fingernails into the palms of my hands.

She bites down on her lower lip, and I feel it all the way to the crown of my dick.

Her movements intensify. She brings her other hand up to cup her tit. She squeezes her nipples through her bra and my balls tighten. My chest feels too full, and my shoulder muscles knot. I set my teeth as she pinches her nipples, turning them this way, then that. All the while she keeps working her fingers in and out of her pussy. I can almost smell the scent of her arousal. Her eyelids flutter down. She parts her lips, and color smears her cheeks. Her fingers jerk. Goddamnit, she tweaked her clit.

The sensations surge under my skin, sparking heat. Fuck this shit. I squeeze my length through my clothes as she pants.

The sound of her breathing fills the room. She raises her hips, shoves her panties down her legs, then kicks them aside. Once more, she spreads her legs.

My fingers tremble and I almost drop the phone. The pink flesh between her thighs is clearly visible. I reach for the app, zoom in further, and goddamn, the moisture clinging to her cunt is right there, in plain sight. My mouth waters. My scalp tingles. I lower my zipper, shove down my pants and boxers, and my cock springs free. I begin to massage myself from base to crown, again and again.

On the screen, she reaches for the box, opens it and pulls out a vibrator. A fucking pink-colored vibrator which, while not as big as the real thing between my legs, is sizable enough that it looks titillating as she runs her tongue down its ribbed length. She lowers it, and switches it on. A buzzing noise reaches me. Then, she slides the vibrator between her legs and holds it to her clit. Her entire body bucks and her head falls back. She writhes her hips, pushing her pelvis forward, and presses her upper body into the pillow. It's as if the sensations elicited by the device are too much for her to bear. She moans again, her chest rises and falls, and color flushes her cheeks. Her shoulders shudder and she raises the vibrator from her center. She lowers her chin and stares straight at me. I swear, she knows I'm watching—she *does* know I'm watching—for her lips curve in a seductive, very satisfied smile. Then she slides the vibrator inside her pussy.

She holds my gaze, and her mouth falls open. A low groan emerges from her lips. Her forearms flex and she slides the vibrator even deeper inside, all the way in.

Fuck. My cock thickens. I can almost feel the wet, hot suction of her pussy as she clenches her inner walls around my column. She pulls the device out, and I swipe my hand up my cock. She plunges it in, and I squeeze my shaft down to the base. And again. And again. I match each movement of hers with a corresponding stroke of my dick with my hand. My thigh muscles harden. The ball of tension at the base of my spine folds in on itself. The still-healing wound in my side protests, but I ignore it. The pressure builds, every cell in my body rigid, every muscle coiled, as I reach for that invisible line on the horizon. The one where I'll finally be with her and taste her, suck on her, squeeze her curves, and bite her lush lips as I fuck her.

Her smile widens. She continues to fuck herself with the vibrator. With her free hand she reaches for the phone next to her on the bed. She swipes the screen.

Then leaves the phone next to her. She reaches up once more to squeeze her tit, continues to shove the vibrator in and out of her.

That's when my phone rings. Her number lights up the screen. I accept the video call, look on the screen to find her surveying me.

"Enjoying the show, Massimo?" Her throaty purr sinks into my blood and arrows straight to my groin.

My balls grow unbearably hard. Fucking vixen, I'm going to teach her a lesson.

"Pull out the vibrator," I growl into the phone.

She hesitates.

"Do it, wife."

She draws in a sharp breath. Her pupils dilate. Then she pulls the device out from between her legs.

"Hold it up."

This time she obliges without hesitation.

"Now shut it off."

"Eh?"

I glare at her. She pales, then does as I ordered.

"Now bring it to your mouth."

"What?" She gapes.

"Do it," I snap.

Her eyes flash, but she does it.

"Now suck on it."

She swallows, glances at the length of the vibrator, then back at me, before she brings it closer to her lips. She pops out her little tongue, then swipes it up the vibrator. She licks it like an ice cream cone then swallows. I swear I feel the suction around my cock. I am so hard now, it's painful.

"*Cazzo*, you're so gorgeous, so beautiful, an erotic vision that I will never forget."

She continues to lick up the length of the device, then curls her tongue around the head. I almost come right then. I drag my fingers to the base of my length and squeeze. I will not come, will not. Not until I have urged her to climax first.

"Lower it to your cunt."

She holds my gaze, then brings the vibrator down to her pussy. She switches it on, and the buzzing sound infiltrates the space again. She holds it to her clit and gasps. Her breathing speeds up, her legs open wider, and she begins to squirm. "Massimo," she pants. "It's too much."

"Keep it right there."

She shakes her head, the color rising up her chest, then her neck, but she obliges. She digs the fingers of her free hand into the coverlet and holds on. A quiver runs up her body, and her arm shakes. An answering tremor grips me. I begin to squeeze my cock from head to base again. And again. And again.

"Massimo, please," she whines.

I twist my lips, and continue to massage my cock.

Another shudder runs up her body. Her entire body jolts. "Massimo, I can't, I have to—"

"Now, stuff that vibrator into your pussy," I order.

Instantly, she slides it inside her cunt and groans. "Oh, my god, oh, my god," she moans.

"Now pull it out."

She tugs the vibrator out until it's balanced at the opening of her slit.

"In," I order.

She shoves it back in; I squeeze my cock from head to base.

"Out."

She pulls out the device; I knead my shaft from base to head.

"Again."

Together we begin to fuck ourselves.

In. Out. In.

My movements grow more frantic. As do hers. The pressure at the base of my spine curls in on itself, growing tighter, compressing into a ball of pure tension that pulls in on itself.

"Fuck," I growl. The sound of wet flesh hitting flesh fills the air. Is it mine? Hers? It doesn't matter. We are one. Together. The climax builds and grows and reaches out to my extremities.

On screen, she gasps. Sweat beads her forehead and shines on her shoulders. She continues to work herself. Her body shudders, her toes curl, and she digs her heels into the mattress. I press my feet into the wooden floor, then squeeze my cock one last time.

"Come," I order.

58

Olivia

"I'm coming. Oh god, Massimo."

"Via," he growls. His shoulders roll forward. His chest heaves. He throws back his head, his gaze not leaving mine. His body grows rigid, every muscle coiled, the planes of his chest stretch the shirt he wears, and then, with a groan, he comes.

So do I. My entire body snaps back as the climax crashes over me. Moisture fills the space between my legs as sensations coalesce, collide, zing up my spine and explode. I see sparks of darkness and of light that dot my vision. Still, I don't close my eyes. I collapse, panting, holding his gaze as spurts of white stream from his cock and all over his shirt and his hands. And still, he continues to milk himself. It's the hottest thing I have ever seen—this man, falling apart, without breaking our connection.

The gray in his eyes bleeds out, leaving a clear, mirrored surface that reflects everything I'm feeling—love, lust, hope, want, need… I need him. I have to have him. Be with him. Within me. Inside me. In my heart. My soul. In my thoughts. I yearn for him. Can't live without him.

He cuts the call and I sink back into the sheets. My fingers tremble. I switch off the vibration, then drop it to the bed. My breath comes in puffs. My vision wavers as I float down from the aftermath of the climax. Every pore in my body seems to have opened. Exhaustion laces my limbs, even as adrenaline laces my blood.

This. This is what I've been missing my whole life. A calm at the end of the storm. The treasure at the end of the rainbow. The applause that greets me when I kill a performance. When I stand there on the stage, sweaty and breathless, with the spotlight in my eyes, blinding me so I can't see the audience, but sense them, their excitement, their euphoria, their adrenaline pumping as they jump to their feet and scream in delight. This...is how I felt right now, as I watched him come apart. As he revealed that vulnerable part of himself that I've always known he has at his core. This... oneness with him... I have never felt with anyone else. Will never feel with anyone else again. Only with him. Him. And it's all for me. Mine. For he belongs to me, the way an audience never can. They'll applaud me, and love me, and worship me when I have a big hit at the box office, and then they'll go home to their families. And me? I'll have him. As he has me.

We belong together in a way nothing else—not fame, not the satisfaction of a career—can replace. Not that this can replace that. I need that, too. But I need him as much. No, more. Penny was right. I need them both to balance me. Forcing myself to choose one over the other would mean I could never be complete.

Then I reach out my hand, toward the mirror. "I need you, Massimo."

"I'm here."

"Eh?" I jerk my head in the direction of the voice to find him framed in the doorway.

"What the—?" I gape. "How did you?" Understanding dawns. "You were never far away, were you? You have a flat in this building. Maybe on this very floor."

"Next door, actually." He prowls toward me. I rake my gaze down his broad shoulders that stretch the T-shirt he's wearing.

He's wearing a T-shirt?

And jeans?

I've never seen Massimo in such a casual getup before. With every step he takes, his jeans mold to his powerful thighs and pull tight across his crotch. His crotch, which is tented, with the bulge of his cock clearly outlined against the fabric. And he came just a few minutes ago. I know, because I saw it on the screen of my phone. Yet here he is, in real life, and completely aroused all over again. Is that even possible? Do men revive that quickly? Apparently, Massimo does. He halts next to the bed. I tilt my head all the way back to meet his gaze, those almost colorless eyes that eat me up with their intensity.

"You couldn't give me this one thing? You couldn't give me space?"

"I did."

"You were in a flat right next door to mine!" I set my jaw. "How is that giving me space?"

"I didn't see you. More importantly, you didn't see me. I didn't put myself in your path." He widens his stance. "Surely, that was enough to allow you to think things through without interference?"

I hesitate, then bite the inside of my cheek. "You had cameras on me in this flat, and I bet you had someone following me around."

"I did," he admits. "But I didn't call you, did I?"

"Big deal. You had access to everything I did. My movements, who I spoke to —" I start. "Did you bug my phone?"

He has the grace to look sheepish.

"You did bug my phone." I stare at him. Seriously, I can't even— I open my mouth to speak but nothing comes out. I raise my hands. "I don't know what to say."

He sits down on the bed next to me. "Don't say anything." He takes my hands in his. "Did you expect me to stay away?"

"Umm, yes?"

He glares at me, and my stomach flip-flops. This… stern, unyielding exterior of his? It's so damn hot. It gets me every time. And he knows it, too. He knows when to play the role of the dominant alphahole to a T. He knows just what it does to me. He runs his thumb across my wrist, and my pulse rate speeds up.

"You're such a liar, Via," he says in that dark, gravelly, thirst-trap voice of his. If I were to record it and sell it, I'd make millions. On the other hand, no way do I want any other woman listening to him. The timbre of his tone alone is enough to bring anyone to orgasm.

"I'm not a liar," I protest, but my voice emerges shaky.

His lips kick up.

"You left, hoping I'd keep tabs on you. That I'd care enough to pursue you, come after you, and convince you that I'm the only one for you."

"Actually, you don't need to do that anymore."

He frowns. "I don't?"

"That last orgasm was explosive enough to clarify my thoughts."

"It was?" he asks slowly.

"Seems the trick was not about putting distance between us, so much as experiencing as many climaxes as possible."

"O-k-a-y," he scans my features. A bemused look on his face.

I grip his hands and rise up on my knees, then swing my leg over to straddle him. His hands instantly come to my hips. I wind my arms about his neck and bring my face close to his.

"I really should be angry with you for stalking me."

"You should," he agrees.

"But I'm not."

He tilts his head. "Oh?" he says, his voice cautious.

How interesting. The moment I go on offense, he gets all confused. Good to know. Something I intend to use in the future. Because we do have a future together, for better or for worse. For richer or poorer. For whether he is in the Mafia or not. As long as he is Massimo… I am his Via.

"Mm… hmm." I rub my nose against his. "I did want some space and time to think, but you were right. Subconsciously, I also wanted you to come after me. And I think, deep inside, I knew you'd never let me just walk away from you. Still, I needed to try."

His lips twist. "And I had to try to let you have your way. I just couldn't stop myself from making sure you were safe."

"By having cameras in my apartment?"

"I'm sorry." He tightens his grip on my hips. "Not sorry," he adds.

I laugh. I can't help it.

His features relax a little. "Maybe I went a bit overboard, but I was taking no chances."

"Is that how it's going to be when we start our married life together? Are you going to stalk me every step of the way."

"Maybe—" He blinks. "Hold on, back up. Did you say married life?"

I nod.

"So, you've forgiven me for everything?" he asks cautiously.

"Not exactly. But I am coming around to the idea that there are some things about you I can't change. Things that aggravate me the most about you are also the very things that attract me to you."

"Don't toy with me, Via." He tightens his grip on my hips. "What are you trying to say?"

"That you have the balls the size of Iceland."

"You mean Texas?"

"When in Europe…" I raise a shoulder.

"Actually, we're in the UK," he points out.

"You know what I mean," I huff. "The point I'm trying to make, is that you're way too confident about yourself. And it's a trait I both loathe and love about you."

"Love, eh?" He hauls me so close that my breasts flatten against his chest.

"Yes, the L-word; that ol' chestnut," I murmur.

"That all you love about me?" His voice is light, but his gaze is intense.

"I also love your gorgeous eyes."

"My eyes?" He blinks.

"They change color with your emotions," I explain.

"My emotions?" He opens his mouth, no doubt, to deny it, but I shake my head.

"No, don't say it. You do have feelings that run quite deep. It's the reason you shot my brother. You were so angry at what he intended to do, and you knew you'd never be able to sway him completely from that route. You wanted to protect me, so you did what you thought was right."

He watches me closely, neither confirming nor denying.

"And I've seen you with your brothers. You'd do anything for your family."

A pulse flares to life at his temple.

"And for me. You'd do anything for me. You'd kill for me again, if necessary."

"In a heartbeat," he says simply.

"It's why you moved to London, even though your life is in Palermo."

"I am where you are. You are my home. When you're happy, I'm happy."

Tears prick the backs of my eyes. Damn. This man, he slays me.

"It's always more than I love you, isn't it?" I smile through the moisture that threatens to spill over. "You'll never be satisfied with the ordinary."

"I'll never be satisfied with anyone but you. If your love were a grain of sand, mine would be a universe of beaches."

"*The Princess Bride*," I exclaim. "You quoted from *The Princess Bride*?"

He smirks. "Now you have one more thing about me to love."

59

Massimo

She loves me. I see it in her eyes. In the way she runs her fingers through my hair. In how she leans even further into me. In how she gazes deeply into my eyes, and shares my breath, and places her lips in front of mine. In how she positions her core over the throbbing shaft at my crotch, in how she grinds down on the column and clenches her thighs around mine.

"Massimo," she breathes, and my cock threatens to tear through the fabric of my jeans.

I wrap my fingers about the nape of her neck and push my forehead into her hers. "You're mine, Via."

"Yours." She swallows. "Only yours."

"There's something I want you to see." I rise to my feet. She wraps her legs about my waist, and I carry her into the bathroom. I place her on the counter near the sink. Then pull a pen knife from my pocket.

"Umm, what's that?"

I merely smile, then pick out a lighter from another pocket. I flip open the blade of the knife, flick the lighter and hold the blade of the knife over it.

"What are you doing?" She laughs nervously.

I continue to burn the blade until every millimeter of it glows red from the flame. I shut the lighter and set it aside, then peer into the mirror over the sink.

"Your happiness is my quest, Olivia. Your sorrows are what I aim to demolish forever. And your pain—" I meet her gaze in the mirror "—I can only hope to experience so I may understand how it feels to be in your skin."

I raise the still glowing blade.

Her gaze widens. "Massimo, no—"

And drag the tip from the side of my eyebrow down to the center of my cheek.

"Massimo!" She shoves off the counter and leaps across the short distance to me. "What the hell?" she yells.

Pain rips through my face, up my temples, and explodes behind my eyes. I gasp. My eyes water. I lower the knife to the counter and carefully place it there.

"Why did you do that? Why, why, why?" Tears pour down her cheeks. "Massimo, your face, your poor face."

I wrap my hand around her waist and draw her to stand in front of me.

"Look," I gesture to the mirror.

"No, Massimo, no," she sobs.

"Look, Via." I pinch her chin, so she has no choice but to glance forward. Her gaze meets mine in the mirror.

"Now we match."

"Massimo." She bites down on her lower lip, and fuck, it's like there's a direct connection between that action of hers and my cock, which thickens further.

"Why?" she bursts out. "Why would you do that?"

"Now I know how it feels," I say simply.

She turns and throws her arms around my waist. She presses her face into my neck and cries even harder.

"You need to put ice on it. And antiseptic. And get a doctor to see to it," she says between her tears.

"I need you, Via."

She glances up. "You have me, Massimo. Remember when you said that when I hurt myself, I hurt you? Now, I understand what you mean by that. I understand why you said I was a part of you because you are a part of me, too."

My heart seems to swell in my chest. My entire body feels like a thousand little fires have engulfed it.

"I love you, you crazy, foolish, obnoxious alphahole." She swallows. "I have loved you from the moment I saw you in that bar. I love you more than I love myself, more than my career."

I quirk my lips. "If all it took was for me to hurt myself to hear you say that, I—"

She places her hand on my lips. "Don't. Please, don't say anything more. I've been stupid, Massimo. And selfish, and—"

"You deserve it all, Via. You deserve to achieve your dreams. You deserve to be celebrated as a woman. You deserve for your talent to be recognized by the world. And I'll be the one cheering you on from the head of the crowd."

"I don't deserve you," she whispers.

"That's true." I smirk. "But you have me anyway."

She slaps my shoulder, then peers into my face. "Please, can we take care of your face now?"

EPILOGUE

Massimo

We walk up the steps of JJ Kane's home. We pause on the top step, and she turns to me. "Does it hurt?" She gestures to the bandage on my cheek.

Yesterday, she wanted to call the ambulance, but I directed her to call JJ's doctor, who came immediately. He dressed the wound without comment—he's probably seen some strange things, considering who he works for—told me it wouldn't need stitches, and left. After prescribing some painkillers, which I, of course, ignored. The pain is good. It's a reminder of just how close I came to losing her.

Not that I would have ever let that happen, but when I saw her face after confessing to stalking her, when she realized I had been in the apartment next door all along… For a second there, I thought she'd leave me. I hoped she wouldn't. Hoped she'd understand why I had to do what I did… But it had been a risk.

So when, instead of getting angry with me, she actually told me she understood my stalker tendencies, I couldn't believe my luck. I don't deserve her. This woman, who has been through so much and come out stronger than she was before… I needed a way to show her just how much she means to me. It had to be what I did… It couldn't be anything else. This way, her stamp of ownership is on me for all the world to see. And I wear it proudly.

"It twinges a little, but otherwise, it's fine," I murmur.

"I hope it doesn't scar." Her brow furrows.

"I hope it does," I retort.

She shakes her head. "I still can't believe you did it."

"I knew I was going to do it as soon as you walked in on the engagement of your sister in that red dress and stood defiantly in the doorway."

"When I stumbled and found myself pressed against your chest, I thought I was imagining things. I had spent the last few days trying to forget you, and there you were, larger-than-life."

"I'll never forget about you lying to me and telling me you were in love with someone else."

"It was always you. I was just afraid of the intensity of my feelings for you." She leans up and smooths the lapels of my jacket.

"I have another surprise for you," I say softly.

She arches any eyebrow. "Does it have to do with guns or knives? Because, if so, I have to warn you, my husband already aced that space."

"Spoken like a true Mafia bride." I chuckle. "No, it's something more personal. Something to do with a horseshoe, actually.'"

"A horseshoe?" Her forehead furrows.

"Look in the inside pocket of my jacket."

She dips her hand inside, and pulls out the chain with the horseshoe pendant. Her gaze widens. "This is—" She squints at it, then at me. "Is this—"

"It is." I take the chain from her, then fasten it around her neck. "There, now you look perfect."

She fingers the pendant. "Where did you find it? It was a gift from my father. I looked everywhere for it. I thought I'd lost it."

"You left it behind in the bed where we first made love."

"Oh." She lowers her eyelids, and when she raises them again, her eyes shine. "All this time, Massimo—" She swallows. "You had it all along?"

"Every part of you belongs to me, *Stellina*. You didn't think I'd ever let anyone else find it, did you? I kept it because it was a link to you, a touchstone. Every time I missed you, I caressed it and felt closer to you. I was sure it would bring us back together, and I was right. I'm never letting you go again, Via."

"Massimo." She searches between my eyes. "I love you."

"I love you, too." I caress her cheek. "And you can thank me properly when we get home, but for now, you can start with telling me how I look."

"Do you even have to ask?" She tugs on the lapels, and I bend my head. She leans up on tiptoes and presses a kiss to my lips. "You look like the most handsome man in the world. I already know, when you remove the bandage, the scar is only going to add to your rakish good looks. I'm going to have to fight to keep the women away from you."

"Women, what women?" I glance around, then back at her. "I only have eyes for you, baby."

"Flattery will get you everywhere." She laughs.

"Thank you for seeing the psychologist earlier today." I brush my knuckles across her cheek.

"Thank you for making me see one. I'm sure it's going to make a difference. Although, I have to admit—" she bites the inside of her cheek "—I think you were right. Since we started fucking again, I haven't cut myself."

"And if I have my way, you'll never be without endorphins in your blood stream. You know what that means, right?"

"What does it mean?"

"That we need to make an appearance and get out of here so I can make love to you again." I wrap my arms around her waist, thankful that the wound in my side doesn't hurt anymore, then haul her to her toes and kiss her thoroughly. She presses her lush body against mine, curves her head back, opens her lips, and allows me to plunder her mouth. I widen my stance, balancing both of our weights as I bend her back.

I hear the sound of the door opening, but ignore it as I swipe my tongue across hers and drink from her. Goddamn, maybe we should have delayed coming, or not come at all. We could have stayed back, and I could have explored every inch of her delicious body all over again. I'll never have enough of her. Not ever.

Someone clears their throat.

"We do have bedrooms here, if you'd like me to show you one," JJ says in a mild tone.

She yelps and tries to pull away, but I continue kissing her for another second or more. By the time I release her, she's flushed, panting, and her eyes have that glazed look I love. She blinks up at me and I smirk.

She scowls back, then laughs, her features lighting up. Goddamn, she's the most beautiful woman in the entire world.

"You guys ready to come in?"

Olivia

"Surprise!"

I walk into JJ's living room and gasp when I see the assembled faces. I recognize Axel and his wife Theresa, who are near the window; Christian, who has his arms around his wife Aurora; Luca, who has Jeanne tucked into his side; Seb, who is on his knees talking to a little girl who looks just like her mother Elsa; and Michael, with Karma, who smiles and waves. The child holds a wriggling Andy in her arm. She bends and places the cat on the ground. He runs over to me and pauses, looking at me warily. I lower myself to a crouch and pet him. He instantly rubs his cheek against my hand and begins to purr. Seb and Elsa's little girl runs over to join me. She drops to her knees and begins to tickle Andy, who snorts. The cat actually huffs a snort.

The girl laughs and picks up the cat, who curls into her chest. She rises to her feet and looks at me with big blue eyes. She reminds me so much of Solene, my heart stutters.

Solene is going to be fine. She's in LA with Declan, who promised to help her find an agent. I trust Declan, and the man, clearly, has feelings for Solene, even though he hasn't come right out and told her. Last Solene told me, the two of them were sharing separate rooms at Declan's place. We'll see how long that's going to last. She's done the right thing, taking him up on his offer to help with her career. She's such a gifted singer. All she needs is the right agent, the right break, and she'll be famous. I know it. And the person best placed to help her is Declan.

I look up from where I'm crouched on the floor. "Hey, baby." I touch the little girl's cheek. "What's your name?"

She stares back at me.

"She's still shy with strangers." Elsa comes over to join us. "Say hello to *Zia* Olivia, Avery."

The girl blinks. "Hello," she says in a shy voice.

"Is this your cat?" I smile at her.

She shakes her head.

"Then whose is it?"

She turns and points at Karma, who walks over to us.

I stand up and heat envelops me, then Massimo's large hands land on my hips. "Who have we here?" His voice rumbles from somewhere up and behind me. My nerve endings instantly seem to fire all at once. I lean back and into him. Avery glances up at him and a smile lights up her face.

"Ma-i-mo," she warbles.

Massimo laughs. "How are you, Sprite?"

She flutters her eyelashes, and I can literally feel Massimo melting. He steps around and holds out his arms, and the girl leans into them. He plucks her and the cat from the floor.

"Well, she already has the men wrapped around her little finger." Karma laughs.

Massimo lowers his head until his mouth is close to my ear. "But you'll always be my favorite girl," he whispers, then kisses my cheek. When he straightens, I see the gleam in his eyes. "I'll go see my brothers." He smiles down at me, before moving away.

"These Sovrano men sure know how to make a woman feel special." Elsa laughs.

"They're hot, dominant, and possessive, but oh-so caring," Karma adds.

I shake my head, trying to get rid of the Massimo daze.

"I know how you feel, girl." Karma nudges me. "I'm still not over the effect Michael's presence has on me. All he has to do is look at me, and my ovaries flutter."

"Mommy," Avery calls out.

"Be right there, sweetie." Elsa looks from Avery to me, then smiles and says, "I'm sorry, motherhood calls. It's wonderful to be able to formally welcome you to the family." Elsa kisses me on both cheeks, then turns to head off after her daughter.

"All of you are being so nice to me." I turn to Karma. "I can't believe you flew out to London for this gathering."

"Michael insisted." Karma hooks her arm through mine. "When he found out what Alvaro had done, he was out of his mind with worry. He had planned to sell a few business assets to fund the money Alvaro had asked for to free you. Then Massimo called and told him you were fine. He mentioned how much JJ had helped them, and Michael decided to come to London to meet with JJ. Then, the rest of the Sovranos wanted to come to make sure the two of you were okay. So, we decided to make an extended family trip out of it."

A warm sensation envelops me. "Still, all of you turning up here?" I shake my head. "You guys are amazing, every single one of you."

"You're family," she says simply.

It's not like my own family doesn't love me, but after my father's death, it seemed like we lost the core of what held us together. My mother always sided with my brother, and while she surprised me on my wedding day with her candid talk, I'm not sure if she sees my alliance to the Sovranos as anything more than one which lends me legitimacy within our immediate community. And now that Solene has left for LA, these people here are my immediate support structure.

I wrap my arms around Karma and hug her. She pats my back. "We'll always be here for you, Olivia."

"Thanks." I swallow the ball of emotion which clogs my throat. When I finally step back, she peers into my face. "You okay?"

I sniffle, then nod. "I am now."

"Good. So, he made sure he has a matching scar, huh?" She touches her cheek.

I stare. "How do you—?"

"It was the logical conclusion to draw, given the placement of the bandage, and somehow, I'm not surprised he did it."

"I'm surprised. I didn't expect him to do that. And—" My chin wobbles. "He didn't even flinch. He just took the knife and—" I shake my head. "He didn't have to do it, you know."

"Maybe he had to do it for himself? Maybe he had to do it for the both of you."

"It… completely floored me. Talk about romantic gestures. That's one I'll never forget for the rest of my life."

"It's a typical Sovrano gesture. When they find the woman of their dreams, they go all out. They won't stop until they've made you theirs completely."

I take her hand in mine. "Thanks, Karma, for everything. You've smoothed my transition into this family."

"You're welcome, you—" She flinches suddenly, then presses her other hand to her stomach.

"What happened?"

"Shh." She flicks a glance sideways to where Michael is deep in conversation with Massimo.

"Come this way." She grips my hand with hers and urges me to follow her to the far end of the spacious living room. She sinks down into a chair, and I sit down in the one next to her.

"You okay?"

"I will be. It's just, this pregnancy. It's causing me a lot of heartburn. Literally." She laughs halfheartedly.

"Do you need to see a doctor?" I frown.

She flicks another glance in the direction of Michael. "Oh, I've been seeing one. There's something I need to tell Michael. I've been working up toward it, is all."

"Nothing serious, I hope?"

She hesitates. "No, nothing serious."

"You sure?"

She glances away then back at me. "I'm sure."

"Karma." I lean closer. "If Michael is anything like Massimo, and I'm assuming he is, then I think he'll want you to share whatever it is that's worrying you "

She shakes her head, her features pinched. "It's really not that big of a deal."

I frown at her, not quite believing her. "Whatever it is, you need to tell him, Karma."

Her brow furrows. She bites down on her lower lip, then nods. "You're right, of course. I'm going to tell him... Very soon."

"Why not right now?"

"Not now. This is your event."

"Your health is more important." I'm about to stand up, but she grabs hold of my arm and tugs me back down. "I promise, I'll tell him. Besides—" She jerks her chin toward the doorway. "I believe there's some drama about to unfold."

"Drama?" I turn to follow the direction she's indicated, then pause when I notice the couple at the doorway. The man is in his early twenties. With dark hair and dark eyes, his build is lean, with broad shoulders. His features are striking. He wears a beard and mustache, and his hair is long enough to brush his shoulders. His jeans are frayed at the edges, his jacket worn out with wear. He also has a scowl on his face. The way he strides into the room reminds me of someone.

The woman is curvaceous, with big brown eyes, auburn hair, and an olive complexion that hints at her exotic heritage. Her eyebrows are furrowed, her gaze slightly angry.

JJ watches them with a narrowed gaze. His shoulders are bunched and strain the jacket he's wearing. The few times I've seen this man, he's always been impeccably dressed. He's an attractive man, with his thick, wavy hair graying at the temples, the lines that fan out from the corners of his eyes, and the bunched tendons at his throat, not to mention, he's every inch an alpha male. He's the same height as the man who stalks past the Sovranos and heads for the bar. Only where JJ has the kind of presence that commands a room and a physique that's as impressive as any of the Sovranos', the other man—who is definitely his son—has yet to fill out the promise of adulthood hinted at in the lines of his body.

The woman—who, I assume, is his son's girlfriend—joins the young man at the bar.

Conversations come to a halt. I glance around the room to find the rest of the Sovranos are watching the unfolding scene with interest. My gaze clashes with familiar gray eyes. I shiver. Massimo watches me from under hooded lids. His lips quirk, and a slow burn begins low in my belly. Will I ever be able to watch him without getting turned on? Probably not.

The muted voices of the arguing couple reach me. I turn to find the girl leaning toward the man. Her body language indicates she's half angry, half trying to appease him. She touches his hand, and he jerks it away. She says something, which only makes him glower. She seems to be cajoling him not to drink, which considering it's not yet noon, is a reasonable ask. The young man tosses his head. He replies in tones too low to hear, but judging by their exchange, which grows more heated by the moment, the two of them are in the midst of an argument.

"You seeing what I'm seeing?" Karma mutters.

"I assume that's JJ's son and his girlfriend?"

"You assume right."

"And they don't seem to be getting along all that well at the moment?" I hazard a guess.

"I'm guessing there's more to it than meets the eye."

She jerks her chin toward the other side of the room. I turn to find JJ with his arms crossed over his chest, his brow furrowed. His features have a look I can only describe as yearning. His gaze is fixed on someone. I follow his line of sight to where his son's girlfriend now has her fingers clasped together. She's biting her lips as if trying hard not to reply back to the other man.

"What's JJ's son's name?" I ask.

"I believe it's Isaac," Karma replies.

Isaac's lips move, he tosses back his drink, slaps his glass on the bar counter, then reaches for the bottle of whiskey again.

She grabs it from him. The two struggle for a few seconds. She manages to wrest it from him, and that's when his features contort. He raises his arm.

Silence descends. I sense Michael tense. Massimo moves forward, but it's JJ who dashes across the room in time to grab his son's arm before his palm can touch the girl.

To find out what happens next read JJ and Lena's story HERE

Read an excerpt

Lena

"Get the hell away from her," a voice reaches me, and a second later, JJ plants his bulk between me and my boyfriend. He grabs Isaac's arm and shoves it down with enough force that he stumbles back.

"What the hell?" I hear Isaac growl in surprise but don't see his face because JJ has his back turned to me. The way he's positioned his body is such that I can't see Isaac. But I hear him when he says, "Did you think I was going to hit her?" He sounds shocked. "Really, JJ?"

Yeah, he calls his dad by his name, or rather, his initials. In the week I've spent at their place, I haven't heard anyone refer to his dad as anything but JJ. Not that I care what his name is; I've had too much on my mind, trying to figure out what the hell I was thinking, moving into my boyfriend's father's house. Not that I'd had a choice.

I completed my internship at an advertising agency, and hoped it would lead to a job. My boss made it clear I was in the running for a role—along with all ten other interns. He asked me what I could do that would set me apart. It didn't take me too long to realize he was asking if I'd sleep with him to get the job.

Of course, I marched right up to HR and told them about it. Naturally, my boss denied it. He was called in for questioning with the CEO, and the last I heard, he lost his role. But then, I didn't get the job, either. I went through the interview process and wasn't selected. A tiny part of me is sure it's because of what I did. They probably saw me as a troublemaker and didn't want me in the company. And truthfully, I'm not sure I'd want to work for a company that would view a whistleblower as a troublemaker. Either way, I wouldn't go back and change anything. My boss got his comeuppance, and he deserved it. At least, any interns coming after me won't be subjected to his brand of sleaziness.

Unfortunately, it still doesn't solve the problem of my employment. So, it's back to emailing my resume and looking for a job. Meanwhile, Isaac lost his job, too—probably because he was too lazy to go into work most days.

If it weren't for the fact that he was there for me during a time in my life when I needed someone in my corner, I wouldn't be with him. But I feel obliged to be there for him now, when he's struggling with whatever issues he's facing. And how much of that is thanks to the man standing between us right now? Well, the jury is out on that.

"Of course you'd believe the worst of me, wouldn't you? Easier to label me the culprit than to give me the benefit of the doubt. Well, you and your so-called friends can go fuck yourselves." He brushes past the both of us and stomps toward the door.

"Isaac." I take a step forward, but he's already marched out of the room. The door slams behind him, and I'm aware of every single person in the room watching the unfolding scene. I don't know any of them, but they seem well-off —well-dressed, the women wearing designer clothes, and the men wearing tailor-made suits like JJ. That's the one thing I noticed right away...

How well-groomed JJ always is, as opposed to Isaac, who seems to live in jeans and T-shirts. Too bad his father's attitude is a thousand times worse than Isaac's. Also, that entire don't-care look Isaac has going for him is a part of what attracted me to him in the first place. Working a corporate job, even as an intern, meant I had to conform to a certain way of dressing, and had to be polite and charming to clients all day long.

In comparison, Isaac's 'I don't give a fuck about anything or anyone' persona was a breath of fresh air. That, combined with his bearded hipsterish look, had been so appealing. But then, I'd also thought he was a struggling artist who took construction assignments on the side to keep some money coming in... When he bothered to turn up on the job, that is.

Many days, he insisted his muse was speaking to him, and he'd disappear for days on end, only to return with the most breathtaking photographs. And his compositions were brilliant, I'll give him that. Only, he hasn't sold any yet. And he's so stubborn, he'd rather hold down a construction job than demean his art by photographing weddings or other family occasions, which pay well. That is, when he managed to hold down a job. And it goes without saying that he refused my help in marketing his work.

So, when I lost my job and we were unable to pay the next month's rent, we were left with little choice but to move in with his father. Which is the first time I found out about his background. Isaac is rich... More specifically, his father's rich. Like, really, really rich, if the size of the house and the grounds around it in the center of prime real estate in London is anything to go by.

Doesn't mean I take kindly to him sticking his nose where it doesn't belong. So, maybe Isaac made it not so personal anymore by walking into a room full of guests and throwing a fit; still, I can manage my own shit.

"Now look what you did." I turn on JJ. "Why did you have to interfere? I had it under control."

"Oh yeah?" JJ looks me up and down. "From where I was standing, it seemed like he was going to hit you, and I'm not going to stand by and watch that happen in my home."

"Isaac is a lot of things, but he has never physically abused me, ever."

"What about emotional and mental abuse?" JJ snaps back.

I hesitate.

"That's what I thought."

"This is your son we're talking about," I point out.

"All the more reason that he behaves." JJ draws himself up to his full height, which means he towers over me. He glances down that arrogant nose of his, from that six-foot-three... or is it four-inch height of his. "As long as the two of you are under my roof, my rules apply. And that includes him being civil to you."

"You have no idea about the relationship between the two of us. I know I'm living under your roof, so I don't want to appear ungrateful—"

"You already do, but that won't stop you from saying whatever it is you're planning to say," he mutters under his breath.

"—but you coming in between us is not helping at all. It's only making things worse. So please, may I request that you stay out of our dealings and let us work things out?"

JJ's gaze widens. He opens his mouth, no doubt, to tell me off, but I don't give him the chance. I turn and head for the doorway, hoping to catch Isaac and try to smooth things over.

"Girl," he calls out after me.

Pompous, stuck-up prick. Would it kill him to call me by my name? Even though Isaac introduced us, grudgingly, his father has refused to acknowledge that I have a name.

It's like I'm a piece of furniture in this house. No, strike that. He lavishes the furniture in this house with a lot more attention. It's more like I'm a piece of gum stuck on his shoe, and every time I'm near him, it's like he's trying to scrape me off. Which suits me fine.

It's not difficult to stay out of his way anyway, in this massive mausoleum he calls home. Honestly, it's no wonder he always looks like he has a stick up his arse. Admittedly, a very well-formed tush for a man of his age. Not that I've looked or anything.

Okay... I may have looked out the window and spotted him swimming in the outdoor pool. It was early in the morning when it was freezing outside, but that didn't deter him. He swam back and forth for at least twenty laps before he pulled himself out the pool and walked over to the towel on the nearest chaise and began to dry himself with his back to me... Jesus, let me tell you, that man has one fine body. He's old enough to be my father, but he sure doesn't look anything like a man his age should. Broad shoulders, sculpted back, narrow waist, and did I mention a heck of a tight arse? My fingers tingled, my skin buzzed, and I pressed my nose into the glass pane and watched avidly. He must have sensed the stare, for he turned around and glanced right up at me. Only, I had ducked to the side and avoided being seen. At least, I think I did… I stayed there for many long minutes before I finally worked up the courage to peek again, by which time, he'd left already. Like I said, he's one fine piece of masculinity—far sexier than my boyfriend. And while I didn't see his front to figure out what he's packing, I wager it must be something out of the ordinary, considering the size of his ego. Clearly, the man must have balls the size of my college debt, if that permanent scowl on his face is anything to go by. Or perhaps, he's just constipated.

"I do have a name, old man," I growl at him over my shoulder.

He seems taken aback, and blinks, as if noticing me for the first time.

"Don't walk away while I am talking to you," he says through gritted teeth.

I laugh, then just because I know it'll antagonize him, and even though he's my host and I'm dependent on his benevolence—or maybe, precisely because of that—I do something very out of character. I show him both of my middle fingers. "Try to stop me."

To find out what happens next read JJ and Lena's story HERE

Read Michael & Karma's story in Mafia King HERE
Read an excerpt from Mafia King

Karma

"Morn came and went—and came, and brought no day…"

Tears prick the backs of my eyes. Goddamn Byron. His words creep up on me when I am at my weakest. Not that I am a poetry addict, by any measure, but words are my jam. The one consolation I have is that, when everything else in the world is wrong, I can turn to them, and they'll be there, friendly, steady, waiting with open arms.

And this particular poem had laced my blood, crawled into my gut when I'd first read it. Darkness had folded within me like an insidious snake, that raises its head when I least expect it. Like now, when I look out on the still sleeping city of London, from the grassy slope of Waterlow Park.

Somewhere out there, the Mafia is hunting me, apparently. It's why my sister Summer and her new husband Sinclair Sterling had insisted that I have my own security detail. I had agreed...only to appease them...then given my bodyguard the slip this morning. I had decided to come running here because it's not a place I'd normally go... Not so early in the morning, anyway. They won't think to look for me here. At least, not for a while longer.

I purse my lips, close my eyes. Silence. The rustle of the wind between the leaves. The faint tinkle of the water from the nearby spring.

I could be the last person on this planet, alone, unsung, bound for the grave.

Ugh! Stop. Right there. I drag the back of my hand across my nose. Try it again, focus, get the words out, one after the other, like the steps of my sorry life.

"Morn came and went—and came, and... and..." My voice breaks. "Bloody asinine hell." I dig my fingers into the grass and grab a handful and fling it out. Again. From the top.

"Morn came and went—and came, and—"

"...brought no day."

A gravelly voice completes my sentence.

I whip my head around. His silhouette fills my line of sight. He's sitting on the same knoll as me, yet I have to crane my neck back to see his profile. The sun is at his back, so I can't make out his features. Can't see his eyes... Can only take in his dark hair, combed back by a ruthless hand that brooked no measure.

My throat dries.

Thick dark hair, shot through with grey at the temples. He wears his age like a badge. I don't know why, but I know his years have not been easy. That he's seen more, indulged in more, reveled in the consequences of his actions, however extreme they might have been. He's not a normal, everyday person, this man. Not a nine-to-fiver, not someone who lives an average life. Definitely not a man who returns home to his wife and home at the end of the day. He is…different, unique, evil… Monstrous. Yes, he is a beast, one who sports the face of a man but who harbors the kind of darkness inside that speaks to me. I gulp.

His face boasts a hooked nose, a thin upper lip, a fleshy lower lip. One that hints at hidden desires, Heat. Lust. The sensuous scrape of that whiskered jaw over my innermost places. Across my inner thigh, reaching toward that core of me that throbs, clenches, melts to feel the stab of his tongue, the thrust of his hardness as he impales me, takes me, makes me his. Goosebumps pop on my skin.

I drag my gaze away from his mouth down to the scar that slashes across his throat. A cold sensation coils in my chest. What or who had hurt him in such a cruel fashion?

"Of this their desolation; and all hearts
Were chill'd into a selfish prayer for light…"

He continues in that rasping guttural tone. Is it the wound that caused that scar that makes his voice so…gravelly… So deep…so…so, hot?

Sweat beads my palms and the hairs on my nape rise. "Who are you?"

He stares ahead as his lips move,

"Forests were set on fire—but hour by hour
They fell and faded—and the crackling trunks
Extinguish'd with a crash—and all was black."

I swallow, moisture gathers in my core. How can I be wet by the mere cadence of this stranger's voice?

I spring up to my feet.

"Sit down," he commands.

His voice is unhurried, lazy even, his spine erect. The cut of his black jacket stretches across the width of his massive shoulders. His hair… I was mistaken—there are threads of dark gold woven between the darkness that pours down to brush the nape of his neck. A strand of hair falls over his brow. As I watch, he raises his hand and brushes it away. Somehow, the gesture lends an air of vulnerability to him. Something so at odds with the rest of his persona that, surely, I am mistaken?

My scalp itches. I take in a breath and my lungs burn. This man… He's sucked up all the oxygen in this open space as if he owns it, the master of all he surveys. The master of me. My death. My life. A shiver ladders along my spine. *Get away, get away now, while you still can.*

I angle my body, ready to spring away from him.

"I won't ask again."

Ask. Command. Force me to do as he wants. He'll have me on my back, bent over, on my side, on my knees, over him, under him. He'll surround me, overwhelm me, pin me down with the force of his personality. His charisma, his larger-than-life essence will crush everything else out of me and I… I'll love it.

"No."

"Yes."

A fact. A statement of intent, spoken aloud. So true. So real. Too real. Too much. Too fast. All of my nightmares…my dreams come to life. Everything I've wanted is here in front of me. I'll die a thousand deaths before he'll be done with me… And then? Will I be reborn? For him. For me. For myself.

I live, first and foremost, to be the woman I was…am meant to be.

"You want to run?"

No.

No.

I nod my head.

He turns his, and all the breath leaves my lungs. Blue eyes—cerulean, dark like the morning skies, deep like the nighttime…hidden corners, secrets that I don't dare uncover. He'll destroy me, have my heart, and break it so casually.

My throat burns and a boiling sensation squeezes my chest.

"Go then, my beauty, fly. You have until I count to five. If I catch you, you are mine."

"If you don't?"

"Then I'll come after you, stalk your every living moment, possess your nightmares, and steal you away in the dead of night, and then…"

I draw in a shuddering breath as liquid heat drips from between my legs. "Then?" I whisper.

"Then, I'll ensure you'll never belong to anyone else, you'll never see the light of day again, for your every breath, your every waking second, your thoughts, your actions…and all your words, every single last one, will belong to me." He peels back his lips, and his teeth glint in the first rays of the morning light. "Only me." He straightens to his feet and rises, and rises.

This man… He is massive. A monster who always gets his way. My guts churn. My toes curl. Something primeval inside of me insists I hold my own. I cannot give in to him. Cannot let him win whatever this is. I need to stake my ground, in some form. *Say something. Anything. Show him you're not afraid of this.*

"Why?" I tilt my head back, all the way back. "Why are you doing this?"

He tilts his head, his ears almost canine in the way they are silhouetted against his profile.

"Is it because you can? Is it a…a," I blink, "a debt of some kind?"

He stills.

"My father, this is about how he betrayed the Mafia, right? You're one of them?"

"Lucky guess." His lips twist, "It is about your father, and how he promised you to me. He reneged on his promise, and now, I am here to collect."

"No." I swallow... *No, no, no.*

"Yes." His jaw hardens.

All expression is wiped clean of his face, and I know then, that he speaks the truth. It's always about the past. My sorry shambles of a past... Why does it always catch up with me? *You can run, but you can never hide.*

"Tick-tock, Beauty." He angles his body and his shoulders shut out the sight of the sun, the dawn skies, the horizon, the city in the distance, the rustle of the grass, the trees, the rustle of the leaves. All of it fades and leaves just me and him. Us. *Run.*

"Five." He jerks his chin, straightens the cuffs of his sleeves.

My knees wobble.

"Four."

My pulse rate spikes. I should go. Leave. But my feet are planted in this earth. This piece of land where we first met. What am I, but a speck in the larger scheme of things? To be hurt. To be forgotten. To be taken without an ounce of retribution. To be punished...by him.

"Three." He thrusts out his chest, widens his stance, every muscle in his body relaxed. "Two."

I swallow. The pulse beats at my temples. My blood thrums.

"One."

Michael

"Go."

She pivots and races down the slope. Her dark hair streams behind her. Her scent, sexy femininity and silver moonflowers, clings to my nose, then recedes. It's so familiar, that scent.

I had smelled it before, had reveled in it. Had drawn in it into my lungs as she had peeked up at me from under her thick eyelashes. Her green gaze had fixed on mine, her lips parted as she welcomed my kiss. As she had wound her arms about my neck, pushed up those sweet breasts and flattened them against my chest. As she had parted her legs when I had planted my thigh between them. I had seen her before...in my dreams. I stiffen. She can't be the same girl though, can she?

I reach forward, thrust out my chin and sniff the air, but there's only the damp scent of dawn, mixed with the foul tang of exhaust fumes, as she races away from me.

She stumbles and I jump forward, pause when she straightens. Wait. Wait. Give her a lead. Let her think she has almost escaped, that she's gotten the better of me... As if.

I clench my fists at my sides, force myself to relax. Wait. Wait. She reaches the bottom of the incline, turns. I surge forward. One foot in front of the other. My heels dig into the grassy surface and mud flies up, clings to the hem of my £4000 Italian pants. Like I care? Plenty more where that came from. An entire walk-in closet, full of clothes made to measure, to suit every occasion, with every possible accessory needed by a man in my position to impress...

Everything... Except the one thing that I had coveted from the moment I had laid eyes on her. Sitting there on the grassy slope, unshed tears in her eyes, and reciting... Byron? For hell's sake. Of all the poets in the world, she had to choose the Lord of Darkness.

I huff. All a ploy. Clearly, she knew I was sitting next to her... No, not possible. I had walked toward her and she hadn't stirred. Hadn't been aware. Yeah, I am that good. I've been known to slit a man's throat from ear-to-ear while he was awake and in his full senses. Alive one second, dead the next. That's how it is in my world. You want it, you take it. And I... I want her.

I increase my pace, eat up the distance between myself and the girl... That's all she is. A slip of a thing, a slim blur of motion. Beauty in hiding. A diamond, waiting for me to get my hands on her, polish her, show her what it means to be...

Dead. She is dead. That's why I am here.

A flash of skin, a creamy length of thigh. My groin hardens and my legs wobble. I lurch over a bump in the ground. The hell? I right myself, leap forward, inching closer, closer. She reaches a curve in the path, disappears out of sight.

My heart hammers in my chest. I will not lose her, will not. *Here, Beauty, come to Daddy.* The wind whistles past my ears. I pump my legs, lengthen my strides, turn the corner. There's no one there. Huh?

My heart hammers and the blood pounds at my wrists, my temples; adrenaline thrums in my veins. I slow down, come to a stop. Scan the clearing.

The hairs on my forearms prickle. She's here. Not far, but where? Where is she? I prowl across to the edge of the clearing, under the tree with its spreading branches.

When I get my hands on you, Beauty, I'll spread your legs like the pages of a poem. Dip into your honeyed sweetness, like a quill pen in ink. Drag my aching shaft across that melting, weeping entrance. My balls throb. My groin tightens. The crack of a branch above shivers across my stretched nerve endings. I swoop forward, hold out my arms, and close my grasp around the trembling, squirming mass of precious humanity. I cradle her close to my chest, heart beating thud-thud-thud, overwhelming any other thought.

Mine. All mine. The hell is wrong with me? She wriggles her little body, and her curves slide across my forearms. My shoulders bunch and my fingers tingle. She kicks out with her legs and arches her back, thrusting her breasts up so her nipples are outlined against the fabric of her sports bra. She dared to come out dressed like that? In that scrap of fabric that barely covers her luscious flesh?

"Let me go." She whips her head toward me and her hair flows around her shoulders, across her face. She blows it out of the way. "You monster, get away from me."

Anger drums at the backs of my eyes and desire tugs at my groin. The scent of her is sheer torture, something I had dreamed of in the wee hours of twilight when dusk turned into night.

She's not real. She's not the woman I think she is. She is my downfall. My sweet poison. The bitter medicine I must partake of to cure the ills that plague my company,

"Fine." I lower my arms and she tumbles to the grass, hits the ground butt first.

"How dare you." She huffs out a breath, her hair messily arranged across her face.

I shove my hands into the pockets of my fitted pants, knees slightly bent, legs apart. Tip my chin down and watch her as she sprawls at my feet.

"You...dropped me?" She makes a sound deep in her throat.

So damn adorable.

"Your wish is my command." I quirk my lips.

"You don't mean it."

"You're right." I lean my weight forward on the balls of my feet and she flinches.

"What...what do you want?"

"You."

She pales. "You want to...to rob me? I have nothing of consequence,

"Oh, but you do, Beauty."

I lean in and every muscle in her body tenses. Good. She's wary. She should be. She should have been alert enough to have run as soon as she sensed my presence. But she hadn't.

I should spare her because she's the woman from my dreams...but I won't. She's a debt I intend to collect. She owes me, and I've delayed what was meant to happen long enough.

I pull the gun from my holster, point it at her.

Her gaze widens and her breath hitches. I expect her to plead with me for her life, but she doesn't. She stares back at me with her huge dilated pupils. She licks her lips and the blood drains to my groin. *Che cazzo!* Why does her lack of fear turn me on so?

"Your phone," I murmur, "take out your phone."

She draws in a breath, then reaches into her pocket and pulls out her phone.

"Call your sister."

"What?"

"Dial your sister, Beauty. Tell her you are going away on a long trip to Sicily with your new male friend."

"What?"

"You heard me." I curl my lips, "Do it, now!'

She blinks, looks like she is about to protest, then her fingers fly over the phone.

Damn, and I had been looking forward to coaxing her into doing my bidding.

She holds her phone to her ear. I can hear the phone ring on the other side, before it goes to voicemail. She glances at me and I jerk my chin. She looks away, takes a deep breath, then speaks in a cheerful voice, "Hi Summer, it's me, Karma. I, ah, have to go away for a bit. This new...ah, friend of mine... He has an extra ticket and he has invited me to Sicily to spend some time with him. I...ah, I don't know when, exactly, I'll be back, but I'll message you and let you know. Take care. Love ya sis. I—"

I snatch the phone from her, disconnect the call, then hold the gun to her temple, "Goodbye, Beauty."

To find out what happens next read Mafia King **HERE**

Read Summer & Sinclair Sterling's story **HERE** in The Billionaire's Fake Wife

Read an excerpt from Summer & Sinclair's story

Summer

"Slap, slap, kiss, kiss."

"Huh?" I stare up at the bartender.

"Aka, there's a thin line between love and hate." He shakes out the crimson liquid into my glass.

"Nah." I snort. "Why would she allow him to control her, and after he insulted her?"

"It's the chemistry between them." He lowers his head, "You have to admit that when the man is arrogant and the woman resists, it's a challenge to both of them, to see who blinks first, huh?"

"Why?" I wave my hand in the air, "Because they hate each other?"

"Because," he chuckles, "the girl in school whose braids I pulled and teased mercilessly, is the one who I—"

"Proposed to?" I huff.

His face lights up. "You get it now?"

Yeah. No. A headache begins to pound at my temples. This crash course in pop psychology is not why I came to my favorite bar in Islington, to meet my best friend, who is—I glance at the face of my phone—thirty minutes late.

I inhale the drink, and his eyebrows rise.

"What?" I glower up at the bartender. "I can barely taste the alcohol. Besides, it's free drinks at happy hour for women, right?"

"Which ends in precisely" he holds up five fingers, "minutes."

"Oh! Yay!" I mock fist pump. "Time enough for one more, at least."

A hiccough swells my throat and I swallow it back, nod.

One has to do what one has to do... when everything else in the world is going to shit.

A hot sensation stabs behind my eyes; my chest tightens. Is this what people call growing up?

The bartender tips his mixing flask, strains out a fresh batch of the ruby red liquid onto the glass in front of me.

"Salut." I nod my thanks, then toss it back. It hits my stomach and tendrils of fire crawl up my spine, I cough.

My head spins. Warmth sears my chest, spreads to my extremities. I can't feel my fingers or toes. Good. Almost there. "Top me up."

"You sure?"

"Yes." I square my shoulders and reach for the drink.

"No. She's had enough."

"What the—?" I pivot on the bar stool.

Indigo eyes bore into me.

Fathomless. Black at the bottom, the intensity in their depths grips me. He swoops out his arm, grabs the glass and holds it up. Thick fingers dwarf the glass. Tapered at the edges. The nails short and buff. *All the better to grab you with.* I gulp.

"Like what you see?"

I flush, peer up into his face.

Hard cheekbones, hollows under them, and a tiny scar that slashes at his left eyebrow. *How did he get that?* Not that I care. My gaze slides to his mouth. Thin upper lip, a lower lip that is full and cushioned. Pouty with a hint of bad boy. *Oh!* My toes curl. My thighs clench.

The corner of his mouth kicks up. *Asshole.*

Bet he thinks life is one big smug-fest. I glower, reach for my glass, and he holds it up and out of my reach.

I scowl, "Gimme that."

He shakes his head.

"That's my drink."

"Not anymore." He shoves my glass at the bartender. "Water for her. Get me a whiskey, neat."

I splutter, then reach for my drink again. The barstool tips, in his direction. This is when I fall against him, and my breasts slam into his hard chest, sculpted planes with layers upon layers of muscle that ripple and writhe as he turns aside, flattens himself against the bar. The floor rises up to meet me.

What the actual hell?

I twist my torso at the last second and my butt connects with the surface. *Ow!*

The breath rushes out of me. My hair swirls around my face. I scrabble for purchase, and my knee connects with his leg.

"Watch it." He steps around, stands in front of me.

"You stepped aside?" I splutter. "You let me fall?"

"Hmph."

I tilt my chin back, all the way back, look up the expanse of muscled thigh that stretches the silken material of his suit. *What is he wearing? Could any suit fit a man with such precision?* Hand crafted on Saville Row, no doubt. I glance at the bulge that tents the fabric between his legs. *Oh!* I blink.

Look away, look away. I hold out my arm. He'll help me up at least, won't he?

He glances at my palm, then turns away. *No, he didn't do that, no way.*

A glass of amber liquid appears in front of him. He lifts the tumbler to his sculpted mouth.

His throat moves, strong tendons flexing. He tilts his head back, and the column of his neck moves as he swallows. Dark hair covers his chin—it's a discordant chord in that clean-cut profile, I shiver. He would scrape that rough skin down my core. He'd mark my inner thigh, lick my core, thrust his tongue inside my melting channel and drink from my pussy. *Oh! God.* Goosebumps rise on my skin.

No one has the right to look this beautiful, this achingly gorgeous. Too magnificent for his own good. Anger coils in my chest.

"Arrogant wanker."

"I'll take that under advisement."

"You're a jerk, you know that?"

He presses his lips together. The grooves on either side of his mouth deepen. Jesus, clearly the man has never laughed a single day in his life. Bet that stick up his arse is uncomfortable. I chuckle.

He runs his gaze down my features, my chest, down to my toes, then yawns.

The hell! I will not let him provoke me. Will not. "Like what you see?" I jut out my chin.

"Sorry, you're not my type." He slides a hand into the pocket of those perfectly cut pants, stretching it across that heavy bulge.

Heat curls low in my belly.

Not fair, that he could afford a wardrobe that clearly shouts his status and what amounts to the economy of a small third-world country. A hot feeling stabs in my chest.

He reeks of privilege, of taking his status in life for granted.

While I've had to fight every inch of the way. Hell, I am still battling to hold onto the last of my equilibrium.

"Last chance—" I wiggle my fingers, from where I am sprawled out on the floor at his feet, "—to redeem yourself..."

"You have me there." He places the glass on the counter, then bends and holds out his hand. The hint of discolored steel at his wrist catches my attention. Huh?

He wears a cheap-ass watch?

That's got to bring down the net worth of his presence by more than 1000% percent. Weird.

I reach up and he straightens.

I lurch back.

"Oops, I changed my mind." His lips curl.

A hot burning sensation claws at my stomach. I am not a violent person, honestly. But Smirky Pants here, he needs to be taught a lesson.

I swipe out my legs, kicking his out from under him.

Sinclair

My knees give way, and I hurtle toward the ground.

What the—? I twist around, thrust out my arms. My palms hit the floor. The impact jostles up my elbows. I firm my biceps and come to a halt planked above her.

A huffing sound fills my ear.

I turn to find my whippet, Max, panting with his mouth open. I scowl and he flattens his ears.

All of my businesses are dog-friendly. Before you draw conclusions about me being the caring sort or some such shit—it attracts footfall.

Max scrutinizes the girl, then glances at me. *Huh?* He hates women, but not her, apparently.

I straighten and my nose grazes hers.

My arms are on either side of her head. Her chest heaves. The fabric of her dress stretches across her gorgeous breasts. My fingers tingle; my palms ache to cup those tits, squeeze those hard nipples outlined against the—hold on, what is she wearing? A tunic shirt in a sparkly pink... and are those shoulder pads she has on?

I glance up, and a squeak escapes her lips.

Pink hair surrounds her face. *Pink? Who dyes their hair that color past the age of eighteen?*

I stare at her face. *How old is she?* Un-furrowed forehead, dark eyelashes that flutter against pale cheeks. Tiny nose, and that mouth—luscious, tempting. A whiff of her scent, cherries and caramel, assails my senses. My mouth waters. *What the hell?*

She opens her eyes and our eyelashes brush. Her gaze widens. Green, like the leaves of the evergreens, flickers of gold sparkling in their depths. "What?" She glowers. "You're demonstrating the plank position?"

"Actually," I lower my weight onto her, the ridge of my hardness thrusting into the softness between her legs, "I was thinking of something else, altogether."

She gulps and her pupils dilate. *Ah, so she feels it, too?*

I drop my head toward her, closer, closer.

Color floods the creamy expanse of her neck. Her eyelids flutter down. She tilts her chin up.

I push up and off of her.

"That… Sweetheart, is an emphatic 'no thank you' to whatever you are offering."

Her eyelids spring open and pink stains her cheeks. Adorable. Such a range of emotions across those gorgeous features in a few seconds? What else is hidden under that exquisite exterior of hers?

She scrambles up, eyes blazing.

Ah! The little bird is trying to spread her wings? My dick twitches. My groin hardens, *Why does her anger turn me on so, huh?*

She steps forward, thrusts a finger in my chest.

My heart begins to thud.

She peers up from under those hooded eyelashes. "Wake up and taste the wasabi, asshole."

"What does that even mean?"

She makes a sound deep in her throat. My dick twitches. My pulse speeds up.

She pivots, grabs a half-full beer mug sitting on the bar counter.

I growl, "Oh, no, you don't."

She turns, swings it at me. The smell of hops envelops the space.

I stare down at the beer-splattered shirt, the lapels of my camel colored jacket deepening to a dull brown. Anger squeezes my guts.

I fist my fingers at my side, broaden my stance.

She snickers.

I tip my chin up. "You're going to regret that."

The smile fades from her face. "Umm." She places the now empty mug on the bar.

I take a step forward and she skitters back. "It's only clothes." She gulps, "They'll wash."

I glare at her and she swallows, wiggles her fingers in the air, "I should have known that you wouldn't have a sense of humor."

I thrust out my jaw, "That's a ten-thousand-pound suit you destroyed."

She blanches, then straightens her shoulders, "Must have been some hot date you were trying to impress, huh?"

"Actually," I flick some of the offending liquid from my lapels, "it's you I was after."

"Me?" She frowns.

"We need to speak."

She glances toward the bartender who's on the other side of the bar. "I don't know you." She chews on her lower lip, biting off some of the hot pink. How would she look, with that pouty mouth fastened on my cock?

The blood rushes to my groin so quickly that my head spins. My pulse rate ratchets up. Focus, focus on the task you came here for.

"This will take only a few seconds." I take a step forward.

She moves aside.

I frown, "You want to hear this, I promise."

"Go to hell." She pivots and darts forward.

I let her go, a step, another, because... I can? Besides it's fun to create the illusion of freedom first; makes the hunt so much more entertaining, huh?

I swoop forward, loop an arm around her waist, and yank her toward me.

She yelps. "Release me."

Good thing the bar is not yet full. It's too early for the usual officegoers to stop by. And the staff...? Well they are well aware of who cuts their paychecks.

I spin her around and against the bar, then release her. "You will listen to me."

She swallows; she glances left to right.

Not letting you go yet, little Bird. I move into her space, crowd her.

She tips her chin up. "Whatever you're selling, I'm not interested."

I allow my lips to curl, "You don't fool me."

A flush steals up her throat, sears her cheeks. So tiny, so innocent. Such a good little liar. I narrow my gaze, "Every action has its consequences."

"Are you daft?" She blinks.

"This pretense of yours?" I thrust my face into hers, "It's not working."

She blinks, then color suffuses her cheeks, "You're certifiably mad—"

"Getting tired of your insults."

"It's true, everything I said." She scrapes back the hair from her face.

Her fingernails are painted... You guessed it, pink.

"And here's something else. You are a selfish, egotistical jackass."

I smirk. "You're beginning to repeat your insults and I haven't even kissed you yet."

"Don't you dare." She gulps.

I tilt my head, "Is that a challenge?"

"It's a..." she scans the crowded space, then turns to me. Her lips firm, "...a warning. You're delusional, you jackass." She inhales a deep breath, "Your ego is bigger than the size of a black hole." She snickers, "Bet it's to compensate for your lack of balls."

A-n-d, that's it. I've had enough of her mouth that threatens to never stop spewing words. How many insults can one tiny woman hurl my way? Answer: too many to count.

"You—"

I lower my chin, touch my lips to hers.

Heat, sweetness, the honey of her essence explodes on my palate. My dick twitches. I tilt my head, deepen the kiss, reaching for that something more... more... of whatever scent she's wearing on her skin, infused with that breath of hers that crowds my senses, rushes down my spine. My groin hardens; my cock lengthens. I thrust my tongue between those infuriating lips.

She makes a sound deep in her throat and my heart begins to pound.

So innocent, yet so crafty. Beautiful and feisty. The kind of complication I don't need in my life.

I prefer the straight and narrow. Gray and black, that's how I choose to define my world. She, with her flashes of color—pink hair and lips that threaten to drive me to the edge of distraction—is exactly what I hate.

Give me a female who has her priorities set in life. To pleasure me, get me off, then walk away before her emotions engage. Yeah. That's what I prefer.

Not this... this bundle of craziness who flings her arms around my shoulders, thrusts her breasts up and into my chest, tips up her chin, opens her mouth, and invites me to take and take.

Does she have no self-preservation? Does she think I am going to fall for her wide-eyed appeal? She has another think coming.

I tear my mouth away and she protests.

She twines her leg with mine, pushes up her hips, so that melting softness between her thighs cradles my aching hardness.

I glare into her face and she holds my gaze.

Trains her green eyes on me. Her cheeks flush a bright red. Her lips fall open and a moan bleeds into the air. The blood rushes to my dick, which instantly thickens. *Fuck.*

Time to put distance between myself and the situation.

It's how I prefer to manage things. Stay in control, always. Cut out anything that threatens to impinge on my equilibrium. Shut it down or buy them off. Reduce it to a transaction. That I understand.

The power of money, to be able to buy and sell—numbers, logic. That's what's worked for me so far.

"How much?"

Her forehead furrows.

"Whatever it is, I can afford it."

Her jaw slackens. "You think... you—"

"A million?"

"What?"

"Pounds, dollars... You name the currency, and it will be in your account."

Her jaw slackens, "You're offering me money?"

"For your time, and for you to fall in line with my plan."

She reddens, "You think I am for sale?"

"Everyone is."

"Not me."

Here we go again. "Is that a challenge?"

Color fades from her face, "Get away from me."

"Are you shy, is that what this is?" I frown. "You can write your price down on a piece of paper if you prefer," I glance up, notice the bartender watching us. I jerk my chin toward the napkins. He grabs one, then offers it to her.

She glowers at him, "Did you buy him too?"

"What do you think?"

She glances around, "I think everyone here is ignoring us."

"It's what I'd expect."

"Why is that?"

I wave the tissue in front of her face, "Why do you think?"

"You own the place?"

"As I am going to own you."

She sets her jaw, "Let me leave and you won't regret this."

A chuckle bubbles up. I swallow it away. This is no laughing matter. I never smile during a transaction. Especially not when I am negotiating a new acquisition. And that's all she is. The final piece in the puzzle I am building.

"No one threatens me."

"You're right."

"Huh?"

"I'd rather act on my instinct."

Her lips twist, her gaze narrows. All of my senses scream a warning.

No, she wouldn't, no way—pain slices through my middle and sparks explode behind my eyes.

To find out what happens next read Summer & Sinclair Sterling's story HERE

Want to be the first to find out when L. Steele's next book releases? Subscribe to her newsletter HERE

Read about the Seven in the Big bad Billionaires series

US

UK

Other countries

Claim your FREE contemporary romance boxset HERE

Claim your FREE paranormal romance boxset HERE

Follow L. Steele on AMAZON

Follow L. Steele on BookBub

Follow L. Steele on Goodreads

Follow L. Steele on Facebook

Follow L. Steele on Instagram

Join L. Steele's secret Facebook Reader Group

For more books by L. Steele click HERE

FREE BOOK

How to scan a QR code?
1. Open the camera app on your phone or tablet.
2. Point the camera at the QR code.

3. Tap the banner that appears on your phone or tablet.
4. Follow the instructions on the screen to finish signing in.

AFTERWORD

FROM L. STEELE (LAXMI)

Hope you enjoyed Massimo and Olivia's story. You can also read Michael & Karma's story in *Mafia King*, Christian & Aurora's story in *A Very Mafia Christmas*, Seb and Elsa's story in *Mafia Vows*, Luca & Jeanne's story in *Mafia Obsession* and Axel & Theresa's story in *Mafia Crown*.

The Arranged Marriage Mafia series starts after *The Billionaire's Fake Wife* in the Big Bad Billionaire Series and the two series then run parallel.

They dovetail with JJ and Lena's story in Mafia Lust. I had a wonderful time writing a scene where I had characters from both the Arranged Marriage Mafia Series and the Big Bad Billionaire series. How many alpha holes can you fit in a room? Read JJ's story to find out!

When I wrote *The Billionaire's Fake Wife* I didn't realize I was actually writing two series. The Seven Billionaires in the Big Bad Billionaires Series, and the Seven Sovrano brothers in the Arranged Marriage Mafia series. And yes I promise a scene at some point when all fourteen alphaholes are in one room... is that even possible? Will their big egos even fit under one roof? :) Wait and see.

Thank you to my editor Elizabeth Connor, my assistant Sophie Koufes, my alpha reader Li Iacobacci, my publicist Sarah Ferguson of Social Butterfly PR who has been so supportive, and my reader group who always cheer me on.

Also big thanks to @bookishfaith0 who inspired the dedication of this book!

Have an opinion on the Sovranos? Share them in my reader group, join Laxmi's team HERE.